Nicholas laughed, ...

Daisy hurried on. "...can be a marriage of convenience. Even so, our marriage would be an obvious sign to the tenants that I accept you and approve of what you're doing."

He shook his head.

"You won't marry me?"

"Not on the terms you've stated."

"On what terms, then?"

"I would want to get full value for *my* sacrifice," Nicholas said. "I would want to have a wife who was a wife."

"I'm not sure that would be a good idea, Your Grace," Daisy said hesitantly.

"Then we're at a stalemate," Nicholas said. "If I have to take a loss on the sale of Severn, that's what I'll do."

"You're really going to sell Severn Manor?" Daisy asked, agonized.

"As quickly as I can, for as much as I can get."

"No. Don't sell just yet. I'll . . . I'll marry you on any terms you ask."

HIGH PRAISE FOR JOAN JOHNSTON AND HER PREVIOUS BESTSELLING NOVELS

OUTLAW'S BRIDE

"*Outlaw's Bride* is a very amusing and imaginative romp that has the Joan Johnston stamp of excellence all over it. The slow unfurling of the real villain and his motives are a subtle counterpoint to the battle of wills that plays out as Patch chases her man and Ethan does his best to resist her. This novel is a highly recommended treat."   —*Affaire de Coeur*

"Patch . . . is strong enough to stand by her man, even when he doesn't know he's hers. All in all, a 'helluva good' western with enough shoot-outs, chuckles, and mystery to draw all sorts of new fans for Ms. Johnston. Keep 'em coming, Joan!"
—*Heartland Critiques*

"Intrigue and passion, combined with a tender love story, make this one delicious, and the subplots promise us closer looks at her riveting characters in future books."   —*Rendezvous*

"Readers who recall Patch and Ethan will rejoice in their return and savor their sensuous, triumphant, and exciting love story. Joan Johnston has created a charming, appealing romance destined to delight readers."   —*Romantic Times*

KID CALHOUN

"4+ Hearts! Powerful and moving . . . Joan Johnston has cleverly merged the aura of the American-style romance with the grittier westerns she has written in the past, making *Kid Calhoun* into a feast for all her fans. This irresistible love story once again ensures Ms. Johnston a place in readers' hearts and on their 'keeper' shelves."

—*Romantic Times*

"This story has surprises at every turn . . . and it's all pulled together with Ms. Johnston's special blend of humor. Plenty of action and adventure to keep you entertained; this is a top-notch western romance with sparkling characters and dynamite dialogue."

—*Rendezvous*

"Not to be missed . . . Joan Johnston peoples the story with unforgettable subplots and characters who make every fine thread of *Kid Calhoun* weave into a touching tapestry." —*Affaire de Coeur*

"This most enjoyable western is packed with spunky women, tough men, rotten bad guys, and ornery kids . . . just the ingredients for a fine read!"

—*Heartland Critiques*

Dell Books by Joan Johnston

The INHERITANCE

Joan Johnston

A DELL BOOK

THE INHERITANCE
A Dell Book

PUBLISHING HISTORY
Dell mass market edition published January 1995
Dell mass market reissue / March 2009

Published by
Bantam Dell
A Division of Random House, Inc.
New York, New York

This is a work of fiction. Names, characters, places, and incidents either are the product of the author's imagination or are used fictitiously. Any resemblance to actual persons, living or dead, events, or locales is entirely coincidental.

Dell is a registered trademark of Random House, Inc., and the colophon is a trademark of Random House, Inc.

ISBN 978-0-440-24551-3

Printed in the United States of America

www.bantamdell.com

OPM 10 9 8 7 6 5 4 3 2 1

*This book is dedicated to
my friend and mentor
Lynda Wojcik.
Thanks.*

1

He could hear her breathing in the next room. It was a painful sound, the air rattling in her chest before it rasped out again between cracked, dry lips. His mother had pneumonia, the doctor had said when he finally arrived, a full day after he had been begged to come. She would most likely die.

It would be a blessing if she did, he thought. She had been sick for a long time from that other disease, the one whores got that gave them sores and turned them blind and finally left them to die as maddened creatures. She hadn't worked for maybe a year or more. He had done odd jobs that kept them from starving, sweeping up sawdust in the saloon and emptying spittoons. He had found an abandoned line shack that gave them shelter. But without heat in the cold of a Texas blue norther, she had fallen ill.

He had turned thirteen a week ago without a celebration, without any acknowledgment at all from her. She hadn't remembered. Her mind was already going. He wanted the pain of watching her die to end. She was his mother, and he hated her, and hated himself for hating her. He prayed the pneumonia would set them both free at last.

"Nicholassss."

He heard the tortured sound of his name pass her lips. He should go to her. He should answer her. But he lay where he was, huddled beneath a thin blanket on the floor, his shoulders hunched against the cold.

"Pleeeease."

The whisper of sound carried to where he lay and shuddered over him. She was his mother. He must go to her. But he lay where he was, feeling the anger sweep through him for what she had done.

She had betrayed his father and given herself to another man. He had been the result. Only her secret hadn't been discovered right away. He had spent eight years as Lord Philip's son. Long enough to know what it meant to have a father. Long enough to be confused and crushed when that same father drove him and his mother from their home in England to exile in America. Long enough to know what it was to be warm and well fed and secure. The contrast, the small cold shack and his empty belly and his mother dying on a pallet on the floor in the next room, was all the more harsh and horrifying.

He covered his ears to shut out the rattling sound as she choked on the fluid that filled her lungs. He waited for her to call him again. He would go then. He would not be able to lie there and listen to her call and not go to her. Even though he hated her. Even though she deserved to die a terrible death.

"Nicholassss."

He leapt to his feet but got tangled in the blanket, which clung like a web, threatening to hold him captive until he could be devoured by some monstrous imaginary spider.

"I'm coming, Mama," he cried. "I'm coming!"

He fought the blanket and freed himself and ran to her. He dropped onto the hard floor, feeling the pain in his knees, which were bare in his shabby pants.

"I'm here, Mama. I'm here," he said, his throat swollen with pain and grief and remorse. "Mama?"

He thought she was dead. Her breathing was so shallow her chest barely rose. She was so thin, so very thin, nothing but skin and bone. He had tried to feed her, but she wouldn't eat. He could see the blue veins in her eyelids in the early-morning light that filtered through the broken-paned window above her.

"Mama?" His voice pleaded with her to answer him. To forgive him for wanting her dead.

"It was a lie," she rasped. "Someone lied."

"Who lied, Mama? About what?"

"You are your father's son," she said in short, ragged bursts of breath. "I never lay with another man."

"What? What, Mama? Mama?"

Her breath soughed out like a bellows that is slowly pressed flat. It took him a moment to realize she was no longer breathing. That she was dead.

"Mama? Mama? Mamaaaaaaaaaaaaaaaaaaa!

Nicholas Calloway sat bolt upright, his hands trembling, his throat painfully constricted, his body bathed in sweat. It was pitch black, and it took him a second to realize where he was, camped out under the sky, not far from Abilene, Texas.

It was only a dream. The same dream. Again.

He raised shaky hands and pressed them against

his eyes. He had learned how to suffer the dream silently, but it had all seemed so vivid, so achingly real. As though it had happened yesterday, even though it had been more than twenty years since his mother had died. He was no longer that frightened boy. He had gone on with his life.

So why couldn't he put his mother's death behind him? Why had he been plagued all these years with the memory of that awful morning?

Was it because of what she had said on her deathbed? Why had she tried to absolve herself from guilt? She should have told the truth at the end.

Maybe she was *telling the truth.*

That was the voice that had kept the dream alive, the nagging voice that told him he might not be a bastard. The treacherous voice that offered him hope.

He should have found a way long ago to return to England, to confront his father with his mother's dying words. But other things—at first, poverty, and later, responsibilities—had conspired to keep him in America. He had a home here now and a son of his own. The past was the past. There was no going back. He just wished there was some way to prevent the dream from recurring, from being so disturbingly real.

The sound of a twig snapping underfoot made him instantly alert. It must have been another, similar sound that had woken him. He reached slowly for the Colt .45 that had never been farther away than the reach of his hand. He pulled it from the holster that lay beside the saddle he had used for a pillow. He moved silently, stealthily away from his camp and concealed himself in a small hollow to wait and watch.

No one would have recognized, in the merciless gray eyes that searched the landscape, the vulnerable boy Nicholas Calloway had been. His mother's death, and the few terrible years that followed, had toughened and hardened him. The lonely, frightened boy of the past existed only in his dreams. The man he had become was ruthless. A killer. Of course, that was a necessary quality in his chosen profession.

Nicholas Calloway hunted men for a living.

Nicholas smiled, a small, cynical tilting of lips that was almost a sneer. He had become a bastard in deed as well as by birth. At least bounty hunting was an honest job, if not a respected one. It was more lucrative than riding line for some ranch, albeit a sight more dangerous.

Nicholas welcomed the danger. The risk made the job more exciting. He wouldn't mind dying, if that was to be his fate. The chances of that weren't as good now as they had been ten years ago, after the War Between the States, when he had begun this sort of work. He had learned how to stay alive. How to kill before being killed.

Nicholas had a good idea who might be out there in the darkness. He had come to Abilene in search of Vince Tolman. The REWARD poster in his pocket promised $1,000 for Vince's capture, dead or alive. Vince had started rustling cattle in Victoria, Texas, but had ended up shooting cowboys. The cattle rustling was enough to get him hanged. The killing had put a bounty on his head and set Nicholas on his trail.

Nicholas believed in letting a man know, through talk around town, that he was being hunted. It invariably made him nervous. And nervous men made mistakes.

Nicholas didn't kill if he didn't have to, but he wasn't above goading a man into a draw. It was easier to account for a dead man than to bring in a live one, and he had no sympathy for the hardened outlaws he hunted down. He didn't delude himself into thinking they would come in peaceably. Not after the first time, when he had nearly been killed by a man he had been bringing back to stand trial.

His eyes had adjusted to the dark, which wasn't as dark as it had seemed when he awoke. There was no moon, but there were stars, and he could make out the bare outline of a Stetson topping the figure of a man. Nicholas had his gun in his hand and an easy target. But there was just the chance it wasn't Vince. He didn't want to kill some fool who was wandering around lost in the dark.

He rose slowly and waited for the stranger to realize he was standing there. "If you're looking for a cup of coffee—"

"Goddamn you, Calloway! How the hell—"

It was Vince all right. Nicholas threw himself out of the way as the outlaw's gun spat fire. He rolled, and when he came to a stop fired once into Vince's body. Vince's hands flew reflexively outward, and Nicholas heard, rather than saw, the outlaw's gun land in the dirt some distance away.

Brush crackled as the outlaw fell, and he swore a muffled "Goddamn!" before all was silent.

Gun in hand, Nicholas walked over to the fire, squatted down, and stirred up the ashes, looking for some embers. He threw a bit of grass into the ring of stones and saw it flare from the corner of his eye. He didn't look directly into the light, knowing that otherwise he would be blind when he needed to see into the darkness again.

The fire bit greedily into the few sticks he added. Vince Tolman was lying ten feet away. Nicholas watched for movement but saw none.

"You still alive?" Nicholas asked.

"Yeah."

"Where are you hit?"

"Belly."

"Too bad."

"I was thinkin' the same thing myself," Vince said with a harsh laugh. The laugh ended in a hiss of pain. "How long you figger I'll last?"

Nicholas left the fire and crossed to the dying outlaw. He lifted the man's vest and shirt aside and looked at the wound. "Daylight maybe."

There was a silence while Vince digested this news.

"I was gonna offer you the thousand to let me go," Vince said at last.

"Wouldn't have taken it."

"Yeah. I heard that. Thought I'd try, anyway."

"Any kin you want notified?" Nicholas asked.

"My ma," Vince said. "Martha Tolman in Seguin."

"I'll take care of it."

Vince exhaled a deep breath. Nicholas recognized the sound. He reached over a moment later and shut the dead man's eyes, knowing it would be harder to do it in the daylight.

"Guess I was wrong," Nicholas said. "Guess you didn't live to see another day."

He took Vince into Abilene to have him identified

by the sheriff so the authorities in Victoria could wire the reward money to him. Then he sent a telegram to Martha Tolman in Seguin.

Your son Vince is dead. His last thoughts were of you.

He didn't sign it. It would be too easy for the woman to find out he was the one who had killed her son. He didn't want her sending some relative to hunt him down. He didn't know why he had asked Vince about his kin. He hadn't done anything like that before, mostly because his first shot was usually deadly. Nor was he sure why he had followed through and sent the telegram. It wasn't going to be much comfort to Martha Tolman.

Three days later, as he headed for his ranch in the hill country west of Austin, Nicholas put Vince and Martha Tolman from his mind. He was looking forward to spending some time with his son. Colin was nearly a man himself, already nineteen. All the same, Nicholas was comforted by the thought that Colin wasn't alone at the ranch. Simp was there with him.

Nicholas didn't know what he would have done if Simp Tanner hadn't crossed his path nineteen years ago. Nicholas had been a boy of sixteen when his three-day-old son had been thrust into his arms. He had been sitting cross-legged on the grass in the middle of the southwest Texas prairie, a bawling baby in his arms, when Simp had come along. The weatherbeaten cowboy had immediately taken on the duty of nursemaid to Colin and had hung around to become a part of the family.

As far as Colin knew, his mother had died when he was born, though Nicholas had made no secret of the fact that he and Colin's mother hadn't been married. He had never told his son the truth about his mother. That was his secret, and he had no intention of ever revealing it to anyone.

The hundred twenty–odd mile ride home, almost due south as the crow flies over rolling, grassy plains, seemed unending. Nicholas stopped each day only when he knew his horse couldn't go any farther without rest. He pushed hard and arrived at his ranch house on the outskirts of Fredericksburg at dusk one evening.

He and Simp had built a simple wood frame house with a central hallway leading to two rooms on either side, then added a kitchen on the back. It was whitewashed and had red shutters that Colin had helped paint. Nicholas smiled as he recalled how Colin had gotten as much paint on himself as on the shutters.

Nicholas pulled his mustang to an abrupt halt when he spotted a single rider approaching the house. It was still light enough from his vantage point on a rise overlooking the house to see the stranger glance surreptitiously around as he dismounted at the front door.

Nicholas felt his heart claw its way up into his throat. He had always known there might come a day when someone would come looking for him—a brother or a father or an uncle—seeking vengeance. No one around Fredericksburg knew what he did for a living. He was just Mr. Calloway who had a ranch and ran a few cattle and raised a few horses outside of town.

They didn't get many visitors at the ranch, and no one Nicholas wouldn't recognize. But he didn't recognize the man walking up the front steps to his house. The stranger turned to look around as though he suspected he was being watched. Nicholas noted he was short and thin with a narrow face and small eyes. Oddly, he was dressed in a city suit and wore a bowler hat. That didn't necessarily mean he hadn't come here with murder in mind. Appearances, Nicholas had learned over the years, could be deceiving.

Nicholas dismounted in the shadows and worked his way around to the porch while the stranger stood at the door, apparently making up his mind whether to knock. Nicholas took the choice away from him.

"Hold it right there," he said. "Put up your hands."

The little man started to move, and Nicholas said, "Turn around and you're a dead man. Drop your gun."

"I'm not armed, I assure you," the little man said.

Nicholas was surprised to hear the clipped British accent. "What are you doing here?" he demanded.

"I'm looking for Nicholas Windermere," he said. "On a matter of utmost importance."

Windermere had been Nicholas's last name for the first eight years of his life. He had taken his mother's name, Calloway, when they arrived in America.

"May I turn around, sir?" the little man asked.

"Go ahead. Just don't make any sudden moves."

Nicholas thought the little man was going to faint when he spied the Colt .45 aimed at his heart. His face paled and he swallowed with an audible sound.

"Whom do I have the privilege of addressing?" the little man said.

"First tell me who you are," Nicholas said.

"Why, I'm Phipps, sir. The Windermere family solicitor."

"Why are you looking for Nicholas Windermere?"

"Because he is now the eighth Duke of Severn. His father left a letter stating Lady Philip's destination in America. It has taken me nearly a year to trace the path to His Grace. It led, if I may be so bold, sir, here."

Nicholas blanched. For him to become the Duke of Severn, his uncle, the previous duke, must be dead, and both his cousins, Tony and Stephen, must have died without male heirs. And his father must be dead. He would never be able to confront him now and ask the questions he needed to ask.

Nicholas felt a tightness in his chest. Surely it wasn't grief at the news of his father's death. He couldn't possibly feel anything for the man after all these years. More likely the pain was caused by the knowledge—the fear—that he would never be able to end the recurring dream that plagued him.

The door opened behind the little man, and a tall, handsome young man with black hair and blue eyes stuck his head out. "Pa? What's going on?"

"Meet Phipps," Nicholas said. "The Windermere family solicitor."

"What's he doing here, Pa?"

"He came to find me."

The little man's eyes widened, and he snapped to attention and bowed low. The gesture was a bit ridiculous because his hands remained high and wide above his head.

"Pardon me, Your Grace. I had no idea it was you I was addressing. May I extend my deepest sympathies, Your Grace, on your loss?"

"It seems a little late for that," Nicholas said. "You can put your hands down now, Phipps."

"Thank you, Your Grace."

"And you can stop calling me that," Nicholas said irritably. "You're in America now."

"Whatever you wish, Your— What shall I call Your Grace if I'm not to call you—"

"Calloway," Nicholas said abruptly. "My name is Calloway."

"Yes, Your—Mr. Calloway, sir. If you wish, sir." But he was clearly unhappy with the breach of etiquette.

"You've found me, Phipps. You can go back to England now."

"But, Your Grace!" Phipps exclaimed, clearly agitated and reverting to the formality with which he was most comfortable. "There's the matter of the inheritance, Severn Manor, the house in London, the lands, and the titles. I couldn't possibly leave just yet, Your Grace!"

"What in tarnation's goin' on out here?" Simp said, shoving the door open farther and forcing Colin out onto the porch. "Who you yammering with, Nick?"

"It's a solicitor from England," Colin explained excitedly. "He keeps calling Pa 'Your Grace,' and he says Pa has an inheritance in England."

"Well, now," Simp said. "That's mighty interestin'. Come on in," he said, grabbing Phipps and ushering—shoving—him inside to the parlor. "Set yourself down." He pushed Phipps down onto a worn horsehair sofa. "Now what's all this about an inheritance?"

Nicholas felt the warmth of homecoming as he closed the front door behind him. The parlor was furnished as simply as the rest of the house with homemade wood and leather furniture. There were no curtains, no frills, no furbelows. It was a male bastion, a bachelors' abode. It wasn't always dusted, but it was neat and clean, a peaceful refuge from the other life he led.

He watched Simp fussing over the Englishman. "It's nice to know you're glad to see me, Simp," he said dryly.

"What?" Simp replied. "Oh, good to see you back, Nick. You know anythin' about what this fella's sayin'?"

"I might," Nicholas replied cautiously.

Phipps bobbed up again. "Would Your Grace care to sit down?"

"No, I don't think I do," Nicholas said. "But make yourself comfortable."

"Oh, no, I couldn't sit, Your Grace, if Your Grace chooses to stand." He remained where he stood at one end of the sofa.

Colin laughed. "He sure is full of 'Your Graces,' Pa."

"Am I to understand you have a son?" Phipps asked as he eyed Colin.

"Yes," Nicholas replied. "Colin is my son."

The little man turned and bowed to Colin. "My lord, may I say what a pleasure it is to meet you."

Colin laughed again. "I'm not lord of anything. Except sometimes I lord it over Simp," he said with a cheeky grin at the old cowboy. He dropped into a rocker by the stone fireplace, while Simp settled himself comfortably on the sofa.

"Excuse me, m'lord, for correcting you," Phipps said, "but as the duke's eldest son, you are the Earl of Coventry."

Colin laughed again, only it was a less confident sound. "Pa? What's he talking about?"

Nicholas sighed and leaned back against the rolltop desk from which he ran his ranch. "I think I can clear things up. I can't be the new duke," he told Phipps. "I'm not my father's son. I'm a bastard," he said so there would be no misunderstanding.

"Your father never legally repudiated you," the solicitor informed him. "And your mother and father were legally wed when you were born. Therefore, Your Grace, I'm afraid I must correct you. You *are* the eighth Duke of Severn."

"Then I renounce the honor," Nicholas said in a harsh voice. "Let someone else have it."

"Oh, no, Your Grace!" Phipps said. "I must beg you to reconsider before you take such drastic action."

"What earthly use could land or a title in England be to me? I'm an American. I have a home here," Nicholas said.

Phipps eyed him consideringly. His forefinger tapped his chin. "I knew your father, Your Grace, and—"

"Nothing my father said or did could be of any interest to me now," Nicholas said, cutting him off.

"The lands are unentailed, Your Grace. And there is considerable wealth. It is all yours to do with as you will."

"What does that mean, Pa? Unentailed?"

"I'm not sure I understand myself, Colin."

"Please allow me to explain, Your Grace." Phipps turned to Colin and said, "It means, m'lord, that there is no restriction on the sale of the land. That it is not a lifetime tenancy, so to speak, but can be sold by the present duke. Unless he wishes to entail it for his heir?" Phipps looked to Nicholas for direction.

"Colin is my son," Nicholas said in a quiet voice, "but I wasn't married to his mother."

"Oh. Oh, dear." Phipps took another look at Colin, his face sympathetic. "Of course, then, you wouldn't wish to entail the properties, not if you would wish your eldest son to inherit them, rather than the heir."

Colin had a frown between his eyes. "I'm confused again, Pa."

"What Phipps means is that under English law you're not my legal heir. Isn't that so, Phipps?"

"Quite so, Your Grace."

"Under those circumstances, Phipps, I don't believe I'd care to entail the properties," Nicholas said. "Assuming I accepted the title, that is."

"Does that mean I'm not an earl?" Colin asked, his face slightly flushed.

"I'm afraid so, sir," the solicitor said, amending his form of address and his level of deference. "Not a lord at all, I'm afraid."

Colin grinned. "Thank goodness. I wouldn't know what to do if I had people bowing and scraping at me all the time."

Simp had been sitting quietly, listening. He turned to Nicholas and said, "I think you ought to take him up on it, Nick. We could use the money to do some improvements around here."

Nicholas raised a black brow. "Use the money from England to improve the ranch? I hadn't thought about that." He turned to Phipps. "Any reason why I couldn't sell everything in England and use the proceeds here?"

Phipps kept his face impassive. The only evidence of his feelings on the subject were the balled fists at his sides. "Of course that is possible, Your Grace. But surely Your Grace won't wish to dispose of Severn Manor. It has been in the family for generations and—"

"That's enough, Phipps," Nicholas said. "How soon can I take control of my inheritance, assuming I agree to do so?"

"There are papers to be signed, Your Grace, some formalities."

"Can I take care of it here?"

Phipps shook his head. "I'm afraid it will be necessary for you to go to England, Your Grace."

There was a moment of silence while Nicholas pondered the strange whims of fate. He was the Duke of Severn. He had wealth beyond his dreams. He could return to England, finally, and put to rest the ghosts of the past.

It's too late. Your father is dead.

But maybe whoever had told the lie wasn't dead. Maybe he could still find out the truth about his birth. And he wanted to see Severn Manor again. He had spent his first eight summers in the palatial manor house, playing with his cousins, Tony and Stephen.

"All right," Nicholas said. "I'll go to England."

The solicitor smiled. "You've made the right decision, Your Grace."

"Really, Pa?" Colin said, leaping from the rocker and crossing the room to his father in three strides. "Are we going to England?"

"Yes, Colin."

"Jehoshaphat!" Colin said. He grabbed Simp's hands and pulled him up from the sofa to dance him around in a circle. "We're going to England, Simp! We're going to sail across the ocean in a ship!"

"Ain't gettin' me off dry land," Simp retorted.

"You have to come, Simp," Colin said, pausing in his celebration. "We couldn't leave you here all alone!"

"Someone has to watch this place," Simp said. "I'll be waitin' right here when you get back."

"Pa? Tell Simp he has to come."

"Simp's right, Colin. Someone has to stay here and take care of the livestock. Besides, we'll be back before you know it. It won't take long to sell Severn Manor and collect my inheritance, isn't that right, Phipps?"

"Exactly, Your Grace. Assuming Your Grace doesn't change his mind and decide to stay in England."

"Don't worry," Nicholas said. "There's absolutely no chance of that."

2

Her Grace, the Duchess of Severn, had been summoned to the library as though she were a naughty child. It wasn't to be borne! Except she had no choice but to bear it. The barbarian who had demanded her presence was none other than His Grace, the new Duke of Severn. From now on he would be making the decisions, guiding the lives and fortunes of all who lived at Severn Manor. And that included her, Margaret, Dowager Duchess of Severn, the previous duke's very young widow.

Margaret, called Daisy by those who loved her, fought back a surge of grief for the husband who had been gone a year, taken by an inflammation of the lungs. She still missed Tony dreadfully. Especially now. Tony would know how to handle the toplofty foreigner who had come all the way from America—where he had hunted down outlaws to make his living—to take the reins of power from her.

Daisy had held those reins for the past year during the search for the missing heir, so she knew how difficult they were to manage. If it were not for her concern that Tony's long-lost cousin wouldn't look after the best interests of the servants and tenant farmers she had grown to care for over the eight years she had been Tony's wife, she would have been long gone to the dower house.

But she wasn't about to leave the premises until she had assured herself that a certain cold, gray-eyed stranger intended to take care of the people whose lives he now held in his callused, unrefined hands.

Daisy halted abruptly at the library door, unaccountably nervous now that the time for confrontation had arrived. Her corset prevented her from taking a deep breath, but as a reigning belle who had once taken the *ton* by storm, she was a creature of fashion, and fashion dictated a tiny waist.

She resorted to several shallow pants to release the tension in her shoulders. She resisted the urge to wipe her sweating palms on the striped skirt of her Worth gown and settled for balling her trembling hands into fists, which she hid in the folds of striped black velvet and yellow satin.

"Is he in there, Higgenbotham?" she demanded of the footman stationed at the library door.

"Yes, Your Grace." There was a short pause before he added, "Pacing like a tiger, Your Grace. If Your Grace wants my advice, you won't go in there alone."

"Thank you, Higgenbotham, but I'm sure he won't do me any harm." *He wouldn't dare!* she thought. But a shiver of foreboding froze her in place.

Her first impression of the duke as he had swept through the front door last night was of a very tall, very dangerous man. Then there were those disturbing rumors about how he had killed so many men in some godforsaken place called Texas. To be

honest, she wasn't sure what a man who had grown
up in the American wilderness would dare. After all,
he had actually drawn a gun on the solicitor who
had been sent to find him. Or so Phipps had claimed.

"I shall be right here, Your Grace," Higgenbotham reassured her. "You need only call for me,
and I shall be instantly at your side."

Daisy wanted to hug the old retainer for his support, but knew he would expire in a fit of apoplexy if
she did anything so impulsive. Higgenbotham was
every inch a duke's footman, which was to say, as
much on his dignity as the man he served. They both
knew that duchesses did not hug the servants.

Nevertheless, she gave him a warm smile before
she squared her shoulders and said, "You may open
the door, Higgenbotham. I'm ready to meet His
Grace."

With an impassive face the old man opened the
paneled mahogany door and closed it with a solid
thunk behind her as she entered the library.

The room smelled of leather and, even after a
year, of the tobacco Tony had smoked. Daisy felt a
pang of self-pity at being left a childless widow at six
and twenty. She remorselessly snuffed it. Tony might
have left this world before his time, but she was still
here, and there was business she must conduct.

Her eyes were drawn to Nicholas, eighth Duke of
Severn, who stood with his back to her, staring out a
window through which the sun streamed in twelve
golden shafts that exactly matched the window-
panes. Tony had often lingered in the same spot, pe-
rusing the vast rolling green lawn that ended at the
edge of a pond bordered by poplar and elm.

As her gaze focused on the duke, she had an impression of strength, of barely leashed energy. She fought a sudden urge to flee as she waited for him to turn and make his bow to her. Instead, he demonstrated his crude lack of manners by neither turning nor bowing before he spoke.

"I understand you've been managing things since my cousin's—since Tony's death," he said.

"I have, Your Grace." Daisy was mortified that her voice broke between the first two words, and that she had to choke out his title. She wasn't going to let that broad, imposing back intimidate her. The Duchess of Severn was entitled to courtesy, and before he left the room, this boorish brute would acknowledge it!

The duke turned to face her at last, and it took all her courage to stand her ground. For if she had thought his shoulders impressive, they were nothing compared to the sight of the man himself. His face wore the most awful frown, but the rest of him was simply awesome.

The collarless white linen shirt beneath his frock coat was open at the throat, revealing a great deal of sun-browned skin. She could even detect the hint of black curls on his chest! It was unforgivable for a gentleman to appear undressed before a lady. The man had just confirmed her belief that he wasn't the least bit civilized.

He radiated an aura of savage power totally unlike the well-bred gentility of his cousins, Tony and Stephen. Stephen had been killed in a hunting accident four years before, but sportsman that he was, Daisy could never remember Stephen looking quite so predatory as the man standing before her now.

In appearance as well as manners the latest duke

was nothing like his cousins. Both Tony and Stephen had been blue-eyed and blond. This man had coal-black hair that hung down over his nape and hooded gray eyes that reminded her of a bleak winter night.

Where Tony and Stephen had possessed the hooked nose, full lips, and thrusting chin of past generations of Windermeres, this man's profile was markedly different. His nose was straight, his chin strong—but hardly jutting—his lips thinned by annoyance or disdain, she wasn't sure which. However, she was forced to admit he was a striking—all right, she conceded in disgust—a handsome man.

He smiled suddenly, revealing a wolfish mouthful of irritatingly straight white teeth.

She flushed, chagrined to discover that he had caught her staring. Color skated across her aristocratic cheekbones as she realized from the improper look of masculine approval in his eyes that he had been giving her an equally thorough appraisal.

"Have you looked your fill, ma'am?" he drawled, lifting a supercilious black brow. Daisy was startled by how much the arrogant gesture reminded her of the old duke, Tony's father.

She stiffened as it dawned on her that the insolent American had failed to accord her the title due her rank. As the previous duke's widow, and until the new duke married, *she* was the Duchess of Severn. How dare he call her *ma'am*! Such address might be allowed between equally ranked friends, but they were strangers and, in her mind, not the least bit equal. She was tempted to address him as *sir*, but forbore to stoop to his level. Maybe it was only ignorance that had made him address her so rudely.

"I am properly referred to as *Your Grace*," she instructed him.

The duke arched one of those devilish black brows. "Oh? I had heard you were called Daisy. Although dressed in those stripes you look more like a bee than a flower."

She couldn't mistake the way his lip curled in mocking amusement. He was laughing at her! She bit back the cutting retort that sought voice, drew herself up proudly, and said instead, "I apologize for staring. However, you must admit, *Your Grace*, that you bear little resemblance to your cousins."

"That is easily explained, *ma'am*," he replied curtly. "I am not my father's son."

Daisy knew the story. She had heard it from several sources, including Nicholas's spinster aunt, Lady Celeste Calloway. Lady Celeste had been a governess for Tony and Stephen and had stayed on in the Windermere household when her duties were completed because she had nowhere else to go. Most recently, Lady Celeste had been a companion to Daisy, since a single woman, even a widowed one, couldn't live alone without opening herself to gossip from the neighborhood.

According to Lady Celeste, Nicholas had been banished at the age of eight from Severn Manor. A hunting crony had nudged Nicholas's father, Lord Philip, in the ribs at the sight of the dark-haired boy, winked, and said, "Your wife has been out hunting a bit of sport for herself, eh, my lord?"

Until that moment, Lord Philip, the old duke's second son, had been unaware of, or had simply ignored, the startling difference in appearance between his son and the rest of the Windermeres. It

was only when it had been brought so uncomfortably to his attention that he had confronted his wife.
She had denied being unfaithful, of course, but the
damage had been done. Thereafter, Lord Philip
could never look at Nicholas without seeing his wife
in another man's arms. Apparently there had been
some evidence—Lady Celeste had been vague about
what it was—to corroborate Lord Philip's suspicions.

In a fit of rage one evening shortly after his crony
had spoken, Lord Philip had banished his wife and
son from his presence. Lady Philip Windermere,
proud and hurt, had left England for America. Lord
Philip had been too stubborn and too angry to call
her back. Even though she never returned, he had
not divorced her. Nor had he disowned his son. Thus
Nicholas, bastard though he was, had become
eighth Duke of Severn, Earl of Coventry, Baron Fen-
wick, and several other lesser titles when his two
cousins had died childless.

A movement to her left caught Daisy's attention.
Her eyes widened in amazement. Standing beside
the Sheraton desk was a younger version of Nicholas. Her gaze streaked from the younger man to the
duke and back again. The tall youth bore a startling
resemblance to the duke, but his eyes were blue
rather than gray, and his features—wide-set eyes under dark brows, a straight nose, wide mouth, and
firm chin—hadn't hardened into the stone mask that
Nicholas wore.

Who was the boy? Since the youth was very nearly
a man, there seemed only one conclusion. Nicholas's mother must have borne another child.

"Your brother?" she asked the duke.

"My son, Colin Calloway." In response to her confused look, he explained, "I took my mother's name, Calloway, in America."

"But he *can't* be your son! He must be at least—"

"Nineteen, ma'am."

"But you're only—"

"Thirty-five, ma'am."

"When he was conceived you must have been a mere *boy* of—"

"Sixteen, ma'am."

Daisy's mouth dropped open. She quickly snapped it shut. She put a hand to her breast in an attempt to calm herself, since her agitation was making her gasp, a dangerous proposition in such a tightly laced corset. "You were *married* at sixteen, Your Grace?" she questioned breathlessly.

"I've never had a wife."

Daisy's heart skipped a beat. "Then the boy is—"

"A bastard," he said coldly. "Like myself, ma'am. And my heir."

"But . . . but . . ."

"He can't inherit the title, of course. But the solicitor who found me in America—Phipps, I believe, is his name—assured me that neither Severn Manor nor the house in London is entailed. The properties and the funds that support them are all entirely mine, to do with as I choose, to dispose of as I will."

Daisy gasped. She knew the entailment of property had to be confirmed legally at each point in the succession, but she hadn't realized until now what the lack of an entailment might mean to her. She had planned to retire to the dower house when she had dealt with this boorish man. But if what the duke had said was true, he could—and probably would—sell the dower house along with the rest of the property. She had a monetary settlement from Tony, but it was sufficient only to cover the expenses of living in the dower house. She stared, disbelieving, at the man who had the power to leave her in dire straits indeed.

"*Not* entailed?" she asked. "Are you sure?"

"*Not* entailed," he confirmed.

"Are you implying that you might actually *sell* Severn Manor?" Daisy asked incredulously. "This house has been the home of Windermeres for generations!"

"As we've already established, I'm not a Windermere. Since I don't share their precious heritage," he said with a sneer that showed exactly how much less than precious he thought it was, "I see no reason why I shouldn't sell."

"No reason!" Daisy was aghast. All her worst nightmares were coming true. "What about the servants? What about the tenant farmers? What will happen to them?" Not to mention her own perilous position.

"Their plight, ma'am, is no concern of mine."

Daisy made one last plea for reason. "What about the title, Your Grace? Surely you wouldn't wish to see the next duke left destitute."

"Since he'll be no relation of mine, I can't see how it matters to me," he said with a shrug. "I'm an American, ma'am. I have no use for titles or the fawning behavior that goes along with them."

"But when you marry—"

The aggravating man interrupted her yet again. His eyes, if possible, turned even colder. "I will never marry, ma'am. You can be sure of that! Now that you've satisfied your curiosity—and I've satisfied mine," he added with a rueful twist of his mouth, "this interview is concluded."

"But—"

"You can go, ma'am."

Daisy stared incredulously as the uncouth barbarian turned his back on her once more. He had interrupted her once too often. Her auburn curls bounced in indignation, and her eyes flashed with emerald fire.

"You may be done with me, *Your Grace*," she said between gritted teeth, "but I haven't even begun with you!"

His back remained turned to her. "There's nothing more to be said. My mind is made up."

"Pa, maybe you ought to hear what she has to say."

Daisy's glance shot to the youth, who hadn't moved from his stand by the desk. Colin's voice sounded peculiar to her ears, the accent broad, an exaggeration of the same drawl his father possessed that was so different from the clipped British speech to which she was accustomed.

Daisy caught herself glaring at Colin and realized she was directing her anger toward the wrong person. She immediately moderated her expression and was rewarded by a smile from the young man who, she was ready to concede, wasn't nearly so boorish as his father.

Daisy took advantage of the opening Colin had given her to say, "There are issues you might be unaware of, Your Grace, that might affect your decision. After all, you've been at Severn Manor less than a day. That's hardly enough time to evaluate the situation."

He turned to face her, but she wasn't encouraged by that small allowance. His mouth had flattened to a forbidding line, and his eyes were narrowed in suspicion. "All right, ma'am. You have my attention. Speak up! What is it you think I should know that will change my mind about selling Severn Manor?"

"In the first place, Your Grace—"

"My name is Calloway. Nicholas Calloway."

Daisy was brought up short by the interruption. "Of course, Your Grace, but—"

"Nicholas."

Daisy pursed her lips. She wasn't the least bit happy about the forced familiarity, but she was willing to try anything that would ameliorate her relationship with the man. After all, he was the one in control. "Of course, Nicholas, if you prefer to be called so, I will abide by your wishes, but—"

"And I'll call you Daisy."

"Hold on one moment, Your Grace—"

"Nicholas," he insisted.

Daisy flushed, appalled at her body's mortifying response to his charming, and quite disarming, grin. She felt the blood rush through her veins, felt her heart pound in an excited tattoo. The man was impossible!

She bit her tongue on the sharp retort that sought voice. She didn't want to lose the boy's goodwill, and she surely would if he listened while she took the father to task for his barbarous behavior.

"Could we discuss this alone?" she asked as politely as she could through clenched teeth.

"I don't have any secrets from my son."

"I'm sure you don't want his youthful ears burned by what I have to say," Daisy retorted.

His grin broadened. "By all means, ma'am. If you're going to tear a strip off my hide, it's best done in private. Colin, will you excuse us?"

"Sure, Pa. I'd like a chance to check on my horse. Send someone to the stable if you want me."

A moment later the door closed with a *thunk* behind him.

Daisy had a moment to regret her impetuous behavior. It was bending propriety to be alone with the duke. It was tempting fate to beard the lion in his den. Only the knowledge that the servants and tenants who depended on Severn for their livelihoods had no other spokesman but herself kept her from bolting.

However, she put as much distance as she could between herself and the duke. She marched over to a settee near the marble-faced fireplace and settled herself imperiously on the brocade seat. "Is there anything I can say to convince you that Severn Manor should not be sold?" she began.

To her dismay, the duke didn't remain where he was. Hands behind his back, he strolled toward her until he was standing directly in front of her. If she sat forward at all, her skirt would brush his knees. She had to crane her neck to see his face. It was set in ominous lines.

"I had one purpose in coming to England, and that was to liquidate the holdings of Severn and take the proceeds back to America with me."

"But you can't do that!" Daisy was on her feet before she could stop herself. Which was when she realized the duke had left her very little room in

which to stand. They couldn't have been more than
an inch apart. Even standing, it was necessary to lift
her chin to meet his eyes. She was close enough to
note the flecks of black that surrounded the gray.
And to feel his heat. And to smell the scents of horse
and leather and man.

She tried to take a step backward and sideways
and nearly tripped on the settee. His hand caught
her elbow to steady her.

"Don't you dare touch me!" she said breathlessly,
jerking herself free. She lurched against the settee
and completely lost her balance. Her eyes flashed to
his. She was going to fall. She was on her way down.
If he didn't catch her . . .

He raised a brow as if to ask whether she wanted
his help, but she set her lips in a mulish line.

He shrugged and let her fall.

She landed on the floor with an undignified
"Ooompf."

It took Daisy a moment to realize what had happened. She was sitting in the middle of the library
floor, her skirt askew, her ankles exposed, her dignity gone. She knew she shouldn't look at him, knew
what she would find if she did, but she couldn't help
herself.

She glanced up and, sure enough, found him
smirking down at her. "Why, you . . . you . . ."
She couldn't think of a word bad enough to call him
and settled for the one that seemed to fit him best.
"You barbarian!"

She tried getting to her feet, but her corset was so
tightly laced it was impossible to bend at the waist.
"Help me up, you dolt!" she hissed.

"Shouldn't that be 'Help me up, *Your Grace*'?"

Daisy was still glowering at him when he set his hands at her waist and lifted her onto her feet. Unfortunately, he didn't let go.

"You can unhand me now," she said, embarrassingly aware of the way she was trembling in his grasp. She wasn't afraid of him, she assured herself, just discomposed by the awkwardness of her situation.

"I must say my cousin had good taste in women," he murmured.

His hooded gray eyes were fixed on her face, and she felt mesmerized, unable to look away. His fingertips tightened at her waist, and it was as though he had touched her in other places, places his hands had no business being.

When Daisy looked down, she was mortified to discover her body had responded to the mere possibility of his touch. She looked up at him again, her eyes glaring daggers. "Let me go," she said in a surprisingly steady voice.

"I don't think I will. Not yet."

There was a moment she could have escaped. He paused as he lowered his head, not long, but long enough so that if she had wanted to turn her face away, she could.

But she didn't turn away. The fires of hell would freeze over before she let him intimidate her. He wouldn't dare kiss her, she thought. He wouldn't dare—

His mouth was warm and damp, and his tongue teased along the seam of her lips seeking entrance. She opened her mouth to protest, and his tongue stroked inside. Her whole body tensed. Tony had never . . . She had never . . .

Daisy was lost in a world of sensation she had never known existed. The duke's hands slid up to cup her breasts and his thumb caught a nipple and made it peak. Of their own accord, her hands inched up the front of his linen shirt and behind his head to tunnel into his too-long hair. It was thick and silky to the touch. She felt his mouth at her throat and leaned her head back with a sensual moan of pleasure.

Somewhere in the back of her brain a warning voice was shouting at her.

What do you think you're doing, Daisy Windermere?!

I'm kissing the duke.

The barbarian duke?

Uh-huh.

The duke who's going to sell Severn Manor? the voice inquired.

Uh-huh.

Are you out of your mind, Daisy?

Daisy jerked herself free and gazed up into the contemptuous gray eyes that stared back at her. "Oh! You . . . you . . ."

"Barbarian?" the duke supplied helpfully.

"How could you do something so . . . so . . ."

"Uncivilized?" he said.

"To take advantage of a woman in such circumstances, it's . . . it's . . ."

"Crass? Crude? Common?"

"You're no gentleman," she accused.

"I never said I was," he replied. "But from what I've seen so far, you're no lady, either."

Daisy flushed painfully. Her hands flew to her cheeks. She had kissed the duke, a complete stranger, like a common trollop, like a harlot from the streets. His accusation stung, but she couldn't deny her behavior had been unladylike. She had probably lost whatever chance she might have had to convince him to keep Severn Manor. But under the circumstances, she had nothing to lose by pleading her case.

Her hands dropped to the folds of her skirt where they curled into white-knuckled fists. Her chin rose so high her neck hurt, and her eyes flashed with the indignation she felt at the situation in which she found herself.

"I came in here this morning to convince you that Severn Manor should not be sold. There are people dependent on the manor for their livelihoods. I had hoped to appeal to your sense of equity, of justice, of right and wrong. I can see now that would have been a waste of time."

His brow arched, and his lip curled cynically.

She ignored the second rush of warmth in her face. "However, I will make the appeal anyway. Is there anything I can say or do that would encourage you to maintain Severn Manor as it has been for generations past?"

He looked her right in the eye, his blunt features implacable. "No, ma'am, there is not. I plan to sell Severn Manor and dispose of everything I can find that has anything to do with the Windermeres." He paused and his curling lip completed the sneer. "You see, it will give me great pleasure to destroy whatever is left of my father's—Lord Philip's—heritage. And now, ma'am, this interview is concluded."

Daisy stood rooted to the spot for another instant. When it appeared the duke might reach for her again, she fled.

3

Daisy paced the length of her bedroom and back, wondering what she could have done differently. For one thing, she shouldn't have stayed in the library alone with the duke. Barbarians were long on action, she had discovered, and short on reason. Oh, Lord. Had she really kissed His Grace? What an idiot she had been to let him corner her like that!

She could still feel his mouth on hers, feel the tightening grasp of his fingers at her waist, feel his hand cup her breast. Oh, Lord. It was happening again. Her knees were ready to buckle. She sank down on her canopied bed and put a shaky hand up to still her heart.

She was too vulnerable. That was the problem. If only things had been different with Tony. But after she had lost the baby, and when the doctor said she would never conceive again, Tony had taken a mistress and left her bed. He had told her he didn't wish to bother her with such a distasteful duty when it would not prove fruitful.

She knew she was supposed to feel grateful. She had been taught that a husband came to his wife to plant his seed, and any other congress was unnatural. And she had been taught that her husband would likely take a mistress to satisfy his baser urges, and that she should look the other way.

Daisy had tried, she had honestly tried not to mind.

But she did. She had loved Tony. When it was plain, after only two years of marriage, that she could never provide him with an heir, she had felt useless. She had needed his reassurance that she still had value to him. She had wanted him to come to her even though she couldn't conceive.

It had been a foolish wish, and Daisy had been utterly unable to speak of the subject openly to her husband. She had lost something of herself in the six years that followed until Tony's death. She had felt undesirable. She had felt less than a woman.

Until His Grace had kissed her.

Daisy had been focused at the time on her own feelings, her own sensations. When she thought back to that kiss in the library, she realized that the duke had been no less aroused than she. The signs had been there. The rapid pulse beating beneath his ear as her hand slid up into his hair, the powerful tautness of his shoulders, his ragged breathing as he stroked her mouth with his tongue.

For the first time in six years she had known what it felt like to be a woman in a man's arms. She had been desired. It was a heady experience. That was why she had let it go so far. She was a weak creature to have succumbed to His Grace. She understood why she had done it, but she found it hard, nevertheless, to forgive herself.

Her surrender to His Grace was even more confusing, because the duke had made it plain he had only one use for her. He had neither the time nor the inclination to hear her suggestions regarding Severn Manor. On the contrary, he was bound and determined to sell it!

Before Tony's death, Daisy had led a very sheltered existence. Her greatest responsibility had been to host dinner parties and make visits to the tenants each Christmas with a charity basket. All that had changed in the past year.

At first she had been overwhelmed by the numbers and kinds of decisions that had to be made. The bailiff, the gardener, the gamekeeper, and the housekeeper all came to her for instructions in those first few days and weeks after Tony's death, when there was no heir to take his place immediately and everything was in such turmoil. Phipps had offered to take charge, but Daisy had desperately needed something to occupy her mind. So she had made the decisions herself.

She had learned several valuable lessons in those early days. She had learned the satisfaction of a job well done. She had learned the fulfillment that comes from helping others. And she had learned how empty her life had been up to that point.

The past year had been a revelation. Daisy had discovered that, contrary to what she had been led to believe by the men in her life, she had a quick and agile mind. There was no difficulty she could not manage, no problem she could not solve. She had always known the day would come when an eighth Duke of Severn would come along to relieve her of the responsibility for Severn Manor and its tenant farmers. If it hadn't been Nicholas Calloway, it would have been a distant Windermere cousin.

But it had been Nicholas. She needed someone upon whom to vent her resentment at having everything she had come to value taken so abruptly from her. His Grace made a very convenient and especially savory target.

During the search for the missing heir, Daisy had let herself hope that the new duke might be willing to accept her help. That he might take advantage of her knowledge of the workings of the estate. It had been a devastating blow to discover that not only would her services not be required, but she would very likely find herself out on the street within the year when he sold the dower house out from under her.

Daisy needed to talk with someone, to put her feelings into words and perhaps find a solution to the dilemma facing her. Unfortunately, the only other female living in the house to whom she might bare her soul was Lady Celeste. In the past, Daisy had found Celeste both judgmental and narrowminded. Consequently, they had never become friends.

She felt sorry for the older woman, who often seemed lonely and sad. Celeste must have been beautiful once upon a time, and Daisy had wondered occasionally over the years why Celeste had never married. She had fine bones and large, heavily lashed hazel eyes. But as long as Daisy had known her she had worn her gray hair in a severe bun and dressed in somber colors that emphasized her pale complexion so that she sometimes looked like one of the walking dead.

No, Daisy couldn't see herself spilling her tale of woe into that spinster lady's ears. Lady Celeste would be horrified at Daisy's lack of discretion in

kissing the duke and appalled at her freakishly un-
feminine desire to remain involved in what were
considered male realms of authority.

There was no help for it. She would have to ride
over and visit her friend Priscilla, who for the past
two years had been the Countess of Rotherham.
Priss would be able to make sense of everything that
had happened this morning. Priss had a way of making even the greatest problems seem small.

Daisy rang for her maid, Jane, and already had
her morning dress unbuttoned down the back as far
as she could reach—not more than three or four
buttons—by the time the young woman got to her.
"Get out my plum-colored riding habit, Jane," she
said. "I'm going to visit Lady Rotherham."

"But His Grace said—"

"Where I go and what I do is not the business of
anyone but myself," she snapped. "Do as I say,
Jane."

Daisy was immediately sorry for taking out her
frustration with the duke on her maid. "I'm sorry,
Jane."

"No apology is necessary, Your Grace. With *that
man* in the house, it's a wonder anyone's got any
nerves left."

Daisy laughed. "*That man* is *His Grace*, the Duke
of Severn, Jane. Beware lest he catch you calling
him otherwise."

"Don't know why I should worry," Jane said. "He
told Thompson to call him Calloway. Just plain Calloway! Can you imagine the Windermere butler calling His Grace anything but His Grace?"

Daisy shook her head. Nicholas Calloway had

picked up some strange habits in the colonies, all right.

Jane found the plum-colored riding costume in the wardrobe and retrieved matching gloves and a feather-trimmed hat before locating Daisy's riding crop, which should have been kept in the stable, but which she invariably brought into the house with her.

The change was accomplished with a minimum of fuss. Daisy adjusted her hat at a jaunty angle, with the feather just touching her cheek, before grabbing crop and gloves. "Thank you, Jane," she called over her shoulder as she headed out the door.

Daisy crept down the stairs, lips pressed flat in disgust that she had been forced to slink around the house to avoid a confrontation with the duke. She breathed a sigh of relief when she saw the library door was closed and quickly made her escape out the front door, which Thompson held open for her.

"Enjoy your ride, Your Grace," he said.

She flashed the butler a quick grin. "It'll be good to get some fresh air, Thompson." Her glance slid to the library door. "The atmosphere has become decidedly stifling."

"Yes, Your Grace," Thompson replied. The austere butler didn't crack a smile, but his eyes had an amused twinkle as he shut the door behind her.

Daisy had forgotten, in her agitation, that Colin Calloway had taken himself off to the stable. Even if she hadn't forgotten, she wouldn't have expected to find him there more than an hour after he had left the library. It was hard to meet his eyes, but she forced herself to smile and say "Hello, Colin."

"Hello, Your Grace." He bowed slightly and a little stiffly. "Did I do it right?"

Daisy's smile broadened in an attempt to relieve the anxious look in his eyes. "Like a true Englishman."

He grinned. "I learned it from Phipps."

"The solicitor?"

"When he came to our ranch in Texas he was forever bowing and calling Pa 'Your Grace.' "

Daisy made a spur of the moment decision. "I'm going for a ride. Would you like to join me, Colin?"

"I've been wanting to take a look around the place, but I didn't want to end up lost. Thanks. I'd like that."

Daisy eyed Colin's clothes askance. He hardly looked the well-dressed Englishman. There was no cravat at the throat of his linen shirt and no collar for that matter. The *de rigueur* waistcoat was missing beneath his black frock coat. His hair was too long, and his boots lacked polish. Yet she felt sure Priss would judge Colin for himself and not his attire. She was less certain how the Earl of Rotherham would react, but she wouldn't allow anyone to embarrass the duke's son.

"What a beauty!" Daisy said as Colin led a gold-colored gelding with a black mane and tail and markings from the stall. The groom was busy saddling her own mount.

"His name is Buck," Colin said, "because he's a buckskin."

"I've never seen a horse quite like that," Daisy confessed. "What breed is he?"

"Buck is a mustang. That's a horse that runs wild in the West. Pa caught him and broke him for me."

"I've never seen a saddle quite like that, either," Daisy said.

"It's what we use in Texas," Colin replied as he hefted the western saddle onto Buck's back. "This horn here is where we dally a rope after we loop in on a steer. This second cinch keeps the saddle from slipping when a longhorn gets other ideas and heads for the brush."

"The designs worked into the leather are certainly beautiful," Daisy said, unwilling to criticize the saddle, even though she believed it lacked the grace and simplicity of the English model.

The groom provided a cupped hand, and Daisy settled into the sidesaddle on her Thoroughbred.

"Oh, Simp did this design on the leather," Colin said as he threw himself onto the buckskin without touching the stirrup.

"Simp?"

"Simp works for my pa, but he's more like an uncle. He's the one who helped my pa raise me."

Daisy wanted desperately to ask what had happened to Colin's mother, but bit her tongue on the question. "Where is Simp now?" she asked instead.

"He stayed home in Texas to keep an eye on the livestock." Colin grinned. "Said he wasn't about to set foot off dry land."

Daisy liked Nicholas's son. The young man had a bright, open face and seemed forthright and honest. How had His Grace managed to raise such a friendly son when he was so cold himself? Perhaps Simp—what an odd name—was responsible for Colin's cheerful outlook on life.

Daisy took Colin on a quick tour of the grounds around Severn Manor, showing off the green rolling hills and the nearby forest that provided a haven for larger game.

"These rolling hills aren't so very different from the ones where I live," Colin said. "Except the land here is more . . . tame. I don't know exactly how to explain it. Nothing grows wild here, like it does back home. It all seems . . . cultivated. You've got hedges and stone walls hemming you in. Texas is all wide open spaces. Does that make sense?"

"Yes, it does," Daisy replied. Apparently the land in America was no more civilized than the people living on it. She kept her thoughts to herself. She had no wish to insult Colin with her opinion of the colonies.

Colin was impressed with Rockland Park, the ancestral home of the Earls of Rotherham. "It's amazing how the ivy grows over the stone on the house like that. It looks almost like a castle with all those odd shapes at the top."

"It looks like a castle because it was a castle, once upon a time," Daisy said, observing the gray stonework that was shaped into crenels along the topmost edge of the house.

"Really? No fooling?" Colin's jaw hung slack. "A real castle. Jehoshaphat! Wait'll I tell Simp about this!"

Even though Daisy wasn't expected, Priss had the butler immediately usher her and Colin to the drawing room, where she was waiting for them.

Daisy always had to choke back a laugh when she entered Priss's drawing room, for the countess constantly filled it with every new decorating idea that came into vogue or that might have been in vogue at some time during the past. Right now the sofa had crocodile arms and feet, and the lamp tables were covered with red cloths fringed in gold. Actually, nearly everything in the room sported a fringe or ruffles, including the heavy, wine-colored velvet curtains. Priss had adopted the cluttered look that was popular, and every bit of space on the walls was covered by some piece of framed art.

Daisy had to confess that the flamboyant decorations matched Priss's personality. Part of the reason she liked Priss so much was that her friend never based her decisions on what other people thought. She was true to her own muse.

Daisy envied her that freedom but had no desire to emulate her. She would have felt suffocated living in such crowded surroundings. Instead, she had chosen the furnishings at Severn for their simplicity and comfort. She ignored the trends and kept the furniture to a minimum so every room felt spacious. She not only had no heavy velvet curtains on her windows, several rooms had no curtains at all. Sunlight was allowed to stream in and brighten the space.

Daisy's attention was drawn back to the matter at hand when Priss spoke.

"Who's this?" she asked, surveying Colin critically.

"May I present Mr. Colin Calloway, from America. This is my friend, the Countess of Rotherham."

Colin practiced his bow again and did a very creditable job of it.

"Well done," Daisy praised.

Colin grinned. "I may just get the hang of this before I return home."

Which reminded Daisy why she had sought out her friend. Colin and his father were planning to be in England only long enough to liquidate the duke's assets. Then they would be returning to Texas. Daisy was wondering how she was going to manage a private conversation with Priss, when the problem was solved for her.

Daisy watched Colin's blue eyes widen and noticed the stricken look on his face as Priss's seventeen-year-old stepdaughter entered the room.

"I heard a male voice," the girl said. "Oh," she said when she noticed Colin.

Colin stiffened as she approached him and looked up into his face—he was a good head taller than she —with open curiosity.

"Roanna," Priss admonished. "Where are your manners?"

The girl flushed and lowered her lashes demurely. "I'm sorry, Priss."

The two young people stood there tongue-tied, unable to move or to speak.

Daisy could see why Colin was bewitched. Lady Roanna Warenne was an English pocket Venus. She had blond curls that framed her face and wide-set blue eyes with long, feathery lashes and a complexion of peaches and cream. She was tiny, but her body curved in all the right places.

She was dressed in a princess sheath that was figure-fitting to below the hips. A row of dark blue buttons began at her throat and led the eye down below her waist. The bodice and skirt were powder blue, while the sleeves and overlay of the skirt were done in a contrasting fabric of dotted blue that matched the buttons. Fine white lace ringed her throat and her wrists.

However, it was Roanna's open admiration of

Colin, as much as her looks, that held the young man spellbound.

Priss appeared undecided whether to introduce Roanna or send her away. Daisy took matters into her own hands. "Lady Roanna Warenne, this is Mr. Colin Calloway, from America. Colin is His Grace's son."

Colin's heels snapped together so quickly they made an audible sound. His bow, only his third so far as Daisy was aware, was as polished as though he had been bowing to ladies for a lifetime.

"It's a pleasure to meet you, Lady Roanna."

Roanna's blush turned her cheeks rosy. Her eyelashes fluttered up once for a quick, impish look at Colin before they lowered once more.

Colin was smitten, Daisy saw. And realized suddenly how she was going to manage her private conversation with Priss. "Why don't you show Mr. Calloway around the gardens, Roanna," she suggested.

Roanna turned to her stepmother for confirmation that a stroll with the young man would be acceptable.

"Take your maid with you and a shawl," Priss said. The countess called a footman to find Priss's maid and to inform the maid to bring the girl's shawl. Luckily, this was accomplished quickly, or the two young people might have burned up from the series of hot flushes that came and went on their cheeks as they tried not to stare at each other.

When Colin and Roanna were gone, Priss settled herself on a winged chair before the fire, which burned even in the summer, and gestured Daisy to the chair opposite her. "I'm not so sure that was a wise thing to do, sending them off together," Priss said. "They're too attracted to each other for my peace of mind. Although, I must say, it isn't like Roanna to be attracted to a young man her own age. And in such disreputable attire! Did I hear you say Colin is His Grace's son?"

"I suspect Mr. Colin Calloway is more mature than an Englishman his age would be," Daisy said. "And yes, he's Nicholas's son, though not legitimate, apparently."

Priss raised a brow. "Does he know how to behave as a gentleman?"

"If he doesn't, I'm sure Roanna will correct him," Daisy said with a smile.

"I suppose you're right," Priss conceded. "Now, I'd like to know what sent you haring over here like this. Obviously, the new duke has arrived. What is he like?"

"He's impossible!"

Priss raised a brow. "Oh?"

Daisy found it hard to sit, as agitated as she felt. She rose and began pacing in front of the fire. "He plans to sell Severn Manor! None of the land is entailed, and he wants to dispose of everything as quickly as he can and return to America."

"Good heavens! What are you going to do?"

"What can I do? Find someplace to live and remove myself from Severn."

"Without a fight?" Priss asked. "That doesn't sound like the Daisy Windermere I've come to know over the past year. That Daisy would be making plans to change the duke's mind."

"She would?"

"She would."

Daisy sat but fidgeted in her seat. "As a matter of fact, I did try arguing with His Grace this morning."

"And?"

"He kissed me."

"Why, Daisy, how wonderful! If the duke is attracted to you, that would solve everything. You can simply convince him to propose and—"

"What!" Daisy leapt from her seat again. "What are you suggesting, Priss?"

Priss sat forward in her chair. "It's perfect, don't you see? If you marry the duke he won't want to go back to America. And if he stays in England, of course he won't want to sell Severn Manor. *Voilá!* All your problems are solved."

"Except I'd be married to that barbarian!" Daisy said. "Besides, I have it straight from the horse's mouth, he doesn't ever intend to marry."

"No man ever intends to marry," Priss said with a shrewd smile. "It's up to us to convince them that they can't live without us."

Daisy chewed worriedly on her lower lip. "I don't know. It sounds like a buffleheaded scheme to me. Besides, I wouldn't know the first thing about attracting a man. I married Tony out of the schoolroom, and the match was arranged by my parents."

"It's easy," Priss assured her. "You've got a head start if he's already kissed you."

"His Grace did that to intimidate me," Daisy said with asperity.

"Did he enjoy it?"

"How should I know?"

Priss made a moue. "Come, Daisy, you aren't that naive."

"All right," she said. "He enjoyed it. Or, at least, he was aroused by it."

"The two—arousal and enjoyment—are connected for men, I believe," Priss confided. "Now, we need a plan of attack."

"I haven't agreed to this," Daisy protested.

"Have you a better idea?"

Daisy stopped in her tracks and stared at her friend. "The benefit to me is obvious if I marry His Grace. What is he going to get out of it? I tell you it won't work."

"Daisy, Daisy," Priss admonished. "Has it been so long since Tony died? What is His Grace going to get out of it, indeed! A charming and beautiful hostess for his table, an able helpmate dealing with his tenants, and a lovely companion in his bed."

Daisy flushed.

"Have I spoken too bluntly? But I thought we could say anything to each other," Priss said. "It also seems to me that this is a time for plain speaking."

"Yes, it is," Daisy said, dropping into the chair across from Priss once more. "I came here today hoping that if I spoke with you I could come up with some course of action that would save me from the disaster that looms, both for myself and the tenants and servants of Severn. I hadn't thought to make so great a sacrifice. . . ."

"You see marriage to the duke as a sacrifice?" Priss asked incredulously. "Is he unhandsome, Daisy? Or cruel, do you think? Or profligate, perhaps?"

Daisy chewed on her lower lip. "He's quite good-looking, in a savage sort of way," she confessed. "I don't think he's particularly kind, but I wouldn't go so far as to call him cruel, either. I have no idea whether he's a wastrel or a spendthrift. To be honest, I don't know very much about him."

Except he makes your toes curl when he kisses you.

Daisy cleared her throat before continuing. "I would gladly sacrifice myself in a marriage to that barbarian if I thought it would make a difference to those who depend on Severn for their livelihoods. Perhaps as his wife I could convince him to stay here." Daisy flushed as she realized what inducements she might use to bind the duke to her and to Severn. "Only I have no earthly idea how to get him to propose."

Priss snorted. It was a totally uncountesslike sound. "You underestimate yourself, Daisy. You're a beautiful young woman. He's a man. There's no reason why you can't get him to propose marriage."

Daisy rose and began pacing again, like a sleek cat in a small cage. "Don't, Priss. Can't you see how impossible all this is? I simply can't do it. I'm not like you. I don't know how to flirt. I haven't the vaguest idea how to attract a man's attention."

"You got him to kiss you," Priss retorted.

Daisy flushed. "That may be true, but I'm not sure exactly what I did to provoke him into it."

"Trust me. You'll figure it out," Priss said.

"Do you really think a savage like His Grace can be tamed enough to make a docile husband?"

Priss shook her head. "No, of course not. But you wouldn't want a docile husband."

"Tony—"

"Tony is dead and best left in the grave," Priss

said. "Whatever he was, he wasn't a husband to you. Not in the year I knew you before he died, anyway."

"How dare you—"

Priss rose and confronted her friend. "I dare because I've come to care about you over the past two years. You're the sister I never had, Daisy. I've never before said a word against Tony, but I'm warning you, don't hold him up to me as the model of a good husband. He wasn't."

"But I loved him!"

Priss put a hand on Daisy's shoulder. "Yes, you did, more's the pity. He didn't deserve you. But that was then, and this is now. You have to start thinking about yourself and what you want."

"I want to stay at Severn Manor," Daisy said. She would never have children, but there were others for whom she could and did care. "I want the servants and tenants to be taken care of. And I want to have some say in the management of the estate. I don't want to give that up." She needed to feel useful. She needed to feel like her life had purpose.

"Fine," Priss said. "What are you willing to do in order to achieve those things?"

"Are you asking whether I'd be willing to marry the duke?"

"If necessary," Priss said.

Daisy's lips firmed. Her shoulders straightened and her chin came up. "I'd do anything to protect Severn Manor. Even marry a barbarian."

"What's that about a barbarian?"

Daisy whirled and found herself facing the Earl of Rotherham. "Nothing of consequence," she said.

He bowed. "Welcome to Rockland Park, Your Grace."

"I wish you would dispense with such formality, Charles," Daisy said with asperity. "I consider you my friend. If Priss is willing to accede to my wishes, I don't see why you won't."

"Very well," he said with a grin. "I'll just ignore you and say hello to my wife."

Gray streaked the earl's black hair at the temples, but even though Charles Warenne was in his early forties, he had the look and build of a younger man. When his dark-brown eyes lit on his much younger wife, they were filled with love.

Daisy was happy that Tony's friend should have found so much joy in his second marriage. Not that the earl's first marriage hadn't been a love match as well, but Charles had lost his wife to childbirth and had been alone for fifteen years before he found Priss.

Priss reached out a hand, and the earl twined his own with hers. Daisy should have felt embarrassed by the demonstration of so much affection between man and wife in public, but she had learned, over the two years since Priss had come into the earl's household, to accept such gestures as natural behavior between them.

Daisy felt a constriction in her chest and realized she wanted that kind of love for herself. There was little chance of that now. Not if she married the duke. And it began to seem more and more likely that she would. If she could just figure out a way to have him propose.

"Has the duke arrived?" Charles asked Daisy.

"Yes, he has."

"I'm looking forward to seeing him."

"Perhaps that can be arranged," Daisy said.

"Would you and Priss be able to join us for dinner later in the week?"

"Name the day," Charles said, "and we'll be there."

The earl's dark brows rose speculatively when his daughter entered the drawing room with a young man close at her heels.

"There's someone else you should meet," Daisy said. "May I present Mr. Colin Calloway, the duke's son. This is the countess's husband, the Earl of Rotherham."

Colin bowed. "How do I address you, sir?" he asked with a hesitant smile.

The earl ignored Colin's inquiry. "Your name is Calloway? How is it you're the duke's son?"

"My father wasn't married to my mother."

The earl frowned as he looked from Colin to his fetchingly pretty daughter and back. "Have you two been out walking together?" he asked his daughter.

"Yes, Papa," Roanna said. "I've been showing Mr. Calloway the gardens."

Charles turned a stern eye on his countess. "And you allowed this?"

"But whyever not?" Priss said.

"I should think that would be perfectly clear," the earl replied, eyeing Colin once more.

"It isn't clear to me, sir," Colin said, his color high.

"You aren't a proper escort, let alone an eligible suitor, for my daughter. I'll thank you not to come here again."

"Charles!" Priss exclaimed.

"Papa!" Roanna cried.

"Oh, no, Charles," Daisy said. "You can't mean

such a thing. I won't believe you would hold the boy's birth against him."

The earl turned flinty eyes on the duchess. "Where my daughter is concerned, I'll do what I must."

When Colin turned to Roanna, his face was bleached white. "It was a pleasure meeting you, Lady Roanna." He bowed formally to her before turning to Priss. "And you, Lady Rotherham." He bowed again before turning to the earl, who got nothing faintly resembling a bow. "No one tells me where I can or can't go. Good day, sir."

A moment later he was gone from the drawing room. They could hear his hurried footsteps on the tiles in the hallway.

Daisy turned on the earl the instant Colin was gone. "How could you do such a thing! I would never have brought Colin here if I'd thought he would have to endure such an insult. I thought you were a better man, Charles."

"A bastard, even the bastard son of a duke, isn't what I have in mind for my daughter," Charles said.

"He isn't here to propose," Daisy said in disgust. "He only came to keep me company. And so long as he's unwelcome here, I won't be darkening your doorstep. Don't bother coming for dinner, either. You won't be welcome!"

Daisy turned to her friend. "I'm sorry, Priss."

"Daisy, don't go like this!" Priss pleaded. She turned her eyes to her husband. "Oh, Charles. Please change your mind. Please."

For a moment Daisy thought Priss might sway the earl. But he turned to Daisy and said, "We all do what we have to do, Your Grace." He bowed, a gesture with not the least bit of condescension in it.

Daisy felt the tears welling in her eyes and fought them back. "Good-bye, Priss."

Priss held herself aloof from both Daisy and the earl. "I won't say good-bye, Daisy. Only *au revoir.* Charles will come to his senses. I'll send a note when he does."

Daisy wanted to laugh at the look of chagrin on the earl's face at his young wife's pronouncement. Daisy hugged Roanna and left the drawing room.

She hurried downstairs, anxious to speak with Colin, to apologize for putting him in such an uncomfortable situation. She found the young American already mounted and holding the reins of her horse.

"Do you need help mounting?" he asked.

Daisy accepted the assistance of the groom who stood waiting nearby. When she was settled she accepted the reins from Colin. "I'm sorry, Colin. Let's go home."

"Severn Manor isn't home to me," Colin said. "And the sooner I see the backside of this place, the better."

"The earl will mellow. Give him time."

Colin looked at her with blue eyes that reminded her of his father, cold and ruthless. "I don't need his approval to see Lady Roanna."

"Oh, but you do," Daisy cautioned. "There are rules about that sort of thing in England."

"I'm not an Englishman," Colin reminded her.

"No," Daisy said, "I suppose you're not." But he might become one if Daisy married the duke and father and son remained in England. She could imagine what Nicholas would have to say about a society that rejected his son because of his birth.

Even more to the point, she wondered how the local English gentry were going to greet Nicholas, the prodigal bastard son. Daisy supposed the duke's case was somewhat different, because he had been born in the parish. And there had never been any proof he was a bastard, only rumors and gossip.

Daisy and Colin rode the rest of the way in silence. Daisy didn't regret her visit to Priss. The countess had forced her to see she had few alternatives if she hoped to save Severn Manor.

Plainly, she would have to marry His Grace.

Daisy fought the rosy heat that raced to her cheeks as she realized what that would mean. She would have to lie with the duke and allow him to make love to her. Daisy found the thought as frightening as it was thrilling. It would be far safer to ask for a marriage of convenience. But she had no real hope the duke would agree to it.

Ashamed as she was to admit it, maybe marriage to the duke wasn't going to be such a sacrifice after all.

4

Nicholas sat behind the Sheraton desk in the library with Phipps on the other side. The solicitor was explaining something about the estate. Nicholas was listening, but he didn't hear a word Phipps said. His mind was totally occupied with Daisy Windermere, or rather, with memories of their confrontation that morning.

He shouldn't have kissed her. It had complicated everything. Not that it hadn't been a gratifying experience. In fact, he couldn't remember a time when he had been so devastated by a kiss. The feel of her defiant little mouth under his, as it softened and yielded, had aroused him beyond rational thought. He had taken liberties with her that were far from acceptable. But she had been right about one thing. He was no gentleman. He had little use for women, and none at all for ladies.

She had gumption, he would give her that. And grit, too. He would have enjoyed taking her to bed. Not that there was much chance of that happening. He imagined all that spit and fire between the sheets, and his body responded accordingly. He shifted and leaned forward at the desk, forcing his mind back to what the solicitor was saying.

"So I'm afraid you're not going to be able to find a buyer for Severn Manor in the immediate future. At least not at a price equal to its worth."

"What?" Nicholas exclaimed. "After you've gotten me here on the pretext of all the wealth to be had from Severn Manor, are you saying I won't be able to sell this place?"

"Not unless you can make it a more profitable undertaking, Your Grace."

Nicholas wished he had been paying attention. "Why isn't it profitable now?"

The look on the solicitor's face made it plain he had already explained the matter. He tugged at his waistcoat and dutifully began again, speaking more slowly, as though that would aid Nicholas in understanding the problem the second time it was presented to him.

"To be frank," Phipps said, "competition from American wheat has depressed prices in England. Since your property is planted primarily in wheat, it's worth less to a potential buyer."

"So we plant something else," Nicholas said. "Something worth more on the market."

"That's not as easy as it sounds, Your Grace."

"Why not?"

"You would need the cooperation of your tenants. You would have to supply them with information about planting and tending crops with which they have no prior experience."

"They'll do as I say, or they'll leave," Nicholas said.

Phipps ran a finger around the buttoned collar at his throat. "Your Grace, if I may be so bold—"

There was a knock on the library door. Daisy entered without waiting for permission. She marched over to stand beside Phipps, her hands laced together in front of her. She looked straight ahead, ignoring Nicholas.

"I'm here, Phipps. Thompson gave me your message when I returned from my ride."

Nicholas raised a brow and focused a hard gaze on the solicitor. "I thought this was supposed to be a private meeting."

Phipps ran a finger around his buttoned collar a second time. "Well, Your Grace—"

"Unbutton the damned thing, Phipps, if you're having trouble breathing."

Phipps stiffened. "I couldn't possibly, Your Grace. It wouldn't be proper."

"Get on with it then," Nicholas said irritably. He refused to look at Daisy, even though she drew his eye.

"To be blunt, Your Grace—"

"Sit down, Daisy."

Nicholas felt a grim satisfaction when her eyes shot to his at the use of her name. She looked lost and vulnerable for an instant, an instant in which he yearned to take her up in his arms and hold her close. The expression in her eyes was gone a moment later, replaced with a look of scorn so contemptuous he felt himself flinch.

Nicholas couldn't keep his eyes off Daisy as she crossed to the other leather chair in front of the desk and sat down. He knew a great deal of the rigidity in her carriage was due to the whalebone corset she wore, but that couldn't account for the regal tilt of her chin or the frost in her green eyes. She perched on the edge of the chair in a different brightly colored gown from the one she had worn that morning, looking like nothing so much as an exotic green and yellow bird about to take flight.

Somehow he knew she wouldn't flee. Her resolve was evident in the set of her jaw, in the tightly clenched hands in her lap, and in the flash of mutiny in her eyes.

"You may continue, Phipps," he said.

"As I was saying, Your Grace, you'll need the cooperation of your tenants to achieve any kind of success in such a monumental undertaking. I mean, to restructure the entire workings of the estate, it's an almost overwhelming task, and nearly unprecedented, I might add. I asked Her Grace to be here this afternoon because I believe she can be of assistance to you."

"I don't want her help," Nicholas said flatly.

"Good," Daisy retorted, rising immediately. "Then I'll excuse myself."

Phipps rose and blocked Daisy's path, but he had to keep backing up to avoid coming in contact with her, which would have been an outrageous breach of decorum. "Please, Your Grace, don't make a hasty decision. Think of the tenants. They'll be the ones who'll suffer if His Grace fails. And he surely will, without your help."

They were halfway to the door when Daisy stopped in her tracks. She kept her hands clasped before her, though she desperately wanted to put them to her temples to stop the pounding in her head. "Surely you're exaggerating," she said to Phipps.

"I'm not," Phipps replied. "Not at all."

"I'd like to know what you think she can do that I can't," Nicholas snapped. He came around his desk and joined the couple at the center of the Aubusson carpet. "Who's in charge here, anyway?"

"You are, Your Grace." Phipps swallowed audibly. "But Her Grace has been managing the estate for the past year, and the tenants have learned to trust her and respect her decisions.

"In short, Her Grace has earned the goodwill of the tenants. To be perfectly frank, they love her, and if I may be so bold, Your Grace, they will do anything for her. Even endure the sort of upheaval this change is bound to cause."

"Are you saying they wouldn't obey the current duke as they would the previous duchess?" Nicholas inquired.

"Begging your pardon, Your Grace, you *are* a foreigner."

"My father grew up in this house. My parents lived here after they were married. I was born in a bedroom upstairs," Nicholas said in an ominous voice.

Phipps flushed painfully. "But your father banished—"

"Am I the duke here, or not?"

"You are, Your Grace," Phipps conceded.

"What I believe Phipps is trying to say," Daisy interceded, "is that your absence has put you in an awkward situation."

"You're telling me," Nicholas muttered.

"Would you excuse us, Phipps," Daisy said. "I

would like to speak to His Grace privately. We'll call you when we need you again."

Phipps looked anxiously from Daisy to the duke and back again. "Are you certain—"

"I'm not going to ravish her, Phipps," Nicholas snarled. "Now get out of here and leave us alone."

"Very well, Your Grace." Phipps showed his disapproval through his icy tone, but he left the room without a backward glance.

"Now, Daisy," Nicholas said, crossing to the door and leaning against it, crossing one booted ankle over the other, effectively blocking her escape. "What did you want to say to me?"

Daisy turned to face him. "Phipps is right," she said, getting directly to the point. "You're going to have difficulty managing the tenants on your own. At least in the near future. I'm willing to help." Her fingers curled until her knuckles were white. "However, there is a price for my services."

Nicholas remained in his lazy pose against the door, but he was anything but relaxed. "Oh?" He felt a bitter taste in his mouth. He knew about mercenary women. He was surprised Daisy hadn't shown her true colors before. He felt more comfortable now that she had taken off her false mask of innocence and vulnerability. She was just another conniving, calculating bitch. Like all the women he had ever known.

His lips curled in contempt. "How much do you want for your . . . services? A quarter of the estate? Half?"

She had the grace to blush. "I don't want money."

He raised a dark brow but said nothing.

"I want you to marry me."

Nicholas laughed, a harsh, raucous sound.

Daisy hurried to speak before he could refuse her. "It can be a marriage of convenience." She felt a sharp pang at the loss, and the long years of loneliness, she would suffer if he agreed to a marriage without intimacy. "Even so, our marriage would be an obvious sign to the tenants that I accept you and approve of what you're doing. We can approach them together as husband and wife, urging them to make the changes necessary for the benefit of everyone."

"And when I sell Severn Manor and return to America? What then?"

Daisy met his mocking gaze. "I would stay here. In the dower house, which you would deed to me."

"Why?" Nicholas demanded.

"What?"

"Why are you willing to sacrifice yourself so nobly?" he asked in a derisive voice. "Because it would be just that, wouldn't it, Daisy? A sacrifice?"

"As I said, it can be a marriage of convenience. In which case, I would sacrifice nothing."

He shook his head.

"You won't marry me?"

"Not on the terms you've stated."

"On what terms, then?"

"I would want to get full value for *my* sacrifice," Nicholas said. "I would want to have a wife who was a wife."

"I'm not sure that would be a good idea, Your Grace," Daisy said hesitantly. She wasn't sure which would eventually cause her more pain, the real marriage or the false one.

"Then we're at a stalemate," Nicholas said. "Shall

I call Phipps back in? If I have to take a loss, that's what I'll do. I can't see the back of this place fast enough!"

"You're really going to sell Severn Manor?" Daisy asked in an agonized voice.

"As quickly as I can, for as much as I can get."

"No. Don't sell just yet. I'll . . . I'll marry you on any terms you ask."

"You realize you're only postponing the inevitable," he said.

"Yes," Daisy said in a voice that quivered with emotion.

"Very well, then. We're agreed. We'll marry."

Daisy nodded, her chin so high her neck was stretched tight. That would explain her inability to swallow, or to speak. But there was one more thing she needed to say to him before she was through. One more painful revelation that needed to be made.

"I can't have children," she said.

He raised a brow, but otherwise his expression didn't change. "It isn't necessary for you to produce any. I have an heir. In fact, under the circumstances, I would say your barrenness is a decided advantage."

Daisy paled. "I've never thought so," she whispered.

Nicholas caught himself wanting to comfort her again. Damn the woman! She was too vulnerable for his peace of mind. He forced himself to stay where he was. "I'll call Phipps back in. He can make all the arrangements."

Later that night, as Daisy stared at the white lace curtains that framed her canopied bed, she wondered how she had allowed herself to get into such a predicament.

She had maneuvered the duke into offering for her, as Priss had suggested she ought. So why did she feel as though she had been the one manipulated? Why had Nicholas agreed to such a pact? What was he going to get out of it?

She knew the answer to that question. He was going to get the only thing he wanted from her: the privilege of her company in bed. Nicholas didn't know it yet, but he had made a terrible bargain. Fortunately, there was no way he could escape once the vows were read between them. She would be his wife. And he would be bound to her for better or worse.

He just didn't know the worst yet.

But she hadn't gotten such a bargain, either. She hadn't avoided the sale of Severn Manor by agreeing to marry the duke, only postponed it.

Unless she could use the little time she had with him to change his mind. Daisy hadn't missed the duke's savage response to Phipps about having been born at Severn Manor. Now that she thought about it, Tony had mentioned how the three cousins had spent their summers together. Which meant Nicholas must have some fond memories of his time at Severn Manor.

Was it possible to revive those memories? Was it possible to make Nicholas care again about a heritage that had been lost to him for most of his life?

Why not?

Daisy listened to the little voice inside that said all things were possible. She knew from her adventures over the past year that she was capable of a great deal. Could she also work a miracle with Nicholas Calloway? Could she teach the duke to love Severn Manor again?

He must have loved it once, she reasoned. Who could live here and not love it? He had been born here, had lived here the first eight summers of his life. Surely she could revive those halcyon days for him.

If she was going to go that far, she might as well go all the way and revive in him—instill in him—a sense of responsibility toward the people of Severn Manor.

But how?

Perhaps there was some way she could make the problems of Severn's tenants real to him. Perhaps if she introduced him to some of them, they would become persons, rather than faceless names. Surely he wouldn't be able to ignore them then. But who should she take him to see? And how was she going to get him to go?

Daisy spent a sleepless night, tossing and turning and thinking. She arose the next morning with a plan firm in her mind. She would do it. By the time she was finished, not only would Nicholas love Severn Manor, but the people of Severn Manor would honor and revere him. In her head, it was all so simple. All that remained was to accomplish the impossible.

Nicholas spent an equally sleepless night—once he got to bed. When he answered the knock on his door after he had retired, he found his son standing before him.

"Come in, Colin. What brings you here this hour of the night?"

Colin hadn't yet learned to hide his emotions, and Nicholas easily perceived his son was upset. Yet the boy didn't immediately launch into speech. He crossed the room and stood at the window, staring out into the darkness. Nicholas stayed by the door, waiting patiently, knowing that Colin would be more likely to reveal his problem if he wasn't pushed into doing it.

"How soon are we leaving here, Pa?" Colin asked.

Nicholas smiled. "We just got here, Colin. Are you homesick already?"

Colin turned and Nicholas saw the tension in his son's face and body. "I'm not homesick at all."

"Then what's the problem?"

"I don't fit in here, Pa."

"What makes you say that?"

"I never once thought of myself as being any different because you weren't married to my mother," Colin said seriously. "That sort of thing matters here."

Nicholas hissed in a breath. "The circumstances of your birth don't make you different from anyone else."

"But I've been treated differently because of it."

"By whom?"

"It doesn't really matter, Pa."

"It does to me," Nicholas said in a dangerous voice. "I asked a question, Colin. Who treated you differently?"

The whole story came pouring out. How Colin had met the most beautiful girl in the world. How they had gone walking in the gardens of Rockland Park.

How he had felt his heart was going to pound out of
his chest when she looked up at him. How they had
returned to the drawing room, and he had been confronted by the earl, Lady Roanna's father, and been
told in no uncertain terms to keep his distance.

"Because I'm a bastard, Pa."

Nicholas's lips flattened. "I'll speak to the earl,
Colin."

"Would you, Pa? I wouldn't ask except I want to
see Lady Roanna again. At first I figured to see her
no matter what her father said. Then I started thinking maybe she wouldn't agree to see me if her father
didn't allow it. It would be easier all around if the
earl changed his mind."

"You're that smitten with her?" Nicholas asked.

Color rose in Colin's cheeks, but he met his father's gaze. "I never met a woman like her, Pa. She's
. . . my heart . . . I can't breathe when I'm
around her, my chest is so tight. I want to protect
her and . . . and hold her."

"I see." Nicholas couldn't keep the frown from his
face. He had known the day would come when his
son fell in love for the first time. Strangely, he hadn't
infected Colin with his disdain for women. Not that
he hadn't warned his son that a woman wasn't to be
trusted, but that admonition had fallen on deaf ears.
Colin trusted everybody. That was Simp's doing,
Nicholas knew. For every bad thing Nicholas had to
say about women, Simp had come up with a story of
something good.

Nicholas saw his son headed for heartbreak and
wanted to step in to stop the disaster before it occurred. Colin was too young to be thinking about
marriage, and young ladies like the earl's daughter

thought of nothing else. He cursed the circumstances that kept them in England. The easiest way
to resolve the problem was to go home to America.
But that simply wasn't possible.

He had another choice besides interference. He
could let his son deal with the problem on his own.
Most likely, the earl would guard his daughter so
closely that Colin would be denied her company.
Nicholas could hope that absence would not make
the heart grow fonder, that if Colin didn't see Lady
Roanna Warenne he would forget about her.

He searched his son's features and scowled at
what he found. He knew that look. It had rested
upon his own face once upon a time. The boy was
besotted. Colin would find a way to see the earl's
daughter. With or without the earl's permission.

His son was looking at him with trust and with
hope. Colin believed he could do anything. Nicholas
wasn't so sure he would be able to resolve this matter to Colin's satisfaction. As he was in a position to
know, Englishmen could be blindly stubborn when
it came to certain social issues. Legitimacy was definitely one of them.

His son was the one thing he loved in all the
world. For Colin's sake, he was willing to try. Nicholas remembered Charles Warenne, who was now the
Earl of Rotherham. He and Tony and Stephen had
played together with Charles as boys. He remembered the earl as a daredevil, as a boy as wild as
Nicholas himself. It seemed strange to consider his
childhood friend in the role of protective father. Perhaps Charles would be willing to ease his restric-
tions for old time's sake.

"Don't get your hopes up," Nicholas said. "The

earl may not change his mind even after I speak to him."

Colin grinned. "I know you, Pa. When you talk to people, they usually come around. Do it soon, will you, Pa? I need to see Lady Roanna again."

"I'll do it tomorrow," Nicholas promised.

"Good night, Pa."

"Good night, son."

They didn't touch each other as they parted, not physically, anyway. But Colin met his father's glance and communicated all the wealth of love and respect he felt. And Nicholas let Colin see his deep affection in return.

A moment later, the door closed quietly behind Colin.

Nicholas stripped—he slept naked when he was at home—and slipped into bed. He had forgotten how soft a bed could be. The mattress threatened to swallow him as he slid into its downy softness.

Nicholas blamed his inability to sleep on the too-soft bed, but it was his thoughts that kept him awake. They didn't concern Colin's problem, nor the tribulations of Severn Manor or its tenants. There was only one star in his sky, and its name was Daisy Windermere.

Nicholas wondered why he had agreed to marry her when he had vowed years ago—when the one and only proposal he had ever made to a woman had been thrown laughingly back in his face—never to wed. Perhaps it was because this wasn't a real marriage. But she was going to come to his bed. That was real enough. If he was honest with himself, there was an easy explanation for his aberrant behavior: he wanted her. And because she was a lady, the only way to have her was to marry her.

Nicholas had taken his share of whores to bed, but he had never gotten involved with a lady. He had seen a few he desired but had never been willing to make the commitment a lady demanded in trade for her virtue. Besides, a lady wanted the desire he felt for the female of the species sugarcoated with words of love and caring. The two women he had loved in his life—his mother and the mother of his son—had each betrayed him. He wasn't going to give another woman that chance.

He had agreed to the marriage with Daisy Windermere because it offered him what he wanted—her body—without requiring that he lie to her about loving her, and without the need for him to surrender anything of himself to a female who was bound to prove untrustworthy in the end.

He would take what he wanted from her and give her what she asked in return. He would work with her to make of Severn Manor the successful enterprise it could be.

Then he would sell it and return to America. It would not matter that he left a wife in England. She would be happy in her dower house. He would go back to his ranch in Texas and forget about her.

They would both be getting exactly what they wanted.

5

Nicholas awoke in a cold sweat. He took several deep breaths in an attempt to calm his racing heart. The dream had come back to haunt him, even here in England. There was no escaping it. He had thought his father's—Lord Philip's—death might ease his desperate need to know the truth. Obviously the dream wasn't going to release him until he sought out answers for the questions that had plagued him over the past twenty-two years. Was he his father's son? And if not, who was his father?

Perhaps Lord Philip had left a journal or some papers that would indicate who had convinced him Nicholas had not sprung from his loins. Nicholas made up his mind to probe Severn's library for information and to question Phipps about the matter. Perhaps the solicitor knew more than he had said on the subject.

More recently, Nicholas had begun to wonder whether someone had purposely misled his father. On her deathbed, his mother had suggested as much. Was there some dark plot against his mother, or his father, or both? If so, who had wanted to hurt them, and why? It might be worthwhile to hire someone to investigate the matter. Certainly there was no reason why he couldn't ask some questions himself. He would start today when he visited Charles Warenne.

Nicholas heard the bedroom door slowly creaking open. The room was shadowed in the predawn light. He could see silhouettes in gray and black, but not much else. He reached for his Colt .45—and realized he had left it in one of the bureau drawers. He had felt naked without it, but the English countryside wasn't dangerous enough to require him to carry a gun, much less sleep with one by his pillow. Yet someone was obviously sneaking into his room. He slowly eased himself out of bed and slipped into the shadows in the corner.

The intruder stealthily approached the curtained bed. An instant later Nicholas sprang from cover and closed one arm around the intruder's neck. His other hand captured a wrist and pulled it high behind the man's back.

"Who are you?" he demanded in a whisper, so he wouldn't wake the house. "What are you doing here?"

Unfortunately, his forearm had cut off the man's air, and all Nicholas heard was a garbled sound in response. He eased off the pressure on his victim's neck and said, "Talk."

"I'm Porter, Your Grace," the man gasped. "Your Grace's valet."

"I don't have a valet," Nicholas said, still not releasing the man.

"I served the previous duke, Your Grace, and his father. I have always served Severn, Your Grace, as my father did before me. I regret to say I was away visiting relatives when Your Grace arrived. Otherwise we might have avoided such an unorthodox meeting."

Nicholas saw no reason not to believe the man. He sounded pompous enough to be a duke's valet. He released the gentleman's gentleman and stepped back. He ought to have felt ridiculous for imagining danger in the English countryside, but Nicholas had lived too many years on the edge, where one mistake could cost him his life. Old habits died hard.

He perused the elderly gentleman who claimed to be his valet as the old man pulled back the heavy curtains from the windows to let in the pinks and yellows of a new day. Porter was nearly bald, with just a fringe of salt-and-pepper hair around his head. His face was gaunt, and his silvery eyes were capped by thick salt-and-pepper brows. He had a beaked nose and a protruding lower lip. He was also impeccably dressed, much more imposingly so than Nicholas had been on his arrival at Severn.

Nicholas tried to remember if he had ever seen Porter as a child, but he couldn't place him. Apparently the duke's valet hadn't ventured into the nursery or onto the lawns, forests, and ponds of Severn where the three cousins had spent most of their time.

Nicholas was convinced Porter was a valet when the man remained totally unruffled as he turned and bowed, even though Nicholas wasn't wearing a stitch of clothing. Apparently, where dukes were concerned, clothes didn't necessarily make the man.

Nicholas grinned wryly. "I'm used to dressing myself, Porter," he said as he dragged on a pair of long johns.

"As you wish, Your Grace. However, someone must take charge of Your Grace's clothing, to make sure it is in the best repair and clean and ready to be worn." He arched a brow as if to say "Don't you agree?"

Nicholas arched one in return. Perhaps clothes did make the man, once he was wearing them. "I see your point. All right, Porter. I guess I have a valet."

Nicholas saw the tension ease in the old man's shoulders and realized Porter hadn't been at all sure of his reception. Apparently word had gotten around about Nicholas's intention of selling Severn. From the frown that remained between Porter's brows, the valet obviously wanted to say more.

"Is there something else, Porter?"

"If I may say so, Your Grace, you require the services of both a London tailor and a bootmaker. May I summon them?"

Nicholas started to deny he needed anything new, then realized that if he planned to start asking questions of the local gentry, he was more likely to get answers if he looked the ducal role. The knee-length frock coat, buckskin trousers, and boots he had bought from a haberdasher in New York before he sailed obviously weren't up to English standards. "All right, Porter. Do as you see fit."

"Now if you will kindly sit over here, Your Grace, I will shave you."

"I shave myself, Porter."

He saw Porter wince, but the valet said, "As you wish, Your Grace. I will take care of procuring some hot water."

Nicholas stood for a second, expecting Porter to leave. Instead the man pulled a cord near the door—

apparently hauling hot water was the chore of lesser servants—then headed for the wardrobe and began removing Nicholas's clothes and laying them out on the bed.

"I said I can dress myself, Porter."

"Yes, Your Grace. I am merely ensuring that everything is in readiness. I understand you will be riding today?"

"I will." Although how Porter could know that was beyond Nicholas. Except, as he recalled from his childhood, the servants always knew everything. They might be an excellent source of information about his birth, Nicholas suddenly realized. Porter, for instance, might have gleaned a great deal about the matter from having served Lord Philip's brother. Nicholas could ask him right here and now what he knew. Only Nicholas's tongue suddenly clung to the roof of his mouth, and he couldn't speak.

Nicholas understood that unless he kicked Porter out right now, he could say good-bye to his privacy in the mornings. One look at the valet, and he couldn't do it. There was great pride in Porter's carriage, and he knew from the things Daisy had said that the servants depended on Severn for their livelihoods. Apparently Porter had been kept on the staff for the past year to be available to serve the new duke once he was determined. What would Porter do if he no longer served the Duke of Severn? Likely the old man would have a hard time finding a new position at his age.

Why do you care?

Perhaps it was because Porter reminded him a little of Simp. That must be it. It wasn't because he cared what happened to the servants at Severn. And it had absolutely nothing to do with Daisy's tirade in the library.

"All right, Porter, as long as you're here, you might as well shave me," he said with a sigh.

He ignored the pleased look that briefly visited Porter's face. "Just don't cut me," he warned.

Porter looked offended. "I have shaved three generations of Windermeres, Your Grace."

"Don't spout history at me, Porter," Nicholas said in an icy voice. "In case you've forgotten, I'm not a Windermere."

Porter didn't contradict him. But he didn't agree with him, either.

Well, Nicholas thought, if he knows the truth, he isn't telling. He wasn't sure he was ready to hear the truth. And in that case, it was better not to ask. But he didn't think he could remain silent, either.

He quickly found himself seated before a mirrored dresser, with a towel around his throat. The hot water was delivered, and Porter began stirring up shaving soap with a silver-handled boar bristle brush.

Nicholas hadn't realized how desperate he was for answers. The words popped out of his mouth before he could stop them. "Were you acquainted with my mother and father, Porter?"

"Yes, Your Grace."

The valet didn't volunteer more, and Nicholas wasn't sure what to say next. He couldn't very well ask outright if his mother had been unfaithful to his father.

"There must have been some gossip at the time," Nicholas said tentatively.

"There was, Your Grace. Could Your Grace remain still? Otherwise I might cut Your Grace after all."

Nicholas took that to mean Porter didn't want to talk about the matter. But if his valet knew enough to admit there had been gossip, there were bound to be others who had heard it as well.

Nicholas felt a little breathless. There were answers here. He knew it. He was only a little frightened to know the truth. Although why it should matter to him after all these years, he didn't know. It wouldn't affect his inheritance, and it couldn't affect his life in America. But it might stop the dreams. And it would be an escape from the dark, horrifying abyss of uncertainty that had swallowed him so many years ago.

He imagined himself coming face to face with the man who had fathered him. What questions would he ask? *Why did you seduce my mother? Why did you abandon her in her hour of need? Didn't you care about me at all?*

Nicholas realized for the first time that he hated the man responsible for the calamity that had forced him from all that was familiar. That nameless, faceless father was responsible for his mother becoming a whore, for their life of poverty and want, for his being rejected by the father he had known and loved until he was eight years old. Nicholas hadn't realized until this very moment the depth of his enmity. If he ever laid hands on the man who had planted the bastard seed in his mother, he would surely kill him.

Nicholas knew he could probably force Porter to tell him what gossip he had heard. But now that the answers were within his grasp, he felt strangely re-

luctant to seek them out. He would be seeing
Charles Warenne within a matter of hours. He
grasped at even that brief respite from the truth.
Because once he knew the truth, he would be bound
to act upon it. Assuming Lord Philip was *not* his
father, Nicholas concluded with a wry twist of his
mouth.

He straightened his features when Porter grimaced disapprovingly at him. Maybe his parents
had simply had a grievous misunderstanding. But
even were that so, there was the possibility that
someone had been making mischief. And if that was
the case, he would somehow, some way have his
revenge.

Nicholas had to admit, half an hour later, that
Porter knew his business. He had dressed himself,
but thanks to Porter his hair was trimmed, his coat
free from dust and lint, and his boots had never seen
such a shine. Still, Nicholas could tell he didn't quite
meet the valet's standards. Undoubtedly Porter
would be happier when Nicholas had been fitted by
an English tailor.

He had planned to escape the house before anyone awoke, but when he reached the dining room he
found Daisy there before him. She was dressed to
ride in a habit of forest green with gold military
braid at the shoulders and a double row of bright
gold buttons down the front. It outlined her figure so
well he began to wish he had asked to be married by
special license rather than agreeing to wait for the
banns to be read. Her copper tresses were pulled
back into a bun at her nape, leaving only a few curls
to frame her face. He marveled anew at how beautiful she was.

She had wide, high cheekbones and a small, straight nose. Her chin was perhaps too square, and she had it raised rebelliously again, which showed off her willowy neck. There were smudges under her eyes, as though she hadn't slept well, and the emerald green orbs that had flashed with fire—was it only yesterday?—met his gaze cautiously.

He realized he wanted to spend some time with her. He was curious about her, about why she felt so much responsibility for Severn and about why she had been so willing to sacrifice herself for the sake of people her class usually didn't bother themselves about. Maybe he could convince her to ride over to Rockland Park with him.

"Where are you headed this morning?" he asked.

"Good morning, Your Grace," she said, providing the courteous greeting he had neglected to offer.

He stared at her intently, silently demanding that she answer his question. Instead, she merely lowered her gaze to her plate.

Don't give up the fight, Daisy, he thought. *I want to see those eyes of your sparkle again with defiance.* She had clearly made up her mind to be everything that was gracious. He became equally determined to provoke a fiery response from her.

"It's a lovely day, isn't it?" she said.

"It is," he conceded. He stalked over and stood just behind her shoulder. He watched the pulse leap in her throat. She gripped her fork more tightly, but raised it and took a bite of food.

He leaned over and murmured in her ear, "Are you riding somewhere in particular, Daisy?"

He noted with satisfaction the shiver that ran down her spine. But again she ignored his question.

She took her time chewing and swallowing before she answered him. He noticed her voice was the slightest bit breathless. She wasn't as unaffected by his presence as she wanted him to think.

"Help yourself to breakfast from the sideboard," she said. "Kidneys, eggs, kippers and herring, some porridge and muffins. I'm sure you'll find something there to your taste."

Nicholas was enjoying the game with Daisy, but just then his stomach growled, reminding him he was hungry. Abruptly he left her and crossed to the sideboard.

He frowned at the food Daisy had recommended to him. Aside from the eggs, he didn't see much that appealed to him. Once upon a time he must have eaten such foods, but his palate had changed over the years he had been gone from England. He would have to talk to Cook about putting some steak and biscuits and gravy on the breakfast menu.

He dished himself up some eggs and several muffins before settling himself on a needlepoint-cushioned chair across from her, rather than at the head of the table. The cherrywood table would easily have seated twenty, and it seemed ludicrous to use it for the two of them. "Why aren't we eating in the smaller dining room?"

"The staff assumed you would rather dine formally. If you prefer, I can direct them to serve our meals in the family dining room."

"I prefer it."

"Consider it done," Daisy said.

"Where did you plan to ride this morning?" he asked for the third time.

For a moment he thought she was going to avoid

the question again. She chewed several more times and swallowed before saying "That's none of your business, Your Grace."

"Wherever it is, we can go together. Then you can ride to Rockland Park with me, since I have to visit the earl this morning, and I would enjoy your company."

Daisy looked for an instant like a trapped creature, determined to fight to the death rather than surrender.

"I won't bite," he murmured, nevertheless allowing her to see that he would have enjoyed a nibble or two at certain portions of her anatomy.

Her green eyes flashed at him. "But I might," she retorted.

Nicholas laughed. "Good for you, Daisy. I'm looking forward to taming you, and I wouldn't like to think you give up too easily."

Daisy flushed painfully when she realized she had risen to his bait and given him the game. He watched her struggle to regain her composure. It turned out to be a losing battle.

She rose and threw her napkin onto the table. "I don't care for company this morning. In fact, I was looking forward to the opportunity of riding by myself."

"But since we're both going for a ride, it seems foolish to ride separately, don't you agree?"

Daisy needed to talk with Priss, but she had vowed yesterday to stay away until Colin was welcome. At least riding with Nicholas would provide the excuse she needed to return to Rockland Park without losing face.

"I . . . oh, very well. Have it your way," she said,

her agitation evident. "But I'm leaving. If you're coming, you'll have to come now."

Nicholas looked down at the plateful of food in front of him. His stomach growled again. It wouldn't be the first time he had gone hungry. "Very well, Daisy. Let's go."

He almost laughed again at the crestfallen look on her face. Obviously she had expected him to choose eating breakfast over a ride with her. He could almost feel the sparks radiating off her as he followed her out to the stable.

Their horses were saddled and waiting. She looked surprised to see he had an English saddle on a Thoroughbred mount. "Colin rode a mustang yesterday with a western saddle," she said.

"I learned to ride on a Thoroughbred. I thought I'd give it another try." Nicholas held his hands cupped, ready to assist Daisy into her sidesaddle. It was apparent she didn't want to touch him, not even with her boot, but she finally conceded that he wasn't going to allow her to ignore him.

Nicholas was amazed at how light she was. She was seated on a large, spirited mount, but was well able to control the animal. "I take it you've done a lot of riding."

"I've done my share. Especially over the past year."

"Yes, you have been a busy little bee, haven't you?"

"If you mean I've done a great deal to make sure Severn Manor was taken care of properly, then yes, *Your Grace*, I have been a busy little bee."

Nicholas groaned. "I thought we'd gotten beyond titles, Daisy. Nicholas, please."

Daisy sat staring straight forward and ignored the duke, incensed at the way he had denigrated her efforts over the past year. He had no idea what she had been through. No idea how difficult it had been to make decisions, not knowing if she was doing the right thing.

From the corner of her eye, she noticed that Nicholas mounted the same way as his son, without touching the stirrup. It looked amazingly graceful, but she didn't want to admire the man. She turned toward Rockland Park and kicked her mount into a trot.

Nicholas quickly caught up to her. "I'm sorry if I insulted you, Daisy."

She angled her head toward him. "An apology, Your Grace? We are making strides, aren't we?"

"No need to be sarcastic, Daisy. Especially not when I'm offering an olive branch."

"Is that what that was?"

Nicholas grinned. Daisy found his smile appallingly seductive. She snapped her head around and faced forward. She wasn't about to let an American savage charm her into doing his bidding.

"I'd like to hear more about what you've done over the past year," Nicholas said.

"I'm sure the bailiff, Mr. Henderson, can tell you anything you need to know."

"I want to hear it from you," Nicholas said.

His request was a hair's breadth from being an order. Daisy thought about denying him, then realized she was glad to have the opportunity to let him know some of the projects she had started which would need his approval to be continued.

"I put new slate roofs on most of the cottages,

many of which were leaking abominably." She glanced at him as though daring him to object to the expenditure.

"That sounds reasonable," he said, denying her the argument she was dying to have with him.

"I opened a school for the tenants' children and hired a young woman to teach them," she said defiantly.

"Education is important," Nicholas said. "We have a number of women teachers in America. I've never found them to be less competent than a man."

"I sold off Tony's racing stock."

"Tony raced horses?"

Daisy nodded. "It was a passion with him. But I didn't see the sense in keeping a stable of blooded animals."

"I would have liked to see them," Nicholas murmured.

"Well, you can't," Daisy said. "I sold them all!"

"What else did you sell?" Nicholas asked, an edge to his voice.

"Nothing that would interest you."

"What?"

"I sold a great deal of outmoded farming machinery." She paused and swallowed before finishing "And bought new."

Nicholas arched a brow. "How did you know what to buy?"

"I read farm journals. And of course I asked Mr. Henderson's advice." She didn't tell him that Henderson had vehemently objected to her "newfangled ideas." He would find that out the first time he talked to the bailiff.

"How did the tenants react to the new machinery?" Nicholas asked.

Daisy started. She hadn't expected Nicholas to be perceptive enough to realize there had been problems with the introduction of modern farming methods. "They were skeptical," she admitted. "At first. But they soon came to see the advantages to be had from the new machinery."

"How do you think they're going to react when I ask them to plant an entirely different crop?"

Daisy wrinkled her nose. "You're going to have your hands full convincing them to make such a drastic change. Most of them have farmed the same land, the same crop, for generations."

"What did you say to get them to try the machines?"

Daisy blushed. "I'm afraid I bribed them."

"Bribed them?"

"I promised to make up from estate funds anything they lost on this year's crops as a result of trying my suggestions."

"Wasn't that a bit risky?" Nicholas asked. "What if the crops had failed?"

There was a long silence.

"The crops did succeed, didn't they, Daisy?" Nicholas asked in an ominous voice.

"Not exactly."

"What exactly?"

"We had rain in the middle of the harvest. The machines broke down, a mechanical failure. Because we relied on the machinery, there weren't enough men to get the harvest in by hand. We lost part of the crop."

"Damn. Damn." Nicholas took off his hat—he

missed his Stetson—shoved a hand through his hair, and settled the small-brimmed English hat back on his head. "How much did that shortsighted idea indebt the estate?"

"Not much," Daisy hedged.

"How much?" Nicholas demanded.

Daisy named a sum that had Nicholas hissing in his breath.

"Good Lord, woman. No wonder I can't sell this place!"

"The machines were a good idea," Daisy said heatedly.

"But the bargain you made with the tenants wasn't."

"We'll make it up next year."

"I won't be here next year," Nicholas reminded her.

Daisy bit her lip. She wouldn't beg him to stay. He could go back to America for all she cared. He was a stupid, ignorant boor. What did he know about running an English estate?

"I can't believe Phipps suggested I marry you as a way of controlling the tenants. Hell, from the sound of things, a few English pounds would have accomplished the same thing!"

"They didn't do it for the money," Daisy said.

"You just got through telling me you promised to make up their losses," Nicholas argued.

"When I offered them the money, they wouldn't take it," Daisy said in a quiet voice.

"What?"

"They said it wasn't my fault, so Severn shouldn't have to pay."

"Are you telling me they turned down the money you owed them."

"That's exactly what I'm saying," Daisy retorted. "And now I've had as much conversation with you as I can stand."

She spurred her horse, and it took off at a gallop.

Nicholas watched her go. She was some woman, all right.

He could imagine a female putting new roofs on homes and creating a school. Home and children were a woman's domain. And he could see her selling the racing stock. Fast horses wouldn't be of much interest to someone who didn't bet on them. But her institution of the new farming methods stunned him.

Imagine a woman having the foresight to implement modern farm machinery. Imagine a woman having the savvy to negotiate an agreement with the tenants to use that equipment. Imagine a woman being so beloved that those same tenants didn't hold her to the foolish, generous deal she had made.

She wasn't like the women he had known. Of course, he hadn't spent much time with ladies, either. Nevertheless, he wasn't at all sure what to make of her. He was certain of one thing, at least. He wanted her in his bed.

That was reason enough to hold to his bargain to marry her.

6

"I can't do it!"

"Daisy? What are you doing here at this hour of the morning? I thought you weren't coming here again until Charles got some sense." Priss was sitting up in bed in her nightgown with a pot of tea and toast beside her. Daisy slammed Priss's bedroom door behind her, making the knickknacks that covered every available surface rattle. "Has something gone wrong?" Priss asked.

"Wrong?" Daisy retorted. "I've only agreed to marry an uncouth, barbaric savage! What could possibly be wrong?"

Priss clapped her hands in delight. "He agreed? However did you get him to say yes so quickly?"

Daisy stopped her impassioned pacing at the foot of Priss's bed and glared at her friend. "You talked me into this. You get me out of it!"

"But you don't want to get out of it, not really, Daisy," Priss said. "You have the duke exactly where you want him now."

Daisy's mouth flattened in disgust. "It feels more like he has me where he wants me! He . . . he frightens me, Priss."

Priss's brown eyes widened in alarm. "Are you suggesting he would use his physical strength against you, Daisy? Because if that's what you're saying, then of course we must rescue you from this situation at once! I'll speak with Charles and—" Priss was already reaching for the bellcord to summon her maid when Daisy took the few steps necessary to grasp her hand and stop her.

"It isn't the threat of physical harm I fear," Daisy said.

"Then what is it?"

"I can't explain exactly." Daisy knew what it was that bothered her about her relationship with the duke. She just wasn't sure she wanted to confess her feelings to Priss. Yet Priss wasn't going to be able to advise her unless she told her friend the truth.

Daisy sighed and seated herself in the upholstered chair beside Priss's bed. "All right," she said. "If you must know, he makes me shiver whenever he gets within a foot of me."

Priss frowned. "That doesn't sound good." Her face brightened. "Unless you're shivering because you're attracted to him. Is that it, Daisy?"

Daisy eyed Priss warily. "I'm not sure. It might be that."

"But that's wonderful! If you like the duke—"

"I never said I *liked* him!" Daisy snapped. She lurched to her feet and began pacing again. "That's the problem. I don't *like* him at all." Her lips pursed in a moue of distaste. "But it appears I . . . I *respond* to him, to his maleness, whenever he comes near me."

Priss's eyes twinkled with humor. "There's nothing wrong with that, Daisy."

"Nothing wrong?" Daisy snorted inelegantly. "We're right back where we started when I marched in here. You have to help me, Priss."

Priss shrugged. "What is it you expect me to do, Daisy? I can't rescue Severn. Only the duke can do that. With your help, of course. You knew marriage to Severn would be a sacrifice, yet you agreed to it. I can't understand your reluctance to marry him now, simply because you're attracted to him. That would seem to make your predicament more palatable, not less."

"But I don't want to be attracted to him," Daisy said with a groan of frustration.

What she couldn't tell Priss, what terrified her, was the thought that she might get to like having the duke for a husband. Then where would she be when he took himself off to America, as he had claimed he would? She would be left alone again. Daisy didn't want to let herself care for someone else who would leave her. She had suffered too much, first at Tony's abandonment of her bed and then at his death. Going through the same thing again would devastate her. The duke wouldn't be dead, of course, but he might as well be if the width of an ocean separated them.

She already had an inkling of what his lovemaking would be like. In the years since Tony had left her bed, she had stopped letting herself yearn for a man's touch. She had stopped dreaming what it would be like to kiss and be kissed. She had stopped hoping to wake and find a man's hard, sinewy body entangled with her own.

Nicholas brought all those yearnings, all those dreams and hopes back to rash and reckless life.

Only this morning when he had leaned over to whisper in her ear, she had felt her blood rush, felt the liquid heat pool between her thighs. She had trembled at the thought he might kiss her. She had felt his heated breath against her face, and even that brush of moist air had been enough to send a shiver of expectation down her spine. It had taken all the self-control she had to continue eating as though nothing were amiss.

Nicholas knew the power he held over her. Daisy was sure of it. If he were any other man, she would be ecstatic with both his attentiveness and her reaction to his suggestive behavior. But the brazen American had only one use for a woman. He had told her so himself. Oh, he wanted her physically, all right. But he had no intention of allowing her to play any other role in his life than that of bedmate. That was what frightened her. She wanted more. She wanted him to recognize, as Tony never had, that she was so much more than a source of pleasure for him, that she had a mind and a will and desires and dreams of her own.

Now, if there were just some delicate way of explaining all that to Priss . . .

"Daisy?"

Daisy saw the worried look on Priss's face and realized she must have been silent for some time. "I'm all right, Priss." For the first time since she had arrived, Daisy took a good look at Priss. It was unusual that her friend was still abed. Furthermore, she looked wan and pinched. Daisy moved to the bed, took Priss's hands in her own, and peered into the young woman's pale face.

"I've been so busy thinking about myself I haven't

given you a thought," Daisy said guiltily. "I've just realized you're still in bed long past sunrise. While that might be common for ladies in London, or even a few in the country, I know you better. What's wrong, Priss? You look terrible!"

Priss laughed. "Daisy, Daisy. Only you would be so marvelously blunt."

"Oh, dear. I didn't mean—"

"It's perfectly all right. There's a reason why I'm still in bed and why I look this way." Priss blushed and said, "Charles and I are expecting a happy event."

It took a moment for the truth to dawn on Daisy. When it did, she paled and then flushed. Her first thought was one of jealous envy, her second was shame that she could be jealous of her best friend, who had been childless for two years. She should be happy Priss was finally going to realize her hope of perhaps giving Charles an heir.

She leaned over and hugged Priss tightly. "I'm so happy for you," she forced past the lump of emotion that clogged her throat. "So very, very happy!"

When she leaned back to look into Priss's face once more, she was stunned to find Priss in tears. "You are happy, aren't you, Priss?"

"Delighted," Priss agreed. "Only I know how badly you've always wanted a child, Daisy. And I wish—"

"Don't worry about me," Daisy chided her friend. "I've learned to live with what I can't change. At least now there will be a baby I can come and play with and enjoy. You will invite me often, won't you?"

"You needn't even ask," Priss said. "I want you to be godmother to our child. If you'd be willing?"

Daisy hugged Priss again and, while her face was hidden, bit her lip to force back the tears of regret and sorrow that burned her nose. "Oh, yes, Priss. Thank you. I would love that."

"Now," Priss said, smiling to lighten the mood, "I think I'd better get up so I can join you and Charles downstairs. I want him to know you've agreed to be godmother to the baby."

"Are you sure you're well enough?"

"I'm only a little nauseous in the mornings," Priss said. "Tea and toast solve that problem. Truly, I feel fine. Certainly well enough to join company downstairs."

"Even if that company includes the Duke of Severn?" Daisy asked.

"He's here?"

Daisy nodded. "He rode over with me. At least, most of the way he did. We had an argument, and I left him behind."

"I wonder why Charles hasn't sent someone up to fetch me."

Daisy wondered herself why she hadn't heard anything from downstairs. Surely the duke hadn't lost his way. Or maybe he had decided not to ride here after all.

She knew that was wishful thinking.

Priss fought her way out of all the ruffles on the bed and pulled the bellcord. "I need to dress. Then we have to get down there, Daisy, and see what's going on."

Nicholas had arrived at Rockland Park only a few minutes behind Daisy. He met Charles Warenne, the

Earl of Rotherham, returning from a morning ride of his own.

The two men drew their horses to a stop before the ivy-covered house and stared for a moment at each other, looking for similarities between their boyhood images of each other and the men they had become.

"You haven't changed," Charles said at last. "You still look like the devil incarnate."

"Thanks," Nicholas said with a wry smile. "May I return the compliment?"

The earl laughed. "I swear you haven't changed one bit, Nick. Or should I say Your Grace?"

"I consider myself an American now, Charles. I don't need or want the title."

"You should at least respect it," the earl said.

"That's difficult, under the circumstances."

One of the grooms approached to take their horses, and Nicholas quickly said, "Why don't we ride a little more? I have a few things I'd like to discuss with you in private."

"Very well." Charles nudged his horse with his spurs and set off at a trot.

They pulled their horses to a stop at the top of a ridge from which they could see the entire valley below them, divided up into plots for farming. Nicholas took off his hat, thrust a hand through his hair, and resettled it on his head.

"I never appreciated this as a child," he mused. "Was it always this beautiful?"

"I suppose it must have been."

Nicholas breathed deeply, smelling the grass and the heather on the wind. "I missed home a great deal at first."

"And later?" Charles coaxed.

"I tried never to think about it. The memories
. . . were hard."

"I never believed the tales they told about your
mother."

Nicholas eyed his friend. "Who did you hear telling tales?"

"I heard my parents talking. My father was sure
Lord Philip was mistaken. He even talked to him
about it. But your fath—Lord Philip was adamant."
Charles looked up and met Nicholas's steady gaze.
"Lord Philip apparently had some firm evidence
that condemned your mother."

"Do you have any idea what it was? Or who provided it?" Nicholas asked.

"Why, no. Does it matter?"

"It does to me."

"What possible difference can it make now?"

"I want to know the truth."

Charles's hands tightened on the reins, and his
horse sidled at the pull on his mouth. Charles relaxed as he apparently came to a decision. "I can tell
you this much. The evidence came from someone
your father knew well, a friend of his."

"Male or female?"

"I can't say."

"Can't? Or won't?"

"It was someone my parents were acquainted
with," Charles said. "I don't know any more than
that."

"Then it was likely someone from the neighborhood," Nicholas said.

"Or someone they knew in London."

"But if it was someone from London, they would

have had to be visiting in the neighborhood," Nicholas said. "It had to be someone who was here."

"Now all you have to do is figure out who was here at the time," Charles said. "That shouldn't give you more than forty or fifty people to choose from. And how will anyone remember who was here and who wasn't? It's been nearly thirty years. Give it up, Nick," he said in a quiet voice.

"I can't." The words were torn from Nicholas and gave away far more of his feelings than he wished. "I have to know, Charles. I have to know."

"All right, then. What can I do to help?"

Nicholas's lip curled in a rueful smile. "I'm not sure. I guess I need to get a list of everyone living in the vicinity at the time and then find out who was visiting them. Who would be most likely to know all that?"

"My mother would know. She's living in the dower house. And your aunt, Lady Celeste. The Reverend Golightly has been here since before we were born. He would have some idea. And there's the squire's wife, Mrs. Templeton. She's the busiest gossip in the county. You could get a list from each of them and compare."

"I had hoped to be a little more subtle than that."

"Why?"

"It has occurred to me that someone might have maliciously slandered my mother."

"Good God! You mean someone lied to your father? But why? What purpose would it serve?"

"I have no idea," Nicholas admitted. "But I intend to find out."

"With the exception of Mrs. Templeton, you could count on the people I've named to be discreet. A list from each of them would give you a place to start. If there is a villain out there somewhere, maybe it wouldn't hurt if he heard you were looking for him. Maybe he would do something to give himself away."

Just like the outlaws he had hunted in the West, Nicholas thought. "All right. If you'll approach your mother and the reverend, I'll speak to my aunt. Let's forget about Mrs. Templeton for now. I'd rather the whole parish didn't know my business."

"Done. Now we'd better be getting back. Priss will be wondering what's happened to me."

Nicholas reached out and caught the bridle on the earl's horse. "There's one more thing we need to discuss."

Charles waited patiently for Nicholas to speak.

"My son. And your daughter."

The earl's face hardened, and his body stiffened. "There's nothing to discuss."

"I hadn't figured you for the sort of man who judges a person by who his parents are. Otherwise, you wouldn't—couldn't—be my friend," Nicholas said in a warning voice.

"I have to think of my daughter," the earl said.

"And I'm thinking about my son," Nicholas responded coolly. "It isn't Colin's fault I didn't marry his mother. He's a good boy, Charles. And after all, I'm not suggesting the two of them marry."

"I should hope not!"

"But there's no reason I can see why they can't enjoy each other's company."

"Except that he's a bastard."

"So am I. Does that mean I'm not welcome in your house?" Nicholas challenged.

"That's ridiculous," the earl said. "You're Severn."

"And a bastard, like my son."

"You don't know that," the earl argued.

"Nevertheless, I don't understand the logic that allows one bastard under your roof, but not another."

"When you put it that way, I suppose it does sound absurd. Is Roanna safe with Colin? I mean, he's not likely to fall in love with her and start making improper advances or anything like that, is he?"

From what Nicholas had seen and heard, Colin was well on his way to being in love with Lady Roanna. But he wasn't about to betray his son to the earl. For a moment Nicholas wondered if he was doing the right thing talking Charles into allowing the two young people to see each other. What if Colin's infatuation with Lady Roanna didn't pass? What if Colin decided he wanted to marry the earl's daughter? Nicholas knew the earl would never allow it. His son would be devastated, and likely Lady Roanna would be hurt, as well.

He was not a prophet. He couldn't foresee the future. He could only do what he thought was right at the moment and hope everything turned out for the best. So he said, "At least let Colin visit. You and the countess can keep an eye on the two of them. If Colin oversteps the bounds you set, you can put a stop to things."

Charles frowned so that his brows met above his nose. "I don't know, Nick. That sounds like playing with fire to me."

Nicholas grinned. "Playing with fire was always

what we did best, as I recall. Where's your spirit of adventure?''

"I left it behind when I became a father. Speaking of which, I have some good news to impart. I'm about to become a father for the second time."

"Your wife is expecting? Congratulations!" Nicholas held out his hand, and Charles shook it.

"Come on back and meet Priss, and we'll have a drink to celebrate." Charles kneed his horse, and the two men began the ride back to the house.

"I'd settle for some breakfast," Nicholas said. "Daisy dragged me away from mine for the ride over here."

"Daisy's at Rockland Park?"

"I presume she's still there. We rode over together this morning. By the way, you may felicitate me, as well."

"What are you celebrating?"

"Daisy has agreed to become my wife."

The earl jerked reflexively on his reins, and his mount reared. It took him a moment to get the Thoroughbred under control. "I don't think I heard you correctly. Daisy Windermere has agreed to marry you?"

Nicholas grinned. "She did. In three weeks, after the banns are read."

"I don't believe it," Charles marveled.

"What's so surprising?"

"You know she can't have children," Charles said cautiously.

"She mentioned it," Nicholas said. "But it doesn't matter. I have my heir."

"Colin? But he can't inherit the title."

"To hell with the title. It doesn't matter to me."

"I don't understand you, Nick. I think maybe you have changed since I knew you last."

"What makes you say that?"

"You forget who you're speaking to, Nick. I played with you and your cousins too many times not to know how much you loved Severn Manor. And how envious you were of Tony that he would be able to live there—'forever and ever' I believe were your exact words—because he would be the next duke."

Nicholas felt his ears burning. "That was a long time ago, Charles. I plan to sell Severn Manor, just as soon as I make a few changes in the place so it will bring a better price."

"I'm sorry to hear that, Nick. I was looking forward to us being neighbors."

"We can enjoy the time we have," Nicholas said.

"How long is that?"

Nicholas shrugged. "Till spring maybe."

"Where will you go then? Back to America?"

"Yes."

"And Daisy? Will she be going to America, as well?"

"Daisy and I have an understanding."

"What does that mean?"

"She'll be staying at Severn, in the dower house," Nicholas said.

"How can you leave your wife like that?"

"I don't have any use for a wife, Charles. What Daisy and I have agreed to is a marriage of convenience. When it's no longer convenient, we'll part."

"You are a bastard, Nick," the earl said in disgust. "How can you use a woman like that?"

"It's easy," Nicholas said in a harsh voice. "I've had a lot of practice."

They had arrived back at Rockland Park, and a groom hurried up to take the reins as they dismounted.

Tension filled the air as they stepped inside the house and headed for the library. Charles sent a servant to find his wife and the duchess and ask them to come to the library. When the two men were behind closed doors once again, the earl turned to Nicholas and said, "I feel sorry for you, Nick. For you and Daisy both."

"Don't waste your time," Nicholas said. "Daisy and I will be just fine."

"You and Daisy will be just fine doing what?" Priss asked as she entered the library.

Daisy entered the library right behind Priss, but she stayed near the door in case she needed to make a quick escape.

Priss walked to Charles and lifted her cheek for his kiss.

"This is my wife, Priscilla, Countess of Rotherham," Charles said, making the introduction to Nicholas.

"It's a pleasure to meet you, ma'am," Nicholas said.

"And you," Priss said with a smile. "I hope you'll call me Priss, because I just know we're going to be great friends."

Nicholas raised a skeptical brow but didn't contradict her.

Priss turned to the earl, looped her arm through his, and said, "What have you two been doing that kept you away so long?"

"The duke and I were enjoying a short ride together." He turned to Daisy and said, "By the way, I've changed my mind about Mr. Calloway. He's welcome to visit Rockland Park any time."

Daisy's glance shot to Nicholas. So that was why he had wanted to come here today. To help his son. It seemed strange for her barbarian to do such a kindness. It gave her pause and forced her to look at the duke with new eyes. "Have you told Nicholas the good news?" Priss asked her husband.

"I have."

"I've asked Daisy to be godmother, and she's agreed," Priss said excitedly. "Did you ask His Grace?"

There was a long silence as Nicholas and Charles exchanged glances. "No, I haven't," Charles said evenly.

"Well, for heaven's sake. What did you two talk about?" Priss turned to Nicholas and said, "Charles and I want you to be godfather to our child."

"I see." Nicholas did see. At some point the earl had decided Nicholas wasn't going to be such a good godfather after all. And in that case, he had to forgo the pleasure—and the responsibility—despite Priss's offer. "I wish I could say yes, Priss, but I've been telling Charles that I'm not going to be in England long enough to stand in that role."

"You're not?" Priss exclaimed.

"I'll be returning to America in the spring."

Priss turned to Daisy, who was still standing by the door. "Oh, Daisy. I didn't know you'd be going to America!"

"I'm not," Daisy managed to say.

Priss looked from Daisy to Nicholas in confusion. "But . . . aren't you two getting married?"

"We are," Daisy said. "I haven't had a chance to tell you yet that it's a marriage of convenience."

"Of *convenience*? That's terrible! You can't do it, Daisy. I won't let you," Priss said, bustling over to her friend and linking their arms. "You are a barbarian, Your Grace, if you can treat Daisy like that."

Nicholas raised a brow. "I never claimed otherwise, ma'am."

"Charles, do something," Priss urged. "Speak to His Grace. Make him change his mind."

"I've already had a talk with Nick," Charles said. "It seemed to me that his mind's pretty well made up."

"There has to be something we can do," Priss said.

"You can mind your own business," Nicholas said.

"Watch how you speak to my wife." The earl's voice was sharp, his body tensed for action.

Nicholas smiled ruefully. "It was only a suggestion."

Charles grimaced. "And not a bad one, I must say. Priss, I think we have to let the duke and duchess make up their own minds what's best for them."

"Charles, how can you defect to Nicholas's side like that?" Priss wailed. "Can't you see Daisy needs our help?"

"Do you need help, Daisy?" Charles asked.

Daisy freed herself from Priss's grasp. "I appreciate what both of you are trying to do, but His Grace and I have discussed the matter thoroughly. We've arrived at a decision that suits us both. I'm sorry if

I've disappointed you, Priss," she said as she faced her friend.

"Oh, Daisy, no!" Priss cried. "I'll accept whatever you decide, truly I will. Only I don't approve. I don't think I can. But I promise not to say another word." She glanced significantly at Nicholas. "To either of you. And now," Priss said, "I think we should all sit down and have a nice hot cup of tea."

"I can't stay," Nicholas said. "I've got work that needs to be done on the estate. Daisy?"

"I'll ride back with you," she said. "There are some other matters we need to discuss."

Priss crossed to Charles, and he slipped an arm around her waist. "You will come back soon, won't you? Both of you?" she said.

"We'll be back," Daisy assured her friend. She eyed Nicholas, but he neither confirmed nor denied her statement.

"I'll take care of that little matter we discussed," Charles said to Nicholas.

"Thanks. Let me know what you find out."

"I'll send word when I know anything."

A moment later Daisy and Nicholas were gone.

Priss turned to her husband and said, "What is it you're doing for His Grace?"

"It's nothing," Charles said. "Some business that's long overdue."

"It's nice of you to help him," Priss said.

"I hope he can handle whatever he uncovers," Charles murmured.

"What's that, dear?"

"Nothing. Have I told you today how beautiful you are, my love?"

Priss smiled. "Why no, Charles. I don't believe you have."

The earl slowly tugged his wife into his arms and lowered his mouth to hers. "Then it's time I did."

7

Daisy held her mount to a slow trot, and the duke kept pace with her. It was easier—and safer—discussing matters with Nicholas on horseback, Daisy mused, because that way there was no chance he could corner her. She had no intention of allowing herself to be compromised before her wedding day, and she wasn't certain she could trust Nicholas not to seduce her. The situation was especially dangerous because she knew herself to be vulnerable to his seduction.

Not that she didn't chide herself endlessly for her attraction to the duke. She simply couldn't help it. When she looked at Nicholas, she felt not only the irritation and aggravation natural under the circumstances, but also the first stirrings of arousal. She was in an untenable predicament, but one from which there was no escape. At least not one that she could see.

"I thought we could visit a few of the tenants," Daisy said. "You could meet them and judge for yourself their reaction to your suggestions for change."

"It doesn't matter whether they like the changes or not," Nicholas said. "They're going to be made."

Daisy forced herself to remain outwardly calm, but her horse curveted, sensing her agitation. She brought the Thoroughbred under control and turned to Nicholas. "It is precisely that overbearing, callous attitude they will expect, Your Grace," Daisy said. "Which is why they will be disinclined to cooperate with you."

"I don't intend to indulge them, ma'am," Nicholas said, returning her icy formality with his own. "It's my understanding that the duke's word is law."

"People have been known to break harsh laws," Daisy retorted.

Nicholas's gray eyes turned cold and dangerous. "If they try, they'll have me to answer to."

"What are you going to do? Shoot them?" Daisy said with a sneer of derision. "I understand you've done a great deal of killing in America. You'll find that sort of behavior won't be tolerated here!"

Nicholas yanked Daisy off her horse and into his lap so fast she didn't have time to protest. No Englishman would have dared accost a lady in such a manner. But, of course, Nicholas didn't play by civilized rules. He had his own code of conduct, which meant that he did as he pleased.

"Put me down!" Daisy said as she struggled in his arms.

"Be still, or I'll drop you."

"Let me go!" Daisy insisted.

She should have known better. The scoundrel let her go.

Daisy landed in a flurry of skirts on the grassy ground. She lay stunned for a moment, uncertain whether she was seriously hurt, or whether she had simply had the wind knocked out of her. A moment later two booted feet appeared in front of her.

"Are you hurt?"

"It would serve you right if I were. I'd see you spent time in gaol for assault! That is, if they put dukes in gaol. They probably wouldn't dare, because you'd give them some story that turned everything around so this was all my fault. Only I haven't done anything!"

"You're fine," Nicholas said with a chuckle, "if you've got enough wind for a tirade like that."

"I hate you!" Daisy said. "I truly despise you!"

"Yeah, it sure as hell looks that way." Nicholas grabbed Daisy by one arm and hauled her to her feet. Her hat had fallen off and pulled a few of the pins from her hair, so the copper mass tumbled magnificently around her shoulders. Her face was flushed, and her green eyes flashed with fury. She had never looked more delectable.

She opened her mouth to scold him again, and Nicholas covered it with his own. Daisy struggled for a moment, but he wasn't about to let her go. He would show her who would be master in his house. He wasn't going to let a fiery redhead dictate to him. Not even if she was a duchess.

His mouth was hard on hers, but it wasn't until he tasted blood that he realized how ruthlessly he was kissing her. He raised his head and stared into her wounded eyes, stunned at the feral behavior she had provoked in him. He hadn't cared enough about a woman to become enraged by one. Yet Daisy had provoked him to act like a savage.

For a moment he felt remorse. He almost let her

go. Until he realized there was something else besides brutality in his kiss. There was need, a desperate need that she fulfilled, a craving that only she could satisfy.

He lowered his head once more, watching her eyes drift closed as he sought out her mouth with his own. His lips met hers in the softest of caresses, and his tongue slid out to soothe the hurt he had done. Her lips were pliant, surrendering to his plunder. But his need was too great for gentle kisses. His hands slid down, and he pulled her close as his tongue urgently stroked her mouth.

Nicholas found it impossible to catch his breath. He had never wanted a woman like he wanted Daisy. Never needed a woman like he needed her. He would surely die if he couldn't have her.

Nicholas tore his mouth from Daisy's and stared down at her with heavy-lidded eyes. She was a witch. She had ensorceled him. That was the only explanation for the way his heart pounded, for the way his body ached. For the inexplicable need he felt.

He had learned never to want anything too much. It was too hard to live with his wishes unfulfilled. He was determined not to fall under Daisy's spell. He could and would resist her siren's call. He forced himself to step back from her. It took an amazing effort to let her go. He was glad when they finally stood a foot apart. He was safe now. She had no more power over him.

"Don't cross me, Daisy," he said in a harsh voice. "You won't like the consequences."

Slowly, and with great contempt, Daisy wiped her mouth with the back of her hand, removing all traces of the duke and his kisses. "I may have to endure your animal urges when we're husband and wife, but until then, I'll thank you to leave me alone, Your Grace."

Nicholas's lip curled in a mocking smile. "Don't pretend you didn't enjoy it, Daisy. I won't believe you."

She flushed, conceding the truth of his allegation. "That's not the point."

"What is the point?"

"If you can't see it for yourself, it won't do me any good to point it out to you," she said in a weary voice.

"Try me."

She searched his face to see whether he was serious. She clasped her hands together in front of her to hide the fact they were trembling and said, "Just now, when you kissed me, you weren't thinking of how I felt, you were thinking only of yourself. And it wasn't pleasure you sought. You were punishing me for daring to contradict you."

This time Nicholas flushed. But he didn't apologize or explain. "You shouldn't have provoked me."

Daisy sighed in exasperation. "Is that how you treat every woman who provokes you?"

Nicholas grinned. "No. Only the pretty ones."

"You deserve every horrible thing that's ever happened to you!" Daisy hissed, enraged by his levity.

The grin faded from Nicholas's face. His features tightened, his lips flattened into a thin line, and a muscle jerked in his cheek.

Daisy was too angry herself to realize she had crossed a line and lit the fuse on a keg of gunpowder. One minute she was opening her mouth to castigate the duke, the next he had her by the arms and was shaking her within an inch of her life. She was so dizzy she would have fallen if he hadn't had a bruising grip on her arms. Her heart pounded with fear when she glimpsed the coldblooded violence in his eyes.

"You know nothing about my life," he raged through gritted teeth. "You know nothing about me. How dare you say I *deserved* to see my mother take up whoring so we could live! How dare you say I *deserved* to watch her die on the floor of a wooden shack when I was only thirteen years old!"

He shoved her away from him with both hands, and she stumbled backward several steps. "Get away from me. Stay away from me. Before I do something to you I'll regret."

Daisy's eyes were bright with unshed tears. She felt the sobs welling in her chest, felt his pain as though it were her own. Dear God! Lady Philip had become a whore? Nicholas had watched her die?

"I'm . . . I'm so sorry . . . I had no idea . . ." she choked out.

Nicholas shoved the heels of his hands against his eyes and sighed raggedly as he tried to bring his tortured breathing under control. "Go home, Daisy. Get out of here and leave me alone."

"Is there anything—"

"You've done enough," he grated out. "Get the hell out of here!"

Daisy looked around with dazed eyes and found her horse grazing not far away. She walked over to him and led him to a stump, which she used to mount. She didn't look back as she headed toward Severn Manor.

What had she done? Daisy wondered. How could she have been so cruel? But how was she supposed to have known how ghastly Nicholas's childhood in America had been? No one had even hinted of the disaster that had befallen Lady Philip. She would never have said a word about Nicholas's past if she had known the truth.

No wonder he was a savage. No wonder he had no respect for the rules of civilized society. Look how that society had treated a helpless, defenseless child. Now that Daisy knew how sensitive Nicholas was about his past, how much pain it held for him, she vowed never to confront him with it again. But how was she going to undo the damage she had done?

She didn't think an apology was going to help. But there had to be some way she could make it up to Nicholas. She would just have to figure something out.

Meanwhile, Nicholas was berating himself for having lost control with Daisy. He of all people knew the importance of always being in control. Somehow, Daisy had touched a wound that was more green and tender than he had ever imagined. Her jabs had awakened all the pain of his youth as though it had happened yesterday. And he had taken out the frustration of years on a woman who was not in the least at fault.

He was going to have to apologize to her. Although he wasn't sure she would be willing to accept his apology. He wondered if she would call off the wedding. He wouldn't blame her if she did. First he had mauled her like a bear, then insulted her, then terrified her. What woman would want a man like that for her husband?

He would promise to keep his distance. He would take back his demand that they have a real marriage. He would keep his hands off her.

No, he couldn't do any of those things. He couldn't leave her alone. He wanted her more now than he ever had. He would have to find some other way to assuage her fears. He couldn't give her up. She had known what he was when she agreed to marry him. Hadn't she named him barbarian more than once? He would find a way to make things right. Then he would sate his need for her body. Once he had satisfied himself with her, the need would ease. Then, when spring came, he would leave her as he had planned.

Nicholas froze when he heard a sound, like an animal in pain, in the underbrush. It was hard not to react with the instincts that had kept him alive as a man who hunted men. He reached for his revolver, only to realize it wasn't there. He felt naked without his Colt, especially since he might be heading into trouble. He looked for another weapon and found a good-size stone that he could throw or use as a club.

Then he went off to investigate the noise he had heard.

Daisy was halfway back to the manor before she realized she had lost her hat somewhere and that her hair had fallen down. She stopped long enough to subdue the riot of auburn curls with the pins she had left and to brush off her skirt, which had picked up several blades of grass when she fell. She only hoped she could sneak into the house the back way so no one would see her dishabille and ask awkward questions.

The groom's eyes widened when he saw her, but he merely tugged his forelock and said, "I'll be taking care of Sunset now, Your Grace." He helped her down, and she realized there was more grass on her skirt where she had been sitting. She quickly brushed it off.

"Did you take a fall, Your Grace?" the groom asked.

"Uh . . . yes, Willie, I did."

"Are you all right, Your Grace?"

"I'm fine, Willie. Take good care of Sunset." Then she escaped into the house.

Unfortunately, Lady Celeste intercepted her before she reached the stairs.

"What happened to you?" Lady Celeste demanded. "Shall I call for the doctor?"

"I'm fine, Celeste." Daisy's hand automatically rose to her hair. She caught a curl just as it fell and stuffed it back into the pinned-up mass. "Really, it was nothing. I took a fall. That's all." Daisy hated lying, but she didn't dare tell Lady Celeste the truth without subjecting herself to a lecture.

Lady Celeste's eyes narrowed as she perused Daisy. "Where's that scalawag nephew of mine?"

"I don't know. I presume he's still out riding."

"You mean he left you alone?"

"Actually, I left him," Daisy said. "I had some things to do this morning, and he wanted to ride awhile longer."

"The first thing you need to do is go upstairs and change. It looks like you've been rolling around in the grass."

"I'll be glad to do so, if you'll excuse me."

Daisy raced upstairs and rang for Jane, who fussed at her for her state of disarray.

"Enough, Jane," Daisy said at last. "It couldn't be helped."

Since Daisy never raised more than her voice to her maid, Jane felt safe in making one more retort. "If you don't mind my saying so, Your Grace, *that man* will be the death of you yet."

Daisy shivered at the maid's words. Nicholas was a dangerous man, but it wasn't death she feared at his hands, it was the way he made her feel more alive than she had in all the years she had been married to Tony.

"Not another word," Daisy said. "Or else."

"Hmmmph," Jane said. It was quite enough to make her point.

By the time Jane was finished, Daisy was elegantly gowned in a dress with a fitted bodice of blue velvet and a skirt of the same color in glossy satin, with at least a foot-long train dragging the ground behind her like a peacock's tail. She had just reached the foot of the stairs when the front door opened, and Thompson ushered the Reverend Mr. Golightly into the house.

Daisy wasn't sure whether to make good her escape back upstairs or stay and greet the reverend.

"Good morning, Your Grace," the reverend said, spying her on the stairs.

Daisy descended the stairs as though that had been her intention all along. It wasn't that she didn't like the reverend, but he tended to preach even when he wasn't behind the pulpit, and since he was long-winded he seldom left after the prescribed period for a visit. She had worked out an arrangement with Thompson. The butler would arrive after a time and announce that Her Grace had some household matter that needed her attention. That way she could escape without the reverend being any the wiser.

Daisy held out a hand to the reverend, who bowed solicitously over it. "Shall we adjourn to the drawing room?" She turned to Thompson and said, "Please inform Lady Celeste that the reverend has arrived. I know she'll want to visit with him. And will you please have Mrs. Motherwell send us some tea and biscuits?" Daisy could always count on her housekeeper to provide refreshments quickly, an important consideration when she was dealing with the reverend, whose reluctance to leave was exceeded only by his appetite.

Daisy settled herself in a chair beside the fire while the balding reverend, who was quite portly, settled himself on the end of the settee closest to her.

"What brings you here today, Mr. Golightly?" Daisy inquired.

"Actually, I came to discuss the wedding ceremony, Your Grace."

Daisy swallowed hard. There was a good chance there wasn't going to be any wedding. Especially after the things she had said to the duke.

"And to speak with Lady Celeste about a note I received this morning from the Earl of Rotherham," he confided.

"Note?" Daisy asked.

"Note?" Lady Celeste echoed as she entered the room.

The reverend rose—not without effort—and greeted Lady Celeste with another bow before help-

ing her to a seat in the chair opposite Daisy before
the fire.

"It is a pleasure to see you, my lady. I was just
telling Her Grace I received a most unusual letter
from the Earl of Rotherham this morning. It seems
he wants to know who was living in the parish
twenty-seven years ago when the duke was banished, and who might have been visiting here from
London.

"The earl urged the utmost discretion in my investigation, but I knew he would want me to speak with
you, Lady Celeste, since you would be the one most
likely to know the information he is seeking about
visitors to the parish."

"Why would he need to know something like
that?" Lady Celeste asked, frowning.

"He didn't explain in his note," the reverend said.
"But I'm sure he will expound upon his thoughts
when I present him with the information I have discovered."

"Can you remember back that far, Celeste?" Daisy
asked.

Lady Celeste drew her shawl closer around her
shoulders as though she were chilled. "I haven't forgotten anything about those few days," she said in a
hoarse voice. "It was awful. Simply awful."

"I can provide a list of those living in the parish
from the church records," the reverend said, ignoring, or simply not perceiving, the anguish in Lady
Celeste's voice. "But I imagine there must have been
a few of Lord Philip's friends here for the hunting. I
know the old duke, Lord Philip's father, usually invited his sons and his sons' friends to stay at Severn

during the season. Can you recall anyone who might have been here at the time?"

Daisy watched Lady Celeste's face pale. The older woman opened her mouth and shut it again without speaking. "Celeste? Are you all right?"

"I was just remembering," Lady Celeste said. "There were a number of young men who came to the house." She swallowed hard and added, "I suppose I can remember their names if I try." She rose and headed for the door.

Both Daisy and the reverend rose along with her.

"Celeste? What's wrong?" Daisy asked.

"I need to be alone to think." Lady Celeste paused before she left the room but didn't turn around. "I'll send the list to you when I have it made, Mr. Golightly." She left the room, closing the door behind her.

"Most unusual. Most odd," the reverend muttered. "She seemed upset, didn't she? I should have realized this would bring it all back for her."

Daisy turned to the reverend and said, "What does Lady Celeste have to do with all this?"

"Lady Philip *was* her sister," the reverend reminded her. "She must have lived through the whole awful episode with her. How thoughtless of me not to have realized what it would be like for her to exhume all those memories."

"Please make yourself comfortable again, Mr. Golightly. I'm sure Lady Celeste will be fine."

"I do hope you're right," the reverend said. "I'm ever so sorry for upsetting her, Your Grace."

Daisy welcomed the footman's interruption with the tea service. "Thank you, Higgenbotham. Please tell Mrs. Motherwell that I'll need to speak with her later about the menus for today. And thank Cook for the fresh biscuits.''

Daisy watched the reverend help himself to a plateful of the butter biscuits that were Cook's specialty. She poured tea for each of them and sat back to wait until the reverend had finished chewing so they could resume their talk.

Not that she was eager to discuss wedding arrangements, but better to make it plain to the reverend now that they preferred a simple service before he got it into his head that they wanted something more elaborate.

"The duke and I want a very small ceremony, with just the immediate family and a few friends present," Daisy said.

The reverend was poised to take another bite of biscuit, but pulled it away from his mouth to sputter, "But Your Grace, your neighbors, the tenants—"

"Will all be invited to attend a reception here at Severn after the wedding," Daisy intoned. "The wedding itself shall remain a private affair. Is that understood?"

"Perfectly, Your Grace."

"And now, Mr. Golightly, since we've concluded our business, I shall have to excuse myself." Daisy rose, giving the hapless man no choice except to stand, as well. He was still holding the biscuit in his hand and seemed unsure whether to eat it or lay it back on the plate.

"By all means, take the biscuit with you," Daisy urged with a smile. "And as many more as you can carry. Cook will be pleased to know you enjoyed them."

"Thank you, Your Grace," the reverend said, picking up several more of the biscuits and stuffing them into the pocket of his coat. "You are generous as always."

He bowed once more before letting himself out.

Daisy sank back in her chair and stared into the fire.

What on earth could the Earl of Rotherham want with information about visitors to Severn Manor so many years ago? It stood to reason that the earl's inquiry had something to do with Nicholas's return to England. But did the earl wish Nicholas good or ill?

Daisy sat down with pen in hand to write a note to Priss. She would know what this was all about.

Daisy had finished her note and sealed it when she heard a commotion in the hall. She rose and opened the door to the drawing room.

The duke had returned at last. But he wasn't alone.

8

Nicholas had approached the thicket as stealthily as he knew how after ten years of hunting a quarry that could just as easily kill him. He wasn't sure what he would find. A wounded animal perhaps, or a wounded felon. It was hard to tell from the sound whether it was man or beast.

What he found made his face contort in disgust.

It was a boy. Caught in a trap made for an animal. His ankle was broken and bleeding, shorn nearly in two by the metal jaws of the trap. He had sandy hair and equally sandy freckles that covered his arms and gaunt, blunt-featured face.

It took a moment for the young man—he was a year or two younger than Colin, Nicholas guessed—to realize he was no longer alone. Nicholas had the stone in his hand, but it wasn't much defense against the shotgun the boy held.

"Stay away or I'll shoot," the boy warned. His voice wasn't frantic, but his forehead was bathed in sweat, and it was obvious he had been trying without success to free his right leg from the trap.

"You look like you could use some help," Nicholas said.

"You're not from around here. Who are you?"

"Does it matter? I'm offering to help free you from that trap. It appears your ankle is broken and that you've lost a great deal of blood. We need to get you to a doctor."

The boy swallowed hard, and his eyes narrowed suspiciously. "You look like the Quality," he said. "Why would you want to help me? You must know what I was doin' here."

Nicholas arched a black brow. "Poaching?" he guessed.

The gun swung around to cover him. "That's right," the young man said defiantly. "I'm not going to end up sentenced to years of hard labor, buried for the best years of my life in some deep, dark coal shaft, for takin' game the bloody duke has no use for. Understand?"

"Perfectly," Nicholas said. "Now, do you want my help or not?"

The boy nodded, his mouth setting mulishly. "Haven't much choice, have I?"

"I guess not." Nicholas dropped the stone in his hand and approached the young man. He bent down on one knee beside him as though to reach for the trap. An instant later he had torn the gun from the trapped boy's grasp. He stood and checked to see if it was loaded. It was.

"Go ahead and shoot me," the boy said bitterly. "I should've know better than to trust the likes of you."

Nicholas laid the shotgun against a tree some distance away and approached the young man again. "I just wanted to make sure I didn't suffer if you had a change of heart once you're no longer hampered by the trap," he said cynically. He had learned not to trust. Those lessons had stood him in good stead.

"Now," he said as he bent once again to examine the young man's leg. "Let's see if we can get you out of this thing."

Nicholas saw immediately why the malnourished boy hadn't been able to free himself. The pressure on the jaws of the trap was immense. This trap hadn't been meant for a small animal, it had been meant to catch a man.

"What kind of person puts a trap like this where a man can step into it?"

"The bloody Duke of Severn, that's who," the young man said caustically. "Doesn't stand for poachin' on what's his."

"Then you knew the risks when you came hunting on his land?" Nicholas asked.

"I had no choice. I'm not one of the rich ones as got food to feed their young'uns. My da died over the winter, and it's up to me to feed my sisters and brothers."

"You have to steal to live, is that it?"

The young man's face was sullen. "And what if I do? You wouldn't know what it's like to go to bed hungry and know there'll be no breakfast in the mornin'."

"You might be surprised at what I know," the duke said in a soft voice. "Scream if you like," he said as he began to apply his strength to the jaws of the trap.

The boy did scream, and Nicholas was dripping with sweat by the time he had pressed the jaws flat and moved the trap away where it could do the boy no more harm.

"I'd send someone back for you, except I suspect you'd bleed to death before they got here. I'll have to carry you back myself." Nicholas took off his silk cravat and used it as a tourniquet to staunch the bleeding.

"Where?" the boy said, his eyes wide with fear. "Where are you takin' me?"

"To the manor, of course."

"No!" The young man shook his head, his body quivering with terror. "No, please! The bloody duke is there. He'll send me away to gaol. My family will starve. Take me home. Please! Take me home!"

"I'm sorry, boy. You need a doctor's care. You'll be well taken care of at the manor."

"But the bloody duke—"

"*I'm* the bloody duke!" Nicholas retorted in disgust. "And you're coming back to the manor with me. So shut your mouth and stop complaining."

The boy began to tremble all over, and Nicholas feared the young man would die of shock if he didn't get some reassurance that he wasn't going to be healed simply so he could be sentenced to hard labor God knew where.

"Look," he said. "I have no intention of prosecuting you for poaching. In fact, I intend to offer you a job so you can support your family."

He lifted the boy in his arms and began marching back toward where he had left his horse. The young man watched him with wide and wary eyes.

"If you're the bloody—if you're the duke, why're you helpin' me?"

"Because you're hurt," Nicholas answered simply.

"But I was robbin' you," the boy said.

"Your life of crime is at an end now that you'll be working for me. What's your name, anyway?"

"Douglas. Your Grace," he added hastily. "Douglas Hepplewhite."

"Well, Douglas, it's nice to make your acquaintance."

The boy managed a shaky grin. "Never thought I'd get this closely acquainted with a duke, Your Grace."

"It appears the day has been full of surprises for both of us, Douglas."

It took a bit of maneuvering for Nicholas to get both himself and Douglas on the English Thoroughbred he had ridden that morning, which spooked at the scent of blood. Nicholas would have given anything for his Western mount and saddle, both of which were better suited to dealing with this sort of emergency. They made the trip at a walk, since the least bit of movement caused the boy to whimper in agony.

When he arrived at Severn Manor, Nicholas sent one groom running for the doctor while he instructed another to hail the house, from which servants quickly poured to assist in helping Douglas from the horse.

"Carry him upstairs and put him in a guest bedroom," Nicholas instructed.

"But, Your Grace—"

Nicholas stared down the dismayed butler who had quickly taken Douglas Hepplewhite's measure and knew the ragged boy ought not to be crossing the front threshold of a duke's home, let alone residing in one of the splendorous guest bedrooms upstairs.

"If you don't care to work here any longer, Thompson, I'm sure we can find someone willing to take your place," Nicholas said.

Thompson squared his shoulders. Nicholas's ultimatum was the first imperiously dukelike thing he had ever said. He almost smiled with delight. "As you wish, Your Grace." Thompson directed two underfootmen to haul the young man upstairs.

"Be careful with him," Nicholas ordered.

"As though he were a newborn baby, Your Grace," Thompson assured him.

It was at this point Daisy opened the door to the drawing room to find out what was causing the disturbance in the hall. "What in the world is going on here?" She gasped when she spied the blood on the tile floor, and her gaze flew in alarm to the young man being gently carried upstairs by two of the underfootmen. "Who is that?"

"One of your precious tenants, ma'am," Nicholas said in a harsh voice. "The ones you supposedly care so much about."

"He's hurt," Daisy said.

"Why, yes, he is," Nicholas replied sarcastically.

"Why did you bring him here?"

"He was hurt on Severn land, ma'am."

"But how? Who?"

"Who authorized mantraps on my land?" Nicholas demanded.

Daisy took one look at the accusing gray eyes staring down at her, and her temper flared. So now it was *his* land. "I know nothing about any mantraps."

"I thought you knew everything that went on at Severn. After all, haven't you been in charge here the past year?" Nicholas asked derisively.

Daisy realized their argument was being observed by the servants, every one of whom had friends and relatives working in houses throughout the neighborhood. "Perhaps it would be best if we retire to the library and discuss this matter privately."

"By all means." Nicholas gestured Daisy toward the library door. "You might want to pick up your tail before I step on it," he said in a snide voice.

Daisy realized he was referring to the train on her dress. "It isn't a tail, it's a train, and the very latest fashion." She let it drag.

"Only animals have tails," he taunted.

"You would know, Your Grace, being one yourself!"

At that moment, Daisy heard the massive library door slam behind her with an ominous *thunk*.

Only then did she realize she had allowed herself to be manipulated into being alone with him again. Unfortunately, as this morning's incident had proven, being in open spaces hadn't necessarily diminished the tension between them. She was going to have to learn how to keep the duke at a distance in any and every situation.

Daisy whirled and found Nicholas not a foot away, towering over her.

"Now, ma'am. I'd like an explanation."

"If there are such things as mantraps on Severn land, I presume the gamekeeper, Mr. Poole, would know something about them."

"Did he ask your permission to set them?"

"He did not."

"Then he acted on his own?"

Daisy frowned. "Mr. Poole has been the gamekeeper at Severn for years. I suppose the or-

der, if there was one, must have come from Tony. Or
from Tony's father, the old duke."

Nicholas shook his head in disbelief. "Why? Can a
few game birds be worth the cost of a man's leg? Or
his life?"

"Will the boy be all right?"

"I don't know. His ankle was crushed by the trap.
He may very well lose his foot. Did you know, Daisy,
he was poaching to feed his family, his brothers and
sisters. Where are these hungry folk at Severn? Why
haven't you pointed them out to me?"

"I didn't think you cared," she said in a quiet
voice. "I thought your only concern was how
quickly you could sell Severn and how much you
could get for it."

Stung, Nicholas retorted, "Since when have those
at Severn gone hungry?"

"Wheat prices have been very low, Your Grace.
There is more poverty now than there was before the
depression in prices began. I've done what I can,
and so has the church, but it isn't possible to feed
them all."

"I want to finish what we started this morning,"
Nicholas said. "I want to see Severn, all of it, the
tenants who are making a living and those who are
not."

Daisy looked down at her hands, which were
knotted before her. "Perhaps first we should discuss
what happened this morning, Your Grace."

Nicholas plowed all ten fingers through his hair
and turned from Daisy to walk over to the window
and stare out. "I owe you an apology, I presume."

"You presume?" Daisy was hard-pressed to keep

her voice level. "I've never in my life been manhandled in such a manner."

Nicholas glanced at her over his shoulder. "Never in my life have I manhandled a woman like that," he confessed. He turned to face her. "I don't seem to have much self-control around you, Daisy. I wonder why that is."

Daisy's lip curled in a cynical smile. "Maybe no other woman has ever dared to contradict you."

"Certainly no other woman has ever challenged me in quite the same way." He paused and said, "Do you want to call off the wedding?"

Daisy raised her eyes to the duke's and searched for the right answer to his question. His eyes were cold, arrogant, and aloof. There was nothing in his expression to encourage her to marry him. Obviously, he was leaving the choice entirely up to her. She lowered her eyes to avoid giving him the chance to discern what she was feeling. She was ashamed to admit—to herself or to him—that despite everything, she wanted to marry him.

Worst of all was the knowledge that she no longer considered marriage to the duke a sacrifice. She wanted from him what his kisses had promised. To feel like a woman in his arms. To experience, for the first time, the caresses of a man who found her sexually desirable. She wanted to lie naked beneath him and have him devour her with his eyes. And she wanted to return the favor.

It was scandalous.

Daisy clasped her hands together to hide her nervousness. "I see no reason why we should call off the wedding," she said in a low voice.

"Good."

Daisy's head jerked up at the duke's response. "You still want to marry me?"

"I still want you," he said in a husky voice.

Daisy felt a flush of guilty pleasure. She knew that someday, somehow she would pay for wanting what no proper woman wanted. She decided to pay that toll when it was exacted and not worry about it now.

"The Reverend Mr. Golightly was here this morning to talk about the wedding. I told him we wanted a small ceremony."

"That sounds fine to me," the duke said.

"But I promised we would have a reception here at Severn Manor for everyone who wasn't invited to the wedding."

"I have no objection to that."

Having once experienced Nicholas's reaction to any mention of his past, she was hesitant to bring up the reverend's other news. But she did. "Mr. Golightly received an unusual note from the Earl of Rotherham."

"Oh?"

"The earl wanted him to make a list of everyone living in the parish when . . . at the time you left."

"Ahhh."

Daisy was relieved that Nicholas wasn't angry, but he didn't seem surprised, either. "Do you know why the earl would be seeking that information?"

"He's doing it as a favor to me. I can see he was mistaken, however, in thinking Mr. Golightly would be discreet."

"You wanted his inquiry to be made in secret? Why?"

Nicholas sighed. He crossed back to the window and looked out over Severn. Everything would have been so much simpler, he thought, if he had stayed in Texas. The ranch was doing fine. And he had made up his mind to retire from bounty hunting. He had been lured to England in the hope of finding a key to unlock the secrets of the past. He had begun to believe he was on a fool's errand.

"If you must know, I'm looking for whoever it was that told my father I was a bastard," he said in a quiet voice. "I want to know what evidence convinced my father that my mother was unfaithful to him." Nicholas turned and faced Daisy. "Because, you see, as she lay dying, my mother told me that someone lied." His lips curved in a bitter smile. "She claimed, poor woman, that I am my father's son."

"Oh." Daisy sank into the nearest chair. "Oh, dear."

Nicholas turned away from the stunned look on Daisy's face and stared out the window. His throat felt swollen, and it hurt to swallow. He recalled the sound of his mother's raspy voice as though it had just slithered over him.

"Why would someone lie to Lord Philip about something so important?" Daisy asked.

"I don't know. Maybe it wasn't a lie."

"Then why would your mother claim otherwise as she lay dying?"

"I don't know that, either." He was aware suddenly of Daisy's presence beside him. He hadn't even been aware of her crossing the room. Which made him think maybe it was a good thing he was in England right now and not in Texas, where that sort of distraction might have gotten him killed.

She reached out a hand and laid it on his arm. "Is there anything I can do to help?"

"I don't see how you can. You weren't even born when it all happened."

"But at some point you'll have a list of people who were here, and you'll want to meet them all, won't you? I could host a party, the reception for our wedding would be perfect, don't you think? It would give you a chance to speak to the most likely suspects."

Nicholas sighed. "If someone was cool and calculating enough to pull off that sort of deception twenty-seven years ago, I can't imagine him revealing himself to me at this point in time."

"Maybe he made a mistake. Maybe he isn't the only one who knows what he did. Maybe he bragged about it to someone," Daisy said.

Nicholas turned to look at her. "I hadn't thought of that. You may be right. All right, I'll make sure you have the list of names when it's available. We'll invite everyone and see what comes out of the woodwork."

"Would it make a difference?" Daisy asked. "I mean, if you really are the duke?" She flushed as she realized how that had sounded. "I mean, would you be more inclined to stay here if Severn is your birthright?"

Nicholas arched his brow in the way that reminded her so much of the old duke. "I won't deny I have a lot of memories here. But it's not where I belong. Not anymore."

"Oh." Daisy's mind was already churning with ideas. There were many ways she could bring Nicholas's past alive for him. There was the portrait gallery, for one. And the attic was full of toys the boys must have played with. And she had Tony's diary. That might bring back some memories for Nicholas. The duke had spent eight summers at Severn Manor. Daisy was going to remind him of every one of them. Nicholas might think he didn't belong here anymore. But she was determined to prove otherwise to him.

At last Daisy saw some hope that her marriage to the duke didn't have to end in the spring. She would make him fall in love with Severn all over again. Of course, it wouldn't be a bad idea if he fell in love with her, as well.

Not that she intended to lose her heart. That was quite another proposition. She knew better than to put herself at risk in such a way. There were too many rough edges to the duke. She was liable to find herself torn apart if she tried to broach his defenses.

"When do you want to visit the tenants?" Daisy asked.

"Let's try again tomorrow," Nicholas said. "Right now I need to go check on my newest employee."

At Daisy's questioning look he explained, "I hired the young man who was caught in the mantrap."

"That was very kind of you, Nicholas."

"It wasn't kind," he contradicted, "it was the smart thing to do. He'll serve me better this way than if I send him off to jail and have to feed his brothers and sisters while he's gone."

Daisy frowned. "Can't you admit you care?"

"I learned a long time ago that caring is for fools and idiots."

Before Daisy could make an appropriate rejoinder, they were interrupted by a sharp knock on the door. Colin came in without waiting for permission. "Well, Pa? What did he say?"

"He said you can visit."

Colin gave a whoop of exultation that was so loud it startled Daisy.

"Excuse me, Daisy," Colin said with a charming grin that was going to be as lethal as his father's someday. "I just got some good news, and I had to celebrate."

Daisy turned to the duke. "There's obviously someone you care for, Your Grace," she said archly, as she looked from father to son. And if there was one chink in his armor, there was bound to be a way to create another.

"I'm glad for you, Colin," she said. "I thought the earl was being unreasonable."

"Thanks, Daisy. Can I go and see her now, Pa?"

"Awfully impatient, aren't you, Colin?"

"I promised Lady Roanna I'd go riding with her today." He gave his father a cheeky smile. "We were going to meet in secret, but now that won't be necessary."

Nicholas felt his heart give a warning thump. "Be careful, Colin. The earl said you could visit his daughter. He doesn't intend for the relationship to go any further than that. Do you understand?"

A surprisingly stubborn look crossed Colin's face and disappeared just as quickly.

"Don't lose your heart to an English girl," Nicholas warned. "Otherwise, you're going to miss it when we head back home in the spring."

"Don't worry, Pa," Colin said. "I know what I'm doing."

He was gone an instant later, leaving Nicholas and Daisy alone once more.

"That sounds like a situation fraught with pitfalls for your son," Daisy said.

"Don't worry. If Colin starts to lose his head over the girl, I'll set him straight."

"What fatherly advice will you give him?" Daisy was chilled by the coldness in Nicholas's eyes when he turned them on her.

"I'll tell him what I've learned over the past twenty-seven years. Never trust a woman. She'll betray you. Never let yourself love one. They're not worth the heartache."

"That's awful!" Daisy said. "You can't tell an impressionable young man something like that."

"Watch me," Nicholas said. "Now, if we've finished our business, I want to check on Hepplewhite."

Nicholas was gone from the library a moment later, leaving Daisy behind with a great deal of food for thought.

9

"I had forgotten how wet England can be," the duke said on the fifth morning he awoke to find the skies gray and a steady rain falling.

"Quite so, Your Grace," Porter said as he moved about the room opening curtains, setting out shaving materials, and retrieving one of the newly tailored frock coats made for the duke over the past week.

"I suppose I've been spoiled living in Texas. When it rains, it pours, but then it's dry again. This weather is a little daunting. Especially since it's kept me from business all week. The duchess and I have made plans every day to visit the tenants, only to have them scrubbed by rain."

"Quite so, Your Grace."

Nicholas was restless. He didn't like being confined by the weather. Of course, he and Daisy could have done their visiting in a carriage, rather than on horseback, but they would have ended up soaked simply getting in and out at each stop. It had seemed a better idea to wait for the rain to break. Nicholas had never imagined it would rain for five days without respite. When it finally stopped it was going to take another day or so for the mud to dry enough to make travel possible with any kind of ease.

However, he had accomplished a great deal over the past five days from behind the desk in his library.

First, he had summoned Mr. Poole and informed him that there were to be no more mantraps on Severn land. He thought the man looked relieved as he agreed to retrieve and dismantle the traps that had been set.

"What do you want done with poachers, Your Grace?" Mr. Poole asked. "Once the mantraps are gone, they'll be all over the place."

"Ignore them."

Mr. Poole's jaw gaped. "But, Your Grace—"

The duke cut him off. "Any man who takes game to feed his family is welcome to it. Make it clear, Mr. Poole, that anyone who abuses the privilege will be treated as a thief and sent before the magistrate."

"Very well, Your Grace."

He called in the bailiff, Mr. Henderson, and asked for his evaluation of the new farming methods Daisy had instituted the previous year. Nicholas could tell right away from the things Henderson said that Daisy had met formidable opposition from the man at first. What he found amazing was that she had somehow manipulated the bailiff into doing what she wanted and then made a convert of him.

"I'm not saying Her Grace was right, and I'm not saying she was wrong in what she did," Henderson said. "But we got the plowing and planting done in a whisker, and the winnowing and harrowing was fast as a snap. The harvest, well, who could have known it would rain? There's good and bad luck, and no one can count on it."

Nicholas had discussed with Henderson his plan to have the tenants plant new crops and saw immediately that the bailiff was as resistant to his "new-fangled ideas" as he had been to Daisy's.

"I'm not saying I don't agree with Your Grace," Henderson said. "But I'm not sure but what the tenants won't revolt."

"Perhaps I should call a meeting and explain the matter to them," Nicholas suggested.

Henderson shook his head. "Begging your pardon, Your Grace, but that would be a waste of time."

"Oh?"

"You see, everyone knows you're only making changes so as to make Severn more profitable so you can sell it, Your Grace." He shrugged. "Which of your tenants is going to want to make it easier for you to put them off land their families have farmed for generations?"

"I see what you mean, Henderson. Well, what would convince them to make the changes I want?"

"If Your Grace was to make some promise not to sell—"

"I can't do that. Because I do plan to sell." His eyes had narrowed and his mouth flattened. "I see I have no choice but to issue an ultimatum," he said. "Make it clear to the tenants, Henderson, that anyone who won't do as I say will be immediately evicted. Is that clear?"

Nicholas saw the fear in Henderson's eyes and the resentment. But the bailiff answered, "Perfectly clear, Your Grace."

Nicholas was confronted by Daisy later the same afternoon.

"You're a fool, Your Grace," she said.

Naturally, he had taken offense. "Pardon me, ma'am. I believe I misunderstood you."

"You heard me," she snapped. "How do you expect to get the tenants to cooperate when you threaten them with eviction? I never heard of anything so stupid in my life."

"Stupid?" A slow flush was crawling up his throat.

"If it's not stupidity, it must be ignorance," Daisy said, her hands perched on her hips.

"Ignorance," Nicholas repeated in a deadly voice. The blood had reached all the way to the tips of his ears. If Daisy had been watching for signs of a volcano about to erupt, she would have seen them on his face.

"Any idiot can see it's going to take some diplomacy to accomplish your goals." Daisy pursed her lips ruefully. "I suppose that's why you're marrying me."

"You can solve the problem, ma'am?"

"It will be more difficult now that you've stirred things up," Daisy said. "But I'll manage somehow, I suppose."

"Manage." He was strangling on bile. And she apparently hadn't the least idea he was upset. She was too busy pacing the library, throwing her hands around in agitated gestures to punctuate her thoughts.

"I'll have to find a subtle way to rescind your ultimatum. It can be done when we make our visit to the tenants. If this damnable rain would only stop!"

She was staring out the library window, so she didn't see his mouth drop at her announcement that she was going to undo what he had done.

"Daisy," he said to get her attention.

She turned abruptly to face him. "Did you have something to say, Your Grace?"

He could see why Henderson hadn't had a chance. Daisy looked perfectly innocent, as if she had no inkling of the enormity of her transgressions against him. He wanted to believe that he had done the right thing in giving the tenants an ultimatum and to fight for his point of view. But he remembered Phipps warning him that he wouldn't get far without Daisy's help. And if Daisy believed he had trod seriously amiss, and obviously she did, then it might behoove him to keep his mouth shut right now.

"You look beautiful today," he said.

Daisy was caught completely off guard by his compliment: Her lids dropped to hide her startled eyes, and her hands twisted into nervous knots. "Uh . . . thank you," she mumbled.

Nicholas was pleased to be the one in control once more. "Come here, Daisy," he said in a husky voice.

"I have to go now, Your Grace." She fled the library like a scalded cat.

Nicholas had the satisfaction of knowing he still had the upper hand in at least one area. He conceded the rest to Daisy. At least for the moment.

On the second rainy day he summoned a bootmaker from the town of Bagshot, who had a reputation for being clever with his hands.

"I want you to make a boot for me," Nicholas began.

"Anything in particular you would like, Your Grace?" the bootmaker asked.

"Yes, there is." The doctor had been forced to amputate Hepplewhite's right foot. Nicholas proceeded to explain his idea for a boot that would fit Hepplewhite's stump and allow the boy to walk again. "Could you make something like that?"

The bootmaker stroked his bearded chin. "I might, Your Grace. Could I see the boy? I'd like to do some measurements on the remaining foot."

Nicholas had accompanied the bootmaker to Hepplewhite's room and then had to leave when he saw the tears in Hepplewhite's eyes as the boy realized that what he hadn't believed possible might be possible after all. He would walk again.

Nicholas had spent the third day searching the library for papers anyone might have left that would give a clue to his true parentage. He searched through Lord Philip's papers, which the solicitor had given him, but found nothing that remotely resembled a journal. Lord Philip's fears and suppositions about his wife had died along with him.

He also spoke with his aunt and got a copy of the list of visitors to the parish she had prepared at the reverend's behest. He tried questioning her further, but she became so anxious and uncomfortable that he gave up the effort.

It had occurred to him that, as his mother's sister, Lady Celeste might be privy to the information he sought. It was equally apparent that if his aunt knew anything, she had kept the secret for nearly thirty years. And she certainly hadn't volunteered any information to him when he had turned up as the newest Duke of Severn. Unless he was willing to use coercion, it was doubtful she would speak. He simply couldn't see himself browbeating an old, gray-haired lady for information. He would have to find out the truth some other way.

He had spent yesterday with Daisy in the attic. She had come to him and suggested he might find something there that would give him a lead in his search for the truth. He had been doubtful, but the memory of all those rainy days spent in the crowded, musty-smelling place as a boy had prompted him to agree.

"You seem to know your way around here pretty well," Nicholas said as Daisy threaded through trunks and stored furniture and rugs to reach a remote part of the attic.

"I've been up here before, Your Grace," Daisy confessed. She reached an open area near a small attic window that let in light. She reached over to unlatch it, and the wind and a mist of rain poured in, as well. "I don't think we'll get too wet," she said. "And the air smells wonderful when it rains, don't you think?"

Nicholas took a deep breath and had to agree. There was a fecund smell that reminded him of the deep forest, of wet leaves and moss and grass.

"Come over here, Your Grace, and make yourself comfortable."

Nicholas was surprised when Daisy settled on the bare wooden floor, but he sat down cross-legged beside her. He wondered what everyone would think if they could see the Duke and Dowager Duchess of Severn now. The humor of the situation made him smile.

Next to him stood a wooden rocking horse that he and his cousins had ridden. Its mane of red yarn had thinned from being yanked on and the black painted saddle and bridle had all but disappeared. He remembered laughter and fights over whose turn it was to ride next.

"I feel like a child again when I'm up here," Daisy said in a soft voice.

Nicholas reached out and smoothed the wood on the rocking horse. "I must have a hundred memories of rainy days spent in this attic."

"There's something here I wanted you to see." Daisy handed Nicholas a small leather book with a brass clasp.

"What's this?"

"Tony's diary," she said. "I thought you might like to read it."

"Is there anything—"

She shook her head. "Nothing about your mother. But there are some anecdotes, memories of his childhood, that you might enjoy."

"Thank you," Nicholas said.

They went through several of the toy boxes, and Nicholas found a whole army of lead soldiers. He showed off a top he found by spinning it for Daisy.

It had been a long time, Nicholas mused, since he had laughed so much, or had so much fun with a woman when he wasn't in bed. Daisy was the one who put an end to their idyll. But it was his fault, because he hadn't been able to resist reaching out to touch her face when she laughed.

There had been a moment when he thought she might remain still for his caress and the kiss that was not far behind it. But she stood abruptly and said in a stilted voice, "I have to discuss some matters with Mrs. Motherwell. You know where everything is now."

Then she was gone.

He hadn't stayed much longer. The memories tore at him, making him ache with longing for the past. Life had been good here.

And could be good here again.

He knew then why Daisy had brought him to the attic. But it wasn't going to work. He put away the toys and with them the nostalgia that had made him consider, even for a moment, staying in England, at Severn.

That was yesterday. Nicholas wasn't sure how many more days of being pent up in this house, with all the memories that clambered for recognition, he could take.

"Do you think the rain will stop today, Porter?" Nicholas asked for the fifth time in five days.

"There's no way to tell, Your Grace," Porter replied.

After a knock on the door, Colin entered Nicholas's bedroom. "Do you want to brave the rain and take a ride with me?"

"Don't tell me you're headed for Rockland Park in this weather," Nicholas said.

Colin grinned. "Actually, I am. Lady Roanna has house guests and sent a note asking me to come and help entertain them."

"Oh? Who's visiting?"

"Friends from London," Colin said. "Her uncle, Lord Willowbrook and his wife, and some cousins."

Nicholas tensed. Lord Willowbrook was one of the London set who had been visiting in the neighborhood, a guest of the Warennes, at the time the accusations had been made against his mother.

"Maybe I will go with you."

"Your Grace—"

He grinned at his dismayed valet. "I'll try not to ruin my new boots, Porter."

"Quite so, Your Grace," Porter said in resignation.

"I want to check on Hepplewhite before we go," Nicholas told his son.

"I've already been by his room," Colin said. In fact, he and Douglas Hepplewhite were in a fair way to becoming fast friends.

"How is he?" Nicholas asked.

"As you might expect. Depressed about the loss of his foot, but grateful for the chance to be able to support his family without stealing."

Nicholas found Douglas sitting up in bed, staring out at the rain. "Good morning, Douglas. How are you feeling today?"

"Better, Your Grace. Ready to be up and about." He bit his lip as he stared at the leg that ended at the ankle. "Not that I'll be much use to anybody for a long while to come."

"We'll have you up on crutches in no time," Nicholas said. "And you'll be amazed how well you can get around once the bootmaker delivers your special shoe."

Douglas wasn't as optimistic. "If you say so, Your Grace." He stared back out the window.

Nicholas put a hand on the boy's shoulder. "Don't worry, Douglas. Things will turn out fine."

The boy didn't answer, but Nicholas didn't expect him to. He joined Colin in the hall and followed him down the stairs. Both men settled capes around their shoulders and tugged down their hats before venturing into the pouring rain.

"He's worried that his girl won't want him anymore," Colin confided as they crossed the threshold and headed for the stables.

"Does she know what happened to him?"

"She does. Nora says she won't come to see him so long at he's at Severn. She says it's because she wouldn't be comfortable in such a grand house, but Douglas thinks it's because she doesn't want anything to do with a cripple."

Nicholas sneered. "That sounds like a woman, all right. Long on promises, short on loyalty."

"You're too cynical, Pa," Colin chided. "It's entirely possible Nora is afraid of coming to the house. You haven't heard the stories being told about the barbarian from America." He wiggled his eyebrows melodramatically.

Nicholas raised a single brow in a devilish arch that only proved his son's point. "Am I that frightening, then?"

"To most of the people hereabouts," Colin confirmed with a grin. "They don't know what to make of you. They're afraid you'll follow through on your threat to sell, and that has them worried. And they've heard a lot of exaggerated stories about the number of men you've killed. They're wondering whether you're a madman or simply prone to violence. In any case, they prefer to keep their distance."

"And what do they think about you?" Nicholas asked.

Colin shrugged. "I haven't much to do with deciding their futures."

"Whereas I do?"

"You haven't asked for my opinion, Pa, but I'll give it to you anyway. I've seen the way you look at this place, even when it's raining. You love it, Pa. It's there in your eyes. I don't understand why you insist on selling Severn. But I have to confess, I wouldn't be happy living here. I would miss Simp, and the ranch, and good old Texas sunshine too much."

His Adam's apple bobbed as he swallowed. "If you need to stay here to be happy, that's all right with me. I can go back—"

Nicholas clutched Colin's arm to keep him from finishing his sentence. He saw his son wince and loosened his hold. He wanted to deny Colin's perceptive words. But he couldn't. He wouldn't lie to his son. He felt a certain affinity for Severn. The green rolling hills pleased his eyes. And there were memories—mostly happy ones—constantly tugging at him to linger. But he wasn't going to stay at Severn if it meant losing his son.

Nicholas felt a queer lurch in his chest at the thought of the separation that would come someday, when Colin set out on his own. But not yet. Not so soon. He wasn't ready to send his fledgling from the nest.

Simp would scold him roundly if he caught him trying to hang on when Colin was ready to go. But these were extraordinary circumstances. There was no need to force Colin to make a choice between his father and America. Nicholas would make that choice easy. They would both be returning to Texas.

"I won't be staying here, Colin. So there's no need for you to worry about leaving me in England when you return home."

Colin managed a puckish grin. "All right, Pa. Whatever you say."

They didn't talk much during the ride to Rockland

Park, preferring to keep their chins tucked into their capes and to make the best speed possible through the heavy weather.

Nicholas took advantage of the quiet time to think about Severn. He needed to get his business taken care of as quickly as possible and get headed home. Perhaps the tenants' fear of him would work to his advantage. Perhaps they would do what he asked, rather than face his wrath. Maybe Daisy wouldn't need to intercede after all. Only time would tell.

He hadn't seen much of Daisy over the past five days beyond their two encounters and the time they spent together at supper. She had stayed out of his way, using the excuse that Mrs. Motherwell had several household matters that needed her attention. It was probably better that way. He had discovered in the attic that he wasn't able to look at her without wanting her. And where Daisy was concerned, he wasn't a patient man.

To Nicholas's disgust, the rain eased just as they arrived at Rockland Park. The sun came out and created a magnificent, misty rainbow. "It's about time."

"You can say that again, Pa. If I ever had any doubts about staying in England, they've been settled over the past five days. Lady Roanna told me it rains all the time here. How come you never mentioned that to me, Pa?"

"I'd forgotten about it." Nicholas and his cousins had simply retired to the attic to play on rainy days, bouncing down the stairs and outside again when the sun returned. The English rain hadn't interfered at all with their enjoyment of life.

Colin was expected, and they were ushered into

the drawing room where everyone had gathered for tea. Nicholas met Lord and Lady Willowbrook, their daughters Lady Hope and Lady Grace, both of an age to be presented to society, and their son, Lord Frederick, who was probably five or six years older than Colin.

Nicholas wasn't aware that he knew Lord Willow-brook, yet the instant he saw the man, he recognized him. And then couldn't take his eyes off him. It was the birthmark on Willowbrook's cheek that drew his eye. He and his cousins had dubbed the man Blotberry because of the blemish, the size and color of a ripe raspberry, positioned close to his jaw. Blotberry had come to the country every year to hunt as a guest of the Earl of Rotherham but had frequently joined parties that included the Duke of Severn and Lord Philip, the duke's brother.

Blotberry looked like a villain, with that ugly mark on his face. Now that Nicholas looked at the man with adult eyes, however, he could see that Blotberry—Lord Willowbrook—had good features, wide-spaced gray eyes, a straight nose, a head of thick black hair laced with strands of silver, a wide mouth with good teeth, and a square chin. He was tall and not too broad at the shoulder, with a wiry frame.

Nicholas froze as he finished his mental recita-tion. He could be describing himself. Except, of course, for the birthmark and the silver in his hair. Nicholas tried to see the humor in the fact he might be Blotberry's son. How Tony and Stephen would laugh at that!

Only Tony and Stephen were dead. And he was the Duke of Severn by default. Nicholas stared at

Blotberry until he realized his scrutiny had been noticed. "You remind me of someone." Nicholas said.
Myself.

He turned immediately to Lady Willowbrook and
said, "You have a charming family, ma'am." Which
gave him a chance to peruse Blotberry's son. He was
relieved to notice the boy didn't look a thing like his
father. He had his mother's brown eyes and hair,
her slightly upturned nose and bowed upper lip.

If Lady Willowbrook was upset by his failure to
address her properly, she didn't show it. Perhaps
word had spread of the barbarian duke's abomina-
ble manners, he thought cynically.

Nicholas desperately wanted a chance to speak
with Blotberry alone. He realized he had better start
thinking of the man as Willowbrook, or he was liable
to accidentally blurt out his childhood nickname for
the man.

"I'd like to see that new stud you bought," he said
to Charles. "Would you like to join us, Willowbrook?"

Since the earl had already shown Nicholas the
stud, he raised a brow in inquiry. At Nicholas's urgent look he picked up his cue and said, "You might
like to see Black Star, Willowbrook. I plan to race
him next year."

"A racehorse? Why didn't you say so?" Willowbrook said. "Lead on, Your Grace, lead on."

Nicholas had never much cared for being called
Your Grace, but he found he especially didn't like it
when a man of Willowbrook's age and stature used
it. Nicholas had learned in America, and especially
in the West, that a man deserved only as much respect as he had earned. In England, Nicholas's title

gave him that respect automatically. He fought the urge to correct the older man. Especially since he planned to use Willowbrook's deference to a duke to get the answers he wanted.

Nicholas bided his time and allowed Willowbrook to admire Black Star's conformation and bloodlines. Then he introduced the subject he had been waiting to discuss.

"I understand you were acquainted with my father," Nicholas said.

"Yes, Your Grace, I knew him well."

Nicholas noted that Blotberry—he was staring at the raspberry mark, and the name kept popping into his mind—seemed nervous. He was a little nervous himself. Hell, he was terrified. He slipped his hands into his pockets to hide their trembling. "Did my father ever speak to you about . . ." Nicholas swallowed over the constriction in his throat. He had to ask. He had to know.

"Did my father ever speak to you about the events that led to his banishment of my mother and me?"

Willowbrook stiffened with his hand outstretched toward Black Star. He slowly withdrew his hand and turned to face Nicholas. His lip curled. "I see you've noticed the similarities in our appearance, Your Grace. Your father was equally perceptive. He noticed the same thing."

"And confronted you? Am I your son?" Nicholas asked in a raw voice.

Willowbrook shook his head. "No, Your Grace. You are not."

"Did my father believe you sired me?"

"He did. For a day. I denied it, of course, but he challenged me to a duel anyway. Before we could meet, he received some new information that he said cleared me of any possible guilt in the matter. He apologized and told me he knew I was blameless."

"Did he tell you who he believed to be my father?"

Willowbrook huffed out a breath of air and wiped the beads of perspiration from his forehead with his handkerchief. "I'm sorry to say I didn't ask, Your Grace. I was too relieved not to be facing him in a duel. Your father was an excellent shot."

Nicholas's face blanched. He had been so sure he was going to find the answers he had sought at last. He wouldn't have liked knowing he was old Blotberry's son, but at least he would have come to the end of the trail. It wasn't over. He had to go on asking questions.

"Do you know . . . Was there anyone . . . Did my mother . . . ?" Nicholas found himself unable to phrase the question he needed to ask.

"I never saw your mother look at another man," Willowbrook said, comprehending very well what concerned the duke. "She was a very beautiful woman. Before she married your father, many men, rich, powerful men, sought her hand. She could have married far above your father. That led me to believe she must have loved Lord Philip a great deal. I don't know what would make him think she would betray him."

"Did my father have any enemies that you know of?" Nicholas asked. "Could someone have purposely poisoned his mind against my mother?"

Willowbrook frowned. "To be honest, I haven't ever considered the matter in that light, Your Grace.

I thought merely that Lord Philip had heard rumors of some liaison that he chose to believe."

"Who started the rumors?"

"That, Your Grace, I cannot say. You might speak to Lord Estleman. He lives in London most of the year. Now, if you'll excuse me, I believe I'll return to the house."

Willowbrook left the duke and the earl standing beside the stall that held Black Star. They were silent long enough for Willowbrook to be out of hearing distance.

"Well?" the earl asked. "Did you get the answers you needed?"

Nicholas grimaced. "You heard him. I don't really know any more now than I did before I started asking questions. Except that I need to speak with Lord Estleman."

"You know you're not Blotberry's son," the earl said.

Nicholas was surprised into laughing. "How did you know we use to call him Blotberry?"

"Tony told me. The name fits, I think. It's amazing how much you look like him. Do you suppose he lied about being your father?"

Nicholas shook his head. "I don't think so. I've learned over the years how to spot a liar. Blotberry was telling the truth."

"How do you know?" Charles asked, intrigued by this insight into Nicholas as bounty hunter.

"I watched his eyes," Nicholas said. "And his hands. The hands always give a liar away, even when his eyes don't."

"How so?"

"Find me a liar, and I'll show you what I mean," Nicholas said with a grin.

"You're going to continue your quest?"

"Why wouldn't I? I haven't got any answers yet."

"I'll invite Estleman to visit from London," the earl said.

"Do you know him?"

The earl stroked Black Star's jaw. "I've had him here to hunt several times over the years."

There was a pause before Nicholas asked, "Does he look like me? Or perhaps I should ask, do I look like him?"

Charles pursed his lips. "He has black hair. He's tall, like you. I don't remember what color his eyes are. But he must weigh a good stone and a half more than you."

"That doesn't mean anything," Nicholas said. "Does he have features similar to mine?"

Nicholas endured the earl's examination as long as he could before he said, "Good God, man, it can't be that difficult to say one way or the other."

"That's just it," Charles said with a sheepish look. "If he were a stone and a half lighter, a slight bit taller, Estleman would look a great deal like you. Of course, I have no idea what color his eyes are. They might be black or green or blue for all I know."

Nicholas forced himself to relax. He reached out and laid a hand on Black Star's neck, knowing he needed to touch something warm and alive. "Invite him soon, please, Charles. I'm going to be married in two weeks. Invite him to come soon. Before the wedding, if possible."

"All right, Nick. Is there anyone else on any of the lists that you want to speak to before the wedding?"

The duke's lips twisted. "Is there anyone on that list who looks as much like me as Blotberry?"

The earl's brow furrowed. "Lord, Nick. I don't even remember what half those men look like. And who's to say you look like your father, anyway? If Lord Philip was your father, you didn't particularly look like him. You have a lot of your mother's facial features, as I recall. In your case, the Windermere blood didn't breed true."

"Assuming I have any Windermere blood," Nicholas said. "My mother had dark brown hair and hazel eyes. My father had blond hair and blue eyes. My hair is black and my eyes are gray. You breed horses. Tell me, could my father have sired me?"

"It's possible," Charles said. "How much do you know about your mother's people? Were they black-haired? Gray-eyed?"

Nicholas realized suddenly that he didn't really know his grandmother and grandfather on his mother's side. They had preferred London to the country, and Nicholas had never made a trip to the city to visit them. But he could go to his aunt and ask her about them. What color were her eyes? Nicholas wondered. He had never looked that closely at her. Her hair had been an even darker brown than his mother's—maybe even black. It was gray now.

He wondered how his aunt had remained so much a stranger to him. She had been Tony's and Stephen's nurse, had lived at Severn Manor year round and stayed with the duke's family on holidays. Perhaps it was because she and his mother hadn't been close. As a result, he simply hadn't paid much attention to her.

He decided to approach her again. She could have

no objection to describing his grandparents to him.
And it might help him in unraveling the mystery of
his birth. "You're right," he said to Charles. "I need
to speak with my aunt. I'd like to do it now, but it's
going to be difficult to convince Colin to leave, when
we just got here."

"Let him stay," Charles said. "With all the females
in the house, Frederick can use the company."

"Are you sure?" Nicholas said, eyeing his friend.

The earl stuck his hands in his pockets before he
answered. "I'm sure."

"Afraid I'll catch you lying?" Nicholas said with a
pointed look at the earl's hands.

Charles laughed. "I'll probably never answer another question with my hands in plain sight. Are you
sure you don't want to give away your secrets now,
Nick?"

"Wait until I speak with Estleman," Nicholas said.
"If you don't notice the signs yourself, I'll tell you
what they are," he said. "Give my regards to the
ladies. They'll appreciate it more from you anyway."

Nicholas found his horse in a stall and the tack
nearby and began to saddle his mount.

"I can get a groom to do that," Charles said.

"I can manage."

"Are you having any second thoughts about marriage?" Charles asked as Nicholas finished and led
his horse from the stall.

Nicholas grinned. "Amazing as it may sound,
none at all."

"What about Daisy?"

Nicholas's features hardened. "It wouldn't matter
if she did. We have a bargain."

"You wouldn't force her—"

"Don't interfere, Charles," Nicholas said in a warning voice. "Daisy and I have an understanding. It doesn't matter if anyone else approves. Do you understand what I'm saying?"

"The duchess is a lady, Nick."

"Yes, she is. And in two weeks, she'll be my wife."

Nicholas mounted in a smooth leap that didn't require touching the stirrup. "Good-bye, Charles. Thanks for your help."

Just as he spurred his horse, the heavens opened again. Muttering imprecations at the weather, Nicholas made his way back to Severn Manor. Where Lady Celeste—and perhaps the answers to a few questions—waited.

10

As he exited the stable at Severn, Nicholas was nearly bowled over by a soggy, caped figure hurrying toward the house. He could tell it was a woman, but no more than that. He reached out to keep the sopping-wet female from falling. When he did, her hood feel back and he realized he was holding Daisy.

"If I'd known you enjoyed the rain so much, we could have gone visiting the tenants days ago," he said dryly.

Daisy shivered. She was wet to the bone. "I had some errands to run, so I took care of them. If you'll kindly release me, I'll go change."

Her face was slick from the rain, and her hair had curled in damp tendrils around her face. He wanted to lick her dry. He wanted to pull her to him and let the steam rise as he warmed her body with his own. He couldn't release her. Not yet. "Where have you been, Daisy?"

"If it's any of your business, I visited the Hepplewhites."

"Why?"

"To take them some food and fuel for their fire.

Douglas told me how famished they would be and how cold. I didn't think I could wait any longer for the rain to stop."

Nicholas thought of the comfort it would bring Douglas to know his family was fed and warm and felt admiration for what she had done. Along with admiration came annoyance. Why hadn't she asked him to come along? He was the one who had taken on the responsibility for Hepplewhite. He felt a little ashamed that he hadn't thought of helping the family himself.

"You should have told me what you had in mind. I would have had someone do it for you. There was no need for you to take a chance with your health."

"I'm perfectly healthy," Daisy protested. "A little cold water isn't going to do me any harm." Her body contradicted her with a violent shiver.

"You're half frozen." Without stopping to think of the consequences, he picked her up in his arms. "It's time I got you inside and dried off."

"I can walk, Your Grace," Daisy protested.

"I know. But I'm enjoying holding you in my arms," Nicholas replied unrepentently.

Daisy knew better than to struggle. Twice before she had tried to thwart him and twice had landed on the ground. Instead, she turned her face into his shoulder and slipped her arm around his neck. At least that way she wouldn't have to face the servants when the duke carried her so ignominiously over the threshold.

As she had known they would, the servants made a to-do over the fact she wasn't walking on her own two feet.

"The duchess is only wet and cold," Nicholas told

Thompson. "I'm going to take her upstairs. Ask Mrs. Motherwell to send up some hot tea," he commanded. "And see about having some hot water brought up for a bath."

Daisy felt the first stir of alarm when she realized the duke had no intention of setting her down at the foot of the stairs. To the contrary, he had just announced to the entire household that he intended to carry her upstairs.

Coward that she was, she kept her face hidden. Well, they were engaged, after all. If the truth were known, she had slept the past week in the suite adjoining the duke's. Not that she hadn't locked the door between them, but she supposed the servants had no way of knowing for sure whether the door remained sealed for the entire night.

Did the duke really intend to carry her all the way into her bedroom? What then? Would he leave without an argument? Somehow, Daisy didn't think so. But what help could he possibly be if he stayed? Daisy shivered at the thought of the duke undressing her.

He tightened his grasp, pulling her even closer, so that she could feel the warmth of his body against hers even through the wool garments that separated them. "I'll have you in your room in a moment, my dear. Then we can get you out of those wet clothes."

Daisy made a sort of whimpering sound and snuggled her nose closer to the duke's neck. He had called her *my dear*. It was appalling to find such pleasure in the endearments of a barbarian. But oh, it felt so wonderful to be held by him! Daisy knew she couldn't let him stay to undress her. That way lay disaster. She would not lie with him until they were married, and she doubted she would have the willpower to deny him if he made even the slightest effort to seduce her.

Of course, she probably looked like a drowned rat, so maybe her concern was premature.

Daisy felt Nicholas lean down to open the door and then heard him kick it closed behind him.

Her heart began to pound. He had actually done it. He had brought her into her bedroom and closed the door behind them. It was outrageous! It was shocking! It was typical of the duke.

She lifted her head from his shoulder and looked him in the eye. "You can put me down now, Your Grace," she said in an even voice.

He shook his head. "Not quite yet."

She saw the kiss coming long before it got to her. She could have struggled. She could have kicked or hit or bitten him. She could have slapped his face. She could have done a dozen things to save herself.

She kissed him, instead.

Daisy wasn't prepared for the tenderness. She had been expecting Nicholas to plunder; instead, he caressed her lips with his, merely touching, barely tasting, then retreating. It was a revelation to feel his gentleness, his reverence, and the banked desire that shimmered through him and left him trembling.

"You're like a potent brandy that warms me to the core," he murmured against her lips. "I take one sip, and I want another." His lips found hers again, and his tongue stroked into her mouth.

Daisy moaned. It was unbelievable that this was happening. He was in her bedroom and she was in his arms and he was holding her close. She clung to his neck and reached for him with her mouth, hungry for what he offered.

"Nicholas."

The sound of his name on Daisy's lips reverberated through him. Nicholas felt her tongue tease the edge of his lips seeking entrance. His blood surged. He felt her hands in his hair and her tongue in his mouth and his knees began to wobble as nature urged him to lay her beneath him, to mount her and claim her as his mate.

He was halfway to the bed when the door opened and one of the female servants appeared. He didn't know who it was and didn't care. "Get out!" he snapped. "Close the door behind you!"

He had no idea how ferocious his face looked, no idea how harsh and commanding his voice sounded. He was, in that moment, every inch a duke. The woman quickly retreated, closing the door with a quiet click.

Nicholas felt Daisy's hand tighten in his hair, heard her tremulous sigh, and knew that she would resist him now. Whatever mood had come over her that had caused her to surrender in those first moments had disappeared and left the headstrong, obstinate, and fractious Daisy behind.

"Nicholas," she murmured.

He felt her breath against his throat, and his groin tightened with need.

"That was Jane, my maid," she said. "Jane would never confront you, but she'll go for your aunt. They'll both be back here any minute. You have to put me down."

He slid her down the front of him, opened his cape, and pulled her tight so she could feel his

arousal. Her eyes widened in surprise, but he saw
the pleasure there, as well. Then he looked down
and realized she had soaked his new frock coat and
that his boots were layered in mud. Porter would kill
him, he thought fleetingly.

He released her, though he didn't want to.

She stepped back, just one step. No more.

"I can't wait two weeks to have you, Daisy," he
said in a low, fierce voice. "And I don't feel like
fending off the servants. I'll make arrangements tomorrow for a special license. We can be married the
day after that."

Daisy's eyes widened in alarm. "You can't do that.
What about our plans for the reception?"

"We can have the reception two weeks after the
wedding. In fact, it only seems fair that we should
have a honeymoon before we entertain a lot of
strangers."

Daisy shivered.

"Damn! You'll catch your death of pneumonia if
you don't get out of those wet clothes. Turn around."

Numb with shock, Daisy did as the duke ordered.
She was to be married in two days instead of two
weeks. And she hadn't even made a peep of protest.

*What's wrong with you, Daisy Windermere? Where
are your guts and gumption?*

I want him. And he wants me.

*For how long? A few days? A week. More likely, one
night in your bed will send him running.*

It won't be like that. It will be different with him. I
know it. I can feel it.

Daisy was so caught up with her thoughts that it
wasn't until she heard the gasp from the doorway
that she realized Nicholas had completely unbut-

toned her dress and drawn it off her shoulders. It
was currently resting in a puddle on the floor. He
was working on the ties of her corset, but his large
hands were finding it impossible to untangle the wet
knots.

"Please leave us, Your Grace! This instant!" Lady
Celeste ordered.

"The duchess was cold and wet. I—"

"I can see exactly what you were doing," Lady
Celeste said in an imperious voice. "That sort of behavior belongs in the boudoir of a mistress, Your
Grace. Not in the bedroom of a duchess. You will
kindly remove yourself from Her Grace's presence."

Nicholas didn't argue, although he certainly dis-
agreed with his aunt. He was truly grateful that he
hadn't grown up with the notion that a lady couldn't
be a whore in bed. He had a lot of plans for the
duchess that included everything he had been taught
about what a woman—and a lady was a woman,
whether his aunt was willing to acknowledge it or
not—wanted in bed.

However, Lady Celeste was reinforced by Daisy's
maid, Jane, and Mrs. Motherwell, who had brought
the tea up herself when she had heard of the shocking goings-on in Her Grace's bedroom, and a maid-
of-all-work, who carried the first pail of hot water
for Daisy's bath. Nicholas nodded his head in defeat
and abandoned the field of battle.

On his way out the door, he remembered that he
had wanted to question his aunt. He wondered
whether she would even agree to stay in the same
room with him after this incident. He retreated
quickly, with as much dignity as he could muster.

"Be sure you get her warm and dry," he intoned in a ducal voice.

Lady Celeste gave him a look that would have melted icicles and shut the door in his face. Behind the door, it was Daisy who received the brunt of the older woman's displeasure.

"I would like to know what you think you're about, Your Grace," she demanded, as Jane set to work untying the knotted strings on Daisy's corset. "Do you care nothing for your reputation?"

Lady Celeste was greatly agitated and wandered about the room picking up several of Daisy's collection of lifelike porcelain and crystal birds and setting them down again. "I would think there has been enough injudicious behavior by both men and women in this family to last a lifetime."

Daisy paused, arrested by what Lady Celeste had said. "What is that supposed to mean? To whom are you referring? Who has been injudicious?" Daisy demanded. "Besides myself, of course."

Lady Celeste threw up her hands, making Daisy long to rescue a Wedgwood robin from her grasp. "I couldn't begin to name them all," she retorted. "From the old duke on down, all the Windermere men have sowed their wild oats without thinking of the consequences."

"Tony?" Daisy said, her face white. "Are you referring to my Tony?" She hadn't thought it could hurt her to hear it spoken aloud that Tony had had a mistress. But it did hurt, terribly, even now.

Lady Celeste seemed to realize all at once the pain she was causing with her indiscriminate accusations. "Oh, my poor dear. I thought you knew. I was sure you did. I didn't mean to hurt you."

"Who else besides Tony were you accusing?" Daisy asked. "Do you know something about Lady Philip? Do you know the truth about the duke's birth?"

Lady Celeste suddenly stilled. She set the robin back on the bureau and carefully folded her hands in front of her. Her face became passive. "There's no sense dredging up the past."

"But Nicholas needs to know the truth!" Daisy crossed to Lady Celeste, but the woman looked so severe, so austere, that Daisy didn't dare lay a hand on her sleeve, even to plead for information. "Please tell me what you know."

"I promised my sister I would keep her secret. My lips are sealed."

"Lady Philip is dead. Her son is alive. Please, Celeste, you have to tell me what you know."

Lady Celeste's eyes focused in the distance as if she were reliving a moment in the past. "There was a man . . ."

"Are you suggesting Lady Philip had a lover, a *cicisbeo*? That she was unfaithful to Lord Philip? That Nicholas is, indeed, a bastard?"

Daisy's words tore Lady Celeste from the past. When her hazel eyes focused they were devoid of emotion. "I know what I know," Lady Celeste said. "If my sister chose to go to her grave with her secret intact, I see no reason to reveal it."

"What secret?" Daisy demanded. "Did she have a lover?"

"That, Your Grace, is no business of yours. Now, get into that tub and get warm before you catch your death of cold."

Daisy couldn't get another word out of the older

woman. It was clear Lady Celeste knew something about the past. Whether she had the answers Nicholas sought was another matter altogether. Daisy made up her mind to seek out Nicholas so that he could question his aunt himself. The old woman might be no more forthcoming, but knowing Nicholas, Daisy was sure he would find a way to encourage her to speak.

Meanwhile, Nicholas had just reached the bottom of the stairs when he realized there was some sort of altercation occurring in the doorway. "What's the problem, Thompson?"

"I've told the girl she should use the servants' entrance, but she won't leave, Your Grace," the butler replied.

Thompson stepped aside and Nicholas saw a short but very buxom young woman. She had carrot-red hair and a face as full of freckles as Douglas Hepplewhite's, only hers were red instead of gold. She was wearing a simple tan wool dress covered by a dark brown woolen shawl. She must have made the walk during a lull in the rain, because only the hem of her dress was wet.

"What's your name, girl?" Nicholas could see she was trembling, and her face got so red it threatened to obliterate the freckles.

She bobbed a quick curtsy. "Nora, Your Grace." She kept her head lowered in fear or deference, or both.

So this was Hepplewhite's lady friend. Nicholas spared a moment of sympathy for the future children of two such vividly freckled parents. But the children should lack nothing in character. He knew Douglas had grit, and Nora had somehow managed to conquer her fear of the beastly duke in order to attend her young man.

"I'll take care of this, Thompson," the duke said.

"Very well, Your Grace."

Nicholas smiled in an effort to ease the girl's anxiety but could see it didn't help. "You've come to see Mr. Hepplewhite, I presume."

"Yes, Your Grace."

Her trembling worsened, but Nicholas resisted the urge to reach out to her. He suspected that would only make things worse. He couldn't even offer her a look of understanding, because she kept her eyes locked on a pair of very sturdy black shoes.

"Follow me, and I'll take you to him." Nicholas turned and started to walk away, but the girl stayed by the door.

"Nora? Are you coming?"

She looked up, and he saw her eyes were as velvety blue as a morning glory, large and innocent. "Are you sure it's all right, Your Grace? I mean, me comin' upstairs and all?"

Nicholas smiled at her naïveté. "If it's all right with me, then I don't see who else can complain." He walked back to her and put a hand on her shoulder. She moved quickly then—to free herself from his touch, he supposed—and hurried up the stairs. When she got to the top she stopped and waited for him to direct her.

"It's this way." Nicholas paused in front of the bedroom where Hepplewhite was staying. "He's in here." He opened the door and waited at the threshold until she scuttled past.

"Douglas, you have a visitor," he said.

Nicholas felt a sharp jab of something—envy or

cynicism, he wasn't sure which—as he observed the reunion of the two young people. He recognized the light in Douglas's eyes. It was love and hope. Poor fool. So what if the girl had come? Who said she would stay when she saw how he was crippled?

Nicholas knew he should go, knew he should leave them alone. But he couldn't tear his eyes away from them. They were totally oblivious to him, caught up in a world of their own.

He saw the tender way Douglas held Nora's hand in his, the way he drew it up to cup his cheek. Heard the soft, caressing tone of his voice as he said in wonder and relief, "Nora. You came."

"Of course I came, Douglas," the girl replied. "I love you. I was only afraid—"

"You needn't be afraid of the duke," he reassured her. "He's given me a job, Nora. We can be married." He paused and said, "That is, if you still want to marry me."

Something turned over inside of Nicholas, something very, very painful, as Nora reached down to touch Douglas's leg below the knee. Her hand trembled as it moved down the sheet to where there was only a stump.

"Nora—" Douglas said in an agonized voice.

She moved the sheet away to expose the bandage over the stump. Then she leaned down and kissed the clean linen. Tears brimmed in her velvety eyes as she raised them to meet Douglas's gaze. "It doesn't matter to me, Douglas. I'll love all of you there is. I won't say you won't miss your foot, but what's done is done. It doesn't change the way I feel."

Douglas held out his arms, and she tumbled into them.

Nicholas pulled the door quietly closed. He was breathing hard, and his nose stung with tears he refused to shed. He moved quickly to his bedroom and let himself inside. He sat in the chair beside his bed and closed his eyes and tried not to remember.

But the memories spilled over the high wall he had erected to keep them at bay. He shoved at them, tried to force them back. But they flowed over him, demanding attention. Bringing it all back.

He was only fifteen, tall and lanky, with a beard that was embarrassing because it refused to grow all over his face. His voice had the disconcerting habit of breaking when he was in the middle of a sentence. And he was in love, with a woman three years older than himself. Her name was Evie.

He had met her in the two-story house on the edge of town where his mother had last worked. The ladies there had taken pity on him when he was orphaned and let him sleep in the kitchen on nights when the wind howled and the snow blew into drifts. Evie wasn't supposed to sleep with him because he hadn't any money to pay her. But she had taken a fancy to him, she said, and invited him upstairs late one night, when everyone else was asleep.

He had come to her a virgin, and she had enjoyed teaching him how to please a woman. He had been so nervous at first that his body was stiff. Fortunately, at least part of him was supposed to be that way. She had made him laugh at himself, and after that first glorious deflowering when he had discovered the pleasure to be had from a woman's body, he had limbered up and quickly learned how to bring her as much pleasure as he enjoyed himself.

They had passed most of the winter that way. He

hadn't been in love with her at first, just grateful for the use of her body. But they were both young and alone, and she began to share her dreams with him. He, young fool, did the same with her.

She was going to marry a rich man some day, a man who could take her away from the house. She was going to wear silk dresses and have a maid to do the housework.

He was going to have a ranch, a place of his own with cattle and horses. He would have a beautiful wife and dress her in silk and have a maid to do the work for her.

He hadn't realized until much later that his dream had incorporated hers. He hadn't realized he was in love with her. Not until spring came, and he had no more excuse to come to the house. He missed her terribly. Not just her body, but the quiet moments after, when they would share their secrets and their dreams.

That was when he realized that if he wanted to make his dream come true he couldn't keep on working in the saloon. He was going to have to learn all there was to know about ranching. He was going to have to become a cowboy.

He had no horse, no saddle, no gun, no rope, no hat, no spurs, no chaps, no bedroll, no slicker—no experience. He had nothing to recommend him at all to Mr. Hardin at the Bar Five. But Hardin must have seen something in him that he liked, because he offered Nicholas a job. Twenty dollars a month and found. Hardin would provide the horse and credit at Stone's Mercantile in town, where Nicholas could buy anything else he needed to do his job.

Nicholas had ridden back to the house where Evie

worked and tied his new Bar Five horse to the post out front. He could still remember the way his eyes had crinkled from the width of his self-satisfied smile. He was so damned happy! He was going to make his dream come true. All he needed was for Evie to wait for him until he could make enough money to buy that ranch.

He hadn't known anything was wrong until he saw Mrs. Greely's face. She was the madam who took care of all the girls. At first he thought it was just because he had used the front door, instead of the back.

"I have a job," he blurted. As though that would make it all right.

"You've been sleeping with Evie," she said. It was an accusation, really.

"I . . ." What could he say? "I have," he admitted. "But not during regular hours," he was quick to add.

"You got her pregnant," Mrs. Greely said. "I'd've never known who the father was, except it could only have happened during that two weeks we had freezing cold and snow and everybody stayed tucked inside so we had no business. You have to be the father. It couldn't be anyone else.

He had been stunned. And then so damned proud. He and Evie had made a child of their own! "I'll take care of her and the child," he said. "Don't you worry."

"I've already made arrangements," Mrs. Greely said.

"What arrangements?"

"To get rid of the child. Evie will be docked what it costs from her pay."

"You can't do that!" he said. "You can't! That's murder!"

He had raced up the stairs to Evie's room, but when he tried the knob, it was locked. He had pounded on it with his fist and yelled, "Evie! Let me in! I'm not going away until you talk to me."

He knew she would let him in because Mrs. Greely hated a rowdy customer more than just about anything. Sure enough, Evie had opened the door. He had gone inside and closed it and locked it behind him, locked out Mrs. Greely and her dastardly plans for his child.

"Have you agreed to this?" he demanded.

She didn't ask him what he was talking about. He could see from the petulant look on her face, from the sullen cast of her blue eyes, that she knew exactly what he was talking about.

"I have," she said. "And there's nothing you can do about it."

He had her by the shoulders before he knew what he was doing. He shook her hard, telling her she couldn't go through with it, that it was murder, and he'd see *her* dead if she tried killing his child. When he let her go, she sank down onto the iron bed where she spread her legs nightly for any man who had the price.

The sound of the springs squeaking reminded him of all the times she had laughingly urged him to be still, not to make so much noise or they would wake up Cass in the next room.

He felt panicked at the thought of losing his child. His eyes were hot and dry, his whole body tensed. He shoved his hand through his hair, trying to make some sense out of everything.

"I thought we were going to get married," he said.

She sat cross-legged on the white chenille spread —which he realized only now that he saw it in daylight bore numerous yellow stains—and shook her head. "Where did you ever get an idea like that?"

"We talked—"

"I want a rich husband, someone who'll take care of me."

"I g-got a job today," he stuttered desperately. And realized how differently he was saying those words than how he had planned to say them. "I'll take care of you."

"How?" she demanded.

"I'll be getting twenty a month and found."

"Where would I live?"

He swallowed hard, knowing she couldn't stay in the bunkhouse with him, and that the only other home he had was the abandoned line shack where his mother had died. "We'll find a place."

"I won't live in a hovel, Nick," she said defiantly. "And I don't want a kid."

"Not even mine?"

She shook her head. "A kid would just be a millstone around my neck. What man is going to marry me if I bring along a whining brat?"

"I would marry you," he said. "I love you." Then he said the words that even today made him cringe. "Don't you love me?"

If there was ever a question that left a man open to being destroyed, that was it. In his youth, in his innocence, he had asked. And she had answered.

With a laugh.

"Good Lord, no, Nick. We just had a good time together. You're good in bed. That's all. I never loved you. If I had it to do over again, I'd think twice about inviting you upstairs. I didn't count on ending up with one in the basket, if you know what I mean."

Somehow he had managed to stand his ground, to keep fighting for the child inside the woman who had laughed at him for being stupid enough to think that what they had shared together had anything to do with love.

"I don't want you to get rid of it."

Evie picked at one of the nubby tufts on the spread. "Mrs. Greely's got it all arranged."

"I'll pay you to have the baby."

Her head jerked up, and her eyes found his. "What?"

"I want the baby, even if you don't. I'll pay you my salary every month you're carrying my child, and I'll take the baby when it's born."

"You're crazy!"

"Not crazy," he insisted in a voice that already held a hard edge he had found somewhere to deflect her ridicule. "I meant what I said before. If you kill my child, I'll kill you."

He saw her shiver and felt a deep satisfaction at the fear that shone in her eyes.

"Mrs. Greely won't let me do it."

"I'll take care of Mrs. Greely. Do we have a deal?"

She pouted, and he tried to remember what he had found so enticing about her lips. She laid her hands on her belly, which he saw was already rounded with his child. "All right," she said. "But I want the whole twenty dollars, every month."

"You'll get it."

He had left the room then, before his anger forced

him to violence against her. After all, she was the mother of his child.

He had paid off Mrs. Greely with the promise of another ten dollars a month. He earned that working odd jobs all over town on weekends and at night when he should have been sleeping. His face grew haggard, and permanent shadows left his eyes looking sunken. Hardin watched him like a hawk, but he did his work and never let on what it was that drove him so hard.

Once or twice Hardin looked him up and asked him how he liked the work, but that was as close as he came to inquiring about Nicholas's situation. No man asked another his business in the West. Nicholas had never shared his problem with Hardin. At first he was too ashamed, and then too determined to manage on his own.

Evie complained the whole time, but she carried the baby to term. He checked up on her, making sure she knew what would happen if she did anything that endangered the child. Mrs. Greely had sent word to him when the baby was born, and he had come to get it.

Fantastic as it seemed, he didn't, until the moment he held his son in his arms, have a thought about how he was going to feed the baby, or even how he was going to take care of it. Evie didn't offer to nurse the child, and Mrs. Greely made it clear she wanted the wailing brat out of her house.

He had gotten on his horse and ridden away with a squalling newborn in his arms. He had felt . . .

Nicholas felt a burning sensation in his nose, the sting of tears at the corners of his eyes as he relived that awful time in his life. Lord, he had felt so desolate. He had ridden the whole day, until late in the afternoon, when he stopped his horse and got off and sat cross-legged on the ground. He had opened the blanket at last to look at his sleeping son, who had finally exhausted himself crying.

And marveled at how perfectly made he was. At his black hair. At his tiny fingernails and toenails—ten of each. At his long eyelashes. He had promised his child that somehow he would make a life for him that was better than his own. But he had known, deep down in some painful place inside him, that he didn't know the first thing about taking care of a baby, let alone raising a child.

That was when Simp had found him.

Nicholas wondered how his life would have been different if Evie had been like Nora, willing to stand by him even in the face of calamity. What if she had loved him enough to endure the hardship of building a life with him, even though they were starting it with a third mouth to feed?

Nicholas hadn't ever allowed himself to become maudlin. Right now he was in danger of being downright sentimental over the past.

He had learned a hard lesson at a young age. He had never offered love to another woman. And never given another woman the chance to hurt him the way Evie had. He had learned a great deal from her. Actually, he owed her a debt of gratitude. He knew how to please a woman in bed. Those lessons had stood him in good stead over the years.

And he had Colin. He could never be sorry for that.

It was amazing that nearly twenty years later he was finally going to be married. It was good to remember the lessons of the past. He would have to keep Evie in mind when he bedded Daisy. And remember why he would be the world's worst fool if he ever let himself fall in love again.

11

Colin had done his best to converse with Lord Frederick Willowbrook, but the young man was pompous and condescending, and Colin had about had his fill of sentences that began with "In London we always . . ." Colin sighed in disgust. He had hoped to spend some time with Lady Roanna, but she had been totally diverted by Lord Frederick's two simpering sisters.

He made his escape when luncheon was announced, excusing himself and heading for the stable. He would rather ride back home in the rain than spend the rest of the day in the company of a London fop. There was a groom available, but Colin preferred to saddle his own horse. He wasn't used to having servants do for him, and he didn't intend to get used to it. He had just finished when he realized the groom was gone, but he wasn't alone.

"Mr. Calloway? Are you leaving already?"

Colin turned and found he hadn't the breath to answer. It was Lady Roanna, looking very, very lovely.

She removed the damp woolen shawl she had used to protect her head and shoulders from the rain and laid it across a stall door. He noticed for the first time that her lavender dress was cut into a V in front. There wasn't much skin exposed, but it was the promise of feminine flesh a bare inch out of sight that left him gulping.

Colin knew it was a dumb move to let himself fall any more deeply in love with her than he already was, but he had no idea how to stop this sort of thing once it had gotten started. He reminded himself he was going back to America in the spring. He reminded himself of his father's warning that no woman was worth the heartache she generally caused.

It did no good. He was already too far gone.

It took a moment for Colin to realize that Lady Roanna had come alone. "Does anyone know you're out here?"

She blushed. "I know it isn't proper. But I couldn't let you leave without telling you how much I appreciate your help entertaining Lord Frederick. Do you really have to go?"

He wasn't about to take the chance of insulting her by admitting his true feelings about Lord Frederick. "My father has some work for me at home," he lied.

"Oh? May I ask what?"

Her question proved what his father had always said. Liars get caught. "The truth is, there isn't any work at home. I just . . . I . . ."

"You don't like Lord Frederick."

He left the stall and stepped into the aisle of the stable, not more than two feet from her. "How did you know?"

She grinned at him, an impish look that suggested

she shared his feelings. "He is a bit affected, isn't he?"

"A bit?"

"All right. He's excessively pretentious."

"Plumb full of foofaraw."

Her grin widened and a dimple appeared in her left cheek. "You have Freddy pegged, I'm afraid. I'm sorry. I should have known better than to force you into his company."

"Freddy? What happened to Lord Frederick?"

Roanna's nose wrinkled in distaste. "I've known Freddy since he was in knee britches. He hasn't improved much with age. His parents and mine keep throwing us together."

"Surely they don't intend for you to marry that clothhead," Colin said, aghast.

"Not right away, of course. But it's been suggested." Roanna lowered her eyes to studiously observe the toes of her patent leather half boots.

Colin acted without thinking. He slipped his arm around her waist and drew her to him, then put his finger beneath her chin to tip it up so he could see her eyes. "That would be a terrible waste."

Her eyes were the color of Texas bluebonnets, more a soft lavender than an actual blue, wide and innocent and not the least bit wary. Colin knew he was playing with fire. *Just a taste*, he thought. *Just one taste*.

He lowered his mouth, waiting for any sign of repugnance from her. Her tongue slicked her lips and disappeared again. She stopped breathing entirely when he lowered his mouth to hers.

Her lips were soft and damp and surrendered to his without resistance. He had barely touched his mouth to hers when her body instinctively arched toward him. His head spun as he tasted her and felt the contours of her body against his own. Her hands slid around his waist and up his back. He lifted his head to look down at her. He wasn't sure what it was he was seeking, something in her eyes, anything in her expression that would tell him what she was thinking, what she was feeling.

Colin hadn't believed himself to be infected with his father's cynicism toward women. And yet it seemed his feelings weren't so virginal, so untouched by skepticism, after all. He couldn't kiss Roanna—in his mind he had dropped the title long ago—without wondering why she was acting in a manner so foreign to what he knew was proper for a young English lady.

Did she care for him at all? Did she love him? Or, because of who he was—a bastard and a foreigner— had she come to the stable merely to seek a diversion, a bit of illicit adventure?

Roanna's eyes were half lidded, and she was pliant in his arms. Obviously she welcomed his embrace, his kisses. But did she want any more than that? Would she be willing to go with him to America when he left? Was she committed to him, as he felt himself becoming committed to her?

"Colin?" she said. "What's wrong?"

At least she was perceptive enough to recognize there was a problem. "Why are you here, Roanna?" He had dropped the title on purpose, to see what she would do and say.

She merely flushed guiltily. "I don't know what you mean."

"I think you do."

Her eyes flashed up at him. "I don't normally do this sort of thing."

"Don't you?" His brow was arched in disbelief, his mouth as cynical as his father's had ever been. "You haven't been kissed before?"

Her flush deepened. "Not like that," she said in a barely audible voice.

"I hope the experiment turned out well for you," he said as he released her and took a step back. "Now, if you'll excuse me—"

She put a hand on his arm to stop him. "Colin . . ."

He felt his blood thrum at the sound of his name on her lips. This was what his father had been warning him about all those years. A woman had weapons a man couldn't imagine. He looked at Roanna and saw them all. Eyes that were so liquid you could drown in them. A mouth so inviting you could lose yourself there. Flesh that was so soft and sweet it made you hunger till you thought you'd die if you didn't taste it.

He looked down to where her hand clutched at his sleeve. "What do you want from me, Roanna?" he asked in a harsh voice. He wasn't happy about having to let her go, even though he knew it was the right thing to do.

"I . . . I'm sorry, Colin," she said. "I didn't mean—"

"You don't have to say any more." He jerked his arm free. "I get the message. I'm not good enough to marry, but a little fling in the hay won't cause any harm. Although I'd like to hear how you're going to explain the slight lack of virginity to Freddy on your wedding night."

He wasn't expecting the slap, and he didn't move quickly enough to stop her hand before she caught his cheek. It stung. He felt the blood rush to his face, heating the spot where she had struck him.

"You're a brute, like your father. I hate you! I'm sorry I ever met you!"

She raced from the stable, but he noticed she didn't head for the house. Likely she wouldn't go back there until she had recovered her composure. Which was a good thing for both of them, he supposed. He had some idea what Roanna's father would do to him if he had an inkling of what had transpired in the stable.

Colin led his horse outside into the rain, mounted, and began the ride back to Severn. He tilted his face so the cool water could get under the brim of his hat and soothe the spot where she had slapped him. For a girl her size, she sure packed a wallop. He had insulted her, so he supposed he deserved her retribution. But he wasn't sure whether she was angry because he was right, or because he was wrong.

Colin wanted to ask his father for advice but realized Nicholas Calloway was the last person he could turn to. He wished Simp were closer. He needed a dose of the old man's wisdom. At least he had learned his lesson. He wouldn't wear his heart on his sleeve again. He would be more careful about where he gave his love.

He wished it were spring already, and they were leaving this place. He liked it better in America, where he knew the rules. Where people were judged by who they were, not who their parents were.

Colin sighed. A few months, and he and his pa

would be on their way home. He would just keep his distance from Lady Roanna Warenne until then.

Colin would have been pleased if he could have seen the confused state in which he had left Roanna. She fled to the gazebo behind the house, which was overgrown with wisteria, creating a private bower in which she could escape detection from the house.

Roanna was agitated and paced the gazebo like a tiger in a five-sided cage. She had never been so insulted by a man! What made it so much worse was the fact that his accusation had been correct. She had been playing with the American, teasing him and hoping to get him to kiss her. She knew he was totally unsuitable as a husband. Her parents had raised her to know her own worth. She was the daughter of an earl. Lady Roanna Christina Warenne would never marry a bastard with no lineage to speak of and no property to his name, even if he could claim a duke as his father.

She touched her lips where Colin had kissed her. She still couldn't believe how it had felt. Devastating. Delightful. Disastrous. Because now that she had tasted him, now that she knew what it felt like to be held in his arms, she knew she would never be able to touch another man without making a comparison.

How had he affected her so deeply, so quickly? She had only been playing, just teasing and trying out her feminine wiles. She had been more successful than she had ever dreamed. To her surprise, Colin was not like the others whom she had coaxed out onto the terrace at some ball in London for a quick kiss. They had been boys. She included Freddy in that number, even though he was twenty-five.

Colin had kissed her with a man's desire, looked at her with a man's hungry need. In his arms, she became a woman worthy of his—

Roanna stopped her thoughts right there. Was there any chance that Colin loved her? Was that what she had seen on his face? Besides the desire, of course. She recognized that for what it was. But the other expression, the one in his searching blue eyes . . . Had that been love?

Roanna plopped down—as much as a woman could plop when she was wearing a breathlessly snug corset—on the wrought-iron chaise longue that sat along one wall of the gazebo.

What if Colin did love her?

She tried to analyze her feelings for the American and discovered they were all jumbled up, the fault of that kiss in the stable, she supposed. Her first thought was that if he had once loved her, he didn't anymore. She felt an ache deep inside, regret that she had ruined everything.

Roanna leapt up and began pacing again. It was foolish to regret something that was never destined to be. Colin had already announced he would be leaving England for America in the spring. Even if he hadn't been a totally ineligible suitor, he wouldn't be staying in England to marry her. So he was as guilty of toying with her feelings as she was of playing with his.

Unless he planned to take you back to America with him.

The thought was stunning. Totally unexpected. And caused Roanna to go hunting for the chaise longue again.

The thought of leaving England permanently had

never entered her mind. Like all young ladies, she had hopes of someday traveling on the continent, of buying clothes in Paris and attending the opera in Vienna. But what on earth did one do in America? The only images that came to mind were of cowboys on horseback and red Indians who took scalps. She supposed those ideas might be a little outdated, but truly, she had no other images to replace them.

Roanna sighed. Her father had kept a very protective eye on her for all of her seventeen years. She had yearned for excitement, for something new and different to replace the sameness of life in the country. Colin had provided that excitement. She felt exhilarated when she was with him. His kiss had been thrilling. She had no way of knowing whether Colin had simply relieved the boredom in her life, or whether her feelings for him amounted to a great deal more.

Perhaps it would be better to keep a great deal of distance between herself and the American until she could sort out her turbulent feelings. Unfortunately, that shouldn't be too difficult. The chances were excellent that, after today's fiasco, he never wanted to see her again.

Daisy found Nicholas in the library. He was standing in the same spot where she had first met him, staring out the window as Tony had been wont to do. She knew now that all resemblance between the two men ended there.

Daisy had spent a great deal of the time in her bath thinking. She had decided to take Nicholas on a guided tour of the portrait gallery. He might find some Windermere ancestor from whom he had inherited his looks, or he might not. In any case, it was past time she began to educate him about what he would be giving up if he sold Severn. She also intended to make known to him her suspicions that his aunt might hold the key to the knowledge he sought.

She had decided *not* to speak to Nicholas about his abrupt decision to send for a special license so that they might marry sooner. She was anxious about what would happen when they were man and wife, but she knew that once Nicholas put the ring on her finger she would be in a much better position to negotiate things for the people of Severn. And that, after all, had been her goal from the first.

Nicholas knew Daisy was there, waiting for him to acknowledge her. He hesitated because he wanted to prolong the moment. He inhaled and caught a whiff of the expensive perfume she had donned after her bath. It was a musky smell, not flowery at all. It reminded him of dark places and sex. He wouldn't have figured Daisy for anything that provocative. Apparently she had depths he hadn't plumbed. He planned to take his time learning all about her soon —in bed.

At last he turned. He kept his hands clasped behind him, so he wouldn't be tempted to reach for her. She was wearing another one of those dresses with a dragging tail, this one a combination of orange and rust that brought out the auburn in her hair and made him want to thrust his hands into it.

"Is there something you wanted, Daisy?"

"I thought you might enjoy touring the gallery with me, since it's still raining."

He glanced out at the gray sky and the drizzle that was still falling. "When do you think it will stop?"

"Tomorrow morning."

His head snapped back around. "You sound sure of yourself."

"I am. I've lived here long enough to be able to tell." She crossed to the window and pointed along the tops of the trees. "See, there. The weather comes from the east. When the sky lightens above the trees, it usually means the end of the rain."

Nicholas spotted a rainbow and pointed it out to Daisy. "It looks like you're right."

He was much more aware of her than he knew he should be. He should never have unbuttoned her dress upstairs. He had seen the curve of her spine, laid his hands on her naked shoulders. Seen the plumpness of her breasts pressed upward by her corset. His fingers knew the way she felt and itched to touch her.

"The gallery sounds like a good idea," he said. At least there would be something to look at besides Daisy.

"Follow me, Your Grace."

He followed her, but he couldn't resist saying "I think, since we're going to be married in two days, it might be better if you began to think of me as Nicholas."

She looked up at him from under her lashes. "If you wish, Nicholas."

Nicholas gazed at her through narrowed eyes. No argument? From his Daisy? That was totally out of character. He wondered what she wanted from him, then chided himself for being so distrustful.

Nicholas thought he knew Severn Manor like the back of his hand, but he wasn't familiar with the

upstairs room where Daisy led him. "Why haven't I
been here before?"

"Probably you weren't allowed here as a child."

Nicholas saw why when he entered the gallery. It
was filled with beautiful brass urns and delicate ce-
ramic vases, with ivory inlaid tables and carvings of
ivory. "Where did all these things come from?"

"India, I believe."

"How did they get here?"

"They were gifts."

"From whom?"

"Lord Estleman, I believe."

Nicholas froze. "What does he have to do with
Severn?"

"He was a friend of the old duke's."

"How long have these things been here?"

"At least two generations, I would say. Tony
showed them to me before we were married. He
said they were here when he was a boy."

"I can't imagine why I was never in this room,"
Nicholas said. "Or why Tony never mentioned it to
me." He paused and stared at the wall of portraits.
"Is Estleman immortalized in any of these paintings?"

"I don't imagine that he is," Daisy replied. "As far
as I know he was no relation to the Windermeres.
Would you like to take a closer look at some of
them?"

"Yes, I would." Nicholas's mind was flying in a
dozen different directions, trying to figure out how
Lord Estleman—he would have to be awfully elderly
by now if he was the old duke's friend—fit into his
past. Especially since Blotberry had specifically
named Estleman as someone he should speak with.

But the Lord Estleman Blotberry had mentioned couldn't be the same Estleman who had given all these gifts to the old duke. Nicholas hissed in a breath. The Estleman he was seeking must be the son.

Nicholas was uncomfortable with the discovery of all these gifts. It betokened a close relationship between Severn Manor and the Estlemans, father and son. He couldn't help wondering what either Estleman had received in exchange for all this splendor. Mere friendship? Had he bought himself the love of a young, impressionable woman? Had he cuckolded one of the old duke's sons—Lord Philip to be precise—and repaid the insult with these fantastic gifts?

"Do you see anyone you recognize?" Daisy asked.

Nicholas forced his attention to the paintings on the wall. He quickly spotted several that looked familiar. "I recognize the old duke." He reached out as if to touch the painting but let his hand fall.

He remembered his grandfather as a gruff, tyrannical old man with bushy brows and snowy white hair. He was bent with age and walked with a cane that made a thumping sound, like a wooden leg. He and Tony and Stephen had called him Pegleg. He had forgotten that.

His grandfather hadn't paid much attention to him, except at Christmas. Then he would hand out candy to all the children. Nicholas had never been fond of him, had never really felt anything at all for him.

He wondered now, as an adult, how his father had become such a good father, with old Pegleg as a model. Lord Philip had been much more accessible than his grandfather. He remembered his father coming to him every night after he was in bed to read to him. He hadn't realized at the time how odd that was for an English gentlemen, most of whom never crossed the threshold of a nursery. But Lord Philip had tucked him in and kissed his forehead every night.

Nicholas had followed the same procedure with Colin, although he hadn't realized until this moment that he had learned it from his father. *From Lord Philip*, he corrected himself. He didn't know yet if the man was truly his father. Because of all those nights, because of what they had meant to him, he hoped he was.

Nicholas remembered fishing with Lord Philip and being allowed to tag along on a hunt the last year he spent at Severn Manor, when he was eight. That, he knew, was the more common way English fathers and sons communed. He had that in common with Tony and Stephen, because they had attended the hunt with their father, the duke's elder son and heir.

"Is this your mother?"

Nicholas was startled from his recollections by Daisy's question. He looked at the painting she indicated. "That's her."

He hadn't meant to sound so curt, but he couldn't help the sharp pain he felt at the sight of the lovely woman in the painting. What he remembered was his mother on the day she had died, wan and pale and gaunt. The woman in the picture was a vivacious beauty.

"Do I look like her?" Nicholas managed to ask through the constriction in his throat.

Daisy looked from Nicholas to the picture and back again. "It's hard to say, really."

"In other words, no," Nicholas said flatly.

"I think you have her mouth, and perhaps her chin," Daisy contradicted. "But it's hard to say where the rest of you came from."

Nicholas perused the picture of the old duke, and his cousins' father, and the picture of Tony and Stephen as young boys with their mother. "Blond and blue-eyed, every last one of them. Where the hell did I get black hair and gray eyes?"

Nicholas lengthened his stride to march from one end of the gallery to the other, his eyes flicking up and down looking for someone who had his darker coloring. "Nobody. Not one of them," he said through clenched jaws.

"There are only Windermeres pictured here," Daisy said. "What did your maternal grandfather look like? Perhaps he's the one you have to blame for looking different."

"I know who to blame," Nicholas said.

"You do?"

"Whoever cuckolded my father."

Daisy frowned. "You don't know your mother was unfaithful." Which reminded her that there was someone who might actually know the truth. "I think you should speak to your aunt. She can describe her father for you. And, as your mother's sister, she's certainly in the best position to know whether there was another man in your mother's life."

"There was," Nicholas said with certainty.

Daisy's fists found her hips. "You keep saying that. Why?"

Nicholas thrust all ten fingers through his hair. "Just now I was remembering how much time my father spent with me as a child. He couldn't—he wouldn't—have abandoned me unless he had some sort of proof that my mother had betrayed him."

"Couldn't he have made a mistake?" Daisy said.

"If he did, it was a mistake with disastrous consequences."

Daisy hesitated to ask, but she was curious about the fate that had befallen his mother. "What happened to you and your mother? I mean, how was she reduced to . . . to . . ."

"To selling herself?" Nicholas finished. "She was robbed on the ship. She didn't realize most of her funds were gone until we arrived in Boston. She wrote a letter asking my father to take her back—at least, that's what she said was in it. We waited at a fishy-smelling inn near the docks for some word. It never came."

Daisy clasped her hands to still their trembling. "What did you do?"

"Six months after we arrived in Boston, we headed West, to the land of opportunity. My mother wasn't a worldly woman. She relied on the Yankee gentleman who befriended her, and when we reached St. Louis, he stole the rest of my mother's money and disappeared. We were destitute. My mother tried getting a job, but she wasn't educated for much more than playing the pianoforte, painting, and embroidering. She ended up playing the piano on a riverboat, the *Lullabelle*, that sailed the Mississippi all the way south to New Orleans.

"Mother was still very pretty in those days, and another man offered her friendship. She thought he wanted to marry her." Nicholas snickered. "He wanted her, all right. For the night. He left some money beside the bed in the morning.

"I remember she cried." He swallowed over the lump in his throat and turned his face away until he could get control of himself. "That was the first time," he continued finally. "It got easier after that.

"We stayed in New Orleans for the winter and slowly drifted over to Texas. Mother found work there, in one saloon after another. We did a lot of traveling in those days." His lips twisted. "Her kind of woman wasn't welcomed by the nice folk.

"We scraped by for four years. But it was clear by the second year that she was sick. It took another three years for the disease to catch up to her. When she died, it was a blessing. You see, the syphilis had already made her a little crazy."

Daisy gasped as he named the dreaded disease that had no cure. It was awful. Horrible. She fought back the disgust and pity she felt. Nicholas didn't deserve to see the disgust, and he wouldn't accept the pity. But she could offer comfort, and did. She took the several steps necessary to close the distance between them and slid her arms around his waist. She laid her head against his shoulder, where his heart beat. She felt it begin to thump erratically.

He's afraid, she realized. *Afraid to believe I can offer comfort with no strings attached. Afraid to accept it.*

Daisy thought for a moment Nicholas might break free. She tightened her grasp. At last his arms crossed behind her, and he clutched her tight, his face buried in her hair.

Nicholas wanted someone to understand, to absolve him for not being grown up enough to keep his mother from the awful fate that had befallen her. Without ever revealing the depth of his failure—that he had hated his mother and wished her dead—he sought forgiveness.

Daisy felt his need and answered it.

She brushed the hair back from his forehead, murmuring words of comfort that were more sounds than substance. "How you must have suffered, Nicholas. How strong you had to be. How alone you must have been. How did you ever survive?"

She wished she hadn't asked the question when he jerked free.

"Do you really want to know?"

She was afraid to hear what he had to say and desperate to know at the same time. She nodded.

"I emptied spittoons and swept the sawdust from the floor of the local saloon. I slept in the whorehouse where my mother had last worked."

"Don't tell me any more," Daisy quickly said. "I've heard enough."

"You wanted to know how the Duke of Severn survived. I'm telling you."

"The past made you who you are."

"A barbarian? Callous? Inconsiderate?" Nicholas taunted.

"A man of conviction. Competent. Capable," she countered.

"You've changed your tune, Daisy," he chided.

"I'm seeing facets of you I hadn't noticed before," she replied.

"Does this mean you don't hate me anymore?" he said in a husky voice.

Daisy recognized the danger. It was time to leave the gallery. Past time. She hesitated an instant too long, and Nicholas reached for her.

Nicholas didn't have seduction in mind when he slid his arm around Daisy's waist. He only wanted to tease her a little. After all, he had sent a man to London for a special license, and they would be married in under two days. But the warmth of her, the scent of that intoxicating perfume, changed his mind.

"Come to me, Daisy," he said. "Hold me."

How could she refuse him? There was something more in his eyes than desire. She knew too much to blame him anymore for what he was. And she simply didn't care anymore who he was. He was Nicholas. That was enough for now.

"How can you kiss me with all these faces looking down on us like this?" Daisy murmured against his lips.

Nicholas's mouth curved against hers. "Close your eyes, Daisy."

"What good will that do?"

"They'll all disappear."

Daisy chuckled. And closed her eyes.

12

It was his wedding day. Nicholas was as nervous as any other groom, and felt like a perfect idiot because of it. After all, it wasn't as though he were marrying for love. It was strictly a marriage of convenience. But after what had happened in the gallery, in full view of all the Windermeres from days gone by, Nicholas had to admit he was looking forward to his wedding night.

His hands had roamed, finding the soft curves that made up Daisy Windermere and claiming them. To his surprise, Daisy had responded with an investigation of her own. He had recognized her shy touches for what they were. Her caresses had been so hesitant, so subdued and cautious, that he soon held himself perfectly still, so as not to frighten her. She had slowly, but surely, driven him out of his mind.

Her eyes were focused on what she touched, so he was able to observe her without being observed. He had seen the pleasure—and wonder—on her face as she caressed the calluses on the palm of his hand, making him tremble. As she trailed her hand up his sleeve, feeling the muscles tighten beneath the wool. As she threaded her fingers through the curls that hung over his collar and then slipped her hand beneath them to find his nape, causing him to shiver.

Nicholas had never been seduced by someone who was totally unconscious of that seduction. By the time Daisy's palm met his cheek, he was completely aroused. As her fingertips traced the line of his jaw, and finally his mouth, his heart was thumping madly, and his lips had parted to seize the air he needed to ease his tortured breathing. He wanted her to look at him, to see in his eyes what she had done to him.

Instead, her lids lowered as she raised herself on tiptoes and pressed her lips against his, where her fingertips had been. It was a kiss of exploration, one that questioned the rightness of what she was doing. It was a kiss of wonder as his mouth opened to hers. It was a kiss of passion as her tongue slid quietly into his mouth and wreaked havoc with his senses.

Somewhere he found the strength to keep from dragging her against him. He feared that if he touched her she would realize what she was doing. Who he was. Who she was. And she would flee. He couldn't bear to let her go, so he surrendered himself to her, allowing her to lead where she would, and happily following after her. Her kiss moved him in ways he had never known a woman could move a man.

Eventually her body arched into his, and his hands gathered her up and held her close. The kiss changed, grew, and changed again to something that swallowed both of them, dragging them into some hidden valley where the wind smelled sweet and the sun shone bright and the grass was green and perfect.

Nicholas wondered what would have happened if Colin hadn't arrived at precisely that moment. They broke apart, or rather, Daisy wrenched herself free. If it had been up to him he would have told his son to take himself away and kept right on kissing her. Daisy had quickly, but with a great deal of hard-won dignity, excused herself.

But not before exchanging glances with him. He had seen the deep, unsatisfied need in her eyes, and it had made him yearn to finish what they had started. He had also seen something else. Something that looked like fear. He didn't know where it had come from or why she had felt it, but tonight, when he made her his wife in fact as well as name, he would find out.

"Pa?"

Nicholas looked up and found Colin in the doorway to his bedroom.

"I called you twice. Are you all right?"

Nicholas grinned ruefully. "As well as any groom ever is an hour before his wedding." He tried tying his cravat, but couldn't get his fingers to do what he wanted. Maybe he shouldn't have dismissed Porter, after all.

"You're nervous!" Colin exclaimed. "Here, let me do that."

Nicholas stood still as Colin expertly folded the cravat into place.

"There, how's that?" Colin asked, as he turned his father to face the mirror over the dresser.

"Perfect. Thanks, Colin. I'm glad you're here to be my best man."

A frown creased Colin's forehead. "Pa, why are

you going through with this if it makes you so uncomfortable?"

"In case you hadn't noticed, Daisy Windermere is a very beautiful woman."

Colin settled on the corner of the bed, near a tall beveled foot post. "But you're not in love with her, are you? I thought people were supposed to marry for love. At least, that's what Simp always told me."

"Simp's a romantic living in a practical world," Nicholas replied.

"So you're marrying Daisy for practical reasons?"

"Not entirely," Nicholas confessed.

"Oh, I see."

Nicholas raised a brow. He wasn't sure if Colin had grasped what he was saying, but he wasn't about to explain to his son that aside from the practical reasons for marrying the Duchess of Severn, he very much desired her and wanted her in his bed. Of course, practically speaking, marriage was the only way to get her there.

He hadn't been entirely honest with his son, but then, he hadn't been entirely honest with himself about his reasons for marrying Daisy, either. He was pretty certain he wouldn't have been so quick to agree to marriage if he had come to Severn and found anyone besides Daisy Windermere in the role of dowager duchess. She intrigued him. She delighted him. She challenged him. She was a woman like none he had ever met. Was it any wonder he was looking forward to making her his wife?

"Are the Earl of Rotherham and his family invited to the wedding?" Colin asked.

"The earl's wife is attending Daisy, so I'm sure the

earl will be there. I'm not sure who else Daisy invited. I left everything up to her."

"Do you think Lady Roanna will come?"

Nicholas turned and faced his son. "You don't sound like you want her there."

"I don't care one way or the other."

Nicholas took one look at the white-knuckled hand that gripped the bedpost and said, "Try again."

Colin noticed how hard he was holding the post and let it go. "The hands give you away every time," he said with a wry twist of his mouth. "The truth is, Lady Roanna and I had a falling out. I'd rather not see her again."

"That might be difficult, since Rockland Park is so close, and since both Daisy and I have ties with the earl and his wife. Would you like to tell me what happened?"

Colin flushed.

"I assume your disagreement involved a kiss."

Colin nodded.

"Did you force her?"

Before his father had finished speaking, Colin was on his feet, ready to fight. "You taught me better than that, Pa. How could you even think such a thing?"

Nicholas laid a hand on Colin's shoulder. He felt the tension in Colin's body and sought the right words to encourage his son to share his problem after the mistaken accusation he had made. "I'm sorry. I should have known better. But if she wanted the kiss, what caused the problem?"

Colin took a step, so that Nicholas's hand fell away. It was difficult for him to admit what he believed to be the truth. He took a deep breath and blurted, "She kissed me like she might have kissed a pig on a dare. To see what it would be like."

"What?" Nicholas simply couldn't believe what he had heard.

Colin turned to face his father, and Nicholas saw the damage Lady Roanna Warenne had done. His son was not so trusting as he had been, and never would be again. The gullible boy was gone, and in his place was a wounded, suspicious man.

"You were right, Pa. About how a woman can be deceitful. Lady Roanna didn't treat me honestly. If she wasn't interested, she shouldn't have pretended she was. I won't be so stupid the next time."

"I'm sorry that happened, son. I'm sure we can find things for you to do around here that will keep you away from Rockland Park."

Colin's experience reminded Nicholas—at a critical time in his relationship with Daisy—that he should beware of his future duchess. She had an agenda of her own where this marriage was concerned. He had to be careful not to let himself trust her. He knew the disaster that awaited a man who trusted—or loved—a woman.

"If Lady Roanna attends the wedding, just ignore her," Nicholas advised. "There's nothing a woman hates worse than that."

Colin grinned. "Thanks, Pa. I knew I could count on you to help me out."

"We'd better get started for the church, or I'm going to be late for my own wedding. Let's go see if my duchess is ready."

Daisy wasn't ready and didn't think she would be for about the next two hundred years.

Last chance to back out, Daisy. Are you sure this is the right thing to do?

No, I'm not sure! But it's too late to do anything about it. We made a bargain.

It's never too late. Just tell the duke you've changed your mind.

How about telling him I'm out of my mind?

A knock on the door interrupted the little voice that warned Daisy to escape while she still could.

"See who that is, Jane," she said to her maid.

Jane opened the door and found the duke and his son standing there. She opened the door wider. "Her Grace is nearly ready, Your Grace."

Daisy closed her eyes and stayed seated in front of her mirror. She wasn't ready. Wouldn't be for maybe *three* hundred years.

"Daisy?"

She felt the callused hand on her bare shoulder, felt the duke's fingers tighten slightly, felt his thumb brush across her flesh. Her body quivered.

Not three hundred years, Daisy. Today. You'll marry him today. Ready or not. Here you go.

She opened her eyes and stared at the man and woman in the mirror. He looked very little like the barbarian she had met—could it have been a mere week ago? Neither did he look civilized. Oh, he wore the trappings, all right. His formal black coat was carefully tailored to fit massive shoulders, and his pristine white cravat was perfectly folded at his throat. A gold brocade waistcoat showed off his flat stomach and tapering black trousers revealed from whence he got his height. He was the epitome of an English gentleman. But it was all an illusion.

The eyes gave him away. And the hands.

He did nothing to hide his feelings, and his gray eyes were heavy-lidded and dark with desire. She knew a savage smoldered behind the careful facade of civilized man. She had seen him leash his passion in the gallery. Had felt his body tremble with need. Had heard his heart thunder.

She felt everything he was feeling through the touch of his hands, which couldn't lie. The moment his fingertips came to rest on her shoulders, they told her that he was anxious and excited. She knew for a fact the callused hands that touched her so gently had killed many men. For her they were tender, coaxing. They told her she was desired. And they were impatient. He wanted her now.

She had called him barbarian. Savage. Uncivilized. He was all of those, but something more. He was a person searching, as she was, for answers to questions that seemed to have no answer. He had survived and become a man in the face of terrible calamity, but at a very dear cost. He had learned to doubt, to suspect and distrust women, to be cynical, sarcastic, and scornful of the fair sex. He would never be an easy man to love.

Not that love was a part of their bargain. Or ever would be. But there were moments when she found him lovable. Times when he allowed her to see his confusion, his perplexity about his birth and his birthright. He was a man who felt deeply, the pain and the passion. He could also be a man of grace and mercy, as she had learned with his rescue of the trapped Hepplewhite boy. Despite everything, he was capable of love. His devotion to his son proved that.

Yet Daisy felt a rising sense of panic, almost hysteria, as her wedding drew near. The source of her distress was easily defined. She wanted to love and be loved but was about to marry a man who not only didn't want her love, but also had absolutely no intention of giving his.

Daisy released a shaky breath.

"What brought that on?" Nicholas whispered in her ear.

Daisy pushed back the fear. Nobody said noble sacrifices were easy. She managed to smile. "I was just wondering how all this will turn out."

"And not seeing a very rosy picture, I presume."

"More like stinkweed and brambles."

The duke's smile flashed and just as quickly disappeared. "We can't know the future, Daisy."

"No, but if one sees a high cliff, one can make the decision not to jump off," she replied with acerbity.

The duke's smile returned, and his hands tightened briefly on her shoulders. "That's my girl. I feel a lot better knowing you don't have any illusions about this marriage." He used his hands to urge her onto her feet. "Come on, Daisy. No more stalling. It's time to go."

Thompson's face remained rigid, as befitted a duke's butler, as he opened the front door for them, but his eyes smiled. "May I offer my congratulations, Your Grace," he said to the duke.

"You may, Thompson. I'm a very lucky man."

"And my best wishes to you, Your Grace," Thompson said to Daisy.

"Thank you, Thompson." *I'm going to need them.*

Nicholas was delighted that the sun had decided to shine on his wedding day, and smiled to show his pleasure as he helped Daisy into the carriage that would take them to the parish church. Colin rode alongside the carriage on Buck.

Once seated across from Daisy inside the coach, Nicholas took time to admire her at his leisure. She kept her eyes glued out the window, supposedly watching the countryside pass them by, which gave him a chance to peruse her.

She was wearing a pale mint-green satin gown that was cut low enough to reveal a tantalizing swell of bosom. He had noticed in her bedroom that it had a row of cloth-covered buttons that ran from her nape to just below her waist. He imagined himself kissing his way down her back as he undid them one by one.

"You look very beautiful, Daisy."

Her head jerked back around so she was facing him. Her face had been rosy since the moment he entered her room, but now two distinct red patches appeared on her cheeks.

"I don't know why you're acting so surprised at the compliment," he said. "You must know how you look."

"Tony never . . ." She stopped, aware of the breach of etiquette in mentioning her late husband in the presence of her future one. "Actually, I haven't received that many compliments. I think my hair—"

He reached over and captured a handful of the curls that lay on her shoulders. "Your hair is lovely. Look how the sun turns it into copper in my hand."

She reached up to free herself and ended up holding his hand. He twined his fingers in hers, refusing to allow her to escape.

"Nicholas, please," she said. "Don't pretend."

"Pretend what?"

"That you care. I know you don't. All these compliments make me uncomfortable. I would rather we got through this with some decorum."

Nicholas withdrew his hand from hers. "Very well, my dear. If you prefer, we can ride in silence."

"That isn't what I meant at all, and you know it," Daisy fired back. Somehow she had hurt him. Nevertheless, she found she could easily match his look of cool contempt.

"You *are* beautiful, Daisy," he said. "I wasn't giving you false coin."

The tone of his voice, the quiet way he said it, made her believe him. Daisy quickly discovered she was no more capable of accepting an honest compliment than she was a false one. She turned to stare out the window, but quickly conceded it was unfair to ask Nicholas to be sincere and then hide from his sincerity. She turned back to him and found him watching her with the cynical look that rarely left his face.

It would have been far easier to stare out the window again. But minutes from now she would be putting her life in this man's hands. It was foolish not to try to deal more easily with him. She forced herself to speak.

"Thank you for the compliment," she said a little breathlessly. "I would be remiss if I didn't return it. You're looking very handsome today, Nicholas."

At first his eyes were wary, but she knew he had decided to accept her words on their face when the cynical twist left his mouth.

"All right, Daisy. We've established that you're

beautiful and I'm handsome. Where would you like to go from there?''

Daisy laughed. ''Fortunately for both of us, we've reached the church. Anything else we have to say will have to wait until we're man and wife.'' She reached out and touched his hand where it rested on his knee. ''Be kind, Nicholas. That's all I ask.''

Nicholas was too stunned to move, and Daisy quickly escaped the carriage before him. The Earl of Rotherham was there to help her down the steps. Nicholas still had a bemused expression on his face when he stepped down in front of the church.

Nicholas wondered what Daisy had meant by her admonition. Was she worried that he would be rough with her in their marriage bed? That was carrying the whole barbarian business a bit too far, he thought. Left with time to mull that thought, he might have gotten angry, but the earl distracted him.

''Second thoughts?'' Charles murmured.

''What? No.'' Nicholas forced himself to smile. ''I'll be glad to have the ceremony over with, but I'm more than willing to marry the duchess.''

Nicholas was pleased to see that Daisy had invited only the Rotherhams. Lady Roanna was there. He watched with narrowed eyes as Colin ignored her, seating himself on the opposite aisle at the front of the simple country church to wait for his father to join him so the ceremony could begin.

Daisy was already at the front of the church with Lady Rotherham beside her. Nicholas left Charles to join his wife before the altar.

''You're trembling, Daisy,'' Priss whispered to her friend. ''Are you frightened?''

"Just excited," Daisy whispered back. "I'm so glad you're here, Priss."

"Me, too," Priss said. "Be happy, Daisy. Oh, please, just be happy."

There was nothing Daisy could say to that. Her happiness was not of primary importance at the moment. The future of Severn Manor and all who depended upon it rested on her shoulders. She was entering a marriage of convenience in order to help a great many people. She was willing to put her own needs aside long enough to ensure the survival of Severn.

Daisy tried to listen to the reverend, but his words jumbled up in her brain. How could she go through with this? She was like a martyr willing to be burned at the stake who had serious second thoughts when someone arrived with torches to light the fire. What steadied her nerves was the painfully honest admission that her motives in marrying Nicholas weren't wholly unselfish.

She wanted the duke to make love to her, and she had every expectation of enjoying herself in bed with him. That made her sacrifice for the tenants of Severn considerably less than noble. But the fact she was going to benefit didn't make the marriage any less necessary.

Daisy heard herself speaking, but had no idea what she said. She felt something cold slide onto her finger and saw Nicholas had put a simple gold band there. She realized with dismay that she had no ring for him. She looked at him in a daze, as if he were a stranger.

He was a stranger. She had known him barely a week.

But she knew more about him, about Nicholas the man, than she had learned about Tony in eight years of marriage. And she wanted him physically in a way she had never imagined wanting a man. And though she was anxious about the night to come, she wasn't as terrified as she had expected to be.

Daisy felt a light kiss on her lips, and it was as if the prince had woken Sleeping Beauty. She blinked and realized the ceremony was over. She was the Duchess of Severn, Nicholas's wife.

She turned and received Priss's hug and then received a gentle kiss on the cheek from Colin.

"Shall I call you Ma now?" Colin whispered in her ear.

"Daisy will do. Or Your Grace if you can't remember that," Daisy said, returning his teasing grin.

"You win," he said. "Daisy it is."

Sometime during all the felicitations Daisy became aware that Nicholas had slipped his arm around her waist. He was leading her inexorably toward the church door.

"Leaving so soon?" The Earl of Rotherham intercepted them and gave Daisy a quick buss on the cheek. He shook Nicholas's hand. "Congratulations. I wish you both every happiness."

"Thank you, Charles. Daisy doesn't know it, but I've planned a short honeymoon for us. We won't be staying for the wedding breakfast, but I hope you'll go back to the house and enjoy it."

"What?" Daisy said. "You've done what, Nicholas?"

"I'm kidnapping you," he said with a roguish grin. "We're going on a honeymoon, my dear."

"But—"

He swept her up in his arms. "For the next two weeks you're mine. I don't want anything interrupting our time together."

"But you can't just—"

"I can and I have," Nicholas said as he settled her in the carriage.

"Where are we going?" Daisy asked. "I haven't packed. I—"

"Jane packed for you."

"Jane knew about this?"

Nicholas grinned. "She did. She and Porter will be joining us in London a few days from now. I'll be your maid until then," he said with a gleam in his eye.

"Who else knows?" she asked, eyes narrowed suspiciously.

"Most of the household. I had to tell them we would be gone so they could take care of things while we're away."

"This must be the first time in history that servants ever kept a secret," Daisy said.

"I wanted to surprise you."

Daisy caught his glance and realized that while he wouldn't have taken no for an answer if she had refused, he nevertheless wanted her to be happy with what he had planned.

And she was, Daisy realized.

Two whole weeks alone, with no thought of Severn. Two weeks alone to discover whether they were compatible. Two weeks alone to investigate the delights of each other's body. It would be wonderful.

Daisy's smile started at the corners of her mouth and ended with a sparkle in her green eyes. "I think it's a wonderful idea, Nicholas. Thank you."

Nicholas tapped the ceiling of the carriage, and it began to move. Before they were even out of sight of the church, he dragged her into his lap and kissed her. Her barbarian wasn't tender. He wasn't gentle. She felt his hunger as one hand claimed her breast and the other captured a handful of copper curls. He arched her head back to give him better access to her mouth.

"Mine," he murmured harshly. "You're finally mine."

Yes, yours, Daisy thought.

The little warning voice inside her head replied, *But for how long?*

13

The duke's kisses consumed Daisy. She gloried in his touch, in the taste of him. She refused to think about the future. They had two weeks alone. She was determined to enjoy every moment of it. Her hand crept into his hair, and her mouth invited him to deepen his kiss. His mouth ravaged hers, and she surrendered to his invasion.

It was Nicholas who finally brought things to a halt.

"We have to stop this," he said, his breathing labored.

Daisy reached mindlessly for his mouth, slipping her tongue between his lips.

Nicholas was so surprised by Daisy's kiss that he let the passion drag him back under. He had his hand on her naked breast, lifting it so he could suckle her, when he realized what he was doing. He didn't want to bed her for the first time in a moving carriage. There wasn't space to do everything he wanted to do. He lifted his head and looked into her face and realized she was going to be upset when he stopped. But stop they must.

"Daisy," he murmured against her ear.

She arched against him, and he groaned as his body tightened with need.

"Please, sweetheart, we have to stop."

"Nicholas?" She was dazed, her eyes heavy-lidded, her lashes creating coal crescents on her cheeks. Her mouth was swollen pink and damp from his kisses.

He resisted the urge to suck on her lower lip. Instead he began to tug her clothes back into some semblance of order. "This isn't the way I want us to make love the first time."

"Oh."

As Daisy regained her senses, embarrassment set in. Nicholas did his best to ease things for her, as he quietly and calmly—as calmly as a man with aching loins could—settled her back onto the seat across from him. His hands were shaking, and he stuck them in his pockets to keep from reaching for her again. He shifted, trying to get more comfortable, and realized he wasn't going to be content until he had eased himself inside her. Fortunately, they would be stopping soon.

"Fix your hair." Nicholas cursed himself for his abruptness. It was just that the sight of all those copper curls made his hands itch.

She didn't say anything, just sniffed and did her best, with the few pins she could find on the seats and the few he found for her on the floor of the carriage, to bring her hair under control.

When Daisy was finished, she checked herself one last time and sat back primly in the seat. "How do I look?" she asked.

Nicholas took the time to admire her naked throat and shoulders and the swell of bosom that rose from her dress. She looked a little disheveled. Her skin was flushed, and her eyes sparkled. She looked like some man had made passionate love to her. "You look exactly like a bride ought to look," he said as an unholy grin split his face.

"What's so funny?" Daisy asked in a sharp voice. She checked her clothing and hair again, but could find nothing amiss.

Nicholas wiped the smirk off his face. "Nothing's funny." Except Daisy probably wouldn't be sitting there looking so calm and dignified if she had any idea there was a perfectly visible love bruise at the base of her throat. He had no idea when he had put it there, and his only regret was that, knowing Daisy, she would likely wear high-necked dresses for the next week or so until it disappeared.

"Will you tell me now where we're going?" Daisy asked.

"London."

"London!" Daisy exclaimed.

"Not today. We'll be stopping shortly in Camberly. Tomorrow morning—not too early, I hope—we'll travel on." Nicholas enjoyed watching the flush rise on Daisy's cheeks. He had every reason to hope they would consume the better part of the night making love and would both sleep well past dawn.

"We'll be spending the rest of our honeymoon at Severn House on Grosvenor Square," Nicholas finished.

"That house has been closed for the past year," Daisy protested.

"I had it opened and cleaned and staffed with servants. We'll be very comfortable, I assure you."

"Why London?" she asked.

"Because I haven't been there before. Because it's the center of the English world, and by all accounts a fascinating place. Because we'll have more privacy there." Nicholas didn't add the final reason he had decided to go to London.

Because Lord Estleman is reputed to be living there.

In the day between sending for the special license and the day of his wedding he had not had an opportunity to speak again with his aunt. Absent any new information from her, he believed a meeting with Lord Estleman was imperative.

The carriage stopped, and Nicholas realized they had arrived at the inn where they would spend the night.

Daisy looked out the window and saw a charming brick two-story cottage with a thatched roof. A hanging wooden sign proclaimed it as The Wolf and the Lamb. The name seemed particularly apt in light of her circumstances.

Nicholas descended the carriage first and realized suddenly that he didn't want anyone else seeing the signs of his lovemaking. So, as Daisy stepped down from the carriage, he picked her up in his arms and tucked her head under his chin so the bruise would be hidden from sight.

"Nicholas, this really isn't necessary," Daisy said, squirming in his arms.

"Trust me, Daisy. It's necessary."

Daisy remembered his unholy grin and realized that something in her appearance must be amiss. Rather than argue with him in the courtyard and draw attention, she reached up and put her arms around his neck, hiding her face against his throat for good measure.

"My wife isn't feeling well. Perhaps you can direct me to our room," he said in a voice that was every bit as arrogant as any duke of the realm.

"Yes, Your Grace," the proprietor said, bowing obsequiously and racing to keep ahead of Nicholas, who was already headed for the stairs.

"Here's your room, Your Grace. The best in the house."

"Send up some water for my wife to wash. We'll have our dinner in the private parlor later. Everything has been arranged?"

Nicholas raised a regal black brow that the proprietor acknowledged with another bow. "Yes, Your Grace. Everything will be ready at your convenience."

"Close the door on your way out," Nicholas said.

The proprietor bowed again and left them alone.

"You can put me down now," Daisy said.

Nicholas eyed the bed. That was where he wanted to put her, but he knew there would be servants coming soon with water for Daisy to refresh herself. When he made love to her, he didn't want to be interrupted. Slowly he eased her down the front of him, enjoying the trembling shiver that shimmered through her.

The eyes that met his weren't the least bit droopy or sensuous. They were downright suspicious.

"All right," she said. "What's wrong with my appearance?"

Nicholas grinned. He couldn't help it. He gestured toward an oval mirror standing in the corner. "Take a look for yourself."

Daisy stalked over to the mirror. In the dusky light from the leaded window she didn't see anything at first. Then she spied it. She took a step closer and leaned in toward the mirror. Her fingertips examined the small bruise on her throat.

"Oh." She turned to face him. At first her lips flattened. Then her eyes crinkled with humor.

Nicholas was surprised and confused by her response. "You aren't angry?" he asked in a wary voice.

"Not if you aren't."

"I don't understand what you mean."

She stood back and gestured toward the mirror.

Nicholas marched over and looked at himself. There, just beneath his right ear, was a small purple bruise. His cravat was askew, and his hair was standing on end.

"Oh." His ears turned pink.

Daisy laughed. When Nicholas turned to her with a frown on his face, she covered her mouth to try to stop her giggles. But they kept coming. And got worse. "Oh, if you could only have seen yourself," she said, hugging her ribs and bending over with laughter. "My wife isn't feeling well," she mimicked. "And all the time . . . all the time . . . he must have known what was wrong with both of us."

Nicholas's mouth twitched, then turned up in a smile. Finally he laughed, a deep guffaw that came up from his belly. "Good Lord! I wonder how many other dukes have arrived here looking like they've come from an orgy?"

"I'll never be able to show my face in this place again," Daisy said.

"Maybe we won't sleep late tomorrow, after all," Nicholas said. "Maybe it would be better if we sneak out at dawn."

Daisy laughed until tears spilled from her eyes. "Oh, Nicholas, I don't know when I've laughed so hard. It's been so long. It feels so *good.*"

Nicholas could no more have stopped himself from taking Daisy in his arms than he could have stopped the rain from falling in England. It seemed the most natural thing in the world to seek her mouth with his. To feel the smile on her lips, to take the joy that bubbled out of her and merge it with his kiss. He reached over without looking and turned the key in the door.

"To hell with water for washing. To hell with dinner. To hell with everything. Except this."

His mouth found hers again, and he took what he wanted, what he needed from her. "Daisy, Daisy," he said in a raw voice. "I need you. Now."

A knock on the door interrupted him.

He tore his mouth from hers, knowing they wouldn't be left alone until he answered. "Go away," he said in his best ducal voice.

"But, Your Grace—"

"Leave us alone!" Nicholas waited until the footsteps in the hall had receded before he returned his gaze to Daisy. Her hands were around his neck, and her body was pressed close to his. Even through the layers of cloth, he knew she must feel his arousal.

"Well, Daisy, we're alone at last."

The fear came and went so quickly in her eyes that he wondered again whether he had really seen it. But she did nothing to stop him as he lowered his mouth to hers and took the sustenance she offered him.

Daisy had already lived through one wedding night. But it had been nothing at all like this. She had experienced more intimacy with Nicholas in the carriage than she had with Tony in all her years of marriage. And she was totally unprepared for the fever Nicholas kindled in her blood.

Tony had kissed her, but only as a perfunctory prelude to the main act. She wondered whether it would be the same with Nicholas, whether having kissed her with such abandon in the carriage he would behave the same way once they were in bed. Her anxiety made her nervous, and her nervousness made her stiffen.

Nicholas immediately noticed the difference. The pliant woman, receptive to his kisses, had disappeared. In her place he held a rigid, unyielding board.

He let her go and stepped away from her. She immediately lowered her eyes to keep him from looking into them. But he wasn't about to let Daisy hide from him. He took her chin in his hand and forced her head up.

"Look at me, Daisy." His fingers tightened. "Look at me."

She lifted her lids, and he saw the fear.

He should have known she would be afraid. She had called him all sorts of names, labeled him a beast. And a beast was certain to be a savage in bed. It made him furious to think she believed he would harm a hair on her head. "What are you afraid of?" he asked in a low, menacing voice.

Daisy swallowed hard. It was more in the nature of a gulp. "It's been a long time."

"Tony's only been dead a year."

"It's been much longer since . . . since he came to my bed," Daisy confessed.

"How long?" Nicholas demanded.

"Six years."

Nicholas's hand circled her throat, where he felt her pulse pounding crazily. "Are you telling me Tony didn't touch you for six of the eight years you were married to him?"

Daisy chose to respond with anger rather than embarrassment. She grasped the wrist of the hand that held her. Her eyes flashed with annoyance that she was being forced to reveal things to her new husband that were not his business. "Once he knew I couldn't give him an heir, he wanted nothing further to do with me."

His thumb brushed her cheek. Gently. Very gently. "He was a fool."

Daisy stared at Nicholas, her heart in her eyes. That wasn't the response she had expected from him. Nor did she expect the bare brush of his finger to send a frisson of sensation streaking to her belly.

"I suppose he had a mistress or two," Nicholas mused. "Although why he would want another woman, when he had you, I can't imagine." His hand smoothed down her throat and over a shoulder bared by her wedding gown.

Daisy flushed with pleasure at what she recognized as a compliment. But she also knew that Nicholas wasn't in possession of all the facts. Now was the time to confess her lack of ability in bed, her undesirability as a bed partner. She might as well. He was going to find out for himself very shortly.

"I couldn't please him," she confessed in a rush. "Tony found me lacking in . . . lacking," she said, unable to be more specific than that.

"Surely not lacking here," Nicholas said as he

brushed a hand across her breast. The tip pebbled before his hand had left her. "Or here," he said, briefly touching her lips with his. "Or here," he said, sliding his hand down to her belly and below.

Daisy trembled. "I don't know exactly . . ."

"He could have taught you what he wanted," Nicholas said, his eyes holding hers, forcing her to meet his gaze and promising her that he would remedy the situation.

"Nicholas. I'm . . . scared." The last word came out as a whisper.

"Of what?" he said. "I won't bite. Too hard," he corrected with a teasing smile.

"That I won't please you."

His hands found her waist and tightened there, his thumbs sliding low to caress her hipbones. "You already please me," he said. "Everything about you pleases me."

"But you can't know—"

"Trust me."

They were strange words for him to utter. Especially when he knew so much more about betrayal. But he gave her no chance to worry further about whether she would please him. He could tell she had worried long enough. He would prove to her that she was exactly what he wanted and needed in a woman.

He set out to seduce her, as she had unconsciously seduced him in the gallery of Severn Manor. He kissed and caressed, seeking the spots that would arouse her ardor, until he knew she was caught up in a sensual maelstrom. He felt too impatient to bother with the thousands of buttons on her dress, but as his hands closed around the material to tear it away, he remembered his fantasy in the carriage.

His hands loosened, and he turned her around so her back was facing him. One at a time, he released the buttons, each time pressing a hot kiss to her flesh. Sometimes his tongue caressed her. Sometimes it was his teeth that grazed her satiny skin. His lips wandered, seeking pleasure and giving it. He had never become so aroused merely kissing a woman, but he forced himself to finish what he had started, down to the very last button, which revealed the two small dimples above her buttocks.

Daisy moaned. "What are you doing to me, Nicholas?"

"Loving you." He slowly shoved the dress down her arms and brushed away her tangled copper curls to press one last kiss to her nape.

An animalistic, guttural sound forced its way out of Daisy's throat.

She wondered how two men could be so very different. Tony had never cherished her as Nicholas just had. He had never kissed her flesh as though it had the taste of ripe strawberries. He had never wanted her so badly he was trembling, as Nicholas was now.

Daisy no longer doubted her ability to please Nicholas. Nor did she doubt her own ability to respond to him. She was willing to bear all the pain she knew would come when he left her in exchange for the passion he offered to share with her. It wasn't love. But it was something equally intimate—the joining of two people in the most primal manner possible.

Nicholas was less patient with Daisy's corset. He

hated the thing, and it bothered him not at all when the ties snapped in surrender to his strength.

Nicholas was unprepared when Daisy stayed his hands on her clothing while she began to undress him. He was staggered when she performed the same ritual on his shirt that he had performed with her dress. His body was quivering by the time she reached his navel.

Daisy relished the chance to taste Nicholas, to feel the crisp hair on his chest. To watch his flat nipples peak as her tongue rasped over them. To watch his belly contract as her teeth slid over his skin. She reveled in the smell of him, the texture and taste of him.

His cousin was a fool, Nicholas thought. He had known from the first moment he saw Daisy that she was a sensual creature. He had wanted her fire, wanted to sink himself into her and be burned up in the conflagration. Her skin was smooth, her hair silky. He couldn't touch enough, couldn't get his fill. He curled his fingers in her hair and pulled her close for a searing kiss.

Then she was touching him, pressing against him. And he burned.

Daisy had never known what it was to want a man this way. Had never known she could be so demanding as a lover. But when she laid both her hands on Nicholas's bare chest she felt a shudder go through him, and she experienced a sense of feminine power such as she had never imagined. She wanted to touch him, to taste him. Her hand slid down, oh, so slowly, to cover the bulge in his trousers.

Nicholas groaned. "What are you doing to me, Daisy?"

She froze. "You don't like it?"

She started to remove her hand, but he caught it and held it against him. His lazy-lidded eyes sought hers. "It feels good. Damn good. Don't stop, Daisy."

She was more hesitant as she continued her exploration across his flanks to his hard buttocks. She soon forgot to be careful. It was fascinating to watch muscle and sinew tense beneath her touch. The rough sounds Nicholas made in his throat caused a corresponding excitement deep within her.

His hands weren't still, either. Daisy felt herself undulate beneath his caresses. It wasn't until she felt his hand on her belly that she realized she was naked.

So was he.

Astonished, she glanced up into his eyes, down at his evident arousal, then back up into his eyes, which by then were alive with laughter.

"Don't tell me you haven't seen anything like it before, because I won't believe you."

"But I haven't!" Daisy blurted. "I mean, it was always dark, and we were under the covers and—" Daisy hid her face against Nicholas's chest to keep from blurting anything more.

"A fool and an idiot," Nicholas muttered.

His arms closed around Daisy, and he held her close. He could feel her nipples harden against his chest. The copper curls between her legs teased his shaft, causing it to throb. He clenched his jaws and forced himself to patience. If he did what he wanted he would terrify her. He had asked for her trust, and he intended to earn it.

His hands roamed her back from her shoulders all the way to the dimples above her buttocks. He wanted to grasp her and pull her close, but he resisted the urge. Barely.

The room filled with shadows as the sun began to set.

"Daisy," he murmured against her ear.

"What, Nicholas?"

"I think it's time to go to bed."

Her fingernails cut into his shoulders. The fear—more of inadequacy now than of him—was back. Kissing was all well and good, but she had been dry when Tony thrust into her body, and it had hurt terribly. She couldn't be sure the same thing wouldn't happen with Nicholas. "I'm afraid," she whispered.

"I know. I'll take care of you," he said. "I promise."

To his surprise, the tension slipped away, and she became pliant in his arms. Her body melted against his, and he felt his pulse begin to race.

He kissed her eyes closed, then kissed each cheek and finally found her mouth with his. It was a questing kiss, seeking permission to enter. She parted her lips and sighed a welcome. His tongue probed, then stroked her mouth, blatantly mimicking the sexual act.

She moaned, and her hips arched against him. Nicholas felt the blood race to his groin but held himself still, letting her thrust against him until he couldn't stand the pleasure any more. He slipped a leg between her thighs and lifted her onto it.

She gasped and leaned farther into him, pressing her breasts against his chest.

Daisy was lost in a euphoria of pleasure. The fear was still there, but buried by layers of want and need and desire. She gave herself up to Nicholas, body and soul, gave him the trust he had asked for, even though she knew he would never give it in return.

She felt a moment of panic when he lifted her and carried her to the bed, but he never gave her a chance to run. One quick thrust and he was inside her.

He paused then.

Daisy kept her eyes closed, afraid Nicholas would see the surprise—and elation—she felt. It hadn't hurt at all. His entry had been slick and smooth. She wanted to shout hosanna. But then she might have to let Nicholas in on her secret.

She should have known he wouldn't let her hide from him.

"Daisy. Open your eyes."

She did, just enough to see him in the twilight. "It isn't at all like I thought it would be." She arched her body experimentally under his, and he bit back a groan. Daisy wiggled her fanny, and Nicholas pressed her flat with his hips.

"If you don't stay still this is going to be over before it's gotten started," he growled.

"No, it's not like I expected at all," she confessed, her fingers walking up his chest to slide confidently into his hair.

Nicholas's grin was slow in coming, but it spread until it reached his eyes. "Oh? What did you expect? Gunfire and Indian drums?"

Daisy smiled, a lazy curl of her lips. "I would have liked that, I think."

He laughed. "No you wouldn't," he assured her. "Too noisy. I wouldn't be able to hear those little purring kitten sounds you make in your throat when I touch you," he said as he began to move slowly in and out of her. "I wouldn't be able to hear you moan," he said as his hands cupped her breasts. "And I wouldn't be able to hear your cry of satisfaction when you reach the pinnacle of desire."

"I would never . . . I don't . . ."

"You do," he assured her. And proved his point by taking her nipple in his mouth to suckle and drawing from her a low, gasping groan.

Daisy had never been so conscious of the sounds that came from her throat. But she couldn't stop them. The gasps. The moans. The groans. And the cry of pleasure he had promised when he arched above her, his body racked with pleasure as he spilled his seed.

Their bodies were slick, their breathing labored as he slid off her. He pulled her into his arms with her buttocks spooned into his groin and slipped a leg over her. Then he fell asleep.

Daisy felt the tears sting her nose and swallowed back the sob of joy that threatened to break free. She had never been so happy. Or so downright miserable. She had finally found a man who made her body sing for him and whom she knew she had pleased, as well. It was wonderful to lie entwined with him, to know they would awaken together in the morning.

That was the good part.

The bad part was, all this was entirely temporary. When Nicholas left England she would have years and years to lie in bed alone and remember this night.

Nicholas's hand tightened possessively around her waist.

Daisy closed her eyes and bit her lip. It was better

not to think about the future. Better simply to enjoy the moment while she could.

She drifted off, expecting to sleep until morning. It was still dark when she heard a match strike, smelled sulfur, and blinked her eyes against the yellow glow of the kerosene lamp beside the bed. Daisy had the fleeting thought that Priss would have loved the ornate lamp. The white globe was circled by at least four inches of red fringe.

"Nicholas? What are you doing up? It's the middle of the night."

Nicholas debated whether to tell her the truth. He had been dreaming, of course. And the dream had woken him, as it always did. Fortunately, Daisy had slept through his restlessness before he awoke. Nicholas felt a tightness in his chest. It was amazing that he should be here as the Duke of Severn, with this lovely, luminous woman lying beside him. It was far more than he deserved, a gift he should treasure.

He reached out and laid a callused hand on Daisy's satiny hip.

Daisy flushed when she realized they were both still naked. And that Nicholas was staring at her with avid eyes. She wasn't sure what part of her most needed covering. When she lifted a hand, he said, "Don't."

"What?"

"Don't hide from me. You're beautiful. Exquisite, really." He laid his hand on her hip and slid it across her hipbone to her belly, then down into the nest of curls between her thighs.

Daisy was mortified. "What are you doing?"

"Making love to you."

"I don't . . . You can't . . ."

"You do . . . I can . . ." he said with a teasing laugh. His fingers slid inside her, first one, then another.

Daisy tensed for the pain, then realized she was embarrassingly wet down there.

"Relax. I promise this won't hurt a bit."

Daisy laughed nervously. "It already does."

He paused and looked at her face. "Really? Does it?"

"It doesn't hurt, exactly. But it feels . . . strange. My body . . ."

"Is responding to mine," Nicholas said in a husky voice.

Daisy felt his thumb move across a particular spot and hissed in a breath of air. Her fingers clenched on the sheets. "That feels good."

"I'm glad," Nicholas said.

"Should I touch you?"

"Do you want to?"

Daisy was torn between wanting to touch and being shy and embarrassed. Nicholas solved the problem when he brought her hand to his chest and slowly slid it down to his abdomen. He stopped there, leaving it to Daisy to decide whether she wanted to do more.

Daisy did.

It was strange, Daisy mused much later, how easy it was to shed her inhibitions with Nicholas. He had no modesty at all and allowed her none. His delight in sex was earthy and natural, and he expected her to enjoy their bedplay every bit as much as he did. Daisy was more than willing to experiment. In fact, she discovered that Nicholas was as vulnerable to being kissed and touched all over as she was. It was a heady experience to reduce him to gasps and groans and cries of pleasure as he had done with her.

It was only when daylight came, when the dawn seeped through the windows, that Daisy realized the folly of what she had done. During the night, Nicholas had demanded everything of her. And she had given him body, heart, and soul.

She had meant to take, not to give.

It was time to step back and reexamine the marriage of convenience she had so blithely entered. It was time to think of self-preservation. Two weeks of this kind of loving and she would never be able to let him go. But he would leave. He had no roots to keep him in England.

Daisy rose from the bed and dressed, careful not to wake Nicholas. This honeymoon was over. He could go to London by himself. She was going home. It wasn't far, and she could probably be there before he roused.

Once she was home, she would be safe from him. He wouldn't be able to force her to do anything she didn't want to do. If he did, she would scream for help. The servants at Severn were her people, and, duke or not, they would come to her rescue.

Daisy took one long last look at the sleeping beast before she closed the door behind her. She knew she had to make her escape quickly. Because when Nicholas awoke, she knew the barbarian would be back.

14

Daisy told John Coachman that a business emergency had made it necessary for His Grace to leave The Wolf and the Lamb during the night and that she was returning to Severn Manor to await his return. She gave no reason for scheduling her departure before it was light enough to see the road, leaving it to the servants to assume it was a simple matter of the Quality being corkbrained and clothheaded.

Daisy gnawed all her fingernails to the quick during the journey home, then was so upset with herself for running away, instead of staying to challenge the duke and demanding new terms for their marriage of convenience, that she burst into tears. She found the handkerchief in her reticule and dabbed at her eyes. It wouldn't do for the servants to see her crying. She was supposed to be a happily married woman. Although it probably didn't matter whether she continued the charade, since Nicholas would arrive very shortly to obliterate it.

He was going to be livid.

Daisy's chin came up a notch at the mere thought of confronting the duke. It had been his idea to take her to bed. She hadn't promised she was going to like it, or that she was going to hop cheerfully between the sheets whenever he ordered it.

She sniffed and wiped her nose with her damp handkerchief. If only it were a real marriage. If only he were in love with her. Then everything would be fine. Because, to tell the truth, she had liked what happened between the sheets just fine. It was the threat of heartbreak that concerned her. Nicholas had the power to destroy her.

Daisy knew it was imperative that the servants believe her story about the duke's business. There was the slim possibility that Nicholas wouldn't come storming in and shatter the illusion she was creating for both their sakes.

"Good afternoon, Thompson," she said as the butler held open the door for her.

"Welcome home, Your Grace."

She saw the questions in Thompson's eyes and blessed the man for not asking them. "Please tell Mrs. Motherwell to send up some water for my bath. Tell Cook I'll have tea in the drawing room in an hour."

Daisy walked up the stairs to her room knowing that word would quickly spread through the house that she had returned from her honeymoon after a single night, and that she had come without the duke.

Jane was scheduled to leave shortly on her trip to London. She was just putting away the last of the laundered and pressed clothing in Daisy's closet, checking as she did for clothing that needed repair, when Daisy walked through her bedroom door.

"Your Grace! Why are you here? Where is His Grace? What happened?"

"Let me close the door first, Jane," Daisy said, as she shut out all the curious ears in the hall. It was a relief to be home, to be in her room, to have made it here at last. She wanted to lie down on the bed and close her eyes and sleep. Three hundred years sounded about right.

"Are you all right?" Jane quickly spied the mark on Daisy's throat, which Daisy had forgotten in her agitation. "That brute! Look what he did to you."

As soon as Jane mentioned it, Daisy's hand flew to her neck. "It's nothing." But she flushed as red as a beet.

"Nothing, is it? That man should be horse-whipped!"

"Then you'd have to whip me, too," Daisy murmured, sinking onto her bed.

"What?"

"I marked him, as well."

"Oh. So that's how it is. Well, if you took to each other so fine, what are you doing back here? Where is His Grace? Did he come with you?"

"I left the duke at The Wolf and the Lamb, the inn where he took me last night," Daisy explained. "He . . . he . . ." She couldn't say Nicholas was going to London, because he might return to Severn. She couldn't say he was returning to Severn, because he might go on to London. "Something came up. The duke asked me to return home and wait for him."

"You had a fight with him." Jane stated it as a fact.

"No," Daisy contradicted.

"He abandoned you on your honeymoon?" Jane was aghast. "I'll murder His Grace myself."

Daisy was moved by her maid's defense of her.

"Don't blame His Grace, Jane. The choice to come home was mine."

Jane didn't presume to sit beside the duchess on the bed. But she had been Her Grace's confidante for too many years not to offer a sympathetic ear. "I wish I understood what all this means."

Daisy lay back on the bed and stared at the ceiling, oblivious to everything around her. Jane began to undress her, as though she were a child.

"There, there now, Your Grace. It will all work out. You'll see. He'll come back home, and everything will be fine."

Daisy wasn't listening. She was back in the soft feather bed at the inn, with the duke's sweat-slick body wrapped around her. She could feel his strong arms and smell the musky scents of their lovemaking on the sheets. She was warm and languorous and felt loved and protected.

Illusion. It was all illusion. He was not what he seemed to be. Their marriage was not what it seemed to be.

Daisy felt the tears well in her eyes and tried to blink them back. One spilled over anyway. She turned her face away so Jane wouldn't see.

Jane had already seen the tears. And cursed the man who caused them. She would let them know downstairs what the duke had done. Then see if his hot shaving water didn't come cold and late, or if his food didn't manage to get burned and if his horse was ready when he wanted it. There was no way to retaliate directly, but His Grace would pay for hurting their darling Daisy.

"Please leave me, Jane," Daisy said. "I want to be alone."

"As you wish, Your Grace." Jane had stripped Daisy to her chemise and pantalets. She had seen where the duke's whiskers had abraded Daisy's fine skin and where his teeth had marked her shoulder. Lord knew what other claims the duke had made on the duchess. He was a savage, all right. No question about it.

Jane unfolded a quilt and laid it over Daisy. "Rest now, Your Grace." As she stepped through the portal to Daisy's bedroom, she looked back and said, "We won't let him hurt you any more."

Daisy slipped into a deep, blessed sleep, unaware of the torrent of gossip and speculation that ran rampant through the house. How she had fallen into bed exhausted, without the bath she had asked for and without taking tea. The entire sequence of events from the moment Her Grace had left the church was dissected and analyzed by one and all. What none of them could figure out was why the duke had sent his duchess home. Why hadn't he taken her on to London with him?

It was Jane who suggested the duchess must have run away from the duke. John Coachman confessed he had only Her Grace's word that His Grace had left in the middle of the night. The duke might very well have been upstairs sleeping at The Wolf and the Lamb when his carriage set out for Severn. In which case, John speculated, he had left His Grace without transport.

John Coachman abruptly rose from the table in the servant's dining hall. "I'd better go back and see if His Grace has need of his coach. It's the least I can do."

"Don't hurry," Jane said. "His Grace deserves to wait, after what he did to Her Grace."

"But you said she marked him, too," Thompson pointed out. "Surely that suggests that whatever passed between them was shared."

Jane frowned. "You didn't see her. He used her . . . cruelly."

"You're exaggeratin'," John Coachman said as he slipped his hat on and headed out the door. "Her Grace looked fine to me."

Jane sniffed. "You're a man. You have no idea of a lady's sensibilities."

John Coachman shook his head. "A mark or two only means they were lost in passion. If you'll join me sometime, I'll show you myself." He winked at Jane.

Jane picked up her teacup and would have thrown it at him except he had already disappeared through the door. "That scoundrel!"

"He's only speaking the truth," Thompson said. When Jane threatened him with the teacup he said, "Hold your horses. I'm only saying maybe it would be better to wait a little while and see what happens when they're together again."

"Then you think he's coming back?" Jane asked.

"Of course. His son is here. He has to come back."

"He could send for the boy. They could sail from London for America."

The two of them sat in silence, contemplating their fate if the duke followed through on his threat to sell Severn while he was in London.

"He'll be back," Jane said in a quiet voice.

"How do you know?"

Jane thought of the marks she had seen on the

duchess. "He won't be able to leave Her Grace without seeing her again."

When Daisy woke, it was morning. She had slept the day and the night away and felt refreshed. She bolted upright, wondering if Nicholas had returned overnight and simply not woken her. She shook her head slightly. No, if he had returned, she wouldn't have been allowed to sleep. He would have woken her and demanded answers.

She pulled the cord to summon Jane and stretched like a cat, groaning as muscles that hadn't been used for seven years protested. She rubbed her jaw where the duke's day-old beard had scratched her face. She winced as she rolled onto her hip. She moved her pantalets and found the imprint of his fingers still on her skin. When he was loving her she had felt no pain, only passion. She wondered if he was feeling equally sore. And hoped he was.

Jane arrived promptly with tea and toast and a boiled egg.

"How did you know I'd be hungry?" Daisy said with a grin.

"As far as any of us could figure out, you haven't had anything to eat since your wedding."

No wonder she felt so empty, Daisy thought. She was half starved. She dug into the food, refusing to speculate on what kind of discussion had rendered up the knowledge that she and Nicholas hadn't even bothered to have supper on the day they were wed, but had retired for the night immediately after they had arrived at the inn. It was humiliating. It was embarrassing. It was all she could do not to close her eyes and relive every single minute of that marvelous, fantastic night.

When Daisy had eaten, Jane helped her to dress. As Nicholas had suspected, she wore a high-necked Worth gown of chocolate velvet and gold satin that hid the mark on her throat. She felt jittery, still not certain that Nicholas wouldn't appear at any moment and demand an explanation.

Both she and Jane started at the quiet knock on her door. Daisy was surprised because she had expected the duke to pound it down. Well, she was as ready as she would ever be.

"See who it is, Jane."

Daisy stood waiting with her hands folded before her. She wouldn't cower. And she wouldn't apologize. She would simply state why she wasn't going to come to his bed again.

The door opened to reveal Colin Calloway. Worry creased his brow, and his eyes looked troubled.

"I'm sorry to bother you, Daisy. Could we talk?"

"Certainly. Let's go down to the drawing room. We can have a cup of tea together."

Daisy preceded Colin down the stairs, wondering exactly how much he suspected, and how much she could tell him about what had transpired between her and his father.

Not much.

Daisy had sent Jane with a message to Mrs. Motherwell for tea and did her best to make Colin comfortable while they waited for the service to come. She wasn't about to start a conversation with him that might be overheard by the servants.

With tea poured and a plateful of sugared biscuits in front of Colin, Daisy said, "What is it you want to know?"

"I know my father planned to take you to London

for a honeymoon. Why are you back here less than forty-eight hours later without him?"

"There was an emergency and—"

Colin dropped his teacup and saucer on the end table with a clatter and rose to his feet. "What kind of emergency? What's wrong?"

"Sit down, Colin," Daisy said. "I'm sorry. I shouldn't have tried lying to you." She waited until he was seated before she continued. "The truth is, your father and I had a disagreement." She grimaced. "Actually, that isn't true either. I . . . I changed my mind and decided I would rather not have a marriage that is . . . quite so convenient. If you know what I mean."

Colin grinned. "Pa's hell on women, all right."

Daisy's head jerked up, and she stared at Colin. "What did you say?"

"Jeshoshaphat! Pa'll kill me if he finds out I said anything like that to you. I'm sorry. Please don't tell him."

In that instant he looked like the boy he was, rather than the man he was becoming. Daisy smiled. "I won't say a word. If you'll explain yourself."

Colin hesitated. "I can't—"

"Please, Colin."

"It's just that, back in Texas where we live there's a place, a brothel I guess you'd call it, where a man can go—"

"I know what a brothel is," Daisy interrupted. She wasn't sure anymore that she wanted to hear Colin's explanation, but curiosity goaded her to say "Go on."

"Anyhow, Pa got kind of a reputation with the women there, for being good in bed, I mean."

"How did you ever find out something like that about your own father?" Daisy asked, appalled and amazed at the same time.

"Oh, well, Trish told me when I went to see her at—" Colin's throat reddened first, then his cheeks, then his ears, until his head looked like a ripe tomato. "Jehoshaphat. I'm sorry, Daisy. I guess ladies aren't supposed to hear about things like that. Pa'll kill me," he repeated.

"Don't worry, Colin. I won't breathe a word of this to your father."

The frown of worry was back on Colin's face. "Did Pa scare you off?" he asked anxiously. "I never heard tell of him hurting a woman. Not once."

Daisy laid a comforting hand on Colin's arm. "He didn't hurt me, Colin." She kept her eyes lowered as she admitted, "The ladies were right about your father. I just couldn't pretend anymore that what we have is a real marriage. It's going to end in the spring. It seemed better not to go through the farce of a honeymoon. Can you understand that?"

From the appraising look on Colin's face, Daisy thought he had things pretty well figured out. And what he didn't know, he suspected.

"Pa really likes it here," he said.

Daisy's eyes widened. "I'm surprised to hear that."

"It's not easy to tell what Pa's thinking. He kind of keeps his thought to himself. But I figure this place must mean a lot to him because he never says a word about it."

"That doesn't make sense."

"Sure it does. Pa never speaks about the things that matter most to him."

"Then how do you know what he's thinking, what he's feeling?" Daisy asked, intrigued.

Colin shrugged. "Mostly you don't. When he's ready, he'll tell you." Colin set his teacup down again. "So where do you suppose Pa went when he woke up and found you gone?"

Daisy shook her head. "I have absolutely no idea."

As the days passed and Nicholas didn't return, Daisy began to worry. She told herself the duke had probably gone on to London to see the sights. She refused to torture herself with images of Nicholas in some other woman's embrace. But she was well aware that Tony had established a mistress in London. There were plenty of actresses and opera singers available to fill the role.

Daisy realized that if she didn't give herself something to do to pass the time, it wouldn't matter when or if the duke returned, because she would already have been carted off to Bedlam. She had in mind two projects, either one of which would have been sufficient to keep her busy. She put the easiest, and the one less likely to irk Nicholas, into action first.

Daisy sought out Lady Celeste and found her in the drawing room, working on new needlepoint cushions for the dining room chairs. Daisy seated herself on a settee across from the older woman and waited to be noticed. She had learned from experience that Lady Celeste didn't like to be interrupted and tended to be sharp and unpleasant when she was.

It took nearly five minutes for Lady Celeste to set down her stitchery and acknowledge Daisy's presence.

"Did you wish to speak to me?" Lady Celeste said.

Daisy reminded herself that Lady Celeste hadn't had an easy life, and that as Nicholas's aunt she was entitled to some say in the arrangements for the reception. "I have a project for which I need your help."

"I've been quite busy with the new chair covers."

"I know that. But this wouldn't take much time. I'd like your assistance planning a party for our neighbors and the Severn tenants to celebrate my wedding to the duke."

Lady Celeste arched a skeptical brow. "Are you sure the duke will be here to attend?"

"He said he would make every effort to be back by then," Daisy lied.

"And if he doesn't return?"

"I'll host the party myself."

Lady Celeste made a small sound in her throat. "I think you're making a mistake. But I'll help you."

Daisy kept her sigh to herself. At least Lady Celeste had decided to get involved with the preparations. "I've already made a list of those I want to invite. I thought we could spend the afternoon writing invitations."

Lady Celeste took a last look at the needlepoint in her lap and heaved a great, aggrieved sigh. "Very well. I shall put my work aside."

Despite her apparent reluctance to help, Lady Celeste worked quickly and efficiently beside Daisy at the dining room table the rest of the afternoon. When they had finished and servants had been sent to deliver the missives, Lady Celeste said, "I've been thinking. You'll want to open the ballroom and hire musicians to play so there can be dancing after supper."

Daisy stared. "There hasn't been a dance in the ballroom since I married Tony."

"Then it's high time there was another, don't you think?"

Daisy chewed on her lower lip. If Nicholas didn't show up and there was dancing, she was going to be left looking very foolish without a partner. On the other hand, the guests she had invited would be delighted by the dance because they would have a chance to see a part of Severn Manor that was rarely used. Stories would fly for weeks after the party about the honor that had been done them. It was exactly the sort of thing she needed to help put Nicholas back in everyone's good graces.

"Thank you, Celeste. That's a wonderful idea," Daisy said. "Now we need to plan decorations and a menu for supper and refreshments during the dance."

Daisy listened while Lady Celeste made suggestions and agreed with everything she said. "I'll be glad to help with the decorations. But do you think you could confer with Mrs. Motherwell and with Cook about the menus yourself?" Daisy asked. "I have some other business I need to take care of."

Lady Celeste looked perturbed for a moment, but Daisy had learned that was her automatic reaction to any request. The older woman pursed her lips and said, "I believe I can make time in my schedule to do that."

Daisy gave Nicholas's aunt an impulsive hug. "Thank you, Celeste."

Lady Celeste frowned. "What are you about, Your Grace? You're going to wrinkle my dress. And yours, too."

Daisy grinned. "If I promise not to hug you again, will you smile?"

Lady Celeste laughed. It was more of a cackle really, and her lips quickly returned to their normal pursed position. "Really, Your Grace. You are incorrigible."

"Oh, Celeste, I feel good again."

Daisy had no explanation for why she felt so carefree. She should have been desolate, considering all the things that could go wrong with her planning. But she just knew the duke would be back. She was counting on it. She had her fingers crossed and decided if necessary she could host the party herself and make excuses for the duke. No one could think any worse of him than they already did.

Daisy was annoyed to discover that she was receiving both sympathetic and pitying glances from the servants. She wanted Nicholas back if for no other reason than to dispel all the rumors that were circulating about his cruelty to her on her wedding night. Unfortunately, the more she protested against them, the more everyone seemed to believe he had ravaged her. She had finally stopped trying to excuse Nicholas and avoided the subject of His Grace whenever it came up.

Meanwhile, she had decided to look on the bright side of things. She was married to the duke. She had nearly nine months to convince him to stay at Severn. And she had the authority, as the duke's wife, to instigate some of the changes that would make Severn more profitable. She intended to do exactly that as her second, more volatile project in the duke's absence.

For this job, she enlisted Colin's help.

"I want to speak to each of the nine tenants about changing his crop from wheat to oats or some other grain that is less competitive with American imports," Daisy explained. "I'd like you to go with me."

"Will they accept me as a surrogate for my father?" Colin asked.

Daisy immediately perceived his problem. "The tenants won't hold your birth against you, if that's what you're asking. It's more likely they'll shun you as a foreigner," she said with a grin. "But since the duke would receive the same treatment, you needn't feel slighted."

Colin grinned. "In that case, I'll be glad to go with you."

Daisy had visited each of the tenants several times over the past year for various reasons. To see how work on the slate roofs was coming, to encourage a tenant to send a child to the new school, to urge a tenant to implement use of the new machinery, or to see a newborn babe. She was friendly without being familiar. She accepted the distance they preserved, and which society demanded, between their world and hers.

Colin ignored the distinction of class and greeted each tenant as friend, shaking hands and charming them with his smile. Daisy watched in awe as he eased his way into each household. She realized that Colin was a far better ambassador than the duke himself ever would have been. Joe Revere would never had relaxed enough to laugh in the duke's presence. Clark Peters would never have invited the duke in for a mug of ale. James Johnson's daughter, Sally, would never have flirted with the duke. Or maybe she would have, Daisy thought, as she watched the girl's shameless antics with Colin.

Daisy and Colin were riding cross country from the Johnsons' cottage to Squire Willingham's more substantial two-story brick house when Colin pulled his mount to a halt.

Daisy quickly brought her horse to a stop beside him. "What's the matter?"

She stared at Colin, whose gaze seemed transfixed on the countryside. She tried to spy whatever it was that had caught his attention, but saw nothing out of the ordinary. "Colin? Why did you stop?"

"I just had an idea."

Colin debated whether he should share it with her. He had suddenly realized what might make living at Severn more appealing to his father. But he wasn't sure whether he wanted to encourage his father to stay in England. It would mean they would spend the rest of their lives separated by an ocean.

The child in Colin was frightened of losing his father. The emerging man knew it was selfish to cling to a parent he no longer needed in the same way. In fact, he looked forward to setting out on his own.

He would miss his father if they were apart, but since coming to England he had seen how his father looked at Severn—and Daisy. He knew that leaving England was going to be much more difficult for his father than he was willing to admit, even to himself.

Colin made a quick decision. He turned to Daisy with a mischievous grin on his face. "You want my father to stay here in England, don't you?"

"Yes," she answered honestly, if cautiously.

"I have an idea how you can get him to do it."

"I'm all ears," Daisy said.

"Cattle."

"What about cattle?"

"My father isn't a farmer, never has been and never will be," Colin said. "But he knows cattle. We've been running a herd of longhorns at our ranch in Texas. This land is perfect for cattle. And horses," he added for good measure. "Some of the land could be used for oats and hay—feed for the stock—and you could sell whatever was left over in the marketplace, since those crops aren't affected by competition from America. What do you think?"

"Would your father allow such a thing?"

"He's not here to tell us no."

"Are you suggesting we buy cattle without his permission and put them on Severn land?"

Colin shook his head. "I'm suggesting *you* buy cattle and put them on Severn land."

Daisy grinned. "That's a positively inspired idea!" Her grin faded. "Except I know absolutely nothing about cattle. I wouldn't know what kind to get, or how many, and my tenants know nothing about how to take care of cattle."

"They don't know how to farm oats or sugar beets, either, but you were going to ask them to learn. Why not have them learn how to herd cattle instead?"

"Who's going to teach them?" Daisy demanded.

"I suppose I can until Pa returns."

"If he returns."

"He'll be back," Colin said.

"How do you know that?"

"I've seen how he looks at you when he thinks nobody's watching."

Daisy turned to stare at Colin. She didn't ask for an explanation of what he meant. She had seen for herself how Nicholas looked at her. With desire. And with hunger. Daisy didn't trust those emotions. They had nothing to do with caring, only with sex.

But Colin's idea appealed to her. She was for anything that could entice Nicholas to stay in England. Because if he stayed, the future was filled with possibilities.

"How would you like to go shopping with me, Colin?"

"What are we going to buy?"

"Cattle."

15

The duke was back.

Word spread quickly among the servants, and Daisy heard it from the gardener as she was strolling in the rose garden behind the house. Her heart began to thump a little faster, and she had to force herself to keep walking along the gravel path, rather than look for someplace to hide.

There was nothing she could do to escape him. If she were truthful, she didn't want to. She felt anxious about how he would react to the changes she had made in his plans for Severn, but that too had already been done and couldn't be undone before he discovered it.

He had been gone for two weeks. The wedding celebration was scheduled for this evening. The house was decorated with bowls of roses from the gardens of Severn, and a wide variety of savory dishes were being prepared. Daisy had come into the garden to seek some peace and quiet before the hectic evening to come.

She wondered whether Nicholas would seek her out, or whether he would wait for her to return to the house. She bent to sniff a brilliant red rose on a bush she had planted when she married Tony. It had bloomed each year, bearing fruit, as she had not.

"I was told I'd find you here."

Daisy jerked upright. She would recognize that voice anywhere. "Good morning, Your Grace."

She had always known he was a dangerous man. His gray eyes were colder than she had ever seen them. His face was gaunt, as though he hadn't eaten or slept. He moved with the grace of a predator, and his muscles seemed tense, ready to spring into action. It gave her no comfort to know she was his likely quarry.

"I wasn't sure you were coming back," she said.

"I almost didn't."

"Where did you go?" she asked, because it seemed safer to keep him talking than to face him in silence.

"London."

She wanted to ask whether he had found a mistress there, whether he had seen the sights, whether he had sold Severn. All that came out was "Oh."

"I thought of you while I was gone."

She was startled into looking up at him. "I don't see how you could have missed me. There's a lot to do in London."

"Why did you run?"

Daisy turned aside from the wrath she could hear in his voice, from the threat she could feel in his body. Trembling, she reached for a rose and stabbed herself with a thorn. She gasped and brought her finger to her mouth, to suck away the pearl of blood.

Before she could do so, the duke grasped her wrist. He was hurting her, but she refused to tell him so. She met his gaze and stood her ground. Slowly, never taking his eyes off her, he raised her hand to his mouth and sipped at her finger until the blood was gone.

Daisy felt the reverberation of his touch all the way up her arm and back down the length of her body. It was as if he were sucking her soul out along with her blood. She forced herself to breathe as naturally as possible and cursed the corset that made it impossible to do even that.

She wanted to jerk away, but knew he would not let her go. "What are you going to do now, Your Grace?" she taunted. "I can guarantee that every servant at Severn is watching you at this moment."

He raised a sardonic brow. "Is that supposed to keep you safe?"

"If you want to keep their goodwill, you'll let me go."

"What if I don't give a damn about their goodwill?"

Daisy's heart skipped a beat and fought its way up to her throat seeking escape. She swallowed it back down again. "I suggest you rethink the matter, Your Grace," Daisy said in the calmest voice she could muster.

He took a step closer, and it was all Daisy could do to hold her ground. His hand threaded through the one he held and angled it behind her back. Then he used the slightest bit of pressure to pull her close so that she could feel the heat of him and the quiver that ran through him as their bodies touched.

His other hand tunneled into her hair, forcing out pins that dropped onto the gravel walk.

"May I remind you the servants are watching?"

"Let them watch."

His mouth covered hers possessively, demanding

a response. He spread his legs and forced her between them until she could feel the hard length of him, the proof that he wanted her.

She hadn't planned on fighting back. But he had frightened her, and like any trapped animal, she was desperate. She bit his tongue until she tasted blood.

He jerked her head back at a painful angle. His gaze was feral, his jaw clenched. "So, my kitten has sharp teeth." He slowly licked his blood from the corner of her mouth.

"Nicholas. Don't," she pleaded. "Don't do this."

She saw something in his eyes, a moment of doubt. Then it was gone, replaced by cynicism and revulsion. "You're no different from any other woman," he said in a guttural voice. "Selfish. Greedy. And dishonest."

"Unfair! Untrue! And when did I ever lie to you?"

"We had a bargain, ma'am. I would marry you. And you would sleep in my bed. Or had you forgotten that?"

"I—"

He didn't give her a chance to make excuses—not that she had any—but continued inexorably with his accusations.

"Where were you on our honeymoon, my dear? With your husband? No. You came running home to Severn. Well, enjoy it while you may," he hissed. "In nine months it will all belong to someone else!"

Daisy cried out in pain, because he had wounded her where she was most vulnerable. "You can't sell!"

His mouth cut off her cry of protest, and his hand came up to force her jaws to open for his tongue. "Don't bite me again," he warned. "Or you'll regret it."

She believed him. And opened her mouth for him.

Daisy could have—and would have—resisted force. But he didn't ravage, he coaxed. He didn't plunder, he cajoled. He groaned deep in his throat as his tongue searched her mouth, seeking the sweetness there. She felt her blood begin to sing, felt the heat pool in her belly. She was furious with him, and he hated her. Yet she could feel his hunger, and it fed her own.

Daisy's free hand slipped up to the duke's nape and held his mouth against her own. Her body arched into his until her breasts flattened against his chest. She felt his heart pounding against her own, felt him gasping for air as his mouth slid from her lips to her throat. She moaned when he increased the suction of his mouth against her skin and she realized if he didn't stop soon she would have a mark there. Again.

Daisy was beyond caring. Beyond thinking.

"Pa. Welcome back, Pa."

Daisy heard the voice and wished it would go away. It returned, louder, more irksome.

"You've got quite an audience, Pa. Maybe you'd like to finish this in the house."

Suddenly she was standing alone. Her eyes wouldn't focus, and it took her a second to realize where she was. And what she had been doing.

"I'll . . . uh . . . wait for you in the library, Pa," Colin said. Then they were alone again.

But not quite alone. A surreptitious glance revealed the truth of Colin's words. The gardener was hoeing not ten rows away. John Coachman had found a reason to walk one of the horses nearby. Mrs. Motherwell was hanging some sheets on the line. And Jane was peering at her from an upstairs window.

Daisy was mortified. She had made a complete spectacle of herself. Thanks to the duke.

"I hope you're satisfied," she hissed at him.

"Not yet," he said in a raw voice. "But I will be tonight."

"If you dare lay a hand on me—"

He grasped her wrist, which was where they had started when he arrived. "You're my wife. A fact I understand we'll be confirming to the neighborhood tonight with a party. I suggest you come here and welcome me home the way a good wife should. Or else."

"The Duke of Severn doesn't subject his wife to public displays of affection," Daisy retorted.

"I'm not going to kiss you, you're going to kiss me," Nicholas replied in a silky voice.

"Or else?"

"Exactly."

"Let go of me first."

Nicholas released her wrist. She resisted the urge to rub it with her other hand to ease the pain. "Stand still," she said. "And bend down so I can reach you."

He leaned down, and Daisy gave him a quick kiss on the cheek.

"I've been gone for two weeks," he said. "Is that the best you can do?"

He shouldn't have taunted her, Daisy thought. She never could resist a dare.

"Welcome home, Nicholas," she purred as her mouth closed with his. Her hands tunneled up into his hair, and she pressed her body against his, rubbing her hips back and forth across the crass evidence of his arousal. She would show him! Her tongue slid along the edge of his mouth without ever going inside. Until he groaned. Then she stroked his mouth with her tongue, probing the roof and the sides and dueling with his tongue until his arms tightened around her, cutting her air off completely.

"Nicholas," she gasped. "Enough. I can't breathe." In another moment she was going to expire.

Daisy felt herself being swept up in Nicholas's arms. She tried to tell him to put her down, but her corset was too tight, and she just didn't have the breath to do it.

"What's wrong with Her Grace?" the gardener asked, stepping in front of Nicholas on the gravel path, hoe in hand.

Nicholas saw the challenge in the man's eyes. Hell, Daisy had tried to warn him. But he wasn't about to answer to anyone for his behavior toward his wife. "She fainted. From excitement," Nicholas growled. "Now get out of my way so I can get her up to bed."

Whether in response to the duke's explanation or the threat of murder in his eyes, the gardener moved out of his way.

A glare kept Mrs. Motherwell at bay. Nicholas used his bared teeth on Thompson and Higgenbotham. But Jane refused to be cowed.

"She'll be more comfortable in her own room, Your Grace," Jane said.

"I want her in mine," Nicholas said.

"Very well, Your Grace. I'll bring some hartshorn and a bowl of cool water to bathe her face."

Nicholas realized that even if he got Daisy to his room, he wasn't going to be allowed any privacy with her there. Perhaps it would be better to wait until after the party tonight to have it out with her. "All right," he conceded. "I'll take Her Grace to her own room."

Jane didn't thank him, merely gave him a look from the side of her eye that warned him to be careful with his precious cargo. Nicholas nearly smiled. He had to respect a woman who didn't allow a man to intimidate her. Which was probably why he had put up with Daisy this long.

He lay Daisy on her bed and leaned down with his arms braced on either side of her head to whisper in her ear. "I know you're awake, so listen to me and listen good. Tonight, after the party, I'll expect you to come to my room. If you don't come, I'll come after you."

He didn't expect an answer, but watching her face blanch was answer enough. He wasn't going to hurt her, but she didn't know that. She deserved a few anxious moments after what she had put him through. He was never going to forget waking up the morning after their lovemaking to find his wife gone.

"Take good care of her," he said to Jane. "She's going to have a very busy night."

Nicholas turned and left the room without another word. He was aware of the eyes that stared at him with various levels of hostility and curiosity. He didn't care. Let one of them say one word, and he would be out on his ear. He'd had a difficult two weeks, and he hadn't the patience to handle any more aggravation. He had endured enough of that in London.

Where he had gotten an offer to purchase Severn Manor.

On his last day in London, Phipps had sent him an urgent message requesting an interview. Nicholas was totally flummoxed when Phipps sat down across from him in the library at the house on Grosvenor Square and said, "I've been approached by a gentleman who wishes to purchase Severn Manor at a price I believe to be somewhat in excess of its actual worth."

Nicholas's brows had shot up. "Why would someone make an offer like that? What does he intend to do with the land that he thinks it's worth so much?"

"Ah." Phipps's estimation of the duke went up a notch. His Grace had immediately seen the fly in the ointment. "I believe, Your Grace, that he intends to divide the land into parcels."

"For what purpose?"

"As you know, Your Grace, because it is in Surrey, Severn Manor enjoys an enviable proximity to London. The gentleman in question intends to sell the land in parcels to provide modest country estates for members of the merchant class who are rich enough to afford such a home, but can't find land close enough to London to make it practical to get back and forth on Sundays and holidays."

"Good God," Nicholas said. "I never imagined Severn broken up like that."

"I thought it my duty to bring the offer to your attention, Your Grace. Financially, it is a sterling opportunity. You need to decide whether you want to take this offer or wait for something from a buyer

who intends to keep the entire estate intact. I should
point out, Your Grace, that there are no guarantees,
whoever buys the land. No one will have the emotional attachment to it that a Windermere would
have."

Nicholas didn't bother telling Phipps he wasn't a
Windermere. He felt possessive enough of Severn to
be one.

"The gentleman doesn't need a decision now,"
Phipps said. "Unless you reject his proposal entirely."

"I do."

"What?" Phipps was surprised by the duke's
quick, harsh response.

"I reject the offer. I'll take my chances on finding
a buyer who'll keep Severn in one piece. Tell the
gentleman my answer is no, Phipps."

"Very well, Your Grace."

All the way from London, Nicholas hadn't stopped
thinking of what he had done. There was no reason
for him to refuse a perfectly good offer for Severn.
Why should he care what happened to the people
there? He was heading back to Texas.

Yet, when Phipps had spoken, when it had been
borne in on him that Severn Manor would be no
more, he had felt such a wrenching in his guts that
he was nauseous. Nothing should mean that much
to him. Severn did.

Nicholas was torn apart, because now he was going to suffer no matter what decision he made. If he
stayed at Severn, his son would be lost to him. If he
went back to Texas, he took a chance that Daisy
would insist on staying in England. And if he con-

vinced Daisy to come to America with him, it would mean giving up Severn.

Nicholas didn't like his choices. But at least he had bought some time. Until spring. Or until he got another offer.

At the foot of the stairs Nicholas remembered that Colin was waiting for him in the library. He headed that way and nodded to Higgenbotham, who opened the door for him. He let out a sigh of relief as he heard the heavy door close with the familiar *thunk* behind him.

"Alone at last," he said, draping himself in the chair behind the Sheraton desk.

"I'm here, Pa," Colin said, turning from his stand at the window.

"You don't count, Colin. You don't want to rip out my throat for manhandling Daisy."

"I wouldn't say that, Pa. I've gotten to like her a lot in the two weeks you've been gone. I'd have to object along with everyone else if you did anything to hurt her."

Nicholas groaned and covered his eyes with his hands. "Believe me, son. That woman doesn't need any help. She does a damned good job of taking care of herself."

"Where were you, Pa? Why didn't you come back sooner?"

Nicholas dragged himself upright in the chair so he could reach the brandy decanter and glasses on a tea cart nearby. He poured himself a drink and swallowed it before answering. The brandy was warm going down, but it was a poor substitute for the two fingers of rye whiskey he needed.

"I went to London," Nicholas said. "I didn't come

back because I was looking for someone. It took me two weeks to find out that he wasn't there."

"Who were you looking for, Pa?" Colin took the few steps that brought him to the mantel and toyed with the miniature portrait of a pretty woman that rested there. It took him a moment to recognize the woman as Daisy. A younger, smiling Daisy. His father's voice drew his attention from the painting.

"During the trip here, I told you the story of how I was banished from England when I was a boy."

"Sure, Pa."

Nicholas forked a hand through his hair in agitation. "I thought, so long as I was here in England, I'd try to find out who my real father is."

"Jehoshaphat, Pa! Why didn't you tell me sooner? Was that who you were looking for in London?"

"There's a man called Estleman, who seems to have spent some time here at Severn Manor about the time . . . And it seems he looks a good deal like me. Or I look like him. Anyway, there's a chance he could be my father." Nicholas sighed. "I heard he lived in London, so I went looking for him there."

"If he lives there, why didn't you find him, Pa?"

Nicholas grimaced. "He lives there, all right. He just happens to be away at the moment. In India."

"India? I don't remember exactly where that is, Pa."

"A long way from England."

"When's he coming back?"

"In the spring."

Colin crossed and dropped onto the settee. "Jehoshaphat! No wonder you were mad as a hornet when you got home. You must have been thinking you'd finally be getting an answer and then got nothing. You shouldn't have taken it out on Daisy, though.''

Nicholas was struck by Colin's words. Was that what he had done? Taken out his frustration with finding Estleman gone to India on Daisy? No. She had deserved everything he had said to her. She had reneged on their bargain.

When he had woken to find her gone from The Wolf and the Lamb, he had thought she might merely have been too shy to face him, and had gone down to breakfast in their private parlor. It wasn't until he dressed and headed downstairs that he realized she had flown the coop, like a chicken that suspects why it's been invited for Sunday dinner. When he found, to his amazement and chagrin, that she had commandeered his carriage, he suspected she had gone home.

His first instinct had been to go after her. But it was humiliating to have to chase after your wife. He wasn't about to face all the servants at Severn with egg on his face. He didn't like lies, and he wasn't sure what the truth was. He had been angry enough that he figured it wouldn't hurt either of them to have some time and distance between them.

But why the hell had she left him in the first place? He hadn't managed to scare the answer out of her this morning, but he intended to find out what had made her flee. Had he been too rough with her? He didn't think so. He would have said she was as satisfied as he had been with their lovemaking. Not that he could recall much except sensations.

He had never lost control with a woman as he had with Daisy. Nicholas frowned thoughtfully. Maybe he had hurt her. But he hadn't meant to. And he

intended to prove to her that he could be gentle.
Tonight.

It never occurred to him not to hold her to their
bargain. He needed her like a desert needed water.
He'd had a taste of her now, and he was a man
starving for more. He hadn't been able to get her out
of his mind in London.

Not that there hadn't been temptations.

He had called on the solicitor, Phipps, and had
him track down Estleman. That had left him with
little to keep him occupied. So he took in the sights
he would have shown to Daisy, wondering how she
would have liked the Thames, with its tide like an
ocean, the Tower of London, the famous tombs at
Westminster Abbey, and the Elgin Marbles at the
British Museum.

Nicholas missed her too much. He caught himself
wanting to turn to her and explain something, or
share some wonder that he found fascinating. He
lost his appetite. He couldn't sleep soundly at night.
He was glad Daisy wasn't with him when he awoke
one night in a sweat, his heart pounding.

The nightmare had come back.

He managed to stay in London only because he
knew he was very close to the end of his sojourn.
That he might very well have an answer to the questions that had remained unanswered for so many
years. And he had realized it was probably a good
thing Daisy wasn't with him. Because he had no
idea how he was going to react when he came face
to face with Estleman at last.

Phipps had very nearly ended up being flattened
when he announced that Estleman was in India until sometime in the spring.

"Pa, there are a few things I think maybe I should mention to you."

"What did you say?"

"Don't get upset until you hear me out."

Nicholas leaned forward across the desk. "Why am I going to be upset?"

"It was my idea."

Nicholas's eyes narrowed. "What was your idea? Spit it out, Colin."

"While you were gone, Daisy went to visit the tenants, to talk about the change in crops, you know. Only, when we were riding over the land, it struck me again how much it's like the hill country in Texas. Except for the stone fences, of course. And really, it's more grass here than brush."

"Get on with it, Colin."

"Anyhow, I had this idea and Daisy liked it, so we did it."

"Did what?"

Colin took a deep breath and said, "Bought some cattle. Herefords, actually. Prettiest white-faced cows you ever saw, Pa."

Nicholas sat back and crossed his legs, a pose that should have given Colin warning that his father wasn't hearing this news for the first time. "Didn't that seem a rather radical step to you? These people are farmers, Colin."

"Not anymore," he replied with a grin. "At least, some of them aren't. Daisy and I figured five of the nine tenants ought to run cattle on their land. The rest can grow oats and hay to feed the stock. What do you think, Pa?"

Nicholas pursed his lips. "It's not a bad idea, Colin. I don't know why I didn't think of it myself."

Colin jumped to his feet. "Then you don't mind, Pa? Daisy thought you'd be upset."

"She did, did she?" Nicholas said, hiding his grin behind his hand. "And she went ahead and did it anyway?"

Colin gulped. "You aren't going to get mad at her, are you, Pa?"

"Don't you worry about Daisy, son. I'll take care of her."

"That's what I'm afraid of," Colin muttered.

"What was that you said?"

"Nothing, Pa."

Nicholas figured it was time to change the subject before he gave away the game. "It looks like everything's set up for the party."

"Yeah. Everyone's coming, Pa. All the neighbors from miles around, and the tenants, too. It's going to be quite a shindig. I promised to help with the decorating in the ballroom, Pa. I've got to go."

"The ballroom?"

"We're having dancing with musicians and everything. I'll get to try out some of the waltz steps Simp taught me. And Daisy helped me practice some English country dances."

Colin knew he wasn't going to be able to avoid Lady Roanna at the reception as he had at the wedding. So he had made up his mind to dance with her, if she would, and enjoy her company. She couldn't hurt him anymore. He had his heart safe behind high walls now.

"It's good to have you back, Pa," Colin said as he headed from the room.

Nicholas didn't say it, but it felt good to be back.

Especially when it had seemed for a moment in London like everything might be ripped away before he was ready to let it go. When he rode up the drive to the manor this morning, it had felt as if he were coming home. It had all looked so familiar. He could almost hear the whoops of laughter from Tony and Stephen. Almost hear his father shouting encouragement as they played cricket. The crack of the ball was real. And shattering glass, as he broke the leaded glass window in his mother's bedroom.

She had come downstairs with the ball, her face aglow with pride. "What a hit, Nicholas," she said. And she had hugged him. His father had hugged her and whispered in her ear, and she had blushed and smiled and hurried back into the house.

Tragically, that wasn't the only happy memory he had at Severn Manor. Sometimes they bombarded him. He would walk into a room and see his family and his cousins' family there. He would ride across a stream and remember lying there on his back, with his father beside him, fishing. It had been a glorious childhood. For eight years. Until some man, someone, had spoiled it all.

Among those on a list Daisy had given him of guests she had invited to the reception were several "suspects" he had compiled with Charles and refined with Phipps in London. He would be terribly remiss not to investigate as many leads as he could at the party. Especially since the elusive Estleman could not be questioned for months. It would be a travesty if he ignored everyone else and then discovered Estleman knew nothing.

Nicholas opened the desk drawer and pulled out

the short list of men who might be able to shed light
on his situation.

Lord Prestyne
Squire Templeton
The Reverend Mr. Golightly
Mr. Dabney
Viscount Linden

He would make the acquaintance of each one of
them this evening. According to Charles, none of the
men bore much resemblance to Nicholas, but that
didn't necessarily rule any of them out as his father.
Except perhaps Mr. Golightly, who was old enough
to be Nicholas's grandfather. But the reverend had
been here long enough to be in a position to know
everything that had happened in the parish for the
past twenty-seven years. Maybe tonight he would
learn something about his past he didn't already
know.

Anything was possible.

Certainly tonight he would get some answers from
Daisy about her flight from the inn. She wouldn't
dare to defy him. If she did, he would keep his promise and come after her. He could already feel her
flesh, smell the scent she wore, imagine himself inside her.

Nicholas laughed, a harsh, self-deprecating
sound. What a fool he was. He wanted her so badly
he was trembling at the thought of bedding her. He
should leave Daisy alone. She was trouble.

He laughed again. When had he ever turned his
back on trouble? He had risked his life a dozen times
for the reward to be had at the end of the trail. The

reward of having Daisy in his bed, in his life, was definitely worth the risk of a little trouble.

Of course, there was always the possibility she would give him more than a little trouble.

Nicholas grinned. He was looking forward to it.

16

Nicholas admired Daisy as she descended the stairs. She was breathtakingly beautiful in an emerald gown that made her dark-lashed green eyes look huge and luminous. She had pulled her hair off her face, leaving only a few enticing tendrils that begged to be touched. Her lips were pink and swollen as though she had been well kissed, but he knew that wasn't possible. He hadn't seen her since early that morning. More likely she had been biting them in agitation. The love bruise he had given her on their wedding night was gone, and the dress exposed her bare shoulders and more bosom than he would have liked. She belonged to him. He didn't care to share even that much of her with other men.

Nicholas didn't know where the possessive streak he felt toward Daisy came from. He certainly hadn't felt that way toward any other woman, not even Colin's mother. Of course, considering her profession, that would have been ridiculous.

"Good evening, Your Grace," Daisy said.

Nicholas noticed her hand trembled slightly as she laid it in the callused palm he extended to her.

"For tonight, do you think you could call me Nicholas? After all, we are husband and wife."

"If ever so briefly," she shot back. Her green eyes flashed, and her swollen mouth flattened in a mulish cast.

Nicholas smiled inside, but the expression never reached his mouth or eyes. This was the Daisy he was most familiar with, the prickly one that gave as good as she got. "Then let's make the most of the time we have, shall we?" Nicholas whispered.

He felt her shiver and saw her glance warily at him from the corner of her eye. There was nowhere she could run tonight. And she knew it.

She reached up and touched a small cut on his jaw, then quickly withdrew her hand. "What happened to your face?"

"Believe it or not, Porter cut me shaving," Nicholas said. "He swore it's the first time his hand has ever slipped."

"Oh, dear," Daisy said.

"It's nothing. An accident."

"Oh, dear. I'm afraid it's only the tip of the iceberg."

"What?"

"You'll see," Daisy said enigmatically. Apparently the servants' revenge for the duke's behavior toward her had already begun.

"Come, wife. Let's go meet our guests."

Daisy wanted desperately to pull free of Nicholas, to run back upstairs and lock herself in her room. But that would accomplish nothing. She didn't think a locked door would do much to hold him back if he wanted in. The best she could do was to put on a brave front and refuse to give him the satisfaction of knowing she was frightened.

Only a few of the neighbors had been invited for supper. Everyone else was scheduled to arrive for the dance afterward. Nicholas and Daisy greeted each couple in the drawing room as they arrived. Charles and Priss were among the first to appear, along with the earl's daughter, Lady Roanna.

Daisy noticed that Roanna had eyes only for Colin, who was standing by the fireplace. As soon as the young woman had greeted Daisy, she headed toward him. Daisy didn't have time to see how Colin greeted her because Priss claimed her attention.

"How are you, Daisy?" Priss asked. "I must say marriage agrees with you," she added after a searching look at Daisy's face.

"What makes you say that?"

"You have a certain glow, of excitement, I suppose."

It was terror, actually. Daisy didn't have time to correct Priss because the next guests were waiting to be greeted. "Hello, Mr. Golightly, Mrs. Golightly. It's good to see you."

Mrs. Golightly dipped a quick curtsy, beaming at Daisy the whole time. "I'm so happy for your Grace. It's wonderful, isn't it? Imagine His Grace returning to Severn after all these years. And the two of you falling in love and getting married—it's like a fairy tale ending."

Daisy stared at Mrs. Golightly, stunned. Where on earth had Mrs. Golightly gotten the impression that she and Nicholas were in love? Again, she wasn't given time for a reply. The next couple to arrive were the first that Nicholas wasn't already acquainted with, and Daisy needed to make introductions.

"Your Grace, may I present Lord and Lady Prestyne?"

Nicholas ignored Lady Prestyne and gave Lord Prestyne a searching look that he could see made the man uncomfortable. Nevertheless, he couldn't help himself. He kept thinking that if he looked hard enough, he would see the answers he sought in some stranger's eyes.

Lord Prestyne was nearly as tall as Nicholas, but he had graying hair, which gave no clue to the color, and not much of that. His eyes were also gray, like Nicholas's, but small and spaced close together. His nose was slightly bulbous, and his lips were thick and fleshy. If this was his father, Nicholas resembled him not at all.

Prestyne also had several affectations that made Nicholas cringe. The older man carried a lace handkerchief, which he waved when he spoke, and there must have been three rings bearing precious stones on each hand, besides a gold watch in his vest pocket that held several fobs. He wore a black formal evening coat, but his waistcoat was a brilliant puce.

"Lord Prestyne owns the land adjacent to Severn on the west," Daisy explained, "but spends most of the year in London."

"It's a pleasure to meet Your Grace," Prestyne said. "Perhaps we can hunt together sometime?"

"Perhaps," Nicholas hedged. That might be a way to get Prestyne alone so he could ask more questions. Assuming he didn't get the answers he wanted tonight. Then his attention was distracted by Daisy's introduction of another guest.

"This is Squire Templeton and Mrs. Templeton," Daisy said. "The squire owns the cottage south of Severn and raises sheep for wool and mutton."

Nicholas hadn't been the subject of much fawning obsequiousness since his arrival at Severn. Squire Templeton made up for that lack. His bow was low enough to show the bald spot on top of his head. His smile spread from ear to ear. And he was garrulous. The man didn't stop talking from the instant Daisy made the introductions. Nicholas was just about to cut him off with an oath when the man's conversation turned in a direction that caught his attention.

". . . so I was saying to the Mrs.—that's Mrs. Templeton, Your Grace—what a good thing it was they found you in America and brought you back home where you belong. I never believed for one instant the rumors that spread about your dear departed mother. If you could have seen Lord Philip in the first days and weeks after Lady Philip left, you'd have sworn he knew what a mistake he'd made.

"Not that he ever forgave her. Stubborn. That's what he was. And her, too. Anyone could have seen it coming. Loved each other too much, if you ask me. Jealousy. Bad thing, that. Ruined them both in the end, didn't it?

"But at least you're here now, and the wrong can be righted." He turned to Daisy as though suddenly realizing that it was only because she had been widowed that Nicholas had been sought out in America. "Begging your pardon, Your Grace," he said to Daisy. "Not to diminish your tragedy. Not at all. But

with you married to His Grace everything turned
out just fine, didn't it?"

According to Charles, it was Mrs. Templeton who
was the parish gossip. If so, Nicholas saw the man
and his wife were well matched. If there hadn't been
someone standing behind Squire Templeton, it was
entirely possible, Nicholas thought, the man might
have kept right on talking for the rest of the evening.
Nicholas intended to get the squire alone later, to
see how much of what he had said was speculation
and how much was based on fact. But it had felt
good to hear someone describe his parents as happily married. Especially since that was the way he
remembered them.

"Viscount Linden and Lady Linden," Daisy said.
"Lord and Lady Linden own the estate to the north,
Linden's Folly."

Nicholas's eyes narrowed as he and the viscount
exchanged nods that sufficed for bows. He wondered how Linden had made Charles's list. The viscount was a mere five to ten years older than Nicholas and still quite a handsome and virile man. He
had wavy black hair that had silvered at the temples.
His eyes were a frosty gray and inscrutable. His lips
were thin, though his mouth was wide. There was a
tension in the man that made Nicholas believe Lord
Linden would be a formidable adversary in a fight.
Here was the first Englishman he had met that he
thought could have held his own in Texas.

"I believe we have something in common, Your
Grace," the viscount said. "We've both recently returned to England from a considerable stay in America."

Nicholas recognized from his flattened accent that

the viscount didn't sound as English as most Englishmen. "Whereabouts in America?"

"Wyoming Territory, Your Grace."

"I'm from Texas myself," Nicholas said, extending his hand. "And please call me Nick."

"I'm Miles," the tall man said with a smile as he shook the duke's hand.

"How long did you live in America?" Nicholas asked.

"Twenty years."

Nicholas raised a speculative brow. He sensed a story in Miles Linden's extended visit to the colonies. "I'd like to talk more with you later."

"I'll look forward to it. This is my wife, Lady Linden."

"Please call me Verity, Your Grace."

Nicholas found himself smiling back at the woman standing before him. "I will if you'll call me Nick." He felt Daisy stiffen beside him and wondered what she didn't like about the woman. Verity Linden had unusual features that made her striking rather than beautiful. She was nearly as tall as the viscount and carried herself with a great deal of dignity and grace. She had an abundance of blond hair bound up in a net and a fine figure that was stunningly shown off in a black velvet gown.

A second look revealed the character lines around Verity's mouth and eyes that suggested she must be very close to the viscount's age. Nicholas knew most English marriages were made between younger women and older, more established men. Which made him wonder whether they had married when they were both young, many years ago, or whether they had met at some later date.

There wasn't time to assuage his curiosity, because the next dinner guest had arrived. Daisy had invited Mr. Dabney to even the numbers, since Lady Celeste was dining with them. Nicholas gave Dabney a cursory glance and dismissed him. He was short and thin, with reddish curls all over his head, which Nicholas recognized finally, incredibly, as a wig. Dabney spoke with a thick Irish brogue that made what he said nearly unintelligible.

"Sorrrry to hear about yourrr mother," the little man said, rolling his r's. "I liked her verrry much."

"You knew her?" Nicholas said, suddenly willing to decipher the brogue.

"I was her music teacher, once upon a time."

"I didn't know she studied music."

"Yourrr mother had the voice of a songbird," the little man said. "Did she neverrr sing for you?"

Nicholas stood transfixed as he remembered a soft, sweet lullaby his mother used to sing to him at bedtime before they had been banished from Severn. Only once could he recall her singing in America, on his tenth birthday.

It had been the very worst year, the poorest year. She had nothing to give him, and they were cold and alone and she had held him close to her as they squatted down against the back wall of someone's house. She had wrapped her shawl around him and crooned the lullaby from his youth.

He had closed his eyes and imagined himself back at Severn, with his mother and his father and his cousins. He had fallen asleep and dreamed, and it had been almost as good as the real thing.

But he could remember waking up the next morning with frost on his eyelashes. Cold and hungry and alone. He remembered vividly what he had said to his mother, his breath creating bursts of fog as he spoke.

"This is all your fault! You brought us here. Why can't we go home? I wish you hadn't sung that stupid song. You keep pretending everything's going to be all right. But it's not!"

The people in the house had heard him shouting and came out to warn them away. He had run, leaving his mother to face the angry woman with the broom. He couldn't remember where he had run, or how long he had been gone. When he returned to search for his mother, he discovered she had gotten a job in one of the houses in town. They had been warm for the first time in weeks, and he had filled his belly for the first time since he could remember. Later he realized it was a house full of women who sold themselves.

She had never sung again.

All of that flashed through his brain in the moments it took Daisy to ask Mr. Dabney about his newest pupil, one of the neighbor's children. Nicholas wasn't even aware that Daisy had slipped her arm through his and that they were leading the guests in to supper. He glanced down and saw her staring up at him, a worried look in her eyes.

"Are you all right?" she asked in a quiet voice.

He swallowed over the thickness in his throat, feeling guilty—much too late to do any good—at how cruel and selfish a child he had been. "I am now. Thanks."

He seated Daisy at one end of the formal dining table and took his place at the other end. He could barely see her for the epergne full of roses in the center of the table and the silver candelabra that provided light at either end. He was pleased and surprised to discover that Lady Linden was seated to his right. At least he would be able to satisfy some of his curiosity about that lovely lady and her husband.

Nicholas tasted one spoonful of his lobster bisque and frowned. "How's your soup, Verity?"

"Delicious."

Nicholas looked back at his bowl. Lukewarm. And very salty. He gestured for Higgenbotham. "You can take the soup. I don't care for it."

"Very well, Your Grace."

Since he wasn't eating, Nicholas turned to Verity and asked, "How did you and the viscount meet?"

"We met in London at my coming-out ball."

"So the two of you went to America together?"

Lady Linden paused. "No. Miles went alone."

She had tawny eyes, angled at the corners like a cat, that were focused somewhere in the distance. Nicholas had the feeling she wasn't even there anymore, but had retreated to some other place. A spoon clattered against a dish, and she returned.

She smiled and said, "Miles and I were only married a year ago."

"I want to ask what happened in the intervening years between your comeout and your marriage, but I have a feeling that's a long story."

Verity Linden laughed. It was a husky, feminine sound that Nicholas knew would bring most men to their knees. He told himself he was unaffected because she was a married woman. The truth was, there had been no other woman for him except Daisy Windermere since the moment he laid eyes on her. Damn her for a witch!

Nicholas greeted with relish the quail stuffed with wild rice that constituted the next course. He was hungry. He tasted a piece of sliced breast tentatively, then savored the juicy tenderness when it turned out to be delicious.

Thus, he wasn't at all careful with his first bite of the wild rice stuffing. He nearly choked when the pepper—lots and lots of pepper—hit his tongue.

His eyes teared, and his mouth burned. He grabbed for his water glass only to discover he didn't have one! Everyone else did, but not him.

He reached for Verity's water glass and swallowed every drop.

"Are you all right, Your Grace?" she asked.

"Thirsty," he replied with a raspy voice.

Nicholas gestured to Higgenbotham. "Lady Linden and I each need another glass of water. Also, will you tell Cook the quail is marvelous, though the stuffing could use something to spice it up." That ought to set the fox among the chickens, Nicholas thought.

Higgenbotham's brows rose. "Very well, Your Grace."

Nicholas wasn't sure what was going on, but it seemed safer to pretend ignorance than to have to confront his servants and punish them for their mischief.

He began to have some inkling of Daisy's remark about icebergs.

Nicholas wasn't aware he was staring at Daisy until Verity said, "She's very beautiful. And very much in love with you."

Startled, he looked back to Verity. "You must be mistaken."

The viscountess shook her head. "I don't think so. She watches you. When you're not looking."

"She does?" Nicholas turned quickly and caught Daisy staring at him. She quickly lowered her gaze and turned to say something to Charles.

Nicholas frowned. "It's more likely she's checking to make sure I don't do something to Charles.

Nicholas frowned. "It's more likely she's checking to make sure I don't do something to embarrass her or myself. The duchess doesn't have a very high opinion of me," he confessed with a rueful smile.

"Perhaps she isn't used to your American customs."

"No *perhaps* about it," Nicholas said. "She thinks I'm a barbarian."

"Are you?" Verity asked bluntly.

Nicholas laughed. It wasn't a question that required an answer. "You remind me very much of Daisy—the duchess, I mean. Frank. Outspoken. Ruthlessly honest. I like you, Verity."

His smile faded as he surveyed the roast beef, peas, and carrots that had replaced the quail before him. His stomach made a growling sound. Nicholas felt a little like growling himself.

He tried a few peas and carrots, figuring they could be more easily swallowed—or spit out—if they turned out to be sabotaged like the rest of his dinner. Happily, they went down without a problem.

It was the meat then, Nicholas concluded. Something was wrong with the meat.

Nicholas pursed his lips in chagrin. It *looked* delicious. And he was starving. But he was afraid to guess what had been done to it.

He almost decided not to try it.

When he did, he gave Cook points for cleverness. The beef was perfect. A lesser man might have left it untouched rather than test dangerous waters for the third time.

Nicholas's glance slid to the foot of the table again, where he found Daisy glowering at him. What had he done now?

Daisy had been watching Nicholas flirt with Verity Linden with mixed emotions. On the one hand, she was glad he was able to converse comfortably with the company she had chosen for dinner. On the other hand, she found herself jealous of the attention he was bestowing on the other woman.

It was her own fault. She had arranged the seating. But she hadn't been thinking of how beautiful Verity Linden was, only of the fact Verity had spent time recently in America. She had thought Verity and Nicholas might find something in common to talk about. Unfortunately, she had been a little more successful than she had intended.

Well, two could play the same game. She turned to Miles and batted her eyelashes.

"Got something in your eye, Daisy?" Miles asked.

"I'm flirting, Miles," Daisy said in disgust. "You're supposed to swoon at my feet."

"Do you mind if I finish supper first? I'm damnably hungry."

Daisy's wrinkled her nose in disgust. "I'm trying to make Nicholas jealous. The least you could do is cooperate."

Miles's glance slid down the table to Nicholas and back to Daisy. "No thank you. I need all my teeth right where they are."

"Nicholas wouldn't—"

"I beg to differ, my dear. You forget, I've lived the past twenty years in America. Cowboys don't take kindly to thieves. Of any kind. And they're plumb serious about their women."

"He's flirting with Verity."

Miles stiffened and searched out his wife at the other end of the table. His eyes narrowed as he saw her head fall back in abandon as she laughed at something Nicholas said. "I trust Verity," he said through tight jaws.

"But do you trust Nicholas?" Daisy taunted.

Miles switched his gaze from Verity to Daisy. "What kind of trouble are you fomenting, Daisy? And why?"

Daisy fought the flush that threatened and lost. "Please forgive me, Miles. I don't know why I'm acting like an idiot."

"You love him," Miles stated flatly.

"I most certainly do not!"

"Head over heels," Miles said as he picked up his fork and resumed eating. "And you're not sure he loves you. That's why you're worried about Verity."

"I'm not worried about Verity. I don't even like the duke, let alone love him. Why, that's the most ridiculous thing I ever heard!"

Miles gave Daisy a perceptive look over the rim of his wine glass. "Oh? Then why were you trying to make him jealous by flirting with me?"

"Hoist by my own petard," Daisy conceded. "It's awful, Miles. What am I going to do?"

"There isn't much you can do. Love isn't something we can control, much as we would like to. I ought to know."

Daisy heard the bitterness in his voice and wondered what had put it there. "Sometime you must tell me about your travels in America."

"Sometime I will," Miles said. "But not tonight. I tell you what I will do, Daisy. I promise to dance the first waltz with you and to hold you close enough to make His Grace of Severn break out in a sweat."

Daisy brightened. "Would you really do that for me, Miles?"

"It'll be my pleasure," he said with a roguish grin. "Now that I'm happily married, I want the rest of the world to be in the same state."

Daisy ignored Nicholas for the rest of the meal, but she felt his eyes on her from time to time. She wore a small, feline smile as she imagined the havoc she planned to wreak with Nicholas's peace of mind when she danced with Miles.

After several toasts to the newlywed couple's happiness had been made, the ladies retired to allow the men an opportunity for brandy and a smoke. Daisy never knew what was said, but Nicholas's jaw was clenched tight when he rejoined the ladies in the drawing room. She shot a quick glance at Miles and saw him looking smug. He had the audacity to wink at her in plain view of the duke.

Oh, Miles, she thought, *what have you done now?*

"I wasn't aware you had so many admirers," Nicholas hissed in her ear.

"I don't know what you mean," Daisy bluffed.

"I'm speaking about Miles."

"Miles is a married man."

"Who finds you very attractive. I want to know whether the feeling is mutual."

"What do you expect me to say? You'd know I was

lying if I said he wasn't handsome. Jealous, Nicholas?"

Daisy hadn't known she was dealing with a leashed tiger. Until he tore free.

Nicholas grasped her arm and yanked her along behind him out of the drawing room and along the hall, looking for an empty room.

"Where are you going? What are you doing? Nicholas, we have guests!"

"They're not going anywhere," he said. "And we have things to discuss." He dragged her into a small sewing parlor and shut the door behind them. "Now, ma'am, you'll tell me exactly what your relationship is to Miles Linden."

Nicholas hadn't realized until this moment in how many ways his mother's supposed betrayal of his father had affected him. He finally knew why he had never let himself love a woman. Because loving meant taking the risk that you might not be loved in return. If anyone had asked, he would have denied emphatically that he loved Daisy Windermere. But he realized now, when he thought her feelings were fixed on another man, that he wanted her to love him.

He felt the clutching fear—and fury—Lord Philip must have felt at the thought that Lady Philip had given herself to another man. Nicholas had killed in the past because it was a job, without letting himself feel the heat of anger or the lust for blood. What he felt now wasn't rational, and it wasn't calm. He could easily have strangled Miles Linden with his bare hands.

"Stay away from Miles, Daisy."

Daisy's chin was up, her hands curled into fists.

She was aghast at the monster she had created—all
by her idiotic self—but determined to brazen it out.
"You're acting crazy, Nicholas. I want to return to
our guests." She tried walking past him, and he
grabbed her arm and swung her around.

"We're not finished here."

"Oh, yes we are!"

"No, Daisy. We're a long way from finished."

He captured Daisy's face in his hands and lowered
his mouth toward hers. "You're mine, Daisy. Only
mine. Always mine."

It was a kiss of claiming that was all the more
effective because his mouth was soft on hers, coaxing an equally hungry response she was helpless to
refuse.

Daisy tore herself free and rasped, "There is no
always for us, Nicholas. Only now."

Desperation. It surged between them, clawed at
them, so they couldn't get enough of each other,
couldn't taste and touch enough to satisfy the needs
of a lifetime in the brief time they had allowed themselves.

Until spring. Just until spring.

Nicholas was stunned by Daisy's passion, overwhelmed by the demands of her mouth and hands.
He hadn't counted on the need that rose in her to
match his own and which threatened to overwhelm
them both.

"Daisy, Daisy," he said as he pressed kisses across
her face. "I need you now. Come upstairs with me
and—"

The quiet knock on the door cut him off. "Ignore
it," he said.

Daisy pressed her palms against his chest, but

they slid up and around his neck. She laid her forehead against his linen shirt and moaned. "We have to go. We have guests."

She lifted her head and stared into eyes that were hot and hungry and impatient. "What are we doing, Nicholas? We're only going to end up hurting each other. I should have told you sooner why I left The Wolf and the Lamb. It was because I didn't think I could spend two weeks making love with you and not lose my heart.

"I'm not strong enough to resist you," she said in a quiet voice. "If you want me, I'll come to you. But I won't fall in love with you, Nicholas. I have to protect myself somehow."

"So you'll give me your body, but that's all," Nicholas said in a harsh voice.

Daisy nodded.

"I'll take it."

Daisy bit her lower lip. "Just my body, Nicholas. Not my heart. Never my heart."

The knock came again. Louder. Insistent.

He let her go, and she stepped back from him.

"I think we should return to the party now." Daisy looked down at herself to make sure she showed no signs of her recent tryst with the duke. "Do I look all right?"

Nicholas brushed a stray curl back from her face. "You look ravishing." And very well kissed. Miles couldn't fail to see that Nicholas had staked his claim on her.

Nicholas opened the door and found Priss standing there.

"Are you two all right? People are beginning to

talk. I thought you might want to return to the party."

"We're coming," Daisy said. She linked her arm with Priss's. "How did you enjoy your supper?" she asked.

Nicholas watched the two women stroll down the hall toward the drawing room. He tried not to think about the agreement he had just made with Daisy, but her words echoed in his mind.

Only my body. Not my heart. Never my heart.

That was fine with him. He didn't want her damned heart. He would be plenty happy with her body in bed. So long as she was his, and only his, for as long as he stayed in England. After he was gone, he didn't care what she did.

Nicholas scowled. It wasn't the best bargain he had ever made. But it was the safest course for both of them. No love. No commitment. It was the way he had always dealt with women. Daisy was no different from all the others. At least, that was what he wanted to believe.

The problem was, he didn't believe it. Not for a second. Only sometimes it was easier to settle for a lie than to probe for the truth. Nicholas found it too difficult to admit to the feelings roiling inside him. He was a man used to being in control, and there was nothing controlled about his relationship with the duchess.

For the first time since his mother had died and left him alone, he was afraid. He wasn't even sure what he was afraid of, except losing Daisy. And that was ridiculous, because how could you be afraid of losing something you had never possessed?

Nicholas shook off the feelings of foreboding that

hung over him like a thundercloud. He had never gone looking for trouble, and he wasn't about to start now.

He shut the door to the sewing room behind him and headed back toward the ballroom, which had filled with people in the short time he had been absent. To his surprise, the orchestra was already playing. He stood at the edge of the ballroom and searched for Daisy. He spied her finally in the middle of the floor. She was dancing a waltz with Miles Linden, and there wasn't more than an inch of space between them.

Nicholas saw red. He ignored the gasps and grunts of surprise as he pushed his way across the dance floor toward his wife.

17

Miles saw Nicholas coming and whispered in Daisy's ear, "You wanted a jealous husband. You've got one."

Daisy had changed her mind about antagonizing Nicholas, but had been so discomfited by the incident in the sewing room that when Miles asked her to dance she had agreed. "Oh, Miles. What am I going to do now?"

"I'm going to turn you over to your husband and let the two of you work it out," Miles said. "Nicholas, I see you want to cut in." Miles released Daisy and backed up a step.

Nicholas had to choose between going after Miles and taking Daisy in his arms. The choice was simple. "Daisy?" He held his arms open, and she reluctantly stepped into them.

His right arm slid around her waist to draw her breathlessly close, and his left hand captured hers as he led her into the waltz. Neither said a word as the music swelled behind them and carried them around the floor.

Daisy could feel Nicholas down the entire length

of her. Her heart batted against her rib cage. "You're holding me too close," she protested.

"Not close enough," he retorted, tightening the arm around her waist.

"I can't breathe."

"Stop wearing those damned corsets."

"Nicholas, please."

He loosened his hold but said, "Don't do that again, Daisy."

She didn't ask what he meant. She knew now that Nicholas wasn't a man to tolerate the sort of games a woman might play with another man. If he thought his claim to her was being challenged, he wouldn't respond with a civilized duel at dawn. Murder would be done.

"I need to speak with some people this evening," Nicholas said. "Can I trust you not to get into trouble?"

"Are you ordering me not to flirt?" Daisy asked, her eyes narrowed dangerously.

"Flirt all you like," Nicholas said. "Just remember that I'll kill any man who lays a hand on you."

"You must joking!" Daisy protested. "What if someone asks me to dance?"

The waltz ended, and his fingers tightened on her waist before he released her. "There are some things a man doesn't joke about." He left her and walked away toward Lord Prestyne.

Daisy wanted to defy Nicholas, but after looking around the ballroom she realized that the only men who would be able to stand up to him in a fight were Charles and Miles. She wasn't about to provoke Nicholas into confronting either one of them, since she didn't want blood shed on her account.

Priss approached her later in the evening and asked, "Why aren't you dancing, Daisy?"

"Nicholas forbade it!" she snapped before she could stop herself.

"Good Lord, Daisy. Why would he do a thing like that?"

"Because he's a barbaric, uncultivated savage. That's why."

"Your opinion of your husband certainly bodes well for a long and happy marriage," Priss teased.

"Oh, Priss. I think I've made a terrible mistake. Everything's gone wrong. The servants dislike Nicholas now more than they did before I married him. The tenants are afraid of him. And I have no idea what he's going to say when he realizes I've bought cattle instead of seeds for new crops with what money we had left."

Priss's jaw dropped. "You did what?"

"Colin suggested it," Daisy said. "And it seemed like a good idea at the time."

"You acted without waiting to speak with Nicholas first?"

"He wasn't here," Daisy said.

"Oh, Daisy. You are in trouble."

"Thanks for the words of comfort, Priss."

"I'm afraid you'll need more than comfort when His Grace finds out what you've done."

"Maybe he won't mind," Daisy said, chewing on her lower lip.

"You don't believe that any more than I do."

"You're right. He'll mind. What am I going to do, Priss?"

"Run for your life?"

"He'd only come after me."

"You're probably right."

"What are you two hens cackling about here in the corner?" Charles asked.

Priss arched a brow. "Hens?"

Daisy matched it. "Cackling?"

Charles held up both hands and laughed. "I take it back. What were you two ladies discussing?"

"Oh, Charles, you'll never believe what Daisy's done."

"Try me. You might be surprised."

"She bought cattle to put on Severn land without consulting Nicholas first."

The earl stroked his chin. "Cattle. I wonder why nobody thought of that before."

"So you think it's a good idea?" Daisy asked eagerly.

"I do. The question is whether Nicholas will agree."

"Whether I will agree to what?" Nicholas asked, joining them.

"That it makes sense to put cattle on Severn land," the earl said.

Daisy held her breath.

"I'd certainly be willing to investigate the idea," Nicholas said.

"It's a little late for that," Daisy said.

"Oh?"

"I've already bought the cattle, and I've put them on Severn land," she said defiantly.

"I know."

"What?"

"Colin told me all about it this afternoon."

"And you let me stand here and worry whether

you were going to lop off my head when you found out?'' Daisy said in an ominous voice.

"Daisy, Daisy, this is no time to argue," Nicholas said with a mocking grin. "We have company. Come on. I'm in the mood to dance."

"I wouldn't dance with you—"

Daisy found herself swept onto the dance floor where the third waltz of the evening—she had noticed Nicholas talking to Lord Prestyne during the second—was playing.

For a few minutes Daisy kept her lips pressed tight, too furious to speak. Then she realized she had won the war without ever having to go to battle. "Do you really think cattle are a good idea?"

"If they're managed properly. At least I know something about cattle. I can give the tenants some direction."

"I've asked a few of the tenants to plant hay and oats to feed the stock," she said enthusiastically. "Severn should be quite profitable in the near future."

"That's what I'm counting on," Nicholas said.

It dawned on Daisy that the more successful the introduction of cattle on Severn land, the sooner Nicholas would be able to put the property on the market. Which meant she had work to do, and fast. There had to be a way to make Nicholas fall in love with Severn all over again. She hadn't found it yet, but by God, she would!

Nicholas didn't like the gleam in Daisy's eye. She was planning something, he could tell. He wondered what she was up to now. So far everything she had done for Severn had turned out surprisingly well.

But he didn't want her getting into the habit of making decisions without talking to him first.

"I should mention to you, I suppose, that Phipps contacted me the day you made the request for funds to buy the cattle," Nicholas said.

Daisy's eyes widened. "He what?"

"You didn't think he was going to release funds without my permission, did you?"

"But he always—"

"I am Severn, ma'am," Nicholas said. "Any decisions that get made from now on go through me. Is that understood?"

Daisy remained silent.

"Daisy, I want an answer."

"Yes, it's understood," she hissed.

Nicholas didn't push for more cooperation from her. His mind had already skipped ahead to the end of the evening, when she would come to his bed. That was all the submission he wanted or needed from Daisy Windermere.

"What did you and Lord Prestyne discuss?" Daisy asked.

"I asked him what he knew about my mother and father."

"Was he able to shed any light on the situation?"

"He mentioned the name of a man he thought might know something."

"Who was that?"

"No one you know," Nicholas said. She wouldn't have known Estleman, he thought. The man had stopped coming to Severn after Lady Philip left for America, Lord Prestyne had said.

Nicholas danced Daisy to the edge of the room. "I

need to speak with Miles. I'll see you later." And left her again.

Daisy fumed. This was supposed to be her wedding celebration, and instead of paying attention to the bride, the groom was off visiting with the guests. Meanwhile, he had made it plain that if she so much as glanced at another man, he would flatten him. Daisy was ready to hit something herself. Preferably Nicholas. In a place where it would hurt.

Nicholas found Miles on the terrace with Verity. "I'm sorry to interrupt you, but I'd like to speak with Miles privately."

"Nick, your timing is terrible," Miles said after his wife was gone. "A party is no time to talk business."

"This isn't business, exactly. I wondered what you might know about my mother and father."

"Oh." Miles turned and stared out over the garden. The smell of roses was overpoweringly sweet. "I remember your mother smelled of roses the day I met her."

"When was that?"

"On the ship that took you to America."

"You were on it?" Nicholas exclaimed.

"I was."

"How old were you then?"

"Seventeen."

"Why didn't I meet you?"

"You were seasick at the beginning of the voyage, if you'll recall. Later I stayed in my cabin during the day and only came on deck at night."

"You spoke with my mother?"

"Often."

"Did she tell you anything about . . . Were my father's accusations true?"

"All I know is that she was a very unhappy woman. She obviously loved your father. And she worried about what was going to happen to the two of you. I think she expected your father to come to his senses and come after her. To be honest, she still seemed to be in shock over the whole incident."

"That doesn't seem the picture of a guilty party," Nicholas said thoughtfully.

"I didn't think so," Miles concurred.

"Unfortunately, her tragic behavior isn't proof of anything," Nicholas said. "She could simply have been upset over getting caught."

Miles shrugged. "I can't help you any more than I have."

"Do you know a man named Estleman? Have you heard of him?"

"No."

"My mother didn't mention him?" Nicholas insisted.

Miles shook his head. "I'm sorry. Believe me, I know how frustrating it can be to wonder about something and never know the truth."

Nicholas recognized the look in Miles's silvery eyes. He had seen it often in his own mirror. "I'd like to get together again sometime. I'd be interested to hear how you like Wyoming."

"You'll have to catch me before the spring," Miles said. "Verity and I are heading home then."

"I thought your home was here."

"I have a ranch in Wyoming that's home for us now. We only came here for a visit. I hadn't been back to England in quite some time. It's interesting how much things change."

"And how much they stay the same."

Miles smiled. "I know exactly what you mean. Do you miss your ranch in America?"

"I didn't leave many friends behind in Texas. Just one really," Nicholas confessed. "I'm amazed to admit it, but I believe I have more memories of Severn than of my ranch in Texas. I was always on the trail. I didn't spend much time at home. My friend, Simp, was there with my son, and I came and went on business."

"What does Daisy think about living in America?"

"I don't know."

When Miles arched a questioning brow, Nicholas flushed. "Daisy and I . . . Daisy's staying in England."

"I see. You need her to keep an eye on things here for a while. I can understand that."

Nicholas didn't correct Miles's inaccurate perception of the facts. He didn't need to explain his life to anyone. But Miles wasn't content to let sleeping dogs lie.

"How soon is she going to be joining you?"

"She isn't," Nicholas said flatly. "Now, if you'll excuse me, there are some people I need to meet."

Nicholas fled, ran like a yellow cur being chased by a broom. He didn't want to answer any more questions about his relationship to Daisy. Because the more times he mentioned to someone he was leaving her in England, the less happy he was about the situation.

Not that he loved her, or anything like that. But he wanted her. She was his wife. He wasn't likely to have another. And if that was so, he would rather have her in his bed than have to find a woman for the night in the sort of house where he had grown up.

He headed back to the party, determined to meet each and every one of his tenants. It was high time he let them know who was going to be in charge of things from now on.

As he stepped into the ballroom Thompson was just passing by him with a tray of half-filled champagne glasses. The tray slipped and champagne spilled across his new formal coat and brocade vest.

"I'm so terribly sorry, Your Grace," Thompson said. "That was terribly clumsy of me."

Nicholas swiped at the fizzy wetness with his hands and perused the butler through narrowed eyes. "I see. There seem to have been quite a few accidents this evening. I don't suppose you know what's at the root of all this clumsiness, Thompson?"

The butler never batted an eye. "I'm sure I can't imagine, Your Grace."

"May I suggest, Thompson, that you pass the word that I've gotten the message?"

"What message was that, Your Grace?" Thompson said.

"It isn't necessary for you—any of you—to retaliate on behalf of the duchess for the way I treated her this morning. Her Grace is perfectly capable of managing the situation by herself. Do we understand each other, Thompson?"

"I believe so, Your Grace. If Your Grace would like to retire to your room, I shall see that Porter attends you there."

The duke's lip curled sardonically. "Thank you,

Thompson. Would you tell Porter I've cried peace before you send him up?"

Thompson's eyes twinkled. "I shall, Your Grace."

Colin's eyes hadn't left Lady Roanna since she entered the drawing room. She was wearing a pink and white striped gown that made her look as soft and pliable as a piece of saltwater taffy. He was surprised when she approached him directly upon entering.

Her eyes met his as she said, "I wanted to apologize for the way I behaved the last time we met."

He didn't want her apology. He didn't want to be anywhere near her. Because when he was, his heart rate slammed out of control and muscle and sinew clenched in all the wrong places. "No apology is necessary."

She laid a hand on his sleeve to keep him from moving away. Her hands were small and dainty. But absolutely capable of keeping him rooted to the spot.

He forced his voice to be harsh. "Was there something else you wanted?"

Her hand trembled on his arm, and her eyes filled to the brim with tears she quickly blinked back. Colin felt like a scoundrel, but he was fighting hard not to succumb to her again.

"Won't you forgive me?"

"You're forgiven," he said in a raw voice. "Now get the hell away from me and leave me alone."

He watched her recoil as though he had slapped her. Her hand fell to her side, and a single tear slipped from the corner of her eye. He kept his face as impassive as granite. He wasn't going to let her tears sway him. She didn't really care about him.

This was all another game. And this time, he didn't intend to lose.

Colin was surprised when Lady Roanna stood her ground. He had expected her to turn and run for cover after the tongue-lashing he had given her. His eyes caught on her lower lip, which she was worrying with her teeth.

"I suppose I deserved that," she said at last. "What I did was rude and . . . thoughtless. I didn't realize until you left that I was also dishonest."

Colin wished she would look up at him again so he could see what she was thinking, what she was feeling. He didn't want to ask, but she had piqued his curiosity. "Dishonest? How?"

She raised her eyes, and he saw himself as a man going down for the third time, drowning in her tears. "I . . . I was afraid to admit to you . . . or myself . . . that I was attracted to a . . ." She swallowed. "To you," she finished.

His heart was thumping so loudly he was surprised she didn't remark on it. She was attracted to him. But she didn't want to be, not to someone like him. "You should call me what I am," he managed to say. "A bastard. That isn't going to change, so I don't see what purpose your apology is supposed to serve."

"It doesn't matter to me."

"Doesn't it?"

He saw the blush that revealed the lie. His voice was soft when he said, "You wish it didn't matter." He paused and added, "So do I."

Her eyes shot to his, and he saw the yearning there, the desire. And knew he would have to be crazy to do anything about it. "No, Roanna. It wouldn't work."

"But—"

Her hand clasped his sleeve again. He glanced over and saw the frown on her father's face. "Let go, Lady Roanna." He had used her title to put some distance between them. It didn't work. When she continued holding on to him, he said in a gentler voice, "Your father is watching us. Let go."

She did, but as her fingertips slid away he fought the shudder of need that tore through him.

She clasped her hands in front of her, which he figured was a pretty good idea, since otherwise he would have been tempted to reach for her.

"Can we be friends, Colin?" she asked, keeping her eyes focused on her hands.

"Friends?" He frowned. "I don't think I've ever had a lady friend before. I don't know. What kind of friendship did you have in mind?"

He watched her brow furrow. She started to speak once, stopped, then pursed her lips in frustration.

"Just friends," she said. "You know. Talk to each other."

"About what?"

"Anything. Everything."

"You have to trust someone to tell them things about yourself." Colin shook his head. "I don't trust you, Roanna," he said bluntly.

"Then let me do all the trusting. At least at first."

"I don't know." Colin knew there was a catch somewhere in what she was suggesting. He just didn't see it right now. He knew he wouldn't be able to avoid her completely for the rest of the time he was at Severn, and the friendship she was offering

seemed safer than any other relationship he could
have with her. To be honest, he liked looking at her,
and he liked the way she made him feel when she
looked at him.

"All right, Roanna. Friends."

She looked up at him with such a surge of joy in
her eyes that it was all he could do not to sweep her
into his arms.

"I promise you won't be sorry, Colin. I'd better go
meet some of the other guests now."

From the look Colin saw on her father's face, he
supposed she was right. "I'll see you later."

She gave him a mischievous smile. "You certainly
will. We're seated together at supper."

He watched, stunned as she turned and flounced
—he couldn't think of a better word—off toward
Lady Linden.

Roanna was ecstatic with the success of her interview with Colin. She had hoped he would forgive
her and agree to come see her again. But she had
underestimated how badly she had hurt him. It was,
she knew, a tremendous concession for him to agree
to try to be friends. Unfortunately, she was as much
in the dark as he was about how a man and woman
who were attracted to each other physically became
friends.

She had grown up as the pampered and protected
daughter of an earl, never allowed to romp and
roam with the neighborhood children. Her only re-
lationships recently had been with the young dan-
dies who had besieged her during her comeout the
past season. She knew how to tease and dissemble.
She knew nothing about honestly sharing her feel-

ings. But if that was what Colin wanted, she was willing to try.

It was fortunate she had been able to persuade Daisy to seat them together at supper. As she laid her hand on Colin's arm, and he led her in to the table, she felt the vibrations that shot between them. She knew it must be happening to both of them. It simply couldn't be one-sided. She debated the wisdom of trying to flirt with him and decided against it. If she was to have a chance at all of earning back his respect, she would have to do it on his terms. As his friend.

Once they were seated and the soup was served, she searched her mind for a topic, any topic, she might discuss with him.

"Are you—"

"Have you—"

They both spoke at the same time, then fell silent, each waiting for the other to speak.

"You go ahead," Roanna said, relieved that she wouldn't have to come up with something intelligent to discuss.

"I was going to ask if you've been riding recently."

"I go every day," Roanna said.

Silence fell.

Roanna wondered whether he wanted to invite her to go riding with him, or whether he wanted her to invite him to join her.

"Would you—"

"We could—"

Roanna laughed. "This is ridiculous. I don't know why I should feel so awkward speaking with you. If you asked Priss I'm sure she'd tell you I can talk all day without taking a breath. Now I'm babbling, so you see she's not far off the mark. Anyway, I wondered whether we might not ride together sometime. What do you think?"

"I was just going to invite you to join me tomorrow. Along with Daisy and the duke of course. We're going to be visiting one of the tenants."

Roanna smiled and Colin felt his stomach do a flip-flop.

"I would love to join you. What time should I be there?"

"Is nine o'clock too early?"

Roanna would have to be up before the crack of dawn to dress and make the ride to Severn, but she said, "Nine o'clock would be fine."

Colin had been wondering what they would find to talk about, but once Roanna got started, it seemed there were a dozen subjects that arose. She had something to say about every one of them. Not that she hogged the conversation. She asked him questions to draw him out, and he was pleased to note that she listened to him and asked even more questions. It surprised him to realize how intelligent she was and how much she had read.

He was grateful for the respite from Roanna's company when the ladies left the men and retired to the drawing room. He paid little attention to the conversation of the men sitting around the table with him; he was too caught up in his own thoughts.

If he were honest, he was forced to admit that Roanna might know more about the world at large than he did, and her interests were more widespread than his. He had always known who he was and what he wanted to do. Life had been simple

because his goals had been simple. He had spent
hours on the range learning everything there was to
know about horses and cattle. He had spent an equal
number of hours learning the business end of the
ranch.

His father had been gone so much he hadn't been
around to do a lot of the bookwork. It should have
fallen on Simp. But Simp hated working with numbers, so Colin had taken over. From a very early age
Colin had assumed responsibilities that would have
staggered some men. He hadn't minded. In fact, he
had found a deep sense of satisfaction from knowing
he was handling a man's job.

But there was no role for him to play here in England except son of the scion. There was a bailiff to
manage the land and a solicitor to manage the business. He wasn't needed here. And the knowledge he
had garnered over the years wasn't valuable here,
the way it was in Texas.

To Colin's dismay, his friendly conversation with
Roanna had only proven how ill-suited he was to
court someone like her. She had been right to reject
him. He had nothing to offer her in England. And he
wasn't sure what she could offer him in Texas—
aside from beauty and stubbornness and an ability
to laugh at herself. Good qualities in a woman, he
conceded. But were they enough for a western wife?

When the men rejoined the ladies and moved to
the ballroom, he still hadn't made up his mind
whether he was going to ask her to dance. The decision was made for him when Daisy said, "Colin, I
hope you'll see that Lady Roanna enjoys a dance or
two."

Since Roanna was standing right there, it would

have been churlish of him not to ask her. "Lady Roanna?"

"I would love to dance," she said.

The problem with being friends with a woman, Colin quickly realized, was that you had to find a way to control the more than friendly feelings you might have for her. In his case, he was deluged with needs and wants and desires concerning Lady Roanna Warenne that had absolutely nothing to do with friendship.

"You're very graceful on your feet," Roanna said, hoping to encourage Colin to relax. Instead, his grasp tightened around her waist, and she was uncomfortably aware of the stern look on her father's face as a consequence.

"Uh . . . Colin . . . I think I need a breath of fresh air. Could we please stop?"

Colin danced her toward the terrace doors and, since they were open, out onto the terrace itself.

Roanna realized that she wasn't nearly so uncomfortable in Colin's embrace without her father's censorious gaze to make her feel self-conscious. She felt Colin's reluctance as he released her, but since she was the one who had pleaded for air, she could hardly demand he continue the dance.

She walked over to the stone balustrade that looked over the rose garden. She took a deep breath and let it out. "The roses smell so lovely."

Before she realized what he intended, Colin had leapt over the stone wall and landed in an aisle between two rows of rosebushes.

"What are you doing down there?" Roanna asked with a laugh.

He plucked a rose—yelping when a thorn caught him—and handed it up to her. "This is for you."

She accepted the rose and said, "Come back up here, and let me see your hand."

Roanna couldn't help being impressed with his strength and grace as he placed his palms on the wall and heaved himself up and over it again. "Your hand," she said, extending hers to receive it.

He had already stuck his thumb in his mouth to suck on it before he relinquished it to her. She cupped his hand in both of hers and lifted it toward her mouth. She put her lips against his thumb, where it was already damp from his mouth.

"Roanna." His voice was raw. She was tasting him, as he wanted to taste her.

Roanna sucked lightly on the spot where the thorn had torn his skin. Then she lifted her eyes to meet Colin's.

His eyes were stormy, his mouth thinned, his body taut.

"To hell with it," he said.

His mouth found hers, and he tasted her as he had been dying to do since he had left her in the earl's stable. To his surprise she met his desire and matched it with her own. Her hands slipped up around his neck and teased into his hair, causing a shiver to run down his spine.

The sound of a man clearing his throat had them leaping guiltily apart. They kept their backs to the ballroom and stared out over the garden.

"Lovely night tonight, isn't it? Lady Roanna, your mother was looking for you. I believe she's ready to leave."

Colin breathed a sigh of relief. It was his father,

not hers. He turned to Roanna, wondering what he would see in her eyes in the golden streams of light from the ballroom.

He saw the same frustration he felt. At business left unfinished. Of desire left unrequited. "I'll see you tomorrow."

"Tomorrow." She left him without another look or another word.

Colin stayed on the terrace and waited for his father to join him at the balustrade. He heard footsteps on the stone, then felt his father's presence.

"I thought you'd gotten her out of your system."

"I thought I had, too."

"Then what was that all about?"

Colin's lips curled in a mocking smile. "We decided to be friends."

"That kiss looked a lot more than friendly to me."

Colin heard the concern in his father's voice. "I know," he said with a sigh.

"You're going riding with her tomorrow?"

Now he heard disapproval. And balked at yielding to his father's judgment of the situation. "I can handle this, Pa. Don't interfere."

"It's hard not to, under the circumstances."

"Don't," Colin warned.

He saw his father stiffen, saw that he had stepped over a boundary that had always been there in the past. He had been a boy, his father a man. His father had given orders, he had obeyed. Only now, somehow, that was all changing. It wasn't comfortable for either of them, Colin thought. But he wasn't able to slip back into the familiar role he had played in the past.

Colin waited to see how his father would react. He

was surprised when his father leaned over with his elbows on the stone balustrade and said, "I wondered when this day would come. How I would feel. What I would do."

He turned and glanced at Colin, then looked out over the rose garden. "I suppose all I have to say is I've always been proud of you. You have a good head on your shoulders. I hope you'll use it."

He stood slowly and turned to Colin and put a hand on his shoulder. "Let's go inside, son. We need to say good night to our guests."

His father had hugged him countless times. To comfort him, encourage him, applaud him. What made this gesture so different was the fact that, although he had called him son, his father had addressed him man to man. He had acknowledged Colin's right to make his own decisions. And to deal with the consequences of his own mistakes.

Colin felt a lump of emotion in his throat that kept him from speaking. He nodded to his father and walked beside him back to the ballroom.

It was the first cutting of ties between father and son, but not the last. Colin fought back thoughts of what it would be like to part from his father in the spring. That was a long time from now. Anything could happen.

18

Lady Roanna arrived at Severn Manor promptly at nine o'clock. She had risen before the sky turned from black to gray and discovered a time of day with which she was unfamiliar—dawn. She had been to enough late parties during her comeout in London to learn about the dark hours after midnight, but mostly she had been tucked into bed by dawn. The morning rewarded her by being absolutely gorgeous. The sky was decorated with breathtaking streaks of pink and gold.

Roanna was feeling very wicked. Her parents had approved her morning ride with Mr. Calloway because the duke and duchess would also be in attendance. But the original plan had been changed. The duke had informed Colin late last night that he and the duchess would not be visiting the Hepplewhites after all. Colin had sent word to her early this morning that they would be riding alone.

She should have told her parents.

But she knew they would have forbidden her to go, or sent a groom along to keep an eye on her. She wanted a chance to talk with Colin when there wasn't someone watching over her shoulder. All right, she had ulterior motives. Yes, she hoped he would want to kiss her. And yes, she intended to let him do it.

She was feeling very wicked, indeed.

"Good morning, Mr. Calloway," Roanna said with a smile that made her dimple show.

"Good morning to you, too, Roanna. I'm a little surprised to see you here. Your parents didn't object?"

"No," Roanna said.

Colin watch her horse dance beneath her, then found the white-knuckled hold on the reins that had caused her mount's reaction. She had just lied to him. For a single second he considered confronting her. But she was a grown woman. She knew the risks and dangers of her behavior. If she chose to ride with him without her parents' permission, he wasn't going to deny himself the pleasure of her company.

"Let's go," he said. "I thought we could take a circuitous route and enjoy a little longer ride."

Having survived the lie, Roanna's second smile was more genuine. "I would love that."

There was still a little dew left on the grass, so the green hills glistened. The smell of heather was in the air, and there was a gentle breeze that kept them from getting too warm as the sun rose higher in the sky.

"You're very comfortable on a horse," Colin noted after a particularly spirited run.

"I spent practically my entire childhood on one," Roanna confessed. "There weren't any other children around that I could play with, so I attached myself to my horse, Victory."

Nicholas frowned. "I can't believe there were no other children your age in the whole parish."

"Of course there were," she said with a laugh. "The tenants all have children I would very much have liked to know. But Father said it wouldn't be fair to them because there would always be a distance between us that could never be erased."

Colin snorted. "That's the stupidest thing I ever heard."

"It isn't stupid," Roanna said. "The class structure in England has existed for generations. It isn't something that can be ignored. Suppose I made friends with the daughter of one of my father's tenants. The girl could never be invited to attend a dinner with people of a higher class. In the first place, she couldn't afford the necessary dress. Second, she wouldn't know how to act in that kind of company, and they wouldn't tolerate her *faux pas*. And it would be cruel to share my own experiences with such a friend, who could never be a part of them, don't you see?"

"I see a system of life I don't much care for and can't approve," Colin said. "Life for the common man is a lot better in America. You might start out poor, working for somebody else. All that can change. A lot of hard work, a little luck, and plenty of determination can raise you above the circumstances of your birth."

"Is that what you plan to do?" Roanna asked.

"It's what I've already done. I'm not anyone's bastard son in Texas. I'm Colin Calloway, rancher. I know the banker's daughter and . . . and a few women who wouldn't be welcome in polite company."

For some strange reason Roanna hadn't imagined Colin with other women. She wasn't worried about the women of the demimonde he had mentioned. He might associate with them, but he was hardly likely to marry one of them. But the banker's daughter concerned her. Did Colin have a sweetheart waiting for him in America? Had he been toying with her affections?

As you've toyed with his? her conscience demanded.

I'm not playing games. Anymore, she corrected.

Would you marry him if he asked?

How can I know? He hasn't asked.

You'd better consider the possibility. It isn't fair to lead him on if your intentions aren't honest.

What if he has someone else waiting for him in America?

Why not ask him and find out for sure?

When Roanna turned to Colin to ask her question, she found him staring at her. "Is something the matter?"

"I was just admiring your . . . dress. The color suits you." Actually he had been admiring the figure inside her dress, but Colin couldn't see himself telling her that. "You've been chewing on your lip for the past five minutes. Maybe I should be the one asking if something is the matter."

"I was just wondering if . . . if you have a sweetheart in America."

Colin laughed. "No, I don't. But if you can ask, so can I. How many beaus have asked for your hand?"

"More than I can count," she said with a twinkle in her eye.

Colin sobered. "Are you serious?"

"Being the daughter of an earl brought more than a few fortune hunters around. Father turned most of them down before they even had a chance to court me. But there's been no one I wanted to have ask me," she added in a soft voice.

They had arrived at the Hepplewhites' small stone cottage at a time when both would have preferred to continue the conversation.

"We can talk more about this later," Colin said, letting her know he wasn't finished with the subject.

"All right," Roanna agreed. She had a few more questions to ask herself.

Douglas was at home and walked out on crutches to greet them. "Hello, Colin." He was surprised to see Lady Roanna Warenne. She wasn't known for her visits to the poor. He touched his forelock. "Lady Roanna."

"You're looking great, Douglas," Colin said. "How soon before you can wear your boot?"

"The doctor says the leg is healing nicely. As soon as I can bear the weight on my stump with a little padding, he says I should do it. I try it every day, just to see. It won't be long now, I'm guessing."

Roanna marveled at the fact Colin didn't seem the least bit self-conscious or uncomfortable talking with a man who was clearly his social inferior, and a cripple besides. She struggled not to cringe from Hepplewhite. She had no experience with anyone who wasn't a whole person. She felt sorry for Hepplewhite of course, but beyond that, she wasn't certain how she should act toward him.

Roanna's reluctance to approach Hepplewhite hadn't gone unnoticed by either man. Douglas accepted it as typical aristocratic behavior.

Colin was disappointed.

"I suppose I should have explained to you why I was coming here today," Colin said to Roanna.

"I thought it was for visit," Roanna said. Although, now that she thought about it, she wasn't sure what that entailed, either.

"I'm going to be helping with some work that needs to be done which Douglas can't do himself until he's back on two feet."

"Oh." Roanna wondered what she was supposed to do while he was working. The expectant, encouraging look on Colin's face told her what he wanted to hear. So she said it. "Is there anything I can do to help?"

She saw the astonishment and cynicism on Douglas Hepplewhite's face and knew she deserved them both. She had never in her life done any manual labor except for the fun of it. Her hands were still soft as a baby's skin and though she was fit from all the riding she did, there was no necessity that she use her muscles for anything more than walking up and down the stairs. Everything else was done for her.

"Do you have something Lady Roanna could do?" Colin asked Douglas.

Douglas was in a quandary. "I can't ask a lady to wash dirty dishes or sweep the floor," he told Colin.

"Why not?" Roanna said. She desperately wanted Colin to be proud of her. And she was willing to do whatever it took to earn his respect. "I can certainly manage those things if you'll tell me where to find the soap and water and the broom."

Douglas scratched his head. "I suppose my sisters

can do that. If you're sure, m'lady, that you really
want to do such menial labor."

"I'm sure," Roanna said. She was even more sure
when she looked at Colin and saw the smile of approval on his face.

What would have been simple chores for Colin
were confusing adventures into realms of the un-
known for Roanna. She was appalled to discover
that seven children, including Douglas, lived in the
house. Mrs. Hepplewhite was confined to her bed
with consumption. While the oldest girl, Patty, did
her best to care for the children and cook and clean,
she was only eleven. The rest were all younger, the
youngest being a year-old baby.

Roanna had never thought much about what it
meant to be poor. The younger children, four girls
and two boys, were dressed in rags that she suspected were cast-off clothing. They were all bare-
foot, but their feet were no more dirty than their
hands and faces and hair. Their bodies were thin, so
she suspected they were hungry. More telling was
the look in their eyes. Hopelessness. Despair.

She thought of her glowing skin, which she
bathed in various lotions every night. Of her glossy
hair, which was brushed daily and washed to keep it
clean. Of the groaning sideboard of food that waited
to be served each morning. Of the silks and velvets
and satins she donned. So many filled her closets
that she would never wear them out.

She felt guilty. For the first time in her life she saw
the unfairness of a system that provided a very few
with so much and everyone else with so little.

But it wasn't her fault. She had only been born
into the system, she hadn't created it. And she had

no desire to change it, even assuming she could. Which was doubtful.

Yet she could help this one family. She had nothing else planned, and she was certainly strong enough and able enough to do what had to be done.

Colin left Roanna in the house and followed Douglas outside. The duke had arranged to have deadwood from Severn's forest delivered to the Hepplewhites for fuel. But there were several large tree trunks that needed to be chopped up. Douglas handed Colin an ax, and he went to work. After Colin chopped the wood, he carted it over to the growing pile beside the house.

Meanwhile, Roanna had her hands full inside. She quickly realized that the children were so in awe of her they would be next to useless in helping her to find what she needed if she didn't do something to ease the tension.

She approached the eldest girl, Patty, and said, "Do you think you could find me an apron?"

"We don't have an apron," Patty said, her wide eyes glued on Lady Roanna's face as if she were an angel come down from heaven.

"A towel then, or anything I could use to cover my dress while I'm cleaning."

"Oh, no, m'lady," Patty protested. "You can't do the cleanin'!"

"Why not?" Roanna said with a teasing smile. "Do you think I'm not strong enough?"

Patty was flustered. "Of course you are!"

"Of course I am," Roanna agreed. "Now, can you find me that apron?"

While they had been talking, the second-oldest girl, Penny, had gone to find a towel they used to dry the dishes. She held it out to Roanna and said, "Here, m'lady."

Roanna took the filthy towel and gamely tucked it around the waist of her riding skirt. It was worse than nothing, but she wouldn't hurt the child's feelings by rejecting it. "What's your name?" Roanna asked.

"Penny, m'lady." The seven-year-old girl dipped a quick curtsy.

"I'm pleased to meet you, Penny. I'm Lady Roanna. Would you introduce me to your brothers and sisters?"

Penny quickly introduced the other two girls, ages six and one, as Peggy and Pippa. The boys, five-year-old twins, were named Diggory and Dolph.

"I see," Roanna said with a laugh. "The girls' names all start with P, and the boys' names all start with D."

"That's because Momma named the girls, and Poppa named the boys," Patty explained. "Momma's name is Polly, and Poppa was called Denis. There were some others, Danny and Darcy and Dana and Phoebe born between Douglas and me. But they all died."

Roanna was appalled to think of any woman having to bear eleven children. But she now knew why there was such a large age gap between Douglas and Patty. The other children had not survived.

Polly Hepplewhite had been sleeping when Roanna arrived, but the sound of a strange voice had woken her. She called to Patty from the other room in the two-room house. "Patty? Who is that you're talkin' to?"

"It's a lady, Momma," Patty replied excitedly. "Will you come meet my mother, m'lady?"

"I'd love to meet her."

When Mrs. Hepplewhite saw Lady Roanna she tried to get up. Roanna hurried over to her and pressed her shoulders back against the pillow. She was already too late to prevent the woman from suffering a horrible round of deep, hacking coughs. Roanna stood helplessly by, even less certain of her ability in a sickroom than of her ability as a maid-of-all-work.

"Are you all right?" she asked when the coughing had subsided.

"Fine, m'lady." Mrs. Hepplewhite wrung her hands for a moment before she asked, "What are you here for, m'lady?"

Roanna grinned. "I've come to clean."

Mrs. Hepplewhite looked alarmed. "Oh, no! You mustn't. A fine lady like you can't be doin' my chores."

"I can and I shall," Roanna said. "Don't worry, Mrs. Hepplewhite. All will be well. I've come with Mr. Calloway."

The woman relaxed then. "Oh. He's a fine man, isn't he, m'lady? So kind and generous and thoughtful. I don't know what we'd've done without him, and the duchess, of course, over these past sorry weeks. And the duke, the Lord bless him. Givin' my son back his foot. And a job!"

It sounded to Roanna like the job was as important, or even more so, than the fitted boot Colin had told her the duke had arranged to have made for Douglas. "I'll be letting you rest now," Roanna said as she backed her way out of the room.

When she turned around, six grimy faces stared back at her. She knew it was futile to wash them first, since they would only get dirty again cleaning. "Let's get started," she said. She began issuing orders like a general.

"Patty, you find a pail and fill it with water. Then put it on the stove to heat so we can wash dishes."

"But there's no fire in the stove," Penny said.

"We're not allowed to have a fire unless it's really cold," Peggy explained.

"Today shall be an exception," Roanna said. "Diggory and Dolph can go outside and collect wood and get the fire started."

The two boys raced out of the house and came charging up to Colin, so he had to catch himself in midswing.

"What's all the excitement?" Colin asked.

"We have to get some wood," Diggory said.

"We're going to make a fire," Dolph said.

"What's that?" Douglas asked.

"The lady said we can have a fire," Diggory told his older brother.

"We have to heat water to wash the dishes," Dolph said.

Douglas and Colin exchanged looks. Then Colin said, "If you boys collect the wood, I'll come help you build the fire."

"We know how to do it," Diggory said.

"It's a fact," Douglas said. "They do."

Colin looked at the two five-year-olds, both of whom had teeth missing from their impish grins. It dawned on him that when you were really poor, you grew up very fast. These boys had learned to do their share of the labor at an early age, which in this case meant learning how to handle fire. "Be careful, then," he said.

Meanwhile, Roanna had sent Penny hunting for the broom, and picked up the baby, Pippa, and taken her into the bedroom where she could play under Mrs. Hepplewhite's watchful eyes.

There was enough work to keep them all busy for most of the morning. Sweeping the floor, cleaning the single window, wiping off the wooden table and chairs and the sideboard, which were the only pieces of furniture, and washing the dishes and drying them and putting them away.

When they were done, the front room sparkled. Roanna then set the children to heating more water to wash the linens, while she went out to see how long Colin planned to stay. She stopped in her tracks when she turned the corner of the house and saw him chopping wood.

He was naked to the waist.

In her very sheltered life, Roanna had never seen a man of her own class with his chest bared. She was fascinated at the play of muscle and sinew as Colin hefted the ax and brought it crashing down. His body was covered with a fine sheen of sweat, and a hank of black hair had fallen onto his forehead. His shoulders were wide and strong and narrowed to a slim waist. There was a patch of black curls between two flat male nipples and a thin line of black down started somewhere midchest and ran into his trousers.

She felt breathless, enervated. He was magnificent. She wanted to run her hands over his sweat-slick body, to feel whether the muscles were as taut as they looked on his belly. To feel the crispness of the hair on his chest. To taste his skin, which was surely salty. She wanted to feel that strength surrounding her, holding her close.

At that moment, Colin happened to look up and caught her gazing at him with mooncalf eyes. It wouldn't have been so bad if he hadn't grinned.

He knew. He knew what she was feeling, and he was laughing at her.

She put her hands on her hips and said, "I only came to see how much longer you can stay."

Colin set the head of the ax on the log and leaned on it. "I've got all day."

"Good. Because I want to do some laundry, and it will take a while for everything to get washed and hung out to dry."

"Take your time," he said. "I've got plenty of wood to chop." Then, knowing she was watching, he lifted the ax and sent it biting into the wood.

Roanna had to force herself to leave. She didn't miss the satisfied smirk on Colin's face before she made her escape.

Roanna put a hand to her aching back as Patty emptied the laundry tub of dirty water. Penny and Peggy were hanging the clean sheets out to dry on bushes in back of the house.

"That's everything, m'lady," Patty said. "I don't think there's another spot of dirt anywhere in the house."

Roanna smiled and touched the tip of Patty's nose. "Except here. I think we need to heat some more water. This time for baths."

"Baths?" Patty said, obviously appalled. "We don't bathe but once a week on Saturdays."

"Today we'll make an exception," Roanna said.

Apparently, working side by side had removed the awe with which Patty had viewed her earlier in the day. The child continued to argue right up until the moment when Daisy dropped her skinny, squirming body into the washtub.

When the girls were finished, the boys took their turns, and finally Roanna settled the baby, Pippa, in the tub and got down on her knees to wash the child herself.

That was how Colin found her.

Her face was smudged with dirt, and several golden curls had unraveled over her nape and by her ears. She had removed her riding jacket and folded up the sleeves of her blouse so they wouldn't get wet. From the looks of the no-longer-white linen, she had done her share of the cleaning.

Her collarless blouse was open at the throat, and he could see just the hint of her breasts. His loins tightened, and his heart began to pound. He clenched his hands into fists to keep from reaching out to touch her.

She was crooning to the baby, and the golden-haired child was looking up at her, a smile on her face, her chubby cheeks ruddy from the warmth of the water. He imagined the child was his. That she was his.

And realized how ridiculous he was being. He could see the blisters every time she cupped her hand for water to pour over the child's shoulder. After today, he didn't think she would volunteer any time soon to visit a tenant with him.

He admitted now that he had been testing her. When he looked around at all she had accomplished, he could see that she had passed with flying colors. She was going to leave everything immaculate, right down to the baby, Pippa.

But gritty as her performance had been, he recognized it for what it was. This wasn't a life she could easily adapt to. And he would be a selfish churl to ask a woman like her to give up her life of ease for him. It would be like sentencing her to a lifetime of hard labor with no chance of escape.

Roanna wasn't aware Colin was in the room until she rose with the soaking wet baby in her arms. "All the towels are wet," she said with a smile of chagrin. "I don't know how I thought I was going to get her dry."

Colin began unbuttoning his shirt, which he had put on only after he had rinsed off with a pail of water. "This ought to be dry enough."

"I can't take the shirt off your back," she protested.

"Why not?"

Roanna's tongue was caught on the roof of her mouth as Colin approached and stood next to her while he surrounded the baby with his linen shirt. She hissed in a breath as his knuckle brushed against her breast, where water had dampened her blouse.

He caught her eyes and held them as he said, "There is nothing quite as fascinating as the look of a woman's flesh through damp cloth."

Roanna swallowed hard. "I . . . uh . . . the baby."

He grinned. "Hurry up and finish, Roanna. It's time to go."

Way past time to go, Roanna thought. "I'll be ready as soon as I dress the baby."

Colin waited outside for her. When she came out of the house, he saw she had removed as many signs as she could of her day's activities. He could see the cuffs of her blouse beneath the riding jacket, which was buttoned to her neck. Her hair was tucked back into its neat bun at her nape, and her face was free of dirt.

He held his hand cupped for her to mount, and once she was in the saddle he leapt onto his horse. The whole Hepplewhite family, with the exception of Mrs. Hepplewhite, stood in front of the house to wave good-bye to them. Just before they left, Penny raced up to Roanna and tugged on her skirt.

"M'lady, please. I have something for you."

Roanna leaned down, and Penny put a tiny doll made of rags and sticks in her hand. "I can't take your doll, Penny."

"But I want you to. Pansy is my best friend. I want her to live in a fine house and be waited on by servants."

Roanna felt a lump growing in her throat. What had been a day out of time for her was a lifetime of everyday hardship for the ragtag bunch of children to whom she had already lost her heart.

"I'll take her," Roanna said. "Only if you promise you'll come to visit her soon. And bring all your brothers and sisters with you."

Penny's jaw dropped. "Do you mean it?" she asked in a voice of breathless disbelief.

"Of course, I do," Roanna said. "You can send a note to me when you have time to come."

"Tomorrow."

"What?"

"We can all come tomorrow," Penny said, her

chin upthrust pugnaciously. It was clear she didn't believe a word of what Roanna had promised. Too few fairy tales had come true in her life.

Roanna smiled. It was a better choice than crying, which was what she felt like doing. "Pansy and I will be waiting. Would around luncheon be all right? We can all have a picnic. How does that sound?"

Penny's eyes were suspiciously bright. "Fine. That sounds just fine."

As they rode away Roanna wondered what her parents would think when six tenant children—or seven if Douglas came—showed up for luncheon. She knew they would understand. She felt certain that Priss would be as moved as she was by the children's plight.

"You've made that child's dream come true," Colin said.

"I had no idea people lived like that," Roanna confessed.

Colin turned away abruptly. Roanna had no idea what she had said to offend him, but she could see by the rigidity in his body that she had. "What did I say? What's wrong?"

When he turned back to her, she saw the sadness in his eyes and felt a moment of stark terror. He had tested her, and she had failed. He confirmed it with the first words out of his mouth.

"That's the difference between us, Roanna. You can't imagine poverty and want. You can't imagine a life where you face struggles and adversity every day. That's how my life is, Roanna. In Texas there are so many things that can kill you. The weather, Indians, outlaws, a cattle stampede, snakes, floods, fire. It's an untamed place where you have to fight to survive.

"That's not the kind of life you could ever live, Roanna."

He didn't say any more. He didn't have to. They rode in silence the rest of the way to Rockland Park.

Which gave Roanna time to think. She realized that for the first time in her life she felt a sense of satisfaction for a job well done. She had helped the Hepplewhites. It had been hard work, but the rewards had been more than worth the effort expended.

Colin was right, she didn't like having blisters or having her back ache from bending over a washtub. But she wasn't the wilting violet he seemed to think she was. She had a great deal of backbone and massive amounts of determination. She was more than a match for Colin Calloway, even in his godforsaken Texas.

Roanna caught her breath when she realized her mother was standing in the circular road that led to the house. Her father was mounted on horseback beside her. There was no way to return home without being detected.

As she rode up to the house, her mother pointed at her, and her father turned around to look at her. At first she saw relief on his face, then, as the earl spied Colin, fury.

"Where have you been?" the earl demanded when she reached his side.

"I went riding with Mr. Calloway. We stopped to visit one of Severn's tenants, the Hepplewhites."

"You've been gone since dawn. It's after one o'clock."

The insinuation was there of what a man and a woman would most likely have done if left alone for all that time.

"I cleaned house," she said defiantly. "I washed dishes and furniture and babies." She laid the reins across her horse's neck while she tugged off her pigskin riding gloves. She held out her hands, palm up, toward her father.

The earl took her hand and ran his thumb across the broken blisters, the patches where soap and water had roughened her hands. He turned an eye on Colin. "What were you doing all this time?"

"Chopping wood, sir. Douglas Hepplewhite is crippled for the time being. He needed some help." He shrugged and said, "I gave it to him."

"Very well," the earl said, mollified. "Next time, young lady, let us know when you have some inclination to help the poor."

"All right, Papa," Roanna said. "The Hepplewhite children will be here tomorrow for luncheon." She kicked her mount and headed for the stable, leaving her father staring, his jaw agape, behind her.

Colin had started to turn his horse for home when the earl stopped him. "Mr. Calloway."

Colin reined in his mount.

"Don't do it again."

"Lady Roanna told me she had your permission, sir." That was the truth, even if he knew Roanna had lied to him. "However, you needn't worry. I've made it clear to Lady Roanna that I don't think we will suit."

With that, he turned his mount and spurred him into a lope. He didn't plan to see Roanna on purpose again. If he ran across her accidentally, he would be polite and courteous. But he wasn't going to pursue a relationship he knew was doomed from the start. He wasn't that much of a fool. But he wasn't a man who easily let go of hope.

Maybe in nine months Roanna could change.

19

Daisy was working in the rose garden, doing the fall pruning. She couldn't believe she had been married three months. It didn't seem possible that so much time had passed. And yet it felt as though she and Nicholas had been married forever. She had spent every night in the duke's bed, as he had commanded her to do. She had not dared to defy him after that first night, when she had hesitated too long in her bedroom, and he had come after her.

The memory of that evening was vivid even now.

She had been standing at the window of her bedroom, dressed in a simple white cotton nightgown that buttoned up the front to the round neck and had sleeves that fell to her wrists. She looked like a virgin sacrifice to some medieval dragon. Only she was no longer a virgin, even if Nicholas did his share of breathing fire.

She heard him try the door to her room, heard his grunt of disbelief when he realized it was locked.

"Open the door, Daisy." He spoke rather calmly, she thought, though she heard the underlying threat.

"No, Nicholas. I've changed my mind."

He didn't argue. He didn't plead. He simply put his shoulder to the door until it crashed open.

She whirled and stood staring at him, stunned at the fact he had forced the door from the hallway, stunned at the look of violence in his eyes.

She shook her head, her eyes wide with fright.

He ignored her fear, ignored her outstretched hands, ignored her one word of protest. "No!"

"There will be no locks between us, wife," Nicholas said as he crossed the room and jerked her into his arms.

His mouth came down without warning, capturing hers. She felt his anger and his desire. It matched her own, which flared to instant life. His kiss urged a response, and she was helpless to resist his entreaty as her body arched into his, giving everything he asked and demanding more.

"Nicholas, don't. I don't want—"

"Don't lie," he said in a harsh voice. "I'm not the idiot you must think me. Your body tells me what you really want."

She had feared it would be like this, that she would be swept up by emotion and carried away by pleasure. Nicholas was a man who knew his way around a woman's body. She was a lamb being devoured by the big bad wolf. His mouth latched on to her breast. She groaned as he suckled her through the damp cotton. His hand came up to cup her other breast, and he grazed the tip with his thumb. His other hand slipped down between her legs and pressed the soft cloth against the dew that had formed between her thighs.

Daisy cried out with surprise and anguished pleasure. He found a place she hadn't even known existed and began to caress her body. She fought the moan that tore its way free. He showed her no mercy, his hands and mouth driving her toward the pinnacle of desire.

She was gasping, sobbing, unable to breathe or speak as her body convulsed with ecstasy. His chest was still heaving, his body still hard and unsatisfied as he lifted her into his arms, unlocked the connecting door, and headed through the door to his room. He stopped long enough to turn the key on the connecting door, locking it behind him, then carried her over and dumped her on his bed.

It wasn't as soft as her own. She rubbed her abused derriere while she glared at him through narrowed eyes. "Haven't you had enough?"

His eyes had a feral light. "I haven't even begun."

He began to strip right in front of her. She should have been embarrassed. She chose instead to stare him into embarrassment.

It didn't work. Nicholas didn't have a modest bone in his body, and it was easy to see why he didn't mind showing it off. He sat to take off his boots, then stood and dragged off his coat before he went to work on his cravat. The waistcoat came next, then his linen shirt.

His chest was broad and muscular, browned by the sun and covered with a wealth of crisp black hair. His belly rippled with muscle and a line of down led her eyes to narrow hips.

He was aroused and made no effort to hide the fact. His shaft stood intimidatingly amid a nest of black curls. He turned his back on her to throw his trousers on a chair, giving her a splendid view of lean flanks and firm buttocks. She had never paid much attention to the male body in the past, mostly because Tony had come to her in the dark. It was impossible to ignore the sheer physical perfection of the man who stood before her.

Something of what she was feeling must have shown in her eyes because he grinned recklessly and said, "If you see anything you like, help yourself."

Daisy turned her back on him and crossed her arms, which was when she felt the wetness where he had suckled her breast. The nipple was plainly visible through the damp cloth. He must have been ogling her the whole time, she realized with a feeling somewhere between thrill and alarm.

She looked back over her shoulder to chastise him and found he had settled on the bed behind her on his knees. His arms circled her, and he captured her breasts with his hands.

"Have I told you how beautiful you are, Daisy?" he murmured.

She shivered as he bit the lobe of her ear. "If we're going to pass out compliments, I suppose I should remark on what a fine male specimen you are," she retorted.

"I'm glad you like what you see."

Daisy harrumphed, then gasped as his mouth slid from her ear to her throat. The way he was holding her, there was no way she could touch him.

"Nicholas, please."

"What is it you want, Daisy? Do you want to touch, too?" he whispered.

The words were torn from her. "Yes. Yes, Nicholas, I do."

He turned her on the bed to face him, then brought her legs around his thighs and lifted her into his lap so they were seated facing each other. "Go ahead, Daisy," he said. "Touch to your heart's content."

She kept her eyes focused on what she touched. His shoulders first, warm and hard. The crisp hairs on his chest. The flat male nipple that peaked much as her own had at a touch. She leaned forward and put her mouth against his skin to taste him. She felt him shudder as her hand slid across his belly and down between the two of them before sliding back up and around his neck.

She drew his head down toward her own and took his mouth in a kiss of possession as fierce as any he had given her. He was hers . . . for a while. She wanted memories for the long days and nights when he would not be there to keep her warm. Physical sensations bombarded her. She fought the emotional response that also threatened. Fought it and won.

She had loved once before and been destroyed when Tony rejected her. She wouldn't allow that to happen again. She would protect herself from that sort of devastation by simply not allowing herself to feel anything except the pure physical pleasure of giving herself to Nicholas and taking him in return.

. He wasn't a patient lover, at least not the first time. He lifted her and impaled her and drove them both to climax.

Enervated, he lowered them both until they were lying entwined side by side, their bodies still joined.

"Don't ever try to lock me out again, Daisy," he warned in a raw voice.

Her hand threaded through his damp hair and brushed it off his brow. "I won't lock any doors," she conceded aloud. But there were other barriers she had put into place to protect herself. Barriers that he couldn't see, and thus presumably couldn't break down.

He made love to her twice more during the night, arousing her to aching passion and then satisfying them both. There was a sense of urgency, of desperation to his lovemaking that she recognized all too well.

It hadn't gone away in the three months they had been married. She gave him her body, but not her heart and soul. He had recognized that dichotomy and had sought, with passion, to take what she would not give him. He had been frustrated, she knew, by the lack of some element in their couplings. But he never voiced a specific complaint, and she never offered an explanation beyond the one she had initially given him.

He could have her body, but not her heart.

Daisy heard the crunch of gravel along the garden path and looked up to find Nicholas striding toward where she sat on the ground. She watched the fluid movement of muscle and sinew and bone as he approached her. She knew his body intimately now and was able to imagine what he looked like without his clothes. Her gaze followed the length of him up to his eyes, which were amused.

"You look busy. Can you take a break to visit one of the tenants with me?"

As Daisy stood, Nicholas reached out a hand to help her up. She felt a frisson of desire that was unwelcome but unavoidable. "I'll be glad to go with you. Just let me change into my riding habit."

"Five minutes," he said.

"Ten," she bargained.

"Five. And I'll leave if you're not ready."

He leaned over to kiss her mouth, and she felt her knees wobble. She backed away from him. How could he do that to her when she didn't love him? Her vulnerability to him was frightening. There had to be a way to get the duke to stay at Severn. She had been meaning to speak to him about it for weeks now. Maybe today would be a good time to bring up the subject.

"Five minutes," she said as she backed away from him.

Nicholas was appalled at how fast his heart was beating after just one kiss. She did it to him every time. Even when he told himself he was prepared for the power she had to bring him to his knees, he was caught by surprise. It hadn't gotten any easier to be around her during the three months they had been married. The more he had her, the more he wanted her. The more he tried to stay away from her, the more necessary it became to spend time with her.

He had already conceded that he couldn't leave her when he returned to America. The only problem now was convincing her to go with him. Not that he couldn't simply kidnap her and take her along. After all, she was his wife. But knowing Daisy, if he used force, she would be on the next ship back to England.

He had been meaning to broach the subject for days now. He hoped there would be time for him to raise the issue during their ride to check on one of the tenants, who was having some problems with his cattle.

One of the things Nicholas had come to admire about Daisy was her seat on a horse. They hadn't gotten far from the house before he offered to race her.

Daisy hesitated. She really ought not to be tearing around the countryside. It wasn't dignified. Furthermore, she had to be more careful now—

"Afraid I'll win?" Nicholas taunted.

Daisy threw caution to the winds. "First one to the cleared field wins," she said.

"Go!" he shouted, spurring his horse.

She was riding an English Thoroughbred. He was riding his mustang. There was no contest over a short distance. The Thoroughbred had speed the mustang couldn't match. But Nicholas had learned over the past few months that if he extended the distance of the race, his mustang outlasted the Thoroughbred and won.

This time Daisy had set the distance, and she was there before him. "You win," he said with a grin as he admired her flyaway hair and windburned cheeks. "What forfeit do you want?"

"Anything?"

"Name it, and it's yours."

"I want you to stay at Severn. I don't want you to go back to America."

Daisy could see she had caught Nicholas totally by surprise. His jaw fell open, and his hands tightened on the reins, causing the mustang to shake his head and back up several steps. Nicholas quickly brought his mount under control. But she could see he was still shaken.

"That's not amusing, Daisy."

"It wasn't meant to be," she said. "You have everything a man could want right here, Nicholas. Power, position, land. Me."

"I have all of that in America. Except the title, of course, which I'd willingly relinquish. And I could have you, if you'd back come to America with me."

This time her jaw dropped, and her eyes opened wide. "Are you asking me to leave England?"

"It's not a matter of leaving England. It's a matter of coming to America."

Her jaw snapped shut. "I'm afraid I don't see the distinction."

"What will you have here when I'm gone, Daisy? You wouldn't be leaving anything behind if you came with me."

"What about Severn?" she asked, her face taut, her body tense. "What happens to Severn?"

He shrugged. "I sell it."

"I see. Oh, I see." At last. Finally. She did see. Nothing she had done, none of the changes at Severn, could entice him to stay. "You really don't care about this place, do you?"

"That's not fair, Daisy. I do care. I just . . . there are too many memories here. Don't you see? Everyone looks at me, and they see a man who might or might not be the real Duke of Severn. Can you imagine what that's like? Can you imagine having to face that for the rest of your life? I would have to do that if I stay here. In America, it doesn't matter who I was. Only who I am."

"And what are you there? A bounty hunter. A man who kills other men for a living," she said scornfully.

His eyes turned cold. "It's an honest living."

"A futile, violent living, you mean."

"And this is better? Raising a few cows, some hay and oats? Where's the challenge in that?"

"The challenge comes in watching things grow. In knowing that you've helped your tenants to prosper. In preserving the past and passing it on to posterity."

"My son intends to live in America. And you can't give me any more children. What posterity, Daisy?"

Nicholas was sorry the moment he saw the stricken look on Daisy's face. It wasn't her fault she couldn't give him children. It wasn't her fault he was a bastard. He reached out a hand to her, but she jerked away.

"It appears we're at an impasse. Again," she said bitterly.

"You could come with me, Daisy."

"You could stay here."

"I've already explained why that isn't possible."

"What if you found out the truth about your birth? Would that make a difference?"

He thought for a long time before he answered her. "It might."

"When is Estleman coming back?"

"In the spring."

"We'll just have to wait until then, to see what he has to say."

"And if he doesn't have any answers? What then, Daisy?"

"We'll worry about that when the time comes. Are we agreed? Until spring?"

"Until spring."

She kicked her horse into a gentle canter, and he spurred his mount after her. They arrived shortly at the small, slate-roofed stone house of James Johnson. When Daisy rode up, Sally was in the yard wearing a blouse that was cut indecently low and that fell off one shoulder. With her dark eyes and dark hair flying in the wind, she looked more like a gypsy than a proper English girl. "Hello, Sally," Daisy said. "Is your father around?"

"He is, Your Grace. If you'd like to come inside, he's working at the kitchen table."

Daisy was ready to slide off her horse when Nicholas arrived to lift her down. He dragged her body along the length of his, and when she met his gaze, she knew he had done it on purpose. He was reminding her of what she would be giving up if she stayed. She rubbed her hips against his. Reminding him of what he would be giving up if he left.

"Touché, Daisy," he murmured, his lips curved in the beginning of a smile.

Daisy turned and found Sally standing in her way. The girl gave Nicholas a sloe-eyed look from beneath lowered lashes and said, "Welcome, Your Grace. If you'll just follow me I'll take you to Papa." Her hips swayed provocatively as she moved away.

Daisy glanced at Nicholas from the corner of her eye, to see if the girl's blatant tactics were working. Nicholas grinned back at her.

"After you." He gestured her ahead of him.

Daisy harrumphed. It would be just like Nicholas to compare her walk to the girl's. Well, if he wanted a show, he was going to get one. She lifted the extra material in her riding skirt and looped it over her arm. Then she headed down the dirt path to the front door, making her hips sway as seductively as she knew how.

She waited for the sound of Nicholas's footsteps

behind her. When she didn't hear them, she turned to peek over her shoulder. Nicholas had a finger in his collar, attempting to loosen it. Daisy laughed, a bell-like tinkling sound that made Nicholas frown.

"Come on," she said. "I promise to be good."

He quickly caught up to her. "That's what I'm afraid of."

James Johnson rose and tugged his forelock and made sure the duke and duchess were both comfortable at his kitchen table before he reseated himself. His wife served tea and disappeared back into the kitchen, and he sent a sulking Sally back outside to feed the chickens.

"What seems to be the problem?" Nicholas asked, getting right to the point.

"I think my cows are sick," Johnson said.

Daisy felt Nicholas tense beside her.

"What symptoms do they have?" Nicholas asked.

Johnson described symptoms that sounded like sick cows, but like no disease with which Nicholas was familiar. He relaxed only fractionally. Hoof and mouth disease had decimated herds in Texas. He wasn't sure if they had something similar in England, but he imagined they must.

"Have you got a local vet?" Nicholas asked.

"A what?"

"A horse doctor. An animal doctor."

"We only have one doctor hereabouts, and he tends people and animals both," Johnson said.

"I think we'd better send for him. Meanwhile, I'd like to take a look at some of your cattle." He couldn't bring himself to call them cows. Cows gave milk. Cattle were bred for beef.

Johnson saddled a tired-looking workhorse, and

the three of them rode out to the field where the
cattle stood listlessly, their heads down. They
weren't eating. Worse, a few of them weren't even
chewing their cud.

Nicholas was baffled by the symptoms he found.
The cattle were sick, all right. He didn't recognize
the disease, if it was one. There was one another
possibility that had to be considered.

"Have these cattle been grazing anywhere besides
this field?"

"No, Your Grace. They've been eating good English grass and naught else."

"What are you getting at, Nicholas?" Daisy asked.

"The cattle might have eaten something, some
weed—like the locoweed we have in Texas—that
made them sick." He turned to Johnson and said,
"If you don't mind, I'd like to take a ride around this
pasture. Maybe I'll see something."

"Certainly, Your Grace. Shall I go with you?"

"That might not be a bad idea. If I do spot something, you'll be able to recognize it yourself next
time."

Daisy noticed how Johnson's shoulders straightened as he rode alongside the duke. Nicholas probably had no idea that dukes were supposed to dele-
gate this sort of thing to their bailiffs. He probably
didn't know that tenants didn't usually ride alongside dukes as equals. It probably had never occurred
to him that it wasn't a duke's job to teach his tenants
to recognize noxious weeds that might be sickening
cattle.

Which was why, over the past three months, Nicholas had made tremendous inroads with the tenants
at Severn. They had moderated their initial opinion

of him. Not that they didn't find him a bit intimidating. The duke's size alone, not to mention his title, accomplished that. But he had made himself accessible to them in the way the nobility rarely did in England.

And he had earned their respect by understanding the basics of what they did and, in at least one other case that Daisy recalled, by working alongside them.

Clark Peters, who liked a jug of ale perhaps a bit too well, had imbibed before he went out to operate a piece of the newfangled machinery that Daisy had introduced the previous year. With the result that he had driven the modern Fowler steam plow, which was fueled by straw, into a ditch at the edge of the field.

There were already several men and a brace of horses trying to rescue the machinery when Daisy and Nicholas had arrived on the scene. Instead of watching from atop his horse, as past dukes had done in days gone by, Nicholas was off his horse in an instant and put his London-tailored shoulder against the huge metal wheel along with the men in muslin shirts.

Nicholas never saw the stunned looks on the faces of Severn's tenants, never saw the consideration that replaced it and the admiration that followed that. Daisy did.

When the steam plow was free, Nicholas asked enough questions to discover the problem and wrangled a promise from Peters to be more careful in the future. He shook hands with the other men—as equals—before mounting his horse and continuing his ride.

Daisy had tried to explain the significance of what

he had done, but Nicholas had brushed off her compliments.

"I only did what any neighbor would do," he said.

Daisy had realized then, for the first time, what growing up in America had done to Nicholas. He had no sense of class, of social distinctions. He judged a man the way he expected to be judged. For who he was. It was a radical proposition, but one that she realized would do the duke no harm in the eyes of his people.

He might treat them as equals, but it would be generations before they would be able to see the duke as anything except what he was. Severn. Whom their parents had served, and their parents before them. And whom their children would serve. It would be interesting to see how those beliefs were moderated over the years.

Daisy's attention was drawn back to the pasture by Nicholas's exclamation.

"By God, here it is! This is what's causing the problem."

Daisy nudged her horse toward the spot where Nicholas was kneeling on the ground with Johnson beside him. He held a small plant with prickly spurs.

"Larkspur. It isn't locoweed, but it's a near cousin," Nicholas said. "You're going to have to move the cattle out of this field until you can get rid of this stuff."

"Move them where, Your Grace?" Johnson said. "I haven't any other field."

Nicholas scratched his head. He turned to Daisy and asked, "Any suggestions?"

Daisy was both pleased and surprised to be consulted. This was what she had imagined it would be like, the two of them working together, making decisions. It was hard to believe it was actually happening.

"Daisy?"

She flushed. If she kept daydreaming he would think she was a nitwit and look elsewhere for advice. The answer to his dilemma came in her next thought. "Squire Templeton has a field he might be willing to lease for a short term."

Nicholas turned back to Johnson, and as the two men rose to their feet he said, "I'll speak to the squire this afternoon. If he agrees, I'll be back to help you drive the cattle over there today."

"That won't be necessary, Your Grace. I can manage."

"You'll need some help, won't you?"

"Well, yes, but—"

"Then I'll be here."

Johnson's eyes skipped to Daisy, and she saw the confusion there. It was hard for his tenants to understand this American duke, who was willing to labor beside them. "As you wish, Your Grace. I'll wait to hear from you," Johnson said.

Daisy noticed an aura of excitement about Nicholas after they had left Johnson's farm. "What has you shifting in your seat?"

His eyes gleamed as he turned to her. "I'm going on a cattle drive. I hadn't thought I missed things like that, but it seems I have. I think I'll ask Colin if he wants to come along. He might enjoy the adventure."

"What about me?"

"Ladies never go on cattle drives," Nicholas stated flatly.

Which only made Daisy more determined to join him. Nicholas must have recognized his mistake because he quickly amended, "Ladies usually don't go on cattle drives. It's dirty, dusty work, Daisy. You won't like it."

"I'll judge for myself," she said.

Nicholas grinned. "This I've got to see."

Daisy never made it to the cattle drive. But neither did Nicholas. Something else came up. Something so amazing, so astonishing, that it took him completely by surprise.

20

Daisy dropped her riding crop in the hallway as she entered Severn Manor with the duke on her heels. Thompson started to retrieve it for her, but she waved him away and bent over to get it herself. "Thank you, Thompson. I can—"

As she stood, the blood drained from her head, leaving her woozy. Afraid she was going to fall, Daisy reached out and caught Nicholas's arm to steady herself.

"Daisy?"

"Nicholas, I—" Everything got dark around the edges. Daisy realized as she fell what was happening. "I think . . . I'm going to . . . faint."

Nicholas bellowed for help as he caught Daisy in his arms. Servants came running from all corners of the house.

"Go for the doctor. Turn down my bed. Get her some tea. Get cool water and bring it to my room." Nicholas shouted orders, then headed upstairs. He wanted to get Daisy alone where he could examine her and find out what had happened.

Fear clawed at him, and he realized how much the woman in his arms meant to him. It was no longer a

matter of simply enjoying her, being intrigued by
her, being delighted with her. He needed her. He
couldn't survive without her.

He loved her.

Nicholas forced that thought away. Now, when
she had fainted for no good reason, was no time to
admit to feelings she probably wouldn't welcome,
nor to feelings he wasn't sure he welcomed himself.

He carried her to his room and lay her on the bed.
Jane was already there and pushed him out of the
way. She unbuttoned Daisy's riding jacket and the
blouse beneath it.

Nicholas's mouth flattened in rage when he saw
how tightly Daisy's corset was tied. No wonder she
couldn't breathe!

"Get that damned corset off her," he said, "before
I rip it off myself. I don't want her wearing another
one, do you understand me?"

Jane didn't cower before him, knowing she had
been hired by the mistress and that it was the mistress she served. "Fashion requires—"

"Be damned to fashion! I won't have her tied up
in one of those again. The woman fainted, for
heaven's sake. It's a wonder she hasn't done so before now."

"It wasn't the corset that caused it!" Jane retorted. She quickly slapped a hand over her mouth.

Nicholas's eyes narrowed. "What do you mean?
What's wrong with her?"

"Nothing's wrong." With Nicholas towering over
her, Jane wasn't so sure of herself as she might have
been.

"If you know anything, you'd best tell me. I've

sent for the doctor, and any secrets you're keeping won't be secret much longer."

"Then he can tell you," Jane said primly.

"Tell me what?" Nicholas roared.

"Her Grace is with child," Jane blurted.

Nicholas stared at her, disbelieving. "She's barren."

"The doctor only said he didn't think she could have another. And His Grace, the previous duke that is, never came to her bed after she lost the child."

"Get out," Nicholas said.

"But, Your Grace—"

"Get out before I pick you up and throw you out."

Jane left the room, closing the door quietly behind her.

Nicholas sank down onto the bed beside Daisy. The jacket of green velvet had been peeled open along with her blouse, and the corset he had blamed for all her trouble pushed her breasts up enticingly. But his eyes were drawn inexorably down below her waist. He laid his palm on her gathered skirt, but couldn't feel any difference in her shape. Her belly was still flat.

Our child is growing inside her.

He hadn't imagined having another child. Hadn't planned on it. Didn't know what to think of it.

Unfortunately, Daisy came out of her swoon too late to keep Jane from spilling the truth and too soon for Nicholas to have come to terms with the cataclysmic news he had just been given.

Daisy raised a hand to her head and opened her eyes slowly to adjust to the light in the room. Everything came back to her, how she had dropped her riding crop and leaned over to pick it up and then

fainted dead away. She decided Nicholas must have
brought her to his bedroom so she could recover.

"Nicholas?"

"You lied to me."

"What?"

"About having children. You lied to me."

He knew. Somehow he knew about the child. Of
course. That was what had caused her to faint. Dr.
Fitzsimmons had warned her to tread carefully, not
to try to do too much. And somehow Nicholas had
figured out the truth. Or someone had told him. She
had seen the doctor when she first missed her
courses, and he had confirmed what she had only
hoped. She had promised to take care of herself, to
eat well and to get enough sleep and to moderate her
activities. He had told her she could continue riding
for a few more weeks. He had also warned her not to
get her hopes up, that it was doubtful she could
carry the child to full term in any event. So she had
been afraid to let herself hope. She had made him
promise not to tell Nicholas, and he had agreed.

But, under the circumstances, maybe he had been
given no other choice. "Did the doctor come?" she
asked.

"Not yet, but he'll be here soon."

"Then how—"

"Jane told me."

"Oh. I wanted to tell you myself."

"When were you planning to let me in on the secret?"

"In another month."

"Why wait?"

"To be sure. I couldn't believe it had really happened at first. Years ago the doctor said I could never have any more children."

"It seems he was mistaken."

Daisy smiled, but had to grit her teeth to keep her chin from quivering. "Yes, it seems so. He also said there's a chance I could lose this child, as well."

Nicholas hadn't given much thought to the fact her first child had died. That this one might die, also. He was torn between feeling elation at this miracle and forcing himself not to care, in case something went wrong.

For Daisy, it was already too late. She already loved the child, though it had been growing inside her a mere two months.

"When will the child be born?" Nicholas asked.

"In the spring."

Nicholas huffed out a breath of air. Suddenly there was a great deal more at stake in the decisions that needed to be made than there ever had been before. He couldn't leave Daisy behind with his child. Wouldn't leave her. If she knew that, she could easily use the child as a means of blackmail to force him to stay. Assuming the child was born alive.

He would never abandon a child of his. He knew too well what the consequences could be. He wondered for an instant if Daisy had planned this all along. It seemed too coincidental that she should become pregnant when she had told him she couldn't have children. It was impossible to know what to believe. He intended to speak with the doctor and find out the truth.

Daisy reached out and touched Nicholas's hand, which lay on the bed beside her. "Nicholas? Are you glad? About the baby?"

"At least this one will be legitimate."

It wasn't the answer she had hoped for. "I'm excited," she said. "And a little frightened." He would never know how much courage it took for her to admit her fear. She looked up and for a flickering instant saw terror in his eyes.

He does care, she thought. *More than he's willing to admit. And he's as scared as I am.*

"Nicholas."

She waited for him to look at her. His expression was masked now. She had no way of seeing past the wall he had put up against her.

"What is it, Daisy?" He sounded annoyed, and she decided this wasn't the best time to confront him about his feelings.

"Nothing. Forget it."

"Dammit! If you've got something to say, say it!"

She hadn't expected the explosion of anger. It was a sign of how just how unsettling he found the prospect of having another child.

Nicholas left the bed and paced the length of the room, tunneling his hands through his hair in agitation. "Talk to me, Daisy. Tell me what you're thinking."

"I'm thinking how lucky we are, Nicholas. Imagine, a child, when I believed it to be impossible."

"A child only complicates things," he said. "You seem to have forgotten we have a little problem."

"What problem?"

"I won't stay in England, and you won't go to America. Who gets the child, Daisy? Tell me that!"

Daisy felt a moment of panic. Surely he wouldn't take the child with him when he left! No one separated a newborn babe from its mother. Yet from the stern look on his face, anything was possible. "We have until the spring, Nicholas. That's plenty of time to make a decision." To come to a compromise, she thought. But she could see no compromise that would work now that a child had entered the picture.

Fortunately, the doctor arrived and their argument was cut short. Nicholas left the room and paced the hallway while Dr. Fitzsimmons examined Daisy. The doctor was an old man, and Nicholas wondered how competent he was. His only comfort came from the knowledge that the doctor had saved Daisy's life once before under similar circumstances.

"How is she?" Nicholas asked as the doctor left the bedroom.

"Her Grace is doing fine. She needs to take better care of herself. There's still a chance she'll fail to carry the child for the full term."

"Is that what happened last time?" Nicholas asked.

"Her Grace miscarried in the fifth month."

"What went wrong?"

"That I cannot say. The child—a boy—was perfectly formed. Unfortunately, Her Grace nearly bled to death. It appeared to me that it would endanger Her Grace's health to become *enceinte* again." He scratched the salt-and-pepper whiskers on his chin. "I spoke to the duke—Her Grace's first husband— about the seriousness of the situation."

"Why the hell didn't you say something to me?"

"I thought Her Grace would have explained everything."

"No," Nicholas said through tight jaws. "She explained nothing."

"The only thing to be done now is to make sure she takes very good care of herself. Plenty of sleep, a bland diet, and absolutely no exertion beyond a short walk. The rest we must leave in the hands of the Almighty."

"Can I . . . can we . . . I don't want to endanger her or the child." Nicholas couldn't stop the flush of embarrassment. He didn't want to ask outright if he could have sexual relations with Daisy. Fortunately, the doctor divined his problem.

"If you are careful, Your Grace. Until the sixth month."

"Thank you, Dr. Fitzsimmons."

"Good day, Your Grace."

Nicholas leaned back against the wall outside Daisy's door, his legs widespread, and digested the doctor's healthy ration of food for thought.

He was terrified. What if Daisy died giving birth to his child?

And furious. He should have been told how dangerous it was for her to couple with him.

He shoved the bedroom door open and marched across the room to confront Daisy, who was sitting up in bed with several pillows behind her. Jane had taken advantage of the opportunity to get Daisy out of her riding habit and into a nightgown.

"Leave us please, Jane," Daisy said.

Daisy never took her eyes off Nicholas. She had some idea, from the muscle ticking in his jaw, of his anger. When the door closed behind the maid, Daisy said, "What has you upset now?"

"I've just spoken to the doctor. He told me how dangerous it was for you to get pregnant."

"Dangerous? For me? You jest."

"It's no laughing matter, I assure you, ma'am. You didn't tell me that you nearly bled to death when you lost the first child."

"I was perfectly healthy until the cramps began. I was weak for a long time afterward, but I recovered completely."

"The doctor doesn't think so."

"I don't understand," she said, confusion clouding her green eyes. "Dr. Fitzsimmons didn't say I *shouldn't* get pregnant, he said that I *couldn't*."

Nicholas shook his head. "Either you heard him wrong, or he wasn't entirely honest with you. He just told me that he explained to Tony that you might die if you had another child."

Daisy's face bleached white. "I swear I didn't know. I had no idea such a danger existed." Now that she recalled the conversation, she realized it was Tony who had given her the doctor's message that she could no longer have children. Tony must have told her the lie to keep her from pleading with him to try anyway, because she would have begged until he gave in to her. It would have been worth the risk. Was worth the risk. Even knowing she might die, she wasn't sorry to be carrying the duke's child.

If what Nicholas said was true, it occurred to her that Tony hadn't left her bed because she couldn't give him an heir, but because it would endanger her life if he planted his seed in her. Leaving her bed might have been as much a sacrifice for him as it was for her. It also meant that for years she had unfairly blamed him for something that wasn't his fault. "Oh, my God," she said. "Oh, God."

Nicholas saw the tears brim in Daisy's eyes, saw one spill over. He sat beside her and drew her into his arms. As soon as he did, she broke into heart-wrenching sobs. He didn't know what to say to comfort her. She must be terrified that she would die. He was the one who had insisted upon a real marriage. He had forced her into his bed. If he had known . . . If she had told him . . .

"Please don't cry, Daisy. I can't bear it when you cry."

He brushed her flyaway hair from her face and kissed the tears from her eyes. Nicholas had never given solace to a woman. The situation had simply never come up. He wasn't sure what to do, so he kept on kissing her. Her cheeks, her chin, her forehead, her ears, until finally he found her mouth.

Hunger. It overrode any other thought as his mouth captured hers. His tongue delved deep. She clung to him, with her mouth and hands and body. He felt her need, urgent and demanding. Her body caught fire and ignited his passion.

He ripped her nightgown, popping buttons that clattered to the wooden floor, and found her naked breasts with his callused hands. They were fuller, he realized suddenly. When she moaned, he realized they must also be more sensitive.

"Daisy, Daisy, I need you," he murmured in her ear. "The doctor said it's safe. I want you."

Daisy felt a tightness in her chest. She wondered if another man would have asked. "I want you, too, Nicholas."

She curled her hand around his nape and drew

him down for her kiss. She arched her body against his, and he groaned as she brushed against his engorged shaft.

"Nicholas."

"What?"

She laughed, a purring sound. "Sweetheart. You need to take off your clothes."

Nicholas frowned in consternation. He ripped off his clothes and threw them helter skelter around the room until he was naked.

By then Daisy was grinning.

"Are you satisfied?"

"Not yet. But I will be soon." She held out her arms, and he came to her.

Nicholas had never been more aware of how much larger he was than Daisy, or how much stronger. *Be gentle. Be careful.* He had to protect Daisy. And their child.

So he moved slowly, his hands caressing her until she writhed in ecstasy beneath him. His palm brushed her nipples until they stood in achingly stiff peaks.

Daisy found herself in the arms of a gentle lover. Where was her barbarian? His face was tense with the effort it took to leash his passion. Daisy didn't want her savage to be civilized. She needed the wild and wanton lover she had come to know and love over the past three months.

So she nipped his shoulder.

He groaned deep in his throat and clenched her hip with his hand.

And bit the lobe of his ear.

He grunted, and his mouth latched onto her

throat to suckle and send shivers of desire shuddering through her body.

Her hands slid down and cupped him.

He hissed in a breath and stilled, waiting to see what she would do. She circled him with her hand.

"Daisy." The word came out as a guttural moan.

She spread her hand and encompassed the sac below.

"Good God." He pressed her hand against him. "I can't . . . You can't . . ."

She circled the tip of his shaft with her thumb, and he nearly came off the bed.

"What are you doing, Daisy?"

"I want to please you," she said, a bit breathless herself.

"You do. You are. I can't . . . I have to be careful."

"I'll let you know if you get too rough, Nicholas. Love me. Please, love me. And let me love you."

He took away his hand and lay still for her. While she drove him to distraction. Until he couldn't bear the pleasure any more and had to be inside her.

Only he didn't enter her right away. He slid a finger inside to see if the passage was wet enough to accommodate him. She wanted him, it seemed, every bit as much as he wanted her.

He sheathed himself slowly, more slowly than he ever had, and enjoyed the wondrous look on Daisy's face as he seated himself to the hilt.

"You feel exquisite," Nicholas said. "Tight and warm and wet. Shall I move, Daisy?"

"Not yet, Nicholas. Not yet."

It was harder than he thought it would be to lie

still within her. He could feel the blood pound in his shaft, feel her muscles contract around him.

"Daisy," he pleaded.

Her lips curled in a catlike smile of satisfaction. "All right, Nicholas. You can move."

He levered himself away from her and slowly returned. Again and again. Until his brow was covered with sweat and beads of perspiration had formed above her lip. Her hands were clasped on his arms. Her legs were banded about his hips. Her eyes were heavy-lidded, and her mouth was open to gasp for air.

She arched up as he lowered himself into her. "How long . . . how long . . . ?"

"All day. All night," he said. "I could love you endlessly and never be satisfied."

She groaned. "I can't . . . I need . . ."

Nicholas slid his hand between them to touch her and felt her immediately convulse around him. Her climax triggered his own, and he arched his body into hers, his face a mask of agony and ecstasy.

He lay atop her for only a moment before he realized what he was doing. "I'm too heavy for you. With the baby, I mean."

Daisy wanted to feel him atop her now, while her belly was still flat enough for that pleasure. But she sighed happily when Nicholas dragged her into his arms and laid his thigh over hers to hold her close.

But when she looked up at him, he was frowning. "Nicholas? What's the matter?"

At first she thought he wasn't going to answer her. When he did, she wished he hadn't.

"I won't let you keep the child in England."

Daisy stiffened. "I won't allow you to take my child away from me."

"Then you'll have to come to America."

"The heir to Severn deserves to be raised here, where his heritage and patrimony lie."

"It might be a she, Daisy, had you thought of that? But even if you give me a son, he won't be a Windermere, because I'm not. Don't you see that, Daisy?"

"You don't know anything for sure," Daisy argued stubbornly. "You haven't spoken to Estleman yet."

"Estleman!" Nicholas snorted the word. "You've got a lot of hopes pinned on someone who may know nothing."

"Maybe I have. But I see no reason to discuss this matter until you've had a chance to speak to the man. Estleman may be able to prove you are your father's son." She paused, took a deep breath and said, "And the baby may not live to be born."

They both lay silent. There was no way they could make any plans until spring. They would have to wait. And try not to love each other any more than they already did.

That was a difficult chore in the months that followed. Nicholas kept an eagle eye on Daisy, making sure she didn't overextend herself. She obeyed him because she wanted the child to be born healthy.

The first time the baby moved, she and Nicholas were in bed together. They had just made love. She took his hand in the darkened bedroom and placed it on her rounded belly.

"Feel, Nicholas. That's our child."

Nicholas laid his fingertips against her bare skin and waited for perhaps a count of ten before he felt it. A small bubble of movement.

"I felt something!" he exclaimed in delight and surprise.

For Nicholas it was the most powerful experience of his life. He hadn't been allowed near Evie while their child was inside her, so this was all new to him. He tried not to regret missing all this with Colin. He made up his mind to enjoy everything with Daisy.

"What does it feel like inside you when she moves?" he asked. "Does it hurt?"

"Not at all. When *he* moves it feels . . . like there's someone stretching, I suppose, inside my skin."

Nicholas laid his cheek against her stomach and waited for it to happen again. "I guess she's gone to sleep."

"So should we," Daisy said with a yawn.

A few moments later they were both wide awake as Nicholas kissed his way across her belly and down between her thighs. They finally fell asleep as dawn was breaking.

Since both Daisy and Priss were pregnant at the same time, it was difficult for the two of them to get together. Neither husband wanted his wife traveling the roads in winter. Priss was nearing term, and Daisy's pregnancy was precarious.

The two women weren't about to be denied each other's company until spring. They got their husbands to agree to a winter picnic on a warm, sunny day in late December, at a hunting box halfway between the two properties. Of course, Colin and Roanna were invited, too.

Servants were sent ahead to make sure fires had been laid to ward of any chill in the house and to prepare food for the picnic. The hunting box wasn't as small as its name implied, and turned out to have four bedrooms upstairs.

"I don't want to imagine the sorts of parties that have been held here through the years," Daisy said to Priss as they rambled through the house searching out all its secrets.

"I can imagine," Priss said with a smile. "My brother has told me a few stories that would raise the hair on your head."

To make it seem more like a picnic, they had moved the furniture out of the main room and laid blankets on the floor in front of a huge stone fireplace big enough to hold the two-foot-wide, four-foot-long log that Nicholas and Charles had dropped into it. There had been a light snow the night before, and snug inside with the crackling fire to lend warmth, it was a perfect site for a picnic.

The three couples, parents and children, had an easy time making conversation. Since both women were expecting, they talked about babies. Having raised Colin, Nicholas was able to add a few war stories of his own.

Nicholas watched Daisy for signs of fatigue, and when he saw them, he insisted they retire upstairs so she could take an afternoon nap. Charles knew a good idea when he heard it, and ushered Priss upstairs, as well.

There were servants around, but otherwise Colin and Roanna were left alone in front of the fireplace.

"I suppose I should get up and seat myself in a chair," Roanna said. She was on the floor with her hands hugging her bent knees.

"I can't see any good reason to move at all," Colin

said. He was lying stretched out in front of the fire with his head held up by one hand.

"Your father takes very good care of Daisy," Roanna noted. "Do you think he's fallen in love with her?"

Colin sat up and leaned an elbow on one knee. "I don't know. Sometimes I think he has. But he hasn't changed his mind about selling Severn. At least, not as far as I've been able to tell."

"What will happen to them?"

"I don't know," Colin said. "I only hope my father comes to his senses soon enough to realize what he's going to lose if he leaves Daisy behind and heads back to Texas alone."

Roanna was silent. She was hoping the same thing occurred to Colin.

"Tell me more about Texas," she said. She listened for an hour to stories of roundups and branding cattle and taming bucking broncs. Texas sounded fascinating.

But the more Colin spoke, the more Roanna realized he had cut her out of any pictures he had of the future. She worried her lower lip, wondering if she should advise him that she had plans for the future that definitely included him.

Whatever she might have said was lost in the commotion that occurred when Charles came racing down the stairs.

"Send someone for a doctor. Priss is in labor."

Daisy and Nicholas quickly joined Charles in the bedroom where Priss lay, her teeth clenched against a powerful contraction.

"I *knew* I shouldn't have agreed to this," Charles raved. "This is all my fault."

The contraction ended, and Priss said with a lop-sided grin, "I'm at least half to blame for my condition, Charles. Although I wish I'd recognized that backache this morning for what it was."

"I knew you didn't feel well. Didn't I ask you again and again before we left if you were feeling all right?"

"You certainly did, Charles. And if I hadn't wanted to see Daisy so much I might have admitted how I really felt. But that's all water under the bridge now. I suppose our first child is going to be born in a hunting box after a December picnic. That will give us a wonderful story to tell our grandchildren, won't it, Charles?"

She grabbed his hand and gasped in pain as another cramp rose and tightened around her belly.

Nicholas had reached for Daisy's hand and held on. He hadn't seen this part, either, when Colin was born. And he didn't like it one bit. He glanced at Daisy and saw the fear in her eyes. He wasn't sure whether she was remembering the loss of her own child, or worrying about Priss.

Daisy was remembering.

Waves of pain, endless pain. Being thirsty, so thirsty, and no one would give her a drink. Clutching the bedsheets and writhing in agony. Screaming.

Feeling the child claw its way out of her body, tearing her apart, leaving her limp and exhausted.

And bleeding. So much blood on the sheets, on her gown. Until her skin was like parchment, and she knew she was going to die. And wanted to die, because she had been told the child, a little boy, was dead.

She had felt like crying, but there wasn't enough

fluid left in her body to make tears. Her throat had ached, and it had been impossible to swallow.

But she hadn't died. She had lived to suffer through the grief of losing her child. And losing her husband, long before he was dead.

Daisy raised her eyes to meet the duke's gaze. It wasn't going to happen like that this time. She was going to bear a healthy child. That way, even if Nicholas left her, she would not be alone. She would always have a part of him with her.

Nicholas's hand tightened on hers, "I never knew it was this hard," he said. "I never knew."

He was afraid for her.

Daisy felt a smile growing on her face. "Women are hardy creatures, Your Grace. Priss will do fine." She paused and added, "So will I."

Five hours later, Priss delivered a healthy baby boy. Charles beamed as he handed Nicholas a cigar. "I have a son. Alexander, Viscount Clifton."

"Congratulations, Charles. I'm happy for you."

"Thanks, Nick. I promise to be there for you when the time comes, and we'll drink a toast to your son or daughter."

Nicholas quickly turned away from Charles. He didn't want his friend to see his terror. What if Daisy wasn't strong enough to suffer through all that pain? What if she didn't survive?

For the first time he forced himself to imagine life without Daisy. It was bleak. Lonely.

What kind of gudgeon was he, to think he could ever leave her? Why did he have to sell Severn at all? Who said he had to go back to Texas? He was Severn. Nobody told him what to do.

But there were risks, serious risks to such a future. She might not ever love him. She might betray him.

Hell, Nicholas thought. What was life without a little risk?

21

"I've always loved the crocus," Roanna said. "Because they're the first sign of spring." She turned to Colin and let her eyes linger on him. "But this year I wish they hadn't searched out the sunlight. At least not so soon."

Colin tethered his horse to a nearby poplar that was just beginning to bud, and Roanna did the same. He reached for her hand, threading his fingers with hers, and they strolled along a rise that overlooked Severn. The early March wind was brisk, and he let go of her hand and pulled her close, slipping an arm around her shoulder so they might share the warmth of each other's bodies.

Over the winter they had managed to see each other. Not often and seldom in private, but it had been enough to allow their relationship to develop into something more than the simple friendship Colin had hoped to maintain between them.

Roanna kept her head bowed, so Colin only had a view of the feathers on her riding hat. "I'll be leaving soon," he said.

"I know."

Colin felt like he had a great weight on his chest.

He couldn't—wouldn't—ask for what he wanted from Roanna, because he knew it wasn't what was best for her. His hand tightened around her shoulder. She stopped and turned and laid her cheek against his chest. His arms slid around her shoulders as her arms slid around his waist. They held each other close, saying nothing, with the early March wind biting at them and the sun doing its best to warm the still-frozen earth.

"Another suitor has spoken to my father," Roanna said. She felt Colin stiffen. "Father gave him permission to court me."

"Who is it?" Nicholas forced himself to ask.

"The Marquess of Brookfield."

"A marquess. That would be quite a coup for you, Roanna."

Roanna pushed herself away from Colin and glared up at him. "You, of all people, should know better than to say something like that to me."

"If the shoe fits—"

"It might have, once upon a time," Roanna interrupted angrily. "But no more. Not since . . . since I met you."

"I'm leaving England, Roanna. You'd better consider the marquess's offer." That wasn't at all what Colin had wanted to say, but he had convinced himself there was no future for the two of them. He felt too vulnerable, knowing he wasn't going to ask her to marry him, to admit how he really felt about her. She had hurt him badly once. He wasn't going to give her the chance to do it again.

Roanna was in an equally uncomfortable position. Over the past few months she had lost her heart to plain Mr. Calloway from America. Her father didn't approve of the match, and as a minor she couldn't marry without his consent. If Colin had given the least sign that he was willing to ask for her hand, she would have moved heaven and earth to convince her father to let her marry him. If that had failed, she would willingly have run away with him.

But she couldn't propose marriage herself. And it appeared Colin wouldn't.

Roanna had one last tactic she hadn't tried to get Colin to declare himself. It was a desperate measure, but time was running out, and it was now or never.

She laid her hand on Colin's jaw and let her fingertips roam up toward his ear.

"What are you doing, Roanna?" The band around Colin's chest tightened a little more so that now he was having serious trouble breathing.

"I'm touching you, Colin."

"I know that. But why? What are you hoping to prove?"

"That you want me. That you need me." Her fingers had found their way into his hair and were stroking their way down to his nape.

Colin shivered. "I don't think this is a good idea, Roanna."

"Why not?" She applied gentle pressure on his nape to draw his head down toward hers. Her eyes were locked on his. She licked her lips nervously, then rose on tiptoes to bring their mouths together.

Their lips clung sweetly, gently. Roanna hadn't realized how soft Colin's mouth could be. She had imagined this moment a hundred times since the last time he had kissed her. But reality was so much better than fantasy.

Colin groaned in frustration as their lips parted.

Roanna swallowed over the lump in her throat and said using his name for the first time, "Please, Colin."

Colin lifted his head and looked down into blue eyes swimming with tears. They both knew what she was asking. Not just for a kiss, but for a promise. It was one he couldn't make.

Colin knew what he had to do. And why. He took a step back from her and let his hands drop to his sides. "No, Roanna."

"Why not, Colin? Give me one good reason why not?"

He raised a hand and brushed exquisitely silky golden curls away from her temple. "Your father is smarter than you think, Roanna. You wouldn't do well in Texas. It's not at all like England. There are no maids to bring you breakfast and dress you in silks and velvets. There are no grooms to saddle your horse and cool him down. There are no tenants to do the work and provide you with an income every year to spend as you wish.

"You weren't raised to suffer adversity and survive hardship. There's no place for an English lady in Texas."

"I can change," Roanna pleaded. "I *have* changed."

Colin sadly shook his head. "Not quickly enough. Not deep down where it counts. You would hate the only kind of life I can offer you. Working with your hands until they had thick calluses, having your skin burned brown by the sun, getting your face chapped by hot winds in summer and blue northers in winter. Building fires, hauling water, cooking, cleaning.

Pretty soon you'd hate me for taking you away from the only life you've ever known."

His hand trailed down to her quivering chin, which he brushed with his thumb. "And I would hate that," he said in a very soft voice.

"I want to remember you like this, Roanna," Colin said. "With your milk-white cheeks flushed by the cold wind and your blue eyes sparkling with the promise of spring."

"Oh, Colin!"

Colin dragged Roanna into his arms and hugged her tight. "You'll thank me for this someday," he managed to say past the lump that had formed in his throat.

"I already hate you for being so reasonable and rational." Roanna swallowed back her tears and said fiercely, "I'll never forget you, Colin."

"I'm not likely to forget you, either," Colin murmured. He pushed her away and took her hand, lacing her fingers with his for the last time. "It's time to go back, Roanna."

"Promise me you'll come say good-bye before you leave," Roanna pleaded.

Colin groaned inwardly as he thought of having to see Roanna once more before he left England. This parting was difficult enough. He wasn't sure he could face her a second time and say good-bye without throwing away all his good intentions. But he couldn't deny her. "I promise," he said.

When he came, Roanna thought, she would get him to tell her on which ship he planned to sail. She planned to be on it, too. With a whole ocean voyage ahead of them, she would have plenty of time to persuade him that she would make him a good wife.

She hadn't bothered denying any of his carefully planned speech about how she wouldn't make him a good wife. He didn't know the Warennes. They had come to England with William the Conqueror and had been fighting ever since. She came of good warrior stock. She could do anything, if she set her mind to it. Surely Colin couldn't ask more of a wife than that.

What was more important, she loved him. And she was almost certain he loved her. He hadn't said the words, but then she didn't need them. Only a man who loved her as much as Colin did would be so ridiculously noble as to try and talk her out of marrying him.

They rode back to Rockland Park in silence. He left her in front of the stable.

"Don't forget your promise," she called as he rode away.

Colin called himself ten kinds of fool as he put some distance between himself and Roanna. She was willing to leave everything behind and go with him to America. And he had refused to ask her to join him. He knew he had made the best choice for her; he wasn't sure he had done himself any favors. He wanted her physically almost more than he could bear. But he knew when he was back in Texas what he would miss most was the woman who had become his best friend.

Colin rode past the manor house at Severn on his way to the stable in back of it. Along the way, he saw his father walking with Daisy in the rose garden behind the house. She was nearing full term, with only three weeks left before she was to deliver. She was huge and unwieldy, and Colin didn't doubt she needed the arm his father was using to support her. She had passed the danger of miscarriage, but he knew his father feared the delivery just as much.

He had seen his father watching Daisy when he thought no one was looking, his eyes shadowed with fear. He hoped for both their sakes that the child was born healthy.

Colin unsaddled Buck and gave him a ration of oats before he headed back toward the house.

His talk with Roanna had been only one of the good-byes he was being forced to endure. He had spoken recently with his father about his desire to return home, to Texas.

"I got a letter from Simp," he had told his father. "He wants to know when we're setting sail for home."

"In the spring," his father had replied.

"When in the spring, Pa? March? April? May?"

"Don't try pinning me down, Colin," he replied irritably. "I can't make any decision until the child is born."

Colin hadn't really been surprised that his father refused to commit to a date for leaving England. He had sensed his father's growing attachment to the land. And to Daisy. Colin had often wondered, as he watched Daisy with his father through the fall and winter and into the spring, how they managed to spend so much time together and ignore the confrontation everyone knew was coming when the baby arrived.

"Hello, Pa, Daisy," Colin said as he strode past the two of them on his way into the house. "How are you, Daisy?"

"Big," Daisy retorted.

Colin laughed. "As a horse."

Nicholas shot his son a warning glance. "You look like all women look at this stage in the game," he consoled Daisy. "No better, no worse."

"Your father is a wonder at compliments," Daisy said wryly.

Colin smiled. "I saw a carriage with a fancy crest in front of the manor when I rode up. Are we expecting company?"

Daisy and Nicholas exchanged glances.

"I certainly wasn't," Daisy said. "I don't want anyone to see me in this condition."

"I wonder who it is," Nicholas mused.

At that moment Lady Celeste appeared on the gravel walk at the edge of the rose garden. Her face was chalky white, and she was clutching her shawl tightly around her shoulders.

"Someone has arrived, Your Grace," she announced to Nicholas.

"Who is it?"

"Lord Estleman."

Nicholas froze. His eyes skidded to Daisy, and he saw that she was as surprised—and distressed—as he was. It was too soon. Now that the moment had come, he wasn't sure he was ready to learn the truth. What if he wasn't entitled to be Duke of Severn? What if none of this rightfully belonged to him? He knew the law would never question his claim, that legally he had inherited the title and the lands.

But Estleman could tell him whether his mother had betrayed his father. Or whether his father had made a horrible and irrevocable mistake in judging his mother.

"Will you come inside and meet him, Your Grace?" Lady Celeste said.

"Why did he come here now?" Nicholas asked his aunt. "How did he know I was looking for him?"

"I'm sure Lord Estleman will be able to answer all your questions."

"I'm coming with you," Daisy said as Nicholas began to stride toward the house.

Nicholas whirled on her. "This doesn't concern you."

"Doesn't it?" she said, eyes flashing, chin upthrust. "I have a right to know who you are. Who our child will be."

It no longer mattered, Nicholas realized, whether she learned the truth now or an hour from now. He had no intention of keeping it from her. He shoved a hand through his hair. "All right. You might as well come along."

Colin didn't ask to come. It mattered not at all to him whether his father was born to the English aristocracy or not. He could love him and respect him no more than he already did. However, he knew that the question of legitimacy had given his father nightmares for years. He hoped for his father's sake that Lord Estleman had the answers his father sought.

Nicholas felt more and more anxious as he approached the library, where Lady Celeste had instructed Thompson to usher Lord Estleman. He wasn't aware of how tightly he was gripping Daisy's hand until she said, "Nicholas. You're hurting me."

Higgenbotham started to open the library door, but Nicholas stayed him. "Wait a moment."

He turned and hauled Daisy a short distance away where they could speak without being overheard.

"Will you come to America with me when the baby's born? I want you with me there."

"Why are you asking me this now, Nicholas?"

"Because I need an answer."

Daisy put a hand on his forearm and felt the rigid muscles beneath her fingertips. "Do you think you don't deserve all this?" she said in a quiet voice. "Are you afraid you love it too much, even though by rights it shouldn't be yours? Who better to be Duke of Severn than you, Nicholas? I've seen how your eyes devour the land, how your heart beats fast when you lay eyes on the house after being gone for a day. It doesn't matter what Estleman says. Severn is yours. It belongs to you."

Nicholas was shaking his head. "Not if my mother betrayed my father. Not if I'm no part of him."

Daisy grasped Nicholas by the shoulders and shook him—as much as someone her size could shake someone his size. "You're being ridiculous. Your father could have repudiated you. He didn't. Doesn't that mean something?"

Nicholas snorted. "That he was a proud man. That he didn't want the world to know my mother had cuckolded him."

Daisy made an exasperated sound deep in her throat. "All right, then. Believe what you will. It's entirely likely Lord Estleman won't be able to shed any more light on the situation than anyone else has."

She turned and started for the door to the library. She paused and looked to see if Nicholas was coming. He walked as though he were on his way to the guillotine. Higgenbotham opened the door and shut it with the usual heavy *thunk*, which somehow possessed a note of finality as it closed behind him.

Nicholas's heart was in his throat as he spied Lord Estleman. The tall man was standing by the twelve-paned window, looking out on the rolling lawns of Severn. If he had once been heavier than Nicholas, he wasn't now. His thick black hair was threaded with silver. When he turned, the heart in Nicholas's throat sank to his toes.

Estleman looked enough like him—in every way— to be his elder brother. Or his father.

Nicholas quickly exchanged a grief-stricken glance with Daisy, whose eyes were full of sympathy. She saw it, too.

Estleman was the spitting image of him.

"I'm Estleman," the man said in a clipped accent. "I heard when I returned to London from India that you were looking for me . . . Your Grace. I believe we have some business to discuss. First, may I say that you've turned into a fine-looking man?"

"Since we look very much alike, sir, that's seems a self-serving compliment."

Lord Estleman chuckled. "Yes, I suppose it does."

Nicholas had been expecting the older man to deny the similarity in their features. It seemed the nail in the coffin that he had only acknowledged it.

"I came here because I'm your—"

"I know who you are," Nicholas said in a harsh voice.

"You do?" Estleman looked surprised.

"I want to know why you never came after my mother. Why you never came after me."

"Oh, I see." Estleman crossed to the fireplace, turning his back to Nicholas. He braced his palms against the marble and rocked back and forth. "I couldn't."

"Couldn't? Or simply didn't?"

"Couldn't," Estleman said as he turned back to face Nicholas. "You see, my father was still alive at the time, but in uncertain health. I couldn't take the chance that he would find out about my relationship to your mother. The shock of learning about such a liaison might have given him a stroke. My mother begged me to use discretion. To my later regret, I acceded to her wishes."

Nicholas felt his heart begin to pump faster as adrenaline sped through his system. He hadn't known how he would feel when he finally learned the truth. Now that the moment had arrived, he felt physically ill. And mortally angry. His hands tightened into fists, his nails digging into his skin. He had to restrain himself from reaching out to strangle the man standing, seemingly unconcerned, across from him.

"So you see, there was no way I could help your mother," Estleman said. "The truth might have killed my father."

"The lie killed my mother," Nicholas said through clenched teeth.

"Lie? What lie?"

"If you had come forward to protect her, she might not have left England. She wouldn't have suffered, and she wouldn't have died. I can't condone what she did to my father, but she shouldn't have been made to forfeit her life because of her affair with you."

Lord Estleman was looking more and more confused. "My dear boy—Your Grace—what are you talking about? Your mother and I never had an affair! The idea is unthinkable!"

Nicholas saw red. His hands closed around Estleman's throat. His strength was superhuman. He wasn't aware of Daisy clawing at his arm. Wasn't aware of Lady Celeste screaming from the other side of the room. "Are you denying that you lay with my mother? That she bore me as a result? Why did you come here if you're not my father?"

"For God's sake, I'm your *uncle!*" Estleman rasped.

Suddenly Nicholas felt as though he were in a long tunnel. He could hear his mother singing a lullaby. He could hear his father shouting at her, accusing her of betraying him. He could hear himself crying, begging his mother to let him stay at Severn, to please not take him away.

"Nicholas. Please, say something. Nicholas."

He was sitting in the chair behind the Sheraton desk. He didn't know how he had gotten there, but he felt Daisy's hands on his cheeks, and when he blinked he saw she was staring worriedly into his eyes.

"Daisy?"

"You're back," she said. "Thank God, you're back."

He looked around and saw Estleman standing at the fireplace and Lady Celeste perched at one end of the settee weeping into her hands. How had she gotten into the room? She must have been there all along, and he had simply not seen her with his gaze focused on Estleman.

Nicholas stood and found his legs wobbly under him. Daisy slid her arm around his waist, and he put an arm around her shoulder, accepting the support she offered. He walked the few steps to Estleman and stared into eyes so very similar to his own. The older man lowered his gaze.

"You're my uncle?" Nicholas said.

Estleman rubbed at the bruises on his neck. "Yes."

Nicholas frowned. "I don't have an uncle, at least not one that I was aware of. Where did you come from?"

"It seems I shall have to confess the whole. Your grandfather, your mother's father, was the one who had an affair . . . with my mother. Your mother found out I was her half brother and insisted on meeting me. We did meet, secretly, several times, because I couldn't take the chance my father would find out the connection between us. You see, my mother had never told him that I wasn't his son. I found out myself only when I caught my mother with her lover. She begged me not to tell my father. She was afraid he would disown her if he ever found out and throw us both out into the street with nothing."

"I understand her concern," Nicholas said bitterly. How unbelievably ironic the whole situation was. It was difficult to blame his uncle for wishing to avoid a fate he had reason to know was more terrible than words could describe.

"When your father made the accusations against your mother, Gloria was naturally hurt. Lord Philip would have forgiven her, I think, if someone hadn't pointed me out to him. He took one look at me—"

"—and one look at me," Nicholas said, "and came to the obvious conclusion. No wonder he believed she had betrayed him." Nicholas still needed a scapegoat. Someone to blame for the tragedy. Someone on whom to take revenge. "Who pointed you out to my father?" he demanded.

"That I don't know," Estleman said.

From across the room, Lady Celeste spoke for the first time. "I did."

Three pairs of stunned eyes focused on the elderly woman.

"Why?" Nicholas demanded in a horrified voice. "Dear God. Why?"

Lady Celeste rose from the settee and walked the few steps to Nicholas. Her hands were clutched like a harpy's claws around her fringed woollen shawl. "She took Philip from me. He courted me first, before he ever laid eyes on Gloria. But he never looked at me again after he met her. I thought . . . I thought if Gloria were gone he might turn back to me."

Nicholas saw the world-weariness in her eyes, the guilt, the regret, and the shame. Overriding them all was the bitterness she still harbored against his mother after all these years.

"He never did, of course," Lady Celeste continued. "He loved Gloria until the day he died. I'm afraid the more he pined for her, the more tightly I held on to the knowledge that would have saved them both.

"You see, Gloria wrote asking me to intercede for her, to explain about her meetings with our half brother and to ask Philip to take her back.

"I burned the letter."

Nicholas grappled with his need to strike out with his fists at the small, gray-haired woman who had ruined so many lives. To bloody her, to mangle her body as she had mangled his life. But killing her wouldn't change the past. He had to live with that forever.

He turned and walked away from his aunt, the woman who had destroyed his family, to stare out the window at Severn. Jealousy. Selfishness. Misunderstanding. Stubbornness. They had all contributed to the tragedy.

He couldn't forgive either his aunt or his uncle for what they had done to him and his mother. But now that he knew the facts, he had no further desire to punish the two of them. They would suffer enough in the years to come. Each of them had to live with the knowledge of how they had betrayed and destroyed their own flesh and blood.

Another truth dawned on him slowly.

I am Severn. I am my father's son.

Nicholas felt the sting of tears in his nose, and his vision blurred. He felt Daisy beside him and clutched at her hand, unable to speak, unable to look at her or at anyone at this moment of revelation. All the questions that had tortured him for so many years had been answered.

In a voice so soft it was almost a whisper Daisy said, "I love you, Nicholas Windermere."

He stared at her for a moment, surprised at her declaration. And not a little distressed by it. Because it felt so good to hear her say the words. Because he could imagine himself saying them back to her.

"I think we should say good-bye to our guest now," Daisy said.

Nicholas saw her wince of pain, the teeth that

caught on her lower lip until it bled. "Daisy? What's wrong?"

"It's the baby. It's coming."

"It takes hours," Nicholas protested. "At least it did with Colin."

"It's been hours," Daisy confessed. "The pains started early this morning. I didn't want to worry you."

Nicholas's hands found her shoulders and tightened. "It's too early, Daisy. Three weeks. You can't—"

"I can and I am!" Daisy snapped back. "Please send for Dr. Fitzsimmons. I think it's past time I retired to my room."

Nicholas swept Daisy up into his arms, no mean feat considering her bulk. "Get the door, Estleman," Nicholas said through tight jaws. "I don't want to see either of you anywhere near Severn, ever again," he said without looking back.

Nicholas swept out of the library through the door Estleman held open. "Send for Dr. Fitzsimmons," Nicholas said to Higgenbotham. "Her Grace's time has come."

Daisy leaned her head against Nicholas's chest and heard his heart careering wildly inside. "Don't worry, Nicholas. Everything will be fine."

"Don't spout platitudes at me, Daisy," he snarled. "I can't take it right now."

"I love you, Nicholas. Barbarian and all."

"This is no time for lovemaking, either."

"I wanted you to know," she said. "In case . . . in case . . ."

He hurried along the upstairs hallway, terrified,

anxious to have her safely in bed. "Nothing is going to go wrong," he retorted. "So shut up."

"You're so tactful when you're angry, Nicholas. I think that's why I fell in love with you."

Nicholas groaned. "Please, Daisy. Don't keep saying that."

"What? That I love you?"

"There. You did it again!"

Jane was there ahead of him to pull the covers aside and Nicholas lay his precious burden on the clean white sheets. Her hands clung to his neck, holding his face close.

"Say it, Nicholas. Say it once."

Nicholas was aware of the eyes and ears listening to him. "This is not the time, Daisy."

She lowered her eyes, so he wouldn't see her disappointment. "I'll be all right, Nicholas. Don't worry. Your son or daughter is sure to come out fighting."

"Just don't . . . Don't . . ."

"Oh, Nicholas." Her fingertips roamed his face, memorizing every character line and crevice. "Don't worry about me. I have every intention of wreaking havoc in your life for many years to come."

Daisy's face contorted as a sharper, harder contraction swept over her.

"Daisy! Darling, what can I do to help?"

Daisy laughed. "Nothing. I have to do this myself."

"You'll have to leave now, Your Grace," Jane said. "The doctor is here and must examine Her Grace."

Nicholas didn't want to leave, but found himself unable to stay and watch Daisy's pain. "Take care of her," he said to Dr. Fitzsimmons as he passed him on the way out.

He was outside the door, and it had been shut behind him before he said, "Don't let her die."

22

Daisy was exhausted. She had been laboring for more than twelve hours with nothing to show for her efforts. The words "weak" and "die" were easily audible despite the fact that Dr. Fitzsimmons was across the room from her.

She saw the duke's face above her and thought she was hallucinating. "Nicholas? What are you doing here?"

"Dr. Fitzsimmons said you were calling for me."

"I was. I didn't think you would come. You don't belong in a sickroom with—" Daisy felt the cramp rising across her abdomen, tightening until she couldn't breathe, couldn't think. She grasped Nicholas's hand.

"I'm here, Daisy. You can hold on to me."

When the contraction was over, Daisy watched as Nicholas shook his chalk-white hand to return the blood to it. There were four distinct red crescents where her nails had bitten into him.

"I'm sorry," she said.

"Don't be," Nicholas replied. "I'm glad I was here for you." Nicholas couldn't imagine the kind of excruciating pain that could take Daisy so far outside herself, that could give her such incredible strength. Especially when, according to the doctor, she was losing the battle against fatigue. If things continued as they were, she would be exhausted long before the child was born. If that happened, it was likely the child would be born dead, or not at all, in which case Daisy was likely to die, also.

Nicholas knew now what it was he wanted. A life at Severn with Daisy and their child. That was his perfect world. He couldn't shake the fear that God wasn't through punishing him yet. That God would think Severn was enough and take the child, or Daisy, or both. Nicholas couldn't let that happen. He wouldn't let that happen.

Nicholas had faced a lot of enemies and never felt fear, because he had confidence in his ability with a gun. Because he knew he had planned for every eventuality and given himself escape routes in the event something went wrong. None of that experience was useful in this situation. His enemy was time, and Daisy's body, which refused to yield up its fruit.

The doctor had said the child was ready to be born, yet it refused to make the trip down the birth canal. When you wanted the pit out of a piece of fruit, Nicholas thought, you squeezed until the pit popped out. He stared at Daisy, trying to figure out how to apply that principle to a pregnant woman.

He put his hands on Daisy's distended abdomen, but his hands, large though they were, couldn't apply pressure evenly.

"What are you doing?" Daisy asked curiously.

"I'm trying to figure out a way to get a pit out of a peach," he said with a wry smile.

"You'd better go see Dr. Fitzsimmons. You sound a little crazy."

"I'm perfectly all right." Nicholas stood and stared at Daisy. "Aha! I see how it can be done." He stepped to the head of the bed and lifted Daisy into a sitting position, bracing her back with his chest.

"Nicholas? What are you doing?"

"Squeezing the pit," Nicholas said.

"Dr. Fitzsimmons," Daisy called.

"We don't need him, Daisy," Nicholas murmured against her throat. "We can do this ourselves."

"Do what?" Daisy asked in exasperation. At that moment another contraction overwhelmed her. She grasped the bedsheets and bit her lip until it bled to keep from screaming. This pain was longer than the others and hurt in a different way. "I think . . . I think the baby's moving," she rasped.

Nicholas could see it himself. The child was lower in her belly. "Dr. Fitzsimmons, I think you should come here."

The contraction ended, and Daisy leaned back against Nicholas. "I can't do it, Nicholas. I can't. It hurts too much. And I'm too tired."

"Only a little while longer, darling."

"Easy for you to say," Daisy snapped. "You're not sitting where I am."

Nicholas grinned. If she had enough strength to argue, she was going to be fine.

Daisy groaned. "It's another contraction. Already. I'm not recovered yet from the last one."

Nicholas lifted her again and forced her upper body forward, putting more pressure on the baby and forcing it down the birth canal.

Daisy's groan became a guttural sound of effort,

as though she were attempting to lift a cartload of
hay along with the horses. "Nicholasssss!"

"I see the child's head," Dr. Fitzsimmons said excitedly. "Only another push or two, Your Grace."

Nicholas wiped the sweat from Daisy's brow with
a cool cloth and pressed it to her bleeding, chapped
lips. "You're doing fine, sweetheart," he crooned to
her.

"Shut up, Nicholas. This is all your fault, you
know. If you hadn't—" The tremendous pressure on
her abdomen cut off Daisy's tirade. Nicholas held
her upright as she pushed, grunting hard as she
worked to free her body from its burden.

She felt the pressure suddenly release as Dr. Fitzsimmons exclaimed, "The head and now the shoulders, that's it, Your Grace. Ah!"

Though it was plain to Nicholas that the child was
no longer inside Daisy's body, there had been no
sound from the other end of the bed. Nicholas felt
Daisy clutch his hand. Both of them waited, not
breathing, hearts pounding, for the child's cry.

It didn't come.

Nicholas had to force words past his swollen
throat. "Is everything all right?" He knew the child
was dead. How would Daisy survive a second tragedy? And then he thought of the bleeding that had
occurred the last time. Was that what kept the doctor silent? Was he trying to stem the flow of blood?

"Doctor?" Daisy whispered. "Is the child—"

The doctor stood with the infant wrapped in linen
and approached the head of the bed. "There were
some other matters I needed to attend to before I
could bring this little one to you," he said.

Nicholas ignored the child and said, "Is Daisy all right? Is she . . . Is there . . ."

"Her Grace is just fine. Came through without any complications at all."

Nicholas allowed himself to look at the child. "Why didn't the baby cry?"

"They don't sometimes. Just come into the world as quiet as you please. She was breathing just fine. I saw no reason to set her to squalling."

"She?" Nicholas said.

"It's a girl, Your Grace."

"Oh, Nicholas, we have a daughter," Daisy cried tearfully.

Nicholas peered at the linen-wrapped child the doctor was laying in Daisy's arms. Her face was a wrinkly, blotchy red, but she had a wealth of black hair and stunning blue eyes.

"She looks like you," Daisy said.

Frankly, Nicholas couldn't see the resemblance.

"What shall we name her?" Daisy hadn't been willing to choose a name before the child was born, because she thought it might jinx the baby's birth. Now that she held her daughter safe in her arms, she turned to Nicholas for help. "You must have been thinking about this," Daisy said.

"I swear I haven't," Nicholas demurred. "Why don't you choose a name?"

"Beatrice," Daisy said. "It means 'one who brings happiness.' She's done that, hasn't she, Nicholas?"

Nicholas rolled the name around in his head, then let it spill off his tongue. "Beatrice. She looks like a bundle of joy, all wrapped up like that." He brushed his finger against the baby's cheek, and Beatrice turned her face toward him. "What do you think, Peaches? How does Beatrice sound to you?"

"Peaches?" Daisy said, arching a brow.

Nicholas grinned. "I'm afraid she's always going to be Peaches to me."

"Where on earth did you get a nickname like that?"

"I'll tell you later," Nicholas said. "When you're feeling stronger and more like arguing."

"Am I going to want to argue?"

"It's possible."

"Your Grace, it would be best if Her Grace rested now," Dr. Fitzsimmons said.

"Get some sleep, Daisy. Everything will be fine now."

"Will it, Nicholas? Have you made a decision? About going back to America, I mean."

"Not now, Daisy. I'll be back as soon as you're awake."

"I won't be able to sleep if I don't know."

But she could barely keep her eyes open. Nicholas merely kissed them closed and said, "Later, Daisy. When you're stronger we can talk."

"Don't leave me, Nicholas," she whispered.

Before he could respond, she was already asleep.

Nicholas turned to the doctor. "Are you sure she's going to be all right? And the baby?"

"Mother and child are both fine, Your Grace. The child is a bit small, but she seems to be breathing well. And Her Grace came through the delivery more easily than I had anticipated."

"Are you saying that whatever went wrong the first time won't happen again?"

"I would have to say that the first birth was extraordinary, and I see nothing that would prevent Her Grace from having other children."

Nicholas felt euphoric and realized he was happy more for Daisy's sake than his own. She would want a lot of children. Now she could have them.

"Thank you, Doctor. For everything."

Nicholas headed downstairs in a daze, where Colin was waiting with Charles and Priss. Priss had brought their son, Alexander, with her and was sitting in a corner of the library with a blanket over her shoulder to conceal the fact she was nursing the child. However, the noises coming from under the blanket made it perfectly obvious what was going on.

"Is Daisy all right, Pa?" Colin asked. "Has the baby been born?"

"Daisy is fine, Colin. And so is our daughter."

Colin let out a whoop. "Jehoshaphat! I'm a brother." He took the few steps that brought him to his father and gave him a hug. Both men were grinning when they separated.

Nicholas turned and shook Charles's outstretched hand.

"Congratulations, Nick," Charles said. "How about a drink to celebrate?"

Nicholas bunched his trembling hands and said, "That sounds like a good idea." It was just beginning to dawn on him that he had a daughter. And that Daisy was going to be fine.

"What did you name the baby?" Priss asked.

"Daisy named her Beatrice." Nicholas swallowed the brandy in a single gulp. It burned like fire all the way down. It didn't do a thing to steady his nerves, so he poured himself another.

"I suppose we'd better be going now," Priss said as she buttoned her bodice under the blanket. "I'm so glad everything turned out all right. Tell Daisy I'll be by to see her and Beatrice as soon as she's feeling well enough for company."

"Thanks for coming to help me through this," Nicholas said to Charles.

The earl grinned ruefully. "I think you just wanted to know there was someone down here pacing the floor in your stead."

Nicholas managed a smile. "Did you wear a hole in the carpet for me? I want to point it out to Daisy when she mentions having another child."

"Damn near did." Charles slipped an arm around Priss and headed for the library door. "We'll come visit soon. Congratulations again, Nick."

"Good-bye, Charles, Priss. I'll send word when Daisy's well enough for visitors."

Nicholas filled his glass a third time and crossed to stare out the twelve-paned window, shifting his gaze outward to the pond and the forest beyond.

"There's a ship leaving for America at the end of the month," Colin said. "I plan to be on it."

Nicholas didn't turn to face his son. It was one of those cruel twists of fate that he had gained a daughter but was losing a son. "I won't be going with you, Colin."

"I didn't think so," Colin said. "I'll miss you, Pa."

Nicholas took a sip of brandy and nearly choked trying to swallow it over the lump in his throat. He turned and threw the glass at the fireplace, where it shattered into a thousand pieces. He continued his turn and found himself hugging Colin. He rocked his son back and forth in his arms, as though he were a young boy instead of a grown man.

There were tears in his eyes. Of relief. Of joy. Of bereavement at the loss of his firstborn to manhood. His fledgling was ready to fly free and alone. He released Colin at last and held him away so he could look at him.

"You're crying, Pa," Colin said in astonishment.

"I've been known to do so."

Colin shook his head. "I never saw you cry before, Pa."

"Everybody cries, son."

Colin stared at his father and saw him for the first time as he was. Not always right. Not invincible. Merely a man with flaws like any other. He could be hurt. He could feel joy. It was all there on his lined and weathered face.

"I'll come visit, Pa, I promise," Colin said. "Maybe someday you and Daisy can come see me and Simp in Texas."

"No maybe about it," Nicholas said. "We will."

"Daisy must be really happy, huh, Pa? I mean, that you're going to stay in England."

"She doesn't know yet."

"You've got to tell her, Pa. Right away."

"I will, son. As soon as she wakes up."

Daisy slept the night through and woke at dawn the next morning. She felt like she had been run over by a beer wagon. Her breasts were tender, her legs felt tied together, and her belly was cramping. She felt plain rotten. She closed her eyes, intending to go back to sleep, which seemed the best state to be in under the circumstances.

Then she remembered. Beatrice.

She leaned over and saw her daughter sleeping soundly in the crib beside the bed. The little girl had woken her once in the middle of the night to be nursed and then had fallen back to sleep. As had her mother.

Daisy's mouth curved in a smug, self-satisfied smile. She had done it. She had borne a living child. A beautiful little girl. And Nicholas had been by her side to experience the miracle with her.

Daisy sat bolt upright. Nicholas had promised he would tell her his decision when she awoke. She pulled the cord to call Jane. She must look a fright. There was no way she was going to allow Nicholas to see her looking anything but her best this morning.

Instead of her maid, Nicholas appeared in reply to her summons.

Daisy covered her face. "Go away! I must look horrible. I wanted to be beautiful for you," she wailed.

Nicholas grinned as he crossed the room and sat beside her on the bed. His arms slid around her, and he kissed her on the forehead. "You look wonderful."

"If you like rumpled sheets," she mumbled against his chest.

"You'll always be beautiful to me, Daisy. Whether you're rumpled or pressed."

"Pressed. As in flat?" Daisy said indignantly. "That doesn't sound very attractive, either."

"There's no pleasing you this morning, is there?" Nicholas teased.

Daisy broke into tears.

Nicholas took her by the shoulders and tried to get

her to look at him. "Daisy? What's wrong, sweetheart? I didn't mean to hurt your feelings, truly I didn't!"

"You're being nice to me," Daisy wailed.

"And that's bad?" Nicholas asked, perplexed.

"I want my barbarian back," she said, sniffling. "At least I knew that he wanted me."

"I want you," Nicholas protested.

Daisy shook her head forlornly. "If you did, you'd be yelling at me."

Nicholas felt his temper slipping. He grabbed for it, but Daisy shoved it out of reach.

"You're a brute and a beast. I don't know why I ever married you!"

"So I'm a brute, am I?" Nicholas snarled. "You nearly died giving birth to a child I planted in you. I was trying to be considerate. I was trying to be kind."

"Kind!" Daisy exclaimed as though he had offered her a snake. "If I'd wanted a kind man I could have married somebody else."

"What the hell *do* you want, Daisy?" Nicholas roared.

"Oh," Daisy said, pleased to see she had provoked him to incivility. "You, Nicholas. Just as you are. For now and always."

She offered her mouth, and he took it like the barbarian he was, with all the hunger and longing he felt. She returned the favor, driving him crazy, making him want her as she wanted him.

Nicholas tore his mouth away, his breathing harsh and ragged. "Don't try that again, Daisy," he warned.

"What did I do?" Daisy said, eyes wide with false innocence.

Nicholas snorted, then broke into laughter. "I love you, Daisy."

Daisy stared at him with her heart in her eyes, her mouth half open with the words she had been about to speak, which had caught in her throat. It was the first time Nicholas had ever declared his love for her aloud. And about time, Daisy thought. She crossed her arms over her chest and demanded, "All right, Nicholas. So you love me. Now what?"

"What?" Nicholas was caught totally off guard by Daisy's attack. "What more do you want from me, Daisy?"

"I want to hear you say it. That you're going to stay at Severn and raise cattle and hay and babies with me."

Nicholas grinned. "Oh, is that all? Well, of course I am."

"Of course you are? How long ago did you make this decision?" Daisy asked.

"The first day I laid eyes on you."

"Oh. You . . ."

"Barbarian?" he offered in a husky voice.

Daisy's eyes welled with tears. "I do love you, Nicholas. So very much."

The duke pulled Daisy into his lap and held her close. "I promise to do something truly primitive as soon as you're able," he murmured in her ear.

"Something savage and uncivilized?"

"Something wild and wanton."

"Oh," Daisy said with a sigh. "That sounds wonderful."

"Wonderful?" Nicholas said with a chuckle.

"Oh, yes." Daisy grinned. "You see, I've developed quite an appreciation for barbarians."

The duke slowly lowered his mouth to meet Daisy's as he did his best to live up to her expectations.

Epilogue

Simp took one of the two diaper pins from his mouth where he had put them for safekeeping and used it to secure the right side of the clean diaper he was putting on Colin's son. "Just be a minute here, young'un, and you'll be right as rain on a desert," he mumbled over the other pin. Then he retrieved the second pin and caught up the cotton on the other side. The baby waved his arms and legs, making the chore more difficult. "Settle down there a minute, Brody, and let me finish."

When he was done, Simp picked the child up and held him high, waggling him from side to side in his hands.

The baby grinned and gurgled.

Simp grinned back. "Look just like your pa and your grandpa both, young'un. Charm oozin' from ya every whichaway."

"Simp?"

Simp turned and greeted Colin's mother as she entered the bedroom he and Colin had built onto the ranch house outside Fredericksburg especially for the baby. She was a purty little gal, full of grit and gumption. Twisted Colin 'round her finger, but no more'n he thought a wife ought to. "Just changin' the boy," he said.

Simp handed the black-haired, blue-eyed baby over to his mother and watched her hug him.

"He's growing so fast! I can hardly believe he'll be a year old tomorrow," Roanna said.

"I'll just be takin' myself off. Got some supper to get started," Simp said.

Roanna stopped him on his way out of the room. "Thanks, Simp. I don't know what we would do without you."

She reached up and gave him a quick kiss on the cheek.

Simp flushed and wiped his cheek clean. "Diapered your husband when he wasn't more'n a few days old. Once you know how, ain't nothin' to it." Simp quickly made his escape. Colin's wife had a way of making him feel mighty good. Come to think of it, life was mighty good lately. 'Specially with the company they had these days.

"Roanna? Where are you?"

"In the bedroom with Brody."

A moment later Daisy appeared with Peaches— the nickname had stuck—in her arms. "Our husbands are planning a picnic this afternoon. Are you interested?"

"That sounds wonderful," Roanna replied. Before she could say more, they were joined by Priss, who had Alex in her arms.

"Your father doesn't think you should be going anywhere in your condition," Priss said to Roanna.

Roanna looked down and patted her rounding belly. Then she looked up and grinned. "He should know by now I'm determined to decide these things for myself."

The three women exchanged rueful glances. There had been hell to pay when the Earl of Rotherham learned from the note Roanna left him that his only daughter had taken ship with Mr. Colin Calloway, bound for America. He had wanted to follow after her, but Priss had forced him to wait.

"She's a woman, Charles," Priss had said. "She knows what she wants."

"A bastard!" Charles had ranted.

"He's a good man. And it won't matter what he is in America. Things are different there," Priss had argued.

Charles had simmered with anger for months before they had word from Roanna that she and Colin were married. Apparently, Colin had tried to get her to return to England, but she had perservered. He had finally admitted that he loved her enough to do whatever it took to make her happy. They had been married by the ship's captain before they made landfall in America.

Thus, the two families that were friends and neighbors in England had been joined by the marriage of their children. When Nicholas suggested it was time to visit Colin, Daisy had immediately suggested to Priss that she and Charles should join them. So they had come together, the two sets of grandparents, to see their children and their grandson, Brody Calloway.

There had been a surprise when they arrived. Roanna was pregnant for the second time.

"I suppose if your father complains too much, we

can always use our other ammunition," Priss said, sending a sly look toward Daisy.

"What ammunition?" Roanna asked.

"Priss and I are each expecting another happy event," Daisy said with a grin.

"What?"

Daisy turned at the sound of a deep male voice. "Uh-oh. I think our secret is out, Priss."

Three men, their husbands, were crowded into the bedroom doorway. "What's going on in here?" Nicholas demanded.

"We were just discussing how much we would enjoy a picnic," Daisy said.

"Daisy," Nicholas said in a warning voice.

"All right," she said. "If you must know, I'm expecting again."

"Me, too," Priss said as Charles crossed the room and put an arm around her shoulders.

Colin had already slipped his arms around Roanna from behind, and his hands rested on her burgeoning belly.

"Good grief," Nicholas said. "We're going to have babies coming out of our ears."

"I don't think that's where babies come from," Daisy teased.

Everyone laughed.

"Shall we all go on a picnic?" Roanna asked. "It sounds like so much fun."

Charles opened his mouth to object, and Priss put a hand over it. "Absolutely," she said.

"I can't wait to enjoy some more of that Texas sunshine," Daisy concurred with a smile.

Daisy and Nicholas were the last to leave the bedroom. Nicholas stopped her and put his arms

around both her and Peaches. "I love you, Daisy,"
he murmured in her ear.

He said the words often now, and she repeated
them back to him. Nicholas Calloway, bounty
hunter, was a man who existed only in memory.
Nicholas Windermere, beloved barbarian, had finally accepted his rightful place as the eighth Duke
of Severn.

LETTER TO READERS

Dear Readers,

I hope you enjoyed my first venture into the English countryside as much as I enjoyed writing it. I'm heading back to the American West for my next book, *Lord of the Plains*, but I'm taking some English characters with me. You've already met Lord and Lady Linden in *The Inheritance*. Their thrilling story also involves a second set of star-crossed lovers. Sparks fly and cultures clash when a half-breed Sioux captures Lady Winifred Worth, a precocious Englishwoman who prefers to wear trousers and is better known to her friends as Freddy. Secrets and past mistakes ensure that the path of true love is strewn with obstacles, all of which you'll enjoy seeing the lovers overcome.

I always appreciate hearing your opinions and find inspiration from your questions, comments, and suggestions. It would be fun to know more about you—your age, what you do for a living, and where you usually find my books—whether new or used.

For those of you who may be interested, I also write contemporary westerns. You can look for The Children of Hawk's Way trilogy from Silhouette Desire, beginning with *The Unforgiving Bride* in September 1994, followed by *The Headstrong Bride* in December 1994, and finishing up with *The Disobedient Bride*, a Man of the Month in April 1995. These books are a spinoff from the original Hawk's Way trilogy, which was published last year.

Please write to me at P.O. Box 8531, Pembroke Pines, FL 33084 and enclose a self-addressed, stamped envelope so I can respond. I personally read and answer all my mail, though as some of you know, a reply might be delayed if I have a writing deadline.

Take care and keep reading!

Happy trails,

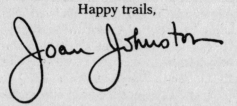

Joan Johnston

January 1995